Blackout

and Other Tales of Suspense

Ethel Lina White

Blackout

and Other Tales of Suspense

Ethel Lina White

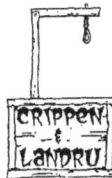

CRIPPEN & LANDRU PUBLISHERS
Cincinnati, Ohio
2025

For information contact:
Crippen & Landru, Publishers
P. O. Box 532057
Cincinnati, OH 45253 USA

Web: www.crippenlandru.com
E-mail: Info@crippenlandru.com

ISBN (softcover): 978-1-936363-91-9
ISBN (clothbound): 978-1-936363-92-6

First Edition: February 2025

10 9 8 7 6 5 4 3 2 1

CONTENTS

Introduction: The Lady Vanished   6
At Twilight   15
River Justice   30
Waxworks   41
Passengers   60
Catastrophe   76
The Gilded Pupil   90
The Cellar   104
Don't Dream On Midsummer's Eve   118
The Holiday   132
Lightning Strikes Twice   146
The Royal Visit   159
Mabel's House   173
Caged   186
Blackout   200
Underground   214
The Baby Heir   228
White Cap   242
The First Day   256
You'll be Surprised   271

INTRODUCTION: THE LADY VANISHED

Ethel Lina White
(1876-1944)

Ethel Lina White was born on the 2nd of April 1876 at what was 4 Derry View, a terrace on Frogmore Street in Abergavenny, Gwent. The house is now a hair salon but White's birth has been marked with a blue plaque mounted by the Abergavenny Local History Society. Ethel was the third child of William White and Eliza Charlotte White, and she had twelve siblings, including three elder step-sisters from William's previous marriage.

William White was a "horticultural builder and general building contractor" who became comparatively wealthy after invent-ing "Hygeian-Rock Building Composition," a bituminous mortar marketed as cheaper and more effective than existing products at strengthening walls and rendering them sound- and damp- proof. In 1881, to showcase Hygeian Rock's capabilities, William designed and built an imposing house in Belmont Road (in the yards of the Great Western Railway station), which overlooks the vale of the river Usk. This is "Fairlea" Grange, an Elizabethan styled enormous house with four reception rooms, a billiards room, and nine bed-rooms, sufficient to accommodate the growing family.

'Fairlea' Grange where Ethel Lina White spent much of her childhood; today it may be rented as a holiday home. (Photograph published in 1917.)

Ethel appears to have been privately educated and enjoyed writing from an early age. Her parents supported the Little Folks Humane Society, which had been instituted in 1881 by the editor of *Little Folks*, a magazine for the young published by Cassell's. As well as Ethel, several of the Whites' other children were regular entrants to the poetry and other literary competitions that appeared in the magazine. In her twenties Ethel also contributed poems and essays to *Hearth and Home*, a publication aimed at adults, on topics such as John Ruskin, China, the Transvaal Crisis, and "The Modern Young Man". Regarding "The Modern Young Man", one critic described it as "a clever poem, full of sarcasm and irony, yet neither exaggerated nor envenomed". Evidently, Ethel's responses foreshadow the spikey and witty commentary on life that would feature heavily in her future thrillers.

It was a leisurely and privileged life but in 1901 Ethel's father, William, died. Her mother, Eliza, took over Hygeian Rock Manufacturers, supported by her children, some of whom — including Ethel — worked for the firm in various capacities. During this time, Ethel continued to write and began selling short stories. These include "An Advertisement Baby," which was published in the *Royal Magazine* in 1906, and over the next twenty years she produced a steady flow of short fiction for magazines such as *The Strand*, *The Idler*, *Pearson's*, *The Lady's Realm*, *Lloyd's*, *The Windsor* and *The London*. During the early twentieth century, the market was enormous for the kind of stories at which Ethel excelled — lightly written romantic entanglements. White had gained the nickname "Dell" as a possible lighthearted reference to the author Ethel May Dell Savage (whose pen name was Ethel M. Dell) – a popular writer of romance novels between 1911 until her death in 1939. White also experimented with tales of mystery and suspense, and eventually gothic and crime narratives. In a letter to her publishers, first discovered by book-seller Mark Sutcliffe, Ethel wrote that her early stories betrayed the lurid tales recounted to her and the other children by their Welsh nurse-maids who in this way had provided "excellent training for a future thrill-writer".

After Eliza's death in 1917, "Fairlea" and Hygeian Rock Manufacturers was sold. Ethel and her two younger sisters, Annis Dora and Marjorie Hilda, moved to Streatham in south London.

With many vacancies created by the war, the three women all found employment: Annis as a secretary; Marjorie as an illustrator; and Ethel as a clerk in the Ministry of Pensions. Ethel confessed in her letter that "I couldn't stand officelife, because of the lack of fresh air"; therefore, in 1919, she "threw up a safe job […] on the strength of a ten–pound offer for a short story". She resigned from the Ministry of Pensions and set out to become a writer on a full-time basis.

Gillian Lind and Harcourt Williams in *The Port of Yesterday*.
(Photograph published in 1928.)

Her first foray into writing novels was *The Wish-Bone* (1927), a lightly satirical tale about love, marriage, and class distinctions that contained subtle allusions to *Jane Eyre*: a bourgeois young woman called Marigold Leaf evades a loveless marriage and absconds middle-class society with a man who has an even more extraordinary name, Hyacinth Smith (who, in turn, wishes to evade the stigma of having a drunken wife).

The following year Ethel dabbled in theatre, completing *The Port of Yesterday*, a play which ran at the Strand Theatre (now the Novello Theatre) in London's West End in April 1928. The play concerns a middle-aged widower who is haunted by recollections — and even, apparently, by the ghost — of his first wife whilst visiting her Godmother's home, the aptly named *Memory Cottage*. Fourteen years later Noël Coward would tread similar ground with his most famous play, *Blithe Spirit*. *The Port of Yesterday* received generally favourable reviews, one describing it as having "a distinct flavour of [J. M.] Barrie" and it contains a moment within which "the impossible was constructed". However, one critic explained somewhat patronisingly that there were "the familiar faults of a writer who has been a novelist before turning to the drama. In other words, Miss White attempts to say too much".

If Ethel's first novel, *The Wish-Bone*, had owed something to Charlotte Brontë, her second was similarly in debt to Charles Dickens. *'Twill Soon Be Dark* (1929), expanded from an earlier 1925 short story of the same name, traces the predicaments of an ambitious dreamer, Oliver, who in his youth desired fame and fortune and, after becoming a famous writer, returns to his home town only to discover that his childhood sweetheart, Emerald, is on trial for murder.

Part satire, part fantasy, Ethel's third novel could be deemed the kindred spirit of Virginia Woolf's *Orlando* (1928) for *The Eternal Journey* (1930) deals with reincarnation and redemption, recounting the life — or, rather, the lives — of a young woman, Ursula, who is accused of being a witch and is drowned in 1794, then sacrifices her own life for a friend in 1931, and marries for love in 2331.

Ethel was writing in the Golden Age of crime fiction and, as she had incorporated murder and suspense in her first three novels, it was not surprising that she should migrate toward detective and thriller fiction. The first result,

Put Out the Light (1931), sees unpleasant spinster, Anthea Vine, murdered, and the killer is amongst a small selection of relatives and acquaintances. The title is a quotation from Shakespeare's *Othello*, and the novel is cleverly constructed. Contrary to the generally accepted convention, the murder occurs three quarters of the way into the narrative. Furthermore, with its focus on the victim's paranoia and dread of ageing, the novel demonstrates what is most distinctive about Ethel's work: her interest in the psychology of her characters and how it shapes their response to the situations in which they find themselves.

In a frontispiece to *Put Out the Light*, Ethel explained that 'Most stories of crime begin with a murder and end with its solution. But as the victim is the dominant character in this novel, she has been retained as long as possible'. Pre-empting criticism that the murderer might be easy to identify, she went on to suggest that 'Readers, therefore, may decide who is going to kill her before the murder is actually committed. They will probably reach the goal before the detective, who is built to last and not for speed.'

This reflects Ethel's approach to writing, which seems to have been almost breezily undisciplined. As she said in the letter to her publisher quoted above:

> "My method of working is so weird that it is a mystery to me that there really is a novel to show for it. I begin, about twelve, with writing materials, write a few lines, then get a glass of water – another line or so – smoke a cigarette – another line – play with the kitten – and then break for a cup of tea. But somehow, a book does get written. I write such an incoherent script that I have to type it roughly in order to realise what it is about – and then I play with the typed version quite a lot before the final typing. All this takes quite a lot of time."

While it would be inaccurate to say that Ethel had a formula, she certainly had a particular approach to writing thrillers, and she is reported to have said that she "treated her craft with all the respect it deserves: she was strongly of the opinion that thrillers should be well written and would write and rewrite her manuscript until she was satisfied." Her thrillers are similar to other writers of neogothic suspense and woman-in-peril stories, like Mary Roberts Rinehart, although Ethel's beautiful and feisty heroines are more likely to say

"Had-You-Believed-Me" than "Had-I-But-Known." And many of her stories have as background a small town, drawing on her childhood in Abergavenny. Indeed, *Some Must Watch* (1933) recounts the predic-aments in a country-house named the Summit, located 'somewhere at the union of three counties, on the border-line between England and Wales', which could be a description of Monmouthshire, Gwent.

During the 1930s and early 40s, Ethel continued to write short stories, some of which were syndicated in the United States, but her reputation rested on her novels, the majority of which are superb examples of what Martin Edwards, *the* authority on the Golden Age of crime fiction, has termed "domestic suspense". Several were expanded from short stories in this collection. The supremely creepy *Wax* (1935) was based on the 1930 short story "Waxworks"; *The Man Who Loved Lions* (1943) took inspiration from her 1940 short story "Caged." Another is *Midnight House* (1942), which was adapted from the 1937 short story "The Cellar"; *They See in Darkness* (1944) was also a reworking of the earlier 1930 short story "At Twilight," which will be reprinted in 2024 by HarperCollins in the second volume in their series *Ghosts from the Library*.

The Wheel Spins (1936) has been filmed multiple times, most notably by Hitchcock as *The Lady Vanishes* (1938). This too was expanded from a short story, "Passengers," and it is effectively a variation on the Victorian urban legend of "The Vanishing Lady" (hence Hitchcock's title!) When the film premiered at the Coliseum theatre in Abergavenny, Ethel attended as the mayor's guest of honour, and said that "Gainsborough made the film and they ought to be on the stage," but that she was there because she "did not take up much room." Hitchcock's film earned Ethel her many plaudits, including being guest of honour one time at Foyle's famous liter-ary luncheons. Unfortunately, however, the film has overshadowed Ethel's original novel, which has also provided an inspiration for other films such as *Flightplan* (2005) starring Jodie Foster. Even when the BBC adapted *The Wheel Spins* in 2013 — with Tuppence Middleton as Ethel's heroine Iris Carr — the producer reportedly said that as Ethel's novel is "a complete delight and beautifully writ-ten ... we decided to go to the book" in order to be 'purists'; *yet* they retained Hitchcock's title.

In the early 1940s, Ethel was diagnosed with ovarian cancer. She died on the 13th of August 1944 at her home in Arlington Park Mansions on Sutton Lane North in Chiswick, West London. Her estate was valued at £5,737 (around £200,000 or $300,000 in today's money). She left this to her sister Annis "on condition she pays a qualified surgeon to plunge a knife into my heart after death". The instruction, which reflected Ethel's genuine fear of being buried alive, is a theme that had featured in her novel *The First Time He Died* (1935), wherein one of the characters makes a similarly worded exhortation to her doctor. Circumventing the risk of a Poe-like entombment, Ethel was cremated and her ashes scattered in the Garden of Remembrance at Mortlake Crematorium in Kew, south London.

They See in Darkness (1944), Ethel's fourteenth and final thriller, was published posthumously and features a chain of murders, an asylum and a sinister cult of nuns. A year after her death, *The Unseen* (1945) was released. This was an adaptation by Raymond Chandler and others of *Midnight House* (1942). Ethel would achieve even greater posthumous success with an adaptation of her serial killer whodunnit *Some Must Watch*. Under the title *The Spiral Staircase* the book has been filmed four times: most memorably in 1946 with Dorothy McGuire; in 1961 with Elizabeth Montgomery; in 1975 with Jacqueline Bisset; and in 2000 with Nicollette Sheridan.

Although her career spanned almost fifty years and produced seventeen fulllength novels, over one hundred and thirty short stories, a play, and at least two poems – and despite the enduring reputation of *The Lady Vanishes* and *The Spiral Staircase* - awareness of Ethel Lina White has undoubtedly receded. One can imagine that this might have pleased the woman who once responded to a request for biographical information by stating that "I was not born. I have never been educated and have no tastes or hobbies. This is my story and I'm sticking to it". Nonetheless, and fortunately for modern readers and researchers, she is experiencing something of a revival. Her fourteen thrillers were reprinted in 2015 by the publisher Murder Room, while her short stories appear in various anthologies, including those edited by Martin Edwards for the British Library's Crime Classics series and the *Bodies from the Library* anthologies published by HarperCollins. However, this present volume, *Blackout and Other Stories*, is the first collection of her short fiction. It is published by Crippen & Landru to mark 80 years since her death.

Happily – after far too long – the lady *un*-vanishes.

Tony Medawar and Alex Csurko
Cyberspace, March 2024

The world seemed to end at Pyman's Corners and pile itself up in a green wash of trees. Although it was still afternoon, the autumn mists had veiled the evergreen shrubs in Miss Luck's moist, leaf-strewn garden so that the lawn seemed peopled with crouching forms.

Standing at her parlour window, Miss Luck thought of church-yard lights—the whisper in the parlour lane—the footsteps on the stairs—all the old nursery tales of horror and fear. In appearance, however, she looked more than a match for man or ghost. A tall, massive woman, she wore an iron grey suit cut on masculine lines; her powerful shoulders and muscular back suggested almost ruth-less strength. She turned her head and the illusion vanished. Her face was a mere handful of little, indefinite features over which peered timid eyes.

"Fay," she bleated, in a small, weak voice, "I saw a—a tree move in the garden."

The younger Miss Luck, a feather-weight of a girl with a small, pale face and short, dark elf locks, laughed. "Did it? Now, that's quite interesting. Suppose we have a look at it."

As she rose and put her arm within that of her aunt the enormous lady felt a sudden gust of courage, for this tiny creature was more than her niece and companion. She was her protector. Together they peered into the gloomy garden, nearly submerged in that strange medium—the shade "between the lights." And immediately the creeping, misted trees stopped in their advance and stiffened into definite holly or laurel.

"Where's your wonderful tree?" asked Fay.

Miss Luck laughed in her relief. She did not know that she was unable to point it out to her niece because it had crept so much closer to the cottage that it was lurking behind the pillars of the porch.

"Draw the curtains and let's be snug, Felicia," she said.

"I love to be called 'Felicia'," commented Fay. "Being small, my name gives such chances to be obvious."

"I know," Miss Luck nodded. "I always wish I'd been called 'Grace.' After Grace Darling, you know. It's my ambition and dream to save life."

She squared her massive shoulders and flung back her head, every inch a heroine. At this moment she could have faced lions or raging seas. Because—at this moment—the witched garden was shut out by thick wine-red curtains; the comfortable room glowed with light from lamp and fire; the gilt clock told her it was only a quarter to five. And, on the rug, was a small, dark girl in a leaf-brown jersey and kilt.

Unfortunately, she saw the smile Fay tried to suppress. It made her writhe with secret shame. It was in vain that she reminded herself that she was a lady of considerable wealth and, as such, an object of interest to her family. She could always depend upon some niece eager to "keep her company" in her Sussex cottage.

In spite of her armour of frigid dignity, she was the meekest soul at heart. A street urchin could make her quail by a shouted insult. She never rode in a bus because she feared the angry glances of the passengers she crushed. She allowed tradespeople to overcharge her rather than risk a scene.

Of course, the poor lady was really to be pitied, since her cowardice was chiefly due to a deficient pituitary gland. Nature had given her the frame of an Amazon with the heart of a mouse. Her fault lay in not trying to control her nerves. Because of this, she was doomed to a terrible moment, when her whole nature hung crucified with suffering and shame.

As Fay remained silent, Miss Luck tried to force her to an admission. "Did you hear how that gardener you—I—discharged described me to Elsie?" she asked. "He said I was a fat old coward. Really fantastic!"

"Really insolent" said Fay severely.

"I confess it made me laugh. . . . Now, would you call me a coward?" Fay noticed that the tip of her aunt's nose quivered, as it always did, in moments of emotion. In spite of her natural contempt, she suddenly felt very sorry for Miss Luck. Fortunately, she was spared a reply by the ringing of the telephone bell from the hall.

"I'll answer it," she said quickly.

When she returned there was a jaded look on her small, vivid face. "Frightfully sorry, Aunt Winny," she said. "I've got to go out immediately."

Miss Luck's mouth dropped. "Leave me all alone?"

"But, angel, it's still afternoon. It's only for half an hour. And you'll have Elsie."

"No. It's her evening out. Where are you going?"

Fay braced her nerves for another scene. "To the police station," she replied. "They've arrested another man, and they want me to identify him."

Miss Luck's face puckered with rage and fear. "Felicia," she gasped, "I forbid you to go."

"I'm afraid it's nothing to do with you," Fay's tone lacked respect. "And I don't see why you should worry. It's my funeral. O, dear, why did I take that walk?"

Her face grew wistful as she remembered that wild wet day of high wind and flying leaves which had tempted her to a ramble in the beech woods. She had been so filled with the joy of living—so unconscious of the horror in store. And, in the midst of her rapture, she had heard a scream. Breaking through the bushes, she had been in time to see a man rushing away from the prostrate form of a woman.

Although she had missed the actual murder and was thus spared the nauseating details—which her aunt devoured in the morning paper—the shock was severe. She re-lived that moment, together with her breathless rush to the police station, in many a nightmare.

What had tried her nerves most, however, was her aunt's attitude. She reproached Fay bitterly for giving information of the appearance of the criminal and thus exposing them to his possible recrimination. "We're a marked house," she quavered.

"You should have kept your own counsel and said nothing at all."

Unfortunately, some of Miss Luck's gloomy prophecy had been fulfilled. The police made an arrest, but Fay failed to identify the man. Although her name was kept out of the papers she must have been seen as she left the station, for the next day she received an anonymous note.

"I seen you. Keep your trap shut or I'll serve you same as I done her." "A Man of His Word."

Fay crushed the note in her indignation.

"Fancy that calling itself a man. Optimist. I'm jolly glad now I saw the little rat."

But some of the poison which lurks in every anonymous letter got under her skin. She could not rid herself of the impression that her movements were dogged. Therefore she was careful to avoid lonely localities and not to go out, unaccompanied, after dark.

Today's message from the police station came as a relief. Her description of a gentleman of brunette colouring, smart appearance, and poor physique applied to more than one member of a razor gang in which the police were interested. But, since the problem boiled itself down to a suspect being unable to account for his movements on a certain fatal Wednesday afternoon, she was hopeful that, this time, she would return to the cottage with the comforting knowledge that the criminal was safely under lock and key.

Her lips were set as she walked into the hall and took down her brown tweed coat from it peg. When she returned to the parlour her aunt looked at her with dog-like, appealing eyes. She had many nieces—all attractive and charming—but this independent chit was the one she cared for most, and was, in fact, her principal legatee. She wanted desperately to win back Fay's respect.

Fay's lips did not relax at her unspoken plea.

"I'm going to the kitchen to tell Elsie that she must stay in for another half hour," she said.

As she spoke, she regarded her aunt with eyes that had grown speculative. Miss Luck was a good and charitable soul, with excellent qualities. At her death she would be missed more than many an attractive personality.

Suddenly Fay felt that she would be really fond of the old thing if she were not such a desperate coward. With the regrettable urge for reformation which animates most young and ardent natures, she wondered if it would be possible to cure her aunt of cowardice. She would have to endure a sharp lesson, but the result would justify any pain. She must be made afraid of some peril which was nonexistent, and thus receive a demonstration of the futility of fear.

"How?" wondered Fay, her eyes brilliant as diamonds.

But, even as she racked her brains, she remembered the classic horror of the man who frightened his wife with a dead snake, only to attract its living mate. Fay shook her head. Her plea held dangerous possibilities. But it spurred her on to reopen the vexed question.

"You asked me, just now," she said, "what I thought of you. Well, I think you are a puzzle. I can understand a rabbit being frightened of a snake, because they're different orders. But it beats me altogether why one human being would be frightened of another human being."

Fay laid down the law with youthful authority, ignorant of the fact that the human species has its rabbits and snakes.

"Wouldn't you be frightened if a man attacked you?" asked Miss Luck.

"No. I'd put up such a fight for it that I'd be too angry to feel afraid, although I'm only a shrimp. And that's why you're such a mystery to me. You know, if you were ferocious, instead of being a darling everyone would be afraid of you. You make me think of some force that doesn't know its own strength. Like an elephant that allows itself to be meekly led by a pygmy."

Fay checked her eloquence at the sight of Miss Luck's face, which was scarlet, while the tip of her nose quivered violently. Too late, she realised that her tactless allusion to her aunt's proportions had mortally offended that sensitive lady.

"Out of her will," she thought, fatalistically, as she went into the kitchen.

She caught Elsie in the act of applying lipstick before the small mirror. Her pretty face had rather a foxy expression. Although it was not yet five o'clock, she wore the Lido blue coat and small felt hat which showed that, temporarily, she was out of service.

"My aunt wants you to stay in until five-thirty this afternoon, Elsie," said Fay.

"Then 'want' must be her master," returned Elsie smartly.

She knew her value as a treasure whose only fault was carelessness, and she had no intention of making herself cheap. By leaving the cottage she could obtain her seat at the cinema for the low price of the afternoon session.

"Where's the sense of me staying?" she argued. "She's set in the drawing room and me here, and she won't see me once all the blooming time."

Suddenly Fay saw a chance of the desired lesson for her aunt. There would be no possible risk in leaving her alone, at this ridiculously early hour, for thirty minutes.

"So long as you can make her think you are here," she said carelessly, "it seems to amount to the same thing."

She brought back the tidings to Miss Luck that Elsie would stay in.

"And they're going to fetch me and bring me back in a car," she added, "so there'll be no risk of meeting the man. I'm sorry to say."

She noticed that Elsie had taken off her coat and hat and was wearing her muslin apron when she announced Sergeant Davis. He was an excellent type of policeman, powerfully built, with a pleasant and intelligent face.

"Sorry to trouble you again," he said, addressing Miss Luck, "but I think we've got our bird this time. We're lucky to have some one like your young lady, who knows her mind right off. Indeed, we're most grateful to both you ladies for your public-spirited attitude and your pluck."

Miss Luck bridled and threw back her shoulders at this praise. She felt every inch a heroine, so tonic was the combination of the policeman's admiration and Elsie's apron.

She accompanied the sergeant and Fay to the hall, and although the front door stood ajar she never shuddered at the garden, wanly visible in the pallid shroud of twilight. It was Fay who remembered the perambulating tree.

"My aunt thought she saw a man lurking 'round," she said.

"If he is, we'll soon have him out," remarked the sergeant, darting across the lawn and ducking around every shrub and tree.

"Not a smell of anyone," he said, returning to the porch. "Well, if your niece identifies this man we'll see the end of a nasty set of cowards. He's the brains, and the gang will fall to bits once he's out of the way, like a slit string of beads."

"Good luck!" beamed Miss Luck, waving her hand.

"Back in half an hour," called Fay, from the car.

As she looked back she saw the front door close on her aunt. She smiled feeling confident that her plan must succeed. Inside was warmth, light and safety. The garden had harboured no reptile. And when Miss Luck knew how she had been tricked she must realise the absurdity of her fears.

For there was nothing to tell Fay that she had just locked up the poor lady in the company of a live snake.

Had Sergeant Davis beaten the garden three minutes previously he would have found the snake. It lurked, coiled up behind the pillars of the porch, a yard away from him, when he rang the bell. When Elsie opened the door to admit the policeman she did not slam it but left it slightly ajar. This was the snake's chance. With the flash of the ferdelance it darted inside and hid behind the row of coats which hung in the recess under the stairs.

In appearance it was not an imposing snake, but among the most venomous of the species are the small reptiles which crawl in the dust. And it carried its sting—a razor in the breast pocket of its smart, plum-coloured suit.

In its flat, black, oiled head, too, was its plan. Spotty—the Brain of the gang, who had croaked the woman in the woods, was now in quod, awaiting identification. The snake had been unable to strike before the advent of the police car. But, upon Fay's return, she would find a perfect gentleman waiting to open the door to her.

With the mentality of his kind he believed that the removal of the chief witness for the crown would cause the case against Spotty to collapse.

Happily unconscious of her anonymous visitor, Miss Luck strolled back to her parlour. She looked around her with pleasure at the warm comfort and rich colouring of the room. The suite had just been recovered with new tapestry—dahlias on a buff ground. None of your cretonne loose covers for Miss Luck.

As she lowered herself cautiously into a deep padded chair Elsie entered carrying a plate with moulds of yellow white sugar.

"I've brought you the sugar from the candy peel," she said loftily. "I've started to mix the Christmas puddings while I'm waiting for Miss Fay, and then when I come back I'll finish them before I go to bed."

Miss Luck beamed her approval.

"And please, mum," went on Elsie, "can I get you anything now? Because I won't want to answer the bell with my hands all mucky with flour."

"I shall require nothing, Elsie," Miss Luck informed her.

Three minutes later Elsie slipped through the hall, unbolted the front door cautiously, and started off at a good pace down the dim grey road towards the tram terminus.

Presently, Miss Luck finished her sugar and walked out into the hall for a little exercise. At its far end was the kitchen door. It was outlined with a crack of yellow light, which together with a smell of nutmeg, told that Elsie was busy at her puddings.

The knowledge gave her such a sense of security that she determined not to disturb her conscientious maid in order to light the bedrooms. Miss Luck explained her illumination of the house by her wish to avoid a possible personal accident in the dark.

She was still so puffed with pride at the policeman's compliment that she did not feel her usual distaste of the hall, which was rather a dim cavern, with mahogany paneled walls. Even though her coat, hanging in the recess, bulged so that it looked exactly as though a man were hiding behind it, she did not quail.

She knew that Elsie was the other side of the kitchen door. So she made an impudent face at it, just to show it that she was not to be bluffed by a mere weatherproof. She even had a sudden childish impulse to punch it, and only refrained because the action involved a loss of dignity.

Up the stairs she ambled ponderously. When she was nearly at the top she slipped and had to hold the balustrade to prevent a fall, as the carpet became suddenly taut beneath her feet. Looking down, she saw that Elsie had failed to put back one of the brass rods, after cleaning.

"Elsie, Elsie," she called.

There was no reply, although the girl must have heard her. Miss Luck was on the point of descending the stairs when she opportunely remembered the Christmas puddings. Because of them, she resolved to accept the fiction of Elsie's deafness.

The staircase ended in a broad corridor. On one side was Elsie's bedroom. On the other side Miss Luck's huge bedroom opened into Fay's smaller apartment.

As a rule Miss Luck hated to open her door in the dusk, because it faced the wardrobe mirror, and it gave her a shock to see a dim figure advance to meet her. But this evening she was forcibly struck by her vast, swaying grey shape.

"Fay's right," she said. "I am like an elephant. What an old fool I was to get so angry with her!"

Her face grew wistful as she remembered how Fay had hinted that she, too, could acquire courage if she would only realise her reserves. From the bottom of her heart she wished that, by some miracle, her cowardly nature might be changed. She had been told that miracles actually did happen. Her silly muddle of features did not look quite as silly as she uttered up a voiceless prayer for a miracle to happen to her. A prayer—to be brave.

Feeling quite gay and confident, she went to her toilet table. To her surprise a cheap blue leather bag lay on her silver tray. She opened it and found, by the evidence of money, key, packet of fags, and sundry cheap aids to beauty, that it belonged to Elsie.

Miss Luck forgot her exaltation in the human indignation of a mistress. This time the careless baggage should stir her lazy bones and come upstairs, in spite of floury hands.

On her way to the bell, however, the thought of the Christmas puddings prevailed. Elsie might get mixed in her quantities, were she called away. Leaving the bag on her toilet table, Miss Luck descended the staircase, treading carefully over the loose carpet on the twelfth step. She was crossing the hall when she glanced at the front door.

It gave her a mild shock of discomfort to discover that the bolt was not drawn. She distinctly remembered doing so herself when she had seen Fay to the police car. Feeling vaguely disturbed she burst into the kitchen to catch Elsie unawares. The homely place reassured her with its glowing fire and snowy table laden with suet and dried fruits. The primrose-enameled walls gleamed in the gas-light and the air was hot and spiced.

But Elsie was not there. Miss Luck's heart began to hammer as she went into larder, scullery, and outhouses, calling the girl by name. When she returned to the kitchen her eye fell upon the empty peg upon which Elsie's coat usually hung. Suddenly she felt blasted by a terrible sense of desolation. Elsie had gone out secretly and left her all alone.

Miss Luck's muddle of features puckered up like a pimpernel on a wet day. To understand her feelings it must be stated that the situation was unique. When she was quite young the doctor had prescribed constant companionship after a nervous breakdown. Being a lady of means, Miss Luck had converted a temporary measure into a permanent one.

She felt helpless as a stranded baby. Fortunately, however, her first flush of indignation left her no room for actual fear. She vowed that Elsie should have her marching orders. When she returned from the pictures Miss Luck would be waiting for her, on the mat. Elsie should learn who was her master.

The kitchen clock, too, provided her with a measure of comfort, for its hands stood at five-fifteen. Already half the time had slipped away and she had survived. Mechanically she scooped up a handful of raisins and put them in her coat pocket. In another quarter of an hour Fay would be back. Meanwhile, she thought she would feel safer in her own bedroom than on the ground floor.

It really seemed as though Fay's strategy were going to succeed, for Miss Luck was careful to curb her unhealthy imagination as she went upstairs. It is true she did not like going through the gloom of the hall and took pains not to look in the direction of the line of coats. On her way she rehearsed the notice that she knew would never be given, for Elsie would not allow it.

"I will not tolerate disobedience."

"No one defies me twice."

"What hurts me most is the deceit."

These fine phrases carried her safely up the corridor, which — in contrast with the hall — glowed with light. It had a red Turkey carpet, two marble busts upon pedestals, one, palm, and a picture after Landseer.

With the exception of the bathroom and her own bedroom all the white enameled doors had their keys on the outside in proof that they were never used. As Fay's sanctum communicated with her own by a door without even a flimsy bolt, Miss Luck locked it and then put the key in her coat pocket. She marched, like a soldier, into her own fortress, where she set about the task of making it impregnable.

It was now more necessary than ever to curb her imagination, for the pictures had made her dread gigantic hands with clawing fingers shooting out from behind curtains and secret panels opening behind her in the hall. She began to give Elsie notice all over again, but this time her phrases were pitched in an ominous minor key.

"O, Elsie, how could you betray me?"

"Haven't I always been a kind and generous mistress to you?"

"Perhaps you'll be sorry when you hear I'm—"

Miss Luck checked herself just in time. Under the beds. Behind the window hangings. Inside the wardrobes. The worst she found was a little fluff. Dusting her skirt, she went to the window and looked out.

She was amazed to find that it was still twilight. The laurels and hollies stood out distinctly against a neutral background and the lamps in the road were not yet lit. Officially, it was afternoon. As she leaned out of the frame in the hope of hearing the car her broad back was towards the door. So she did not see the handle turn slowly, as though someone on the other side were trying to enter.

But she looked around at the sound of footsteps, creeping along the corridor. She put her hand automatically to her heart and then withdrew it proudly as she remembered the locked doors. Besides, she knew how much mimicry there was about the noises of an empty house at dusk. That creak, for instance, exactly resembled the opening of Elsie's door.

She looked at her watch and heaved a sigh. It was nearly twenty-five minutes past five. Of course, she could not count upon Fay returning to the dot—but her vigil would soon be over. A car purred down the road, and although it did not stop it seemed a link with the outside world.

She determined not to let her thoughts get out of hand. Little bits of cotton wool in her ears would be helpful. Nourishment, too, seemed a good plan. As she began to crunch her raisins she wondered why people hinted that she was greedy. Once she had taxed Fay with the question and had been comforted by her tactful reply.

"Not greedy, darling. But, perhaps you give the impression of someone who's been kept short."

That was it. Miss Luck nodded vehemently at her reflection. She had been half starved at her expensive boarding school.

Meanwhile it was tonic to look about her room, which was furnished in florid taste, with an imitation Empire bed, a rose-pink carpet and pink wall paper, picked into panels with silver beading.

No one should feel nervous in such surroundings. Those curious scraping noises were plainly made by a mouse. Any minute now Fay would return. And here she was in a cheerful, brightly lit room, from whence she would step into a cheerful, brightly lit corridor, down into a cheerful, brightly lit ground floor.

Luckily, she did not know of the startling change which had taken place just outside her closed door. The white doors and red carpet were blotted out by a pall of darkness, transforming the homely passage into a jungle, wherein crept and rustled some creature of the night. Miss Luck began to yawn. She played with the idea of going downstairs to ring up the police station and ascertain the exact time at which the car had started. Only—that might look like nerves. It was rather late in the day to wear the white feather, now that the hands of her watch were past the half hour. Besides, she did not quite like the idea of passing that line of coats in the hall.

Suddenly her expression grew intent. In the distance there was a pinging note, like the buzz of an insect. It might be the car returning with Fay. In order to listen better she removed the plugs of wool from her ears.

Her face paled. Someone was moving inside Fay's room.

This time it was not fancy. There were unmistakable footsteps on the other side of the thin wall. Intelligent footsteps, too, that paused when she moved, in order to mark her down.

In an agony of fear, Miss Luck told herself that it was impossible. She had, herself, locked Fay's door, and the key was in her pocket. Besides, there were old fashioned lustres on the mantelpiece which always rattled when anyone walked over a loose board in the middle of the room. As the thought flashed through her mind it came—the thin, icy tinkling of cut glass.

Miss Luck's terror was too acute to endure. She was timid of most tangible things, but her practical mind rejected sheer impossibilities. She did not believe in ghosts. And no human being could pass through a locked door.

It was Elsie's bag, lying on her table, that suggested the solution. The girl must have discovered her loss, directly she reached the tram. What was more natural than for her to return and stealthily creep about the house to find her bag?

Miss Luck knew that she was on the right trail, for Elsie had informed her of her discovery that the bathroom key fitted the lock of Fay's room. She determined to give her deceitful domestic the fright of her life.

"Come out," she called, in a loud voice. "I know you are there."

There was silence, as the footsteps stopped dead. Miss Luck advanced towards the door of communication.

"Come out and show yourself," she repeated, "I'm waiting for you."

But as she stood, in expectant majesty, her attention was distracted by the hooting of a motor horn outside the gate. She hurried to the window to see a car stationary in the road. This time there was no mistake for Fay's voice floated faintly on the air.

The person in the adjoining room had caught the sounds even sooner than herself. Returning from the window, Miss Luck looked inside, to find the bird flown.

She smiled grimly. Elsie could wait her pleasure, with Fay at the gate. Humming tunelessly, she opened her door, only to step back in surprise at the belt of darkness which lay beyond the area illuminated by her room.

She nodded sagely. Another of my lady's tricks. The fresh demonstration of guile was typical in Elsie's mentality. Since her mistress could not actually see as she stole upstairs, she would swear by all her gods that, all the time, she was in the kitchen.

As the electric switches were in the hall, Miss Luck groped her way along the wall until her outstretched hand touched the balustrade. Stepping cautiously into the gulf, she started to descend, peering the while into the well of darkness. Suddenly she stopped and stared more closely, blinking her eyes the while, as though to clear some flaw of vision. Against the dark panel of the front door was a denser shadow, like the blurred shape of a man.

The light from the porch filtering through the fanlight fell upon a flat, shiny black head, a peaked evil face, rotten teeth. A corrupt soul peered out of small, flickering eyes.

"Like something from a sewer," flashed across Miss Luck's mind.

As she stood, petrified with shock, her brain worked rapidly. She realised that Elsie had not come back after all. Below her crouched the actual source of the mysterious happenings—the scratching.

Probably, following some predatory urge, he had crept about the house under cover of darkness His cunning would soon detect which key fitted the lock of Fay's door.

Her hands grew sticky and her throat dry as she thought of the boltless door of communication. Only a few frail panels of wood divided her from him. She remembered the murder in the wood and those newspaper details which Fay had been spared. Had she confronted the man she knew that he would have attacked her, like a cornered rat.

Even as she thought of the danger she had just escaped she heard Fay's voice ringing out from the garden path. She was evidently calling to her escort in the car.

"Don't wait. I'm all right. My aunt will be frightfully thrilled at the news. She's been windy about me."

Miss Luck made an impotent gesture as though to arrest the car. But she heard its exhaust roar as it hummed down the road like an express train.

Cheerily Fay's signal knock sounded on the front door. In imagination Miss Luck could see her standing outside—her cheeks coloured by her ride, her dark elf locks blown, and her eyes shining with excitement. She had a tale to unfold.

Instantly the dark figure crept forward, while the light flashed upon something in his hand. Then Miss Luck understood the ultimate horror. A gentleman with a razor was waiting to open the door to Fay.

That moment was to remain as her bitterest memory. She recognized it as the peak of her life. All these events had led up to this climax, when she would expiate her cowardice in a blaze of heroism. She had prayed for a miracle to happen. . . .

But miracles follow the working of the natural law. Because Miss Luck had violated this law—starving each feeble flicker of courage while she pampered her nerves—the moment of trial brought its logical fulfillment.

No rush of mysterious power flooded her veins. Instead, she stood paralysed, like a rabbit hyponotised by a snake. She tried to move, but her limbs were stiffened as though her muscles were tied. Her strength oozed away through every pore. Her tongue felt so swollen that it seemed to stopper her throat.

"Fay! Don't open the door!"

Her lips framed the words—but the only sound that issued from them was a tiny gasp.

With the sensitsed ears of his species, the snake heard. He darted forward, the razor flashing in his hand. As he sprang, terror snapped the spell which bound Miss Luck. All thought of Fay was swept away by sheer, blind panic. She turned to run. As she did so, the loose carpet unrolled under her foot and the tense moment of climax slurred down into anti-climax.

Miss Luck fell down the stairs.

She dropped, like a stone, with twice the force of her stupendous weight, hitting the snake just over his heart so that he collapsed, like a crumpled paper bag. Winded and prostrate, Miss Luck awaited her end... Then, as nothing happened, she opened her eyes. Underneath her lay something which felt boneless as pulp. Peering down, she saw a narrow-chested, putty-faced creature—an adder crashed flat by an elephant's foot. His sting was drawn for his razor gleamed two yards away.

Miss Luck stared in astonishment at her handiwork.

"I—did—that!" she gasped.

It was in this moment that the miracle actually happened. As she gaped at the puny form, now beginning to twitch feebly under the weight, she suddenly realised her own strength.

A wondrous sense of release swept over her. She felt mighty and dominant, as though she were sitting on top of the world.

Outside the door Fay hunted for her key. She had just remembered that Elsie was out, so could not answer to her knock.

As she entered the hall she was startled by the unfamiliar darkness. But her alarm was lost in surprise when she heard Miss Luck's feeble bleat magnified to a trumpet blast of triumph and scorn.

"Fay, bring the laundry cords, quick! I've squashed something here!"

RIVER JUSTICE

When Miss Nile realised that Chadwick Morris was poisoning his wife, she tried to realise her duty, in the cause of humanity.

It was a morning of sparkling summer when the sky was a clear wash of blue, and the air tasted like wine. The balcony of Miss Nile's bedroom hung out over the glacier-fed river which rushed below in a boiling green torrent. On each side were picturesque wooden houses with sometimes a door or flight of steps leading directly down to the water.

In appearance Miss Nile was a small, bleached English spinster with grey hair and blue eyes, mild as milk. She was shabby, insignificant, and poor, and she lived in a *pensione* in a beautiful but primitive European town. In her youth, however she had been a pretty, golden-haired girl, with many lovers. She had known romance, but destiny had turned her into a nursery governess—in the best families only to propitiate her family pride.

The best families had meant back bedrooms, solitary meals, and an existence suspended midway between the drawing room and the servants' hall. But she kept her spirit and preserved her ideals until a legacy had given her freedom and belated happiness. Although she chose to live abroad, on account of the central heating, she remained a patriot, but she had lost her heart to the quaint town with its flower boxes and its dark arcaded streets.

And she grew to love the river. Just opposite to the *pensione* and under the door of a large sepia-brown house with green jalousies, the current flowed down a steep, glassy wall toward the pillars of the low bridge, against which it broke in a smother of foam. Miss Nile's landlady, in her courageous English, had warned her boarder against the danger of leaning too far over the rails of her veranda. She had pointed to the bridge and made swimming movements.

"No good," she said. "Current, him big and strong. Smash."

Here the landlady touched her head, clapped her hands, and grimaced horribly and expressively.

Miss Nile promised to take care but she spent most of her time on her veranda. She loved running water and when she closed her eyes she could imagine that she had slipped back into her youth and was beside the river at home.

Looking back, it seemed to Miss Nile that the sun always shone then and the month was a permanent June. Her memories were all of the river—boating, bathing, fishing. Sometimes she chuckled over the recollection of a practical joke they had played on Captain Terry Blake.

Terry was a bad boy, but he was also her romance, for she had remained single for his sake. One summer evening when they were all sitting in the little summer house, built out over the river, he fell asleep and she was afraid from the grins of the other young men that the origin of his slumber was wine.

It was the day of Spoof, and they had combined to trick him by reversing the position of the furniture—looking-glass fashion, putting on the hands of the old clock, and turning his chair completely round. When he awoke to find himself staring at the hour of midnight he had staggered to what was apparently, on the evidence of its faded green curtain, the door and stepped instead through the open French windows, down into the river.

Presently on the veranda of the big house opposite she found a romance of real life. A slim, radiant girl, with a vivid face and golden hair, used to lean over the rail and look down at the river. From her landlady Miss Nile gleaned the fact that she was a bride and that her husband was big and rich.

Instantly she saw the girl through a veil of glamour. Although she rouged her lips and smoked cigarettes, she was a darling with the gay spirit and eager eyes of her own youth. It gave her a sharp thrill of pleasure when young Mrs. Morris grew to recognise her and to wave and smile across the river.

One day, as she stopped to buy peaches at a stall, Miss Nile met the bride engaged in the same pantomimic performance. Instantly she gave the little spinster a friendly greeting.

"You're English, aren't you? We're neighbours, too, across the river. Doesn't it talk? It is saying something to me, if I could understand . . . Won't you call on me?"

"I shall be very pleased," Miss Nile replied primly.

"Then come now, for coffee!" pleaded the girl impulsively. "I am just dying to talk again."

She looked so eager that Miss Nile could not resist her, although she was doubtful of the propriety of her course, since she did not know the lady's husband. But that obstacle was removed, for, as they mounted the steps of the house, they met a tall, massive man with a big, clean-shaven face, dead eyes, and a monocle. He gave the impression of being hard and slippery as glass, and Miss Nile noticed that his head was too small for his body and that one of his eyes was grey and the other hazel.

The golden-haired girl introduced them. "My husband, Chadwick, I'm in luck, for I've captured an English resident."

Miss Nile had a sharp pang of repulsion as she remembered her mental pictures of the big, rich bridegroom. In that moment she felt herself superior to this radiant girl. She, at least, had not dipped her colours.

The girl led her to the river room, the walls of which were speckled with dancing reflections of light from the water and murmurous with the big voice of the river.

"So you don't like him, either?" she said to Miss Nile. "I wish I was as quick as you. I had to marry him to find him out." Then she burst out laughing.

"Oh, don't look so shocked," she pleaded. "You know, you're not like a stranger to me. You make me think of my darling Miss Ward, my governess. No one's been so good to me and she was the only person who never spoiled me. Please don't be stiff and formal. If you only knew the relief of talking to someone who understands!"

Her eyes were filled with tears, in spite of her smile, so that Miss Nile took her to her heart. Very soon she was listening to the flood of dammed-up confidences. It was a common enough story of matrimonial misfit. The girl, whose name was Delphine, was the only child of a rich man who had big interests in South America, where they lived. The girl was thoroughly spoiled and autocratic. Because of a quarrel with her lover, Chester, she had married Chadwick Morris in a fit of pique and anger.

"I was so spoiled and vain," confessed Delphine, "that I never dreamed he was marrying me for the money my mother left me. But I'm getting a divorce, almost immediately. Daddy is coming over to arrange it and then I'm going to marry Chester. Isn't he a darling?" She showed Miss Nile the photograph of a youth in R.A.F. uniform. Instantly the little spinster's heart leaped in response to the call of romance. This young man with the eager eyes and clear-cut lips was the husband she would have chosen for Delphine.

"How does Mr. Morris feel about it?" she hinted.

"My dear, he's a man of the world and he's quite decent about it and remarkably resigned to my loss. You see, he's specially—sophisticated, and I think I've been rather a drag on him."

"Do you know, his face is curiously familiar to me? Ever since you introduced him I've been puzzling over where I've seen him before."

"Perhaps it's someone on the screen," suggested Delphine.

"No," dissented Miss Nile. "I never forget a face. And sooner or later I shall remember."

Then, yielding to impulse, she opened her big black bag and drew out a worn leather case which contained the faded photograph of another young man in uniform.

"That's my boy," she said.

"Is he dead?" asked Delphine tenderly.

"No, but we drifted apart. He was wild and he drank. But the kindest and most generous men have that weakness. You are not to blame him."

"I don't, bless him," said Delphine. "I love his eyes. Tell me about this bad boy."

Miss Nile began to laugh. "Oh, my dear," she said, "we once played such a trick on him when—when he was like that. We altered the furniture of the room and he walked right into the river and pulled me in after him. In fact, we all ended up in the water."

She was a girl again as she related the story with full details, and Delphine laughed with her.

"I'll try that one on Chester if ever I get a chance," she declared.

Miss Nile left Delphine after promising to come again soon. But the next time she called at the house a servant gabbled a fluent and unintelligible explanation and resolutely shut the door in her face.

As the days passed without news or sight of Delphine, Miss Nile began to grow worried. She wrote to her, but received no reply, and she called at the house only to be repulsed.

Presently she managed to understand from her landlady that the bride was ill. As far as she could gather it was some form of dysentery, for which the local water was blamed.

"But I drink it," cried Miss Nile in alarm. "Is it bad?"

"You trink him." The landlady nodded vehemently. "I trink him, is us bad? No, no, not at all."

Her landlady's scepticism as to the cause of Delphine's illness was not reassuring and Miss Nile grew still more worried. She was hungry for the sight of a slim gay figure, waving to her across the river. One day in her anxiety she deliberately forgot that she had taught in the best families only and descended to regrettable tactics.

"It's humiliating," she told herself, "but I am forced to—snoop."

So Miss Nile snooped. She concealed herself in a clump of chestnuts at the corner of the street until she saw Morris pass through the door. He wore a carnation in his buttonhole and he twirled his cane as though he were in excellent spirits. After he had disappeared Miss Nile loitered on the pavement until the first tradesman called at the house. As the door was opened the respectable spinster dodged under the servant's arm, scampered up the stairs, and scuttled into the front bedroom like a demented mouse.

Delphine was in bed listlessly staring at the wooden ceiling. At the sight of Miss Nile she gave a faint scream of joy.

"Oh, darling, darling, it's wonderful to see you again! Why didn't you come before after all my messages, you little brute?"

Notes? Miss Nile felt aghast at this revelation of treachery. Then she recollected Morris's alleged dislike of women friends and reminded herself that, in his eyes, she probably was some gossip-mongering old maid. Suddenly the girl seized Miss Nile's wrist and began to whisper.

"Wardie, dear, stay with me." Although she used her old governess's name, Miss Nile was positive that her mind was lucid. "I'm afraid, I've never been ill before. Sometimes I feel numb as if my body was already dead, but my brain keeps on working. And I've a terrible fear that, just because everything is coming right so soon, something will happen to me first."

As she looked at her, Miss Nile felt a shadow of the same dread. She was shocked by the change in Delphine. The bone of the girl's nose rose sharply from a pinched white face and her blue eyes were brilliant from temperature.

"When will your father be here?" she asked.

"In a few days. I'm going to be wonderfully happy, soon. But, Wardie, suppose I don't get well? Oh, please, please stay with me!"

Even as she spoke the door was opened and Morris, followed by a panting servant, entered. His eye glittered like ice behind his monocle.

"How dare you force an entrance against the doctor's orders?" he asked. "If you have endangered my wife's condition the responsibility will be yours. Kindly go at once."

But the mild looking little spinster showed unexpected fight.

"I'm an Englishwoman," she said, "and consequently the right person to nurse your wife. It is her wish. I have undertaken a duty and wild horses will not drag me from my post."

Wild horses were not needed for the big man merely gripped the featherweight Miss Nile by the arm and, between her indignant gasps, ran her down the stairs and out into the street. Her shattered faculties revived as she looked up at the scowling face that frowned at her just before the slam of the door.

"Where have I seen you before?" she asked herself. Then suddenly her knees felt weak, for at that moment she suddenly remembered Chadwick Morris was Dr. Burton of Westmoreland, England, who had been prosecuted by the crown on the charge of murdering his wife, Amy Amelia, by poison, but had been acquitted for lack of sufficient evidence.

Miss Nile had reason for her claim that she never forgot a face and she had seen a photograph of Chadwick Morris in a *Daily Mail* about three years before.

It is true that the portrait had shown a full beard and moustache and no monocle, but the features were identical, while his personal peculiarity in possessing eyes of a different colour was mentioned in his description.

Miss Nile thought of two things. First, that a man in such a case must go somewhere and South America is as good a place as another to hide a changed identity. Second, that a poisoner will usually try the same game again.

Chadwick Morris was poisoning his wife. . . . She roused herself from her torpor and walked home quickly, feeling there was no time to be lost. If Delphine died intestate her money would pass to her husband, but the divorce proceedings would cheat him of the prize for which he had worked.

Since her father was expected so soon, the inference was that he would arrive to find his daughter dead and buried. The doctor would diagnose a sudden relapse and fill in a certificate according to the symptoms which he had treated. A water-tight plan—only Morris had not reckoned with little Miss Nile.

But when she reached her bare bedroom at the *pensione* she was acutely conscious of her helplessness, mental, physical, and material. She was without money, influence or experience of the world. Her lips trembled pitifully and she blinked away a tear.

"I must be a man," she whispered. Suddenly she felt a small explosion in her head and her chaotic muddle of thoughts was blown clean out, leaving her with a desperate plan to save Delphine. It was so daring and fraught with so much personal danger that her legs began to shake, so that she clung to the parapet to save herself from slipping to her knees.

She must kidnap Delphine and hide her for a few days, until she could safely hand her over to her father. It would be an expensive undertaking, for it would be useless to take her anywhere in the locality, since her husband could easily trace the fugitives through the taxicab driver. Miss Nile decided that they must catch the midnight express to Berlin, where she was confident that she could confuse their trail.

She began to count the cost. Two second-class railway tickets, for she dared not allow. Delphine to travel third class—and then, money to keep them at a hotel until they could get in touch by telegram with Delphine's father. Fortunately, her own passport was in order and she could count on Delphine possessing one apart from her husband, as she had done so much travelling before her marriage.

There only remained the detail of removing the lady's husband, while she kidnapped his wife. Drunk with power, she played with the idea of first stunning him and then trussing him into a bundle, an operation which always appeared so easy in the pictures. But common sense revived in time to suggest the subtler method of a sleeping draught.

Its administration would be a possibility, as she reviewed her knowledge of Morris's habits. From the shadow of her veranda she could see down into the river room, where he was accustomed to sit until a late hour, drinking. Since Delphine's story of their ill assorted marriage she used to watch him, for she had a dim idea that all knowledge is power.

She knew, therefore, that at a certain time he invariably dropped off to sleep for a few minutes. And since she was in the habit of taking her letters to the pillar box in time for the last collection, she had remarked the fact that the Morrise's servant used to slip out of the house on the same errand, and generally left the door ajar. She had only to wait her opportunity to slip into the hall and to pour her sleeping draught into the whisky of the unconscious man.

"And then," she thought.
"I shall go upstairs to Delphine, and exert my authority as a governess. She'll respond to it, whatever her condition, for she was used to obeying her own Miss Ward. . . . It will be a risk removing her in her weak condition, but if necessary I'll carry her down to the street myself. And there's a cab rank at the corner."

Miss Nile came out of her dream and realised that she was stewing in the sunshine beside an ancient fountain gay with boxes of small pink begonias. Crossing the cobbled square to the deep shadow of the arcade, she entered the dark cave of the chemist's shop where English was spoken.

She was a frequent customer—for patent medicine was her only vice—and the youth possessed her prescription for a sleeping draught.

"Double strong," she told him. "It's for my—my husband."

Although the assistant understood English he stared at her in such blank surprise that she hastily corrected herself and added. "I mean a—a man."

Very soon she came out of the shop with a small bottle in her hand. Walking quickly despite the broiling heat, she next visited the bank, from which she emerged with an opulent bust and six months' income in notes lying on her meagre chest.

It was not until she was back again at the pensione that she was sucked into the undertow of reaction. She had missed her tea and had a racking headache. Suddenly she realised that she was only a weak elderly woman who had pledged herself to a dangerous mission.

And now that she stood to lose everything, she realised the sum of her overdue happiness. She loved her life in this fairy-tale town. She even loved her bare room with its radiator and its constant hot water, which enabled her to do her laundry on the sly.

Unable to eat dinner, she sat alone listening to the roar of the river. Its voice was louder with a triumphant under-current, as though it knew something.

In every particular of her delirious melodrama, Miss Nile had guessed right. Morris had the usual poisoner's confidence to get away with another crime, and he wanted Delphine safely under the soil or, better still, cremated, before her father arrived. He knew that his preliminary administration of poison had simulated symptoms which would enable the doctor to pronounce the cause of death as botulism.

He had decided to kill her that night, and to pour the fatal dose into her barley water. The servant made a fresh supply every evening and left the jug in an ice-packed tub standing on a table outside the bedroom in order to keep it fresh and cool. On this particular occasion the woman was unusually late in bringing it upstairs. She had run out of barley, so had had to go out of the house to borrow from a neighbour. As he waited for the sound of her footsteps clumping over the wooden flooring of the hall, Morris dropped off into his customary nap.

Upstairs in her room Delphine was lying awake listening for the tinkle of glass which heralded her cooling drink. As she was very thirsty she soon grew impatient and then worked herself up into a fever of irritation. She had actually recovered from her first dose of poison and was full of hope for the future. All her fear of premature death had passed away. But she was still weak and—toward evening, when her temperature rose—was inclined to be light-headed. As no one answered the bell, she determined to fetch her barley water herself. Sliding out of bed, she walked rather unsteadily to the door but by the time she reached the hall her legs felt normal again. The door of the river room was open, so that she could see her husband asleep in his chair. His mouth was open and he was snoring. He looked so grotesque as he puffed his lips that Delphine began to giggle. And then an impish recollection, born of a practical joke swam into her head.

The voice of the river rose—loud and triumphant. It knew. Miss Nile's sacrifice was rejected of fate because this drama had been already played out, years ago, in the comedy of an English summer house.

Delphine's brain was still slightly cloudy with delirium, so that Miss Nile's juvenile buffoonery seemed converted to a pitch of utmost wit and brilliancy. As she looked around her she saw how easy it would be to play the looking-glass game with his room. Halfway up the wall, a broad shelf ran around it, so that she had but to change the distinctive articles which were placed upon it, and to alter a few light pictures. Both doors were painted the same colour and so assisted in the conspiracy.

On one side of the hall entrance was a tantalus with a couple of siphons and a smoking cabinet on the other. As she placed these on the river wall, a corner of her brain remained lucid and dictated a policy of caution.

"It's dangerous. I mustn't carry the joke too far."

She decided, between her smothered chuckles, that she would wake her husband and ask him to open the water door, as she was feeling faint. They were quite good friends, now, although completely detached, and he would enjoy a joke at his expense, when—instead of the foaming river—he saw before him, the parquet floor of the hall.

Delphine's work was done. There only remained the operation of tilting back the chair on its castors and turning it round. She managed to do this, but the exertion overtaxed her strength.

Suddenly the room began to spin around her and then darkness rushed down on her, and she slipped to her knees and lay unconscious on the floor behind the big chair. The slight scuffle aroused Morris, so that he opened his eyes with a start and stared stupidly at the familiar tantalus and portrait of Wilhelm I. Instantly his clouded brain began to click again at the point at which it had been arrested. Murder!

Heaving himself out of his chair, he lurched blindly across the room and threw open the door. In one bewildering moment he saw instead of the wooden floor a raging sheet of water, as—too late to save himself—he stepped into the river. Instantly the current seized him in its grip, spinning him round like a leaf as it sucked him toward the death trap of the bridge. When Miss Nile, with leaden limbs and heart of ice, reached the house it was blaring with lights and humming with the news of the tragedy. So she crept upstairs and looked after the unconscious widow, who had suffered a severe relapse. Fortunately, she was delirious and so would never remember her own madcap frolic. The servants, too, when they noticed the alteration of the room, attributed it to some freak of the master's fancy. Only the river knew.

When the doctor pronounced Delphine out of danger Miss Nile walked back to her pensione under the grey sky of dawn. After she was in bed, the happiest woman in the world kept switching on her electric light for the joy of seeing her wooden walls and the portrait of little Princess "Lilibet."

And far away in England a river sucked at the willows as it rippled and chuckled over its memories of ancient jests.

S onia made her first entry in her notebook:

"Eleven o'clock. The lights are out. The porter has just locked the door. I can hear his footsteps echoing down the corridor. They grow fainter. Now there is silence. I am alone."

She stopped writing to glance at her company. Seen in the light from the street lamp, which streamed in through the high window, the room seemed to be full of people. Their faces were those of men and women of character and intelligence. They stood in groups, as though in conversation, or sat apart in solitary reverie.

But they neither moved nor spoke.

When Sonia had last seen them in the glare of the electric globes, they had been a collection of ordinary waxworks, some of which were the worse for wear. The black velvet which lined the walls of the Gallery was alike tawdry and filmed with dust.

The side opposite to the window was built into alcoves, which held highly moral tableaux, depicting contrasting scenes in the careers of Vice and Virtue. Sonia had slipped into one of these recesses, just before closing time, in order to hide for her vigil.

It had been a simple affair. The porter had merely rung his bell, and the few courting couples that represented the public had taken his hint and hurried towards the exit.

No one was likely to risk being locked in, for the Waxwork Collection of Oldhampton had lately acquired a sinister reputation. The foundation for this lay in the fate of a stranger to the town—a commercial traveller—who had cut his throat in the Hall of Horrors.

Since then, two persons had, separately, spent the night in the Gallery and, in the morning, each had been found dead.

In both cases the verdict had been "Natural death, due to heart failure." The first victim—a local alderman—had been addicted to alcohol, and was in very bad shape. The second his great friend— was a delicate little man, a martyr to asthma, and slightly unhinged through unwise absorption in spiritualism.

While the coincidence of the tragedies stirred up a considerable amount of local superstition, the general belief was that both deaths were due to the power of suggestion, in conjunction with the macabre surroundings, the victims had let themselves be frightened to death by the Waxworks. Sonia was there, in the Gallery, to test its truth.

She was the latest addition to the staff of the *Oldhampton Gazette*. Bubbling with enthusiasm, she had made no secret of her literary ambitions, and it was difficult to feed her with enough work. Her colleagues listened to her with mingled amusement and boredom, but they liked her as a refreshing novelty. As for her fine future, they looked to young Wells, the Sporting Editor, to effect her speedy and painless removal from the sphere of journalism.

On Christmas Eve, Sonia took them all into her confidence over her intention to spend a night in the Waxworks on the last night of the old year.

"There's copy there," she declared. "I'm not timid and I have fairly sensitive perceptions so I ought to be able to write up the effect of imagination on the nervous system. I mean to record my impressions every hour while they're piping hot."

Looking up, suddenly, she had surprised a green glare in the eyes of Hubert Poke. When Sonia came to work on the *Gazette*, she had a secret fear of unwelcome attentions since she was the only woman on the staff. But the first passion she awoke was hatred. Poke hated her impersonally, as the representative of a force, numerically superior to his own sex, which was on the opposing side in the battle for existence. He feared her too, because she was the unknown element, and possessed the unfair weapon of charm. Before she came, he had been the star turn on the *Gazette*. His own position on the staff gratified his vanity and entirely satisfied his narrow ambition. But Sonia had stolen some of his thunder. On more than one occasion she had written up a story he had failed to cover, and he had to admit that her success was due to a quicker wit.

For some time past, he had been playing with the idea of spending a night in the Waxworks, but was deterred by the feeling had felt a hot, thick taste in his throat, as though of blood. He knew that his jealousy of Sonia was accountable. It had almost reached the stage of mania and trembled on the brink of a homicidal urge.

While his brain was still creaking with the idea of first-hand experience in the ill-omened gallery, Sonia had nipped in with her ready-made plan.

Controlling himself with an effort, he listened while the sub-editor issued a warning to Sonia.

"Good idea, young woman, but you will find the experience a bit raw. You've no notion how uncanny these big deserted buildings can be."

"That's so," nodded young Wells. "I once spent a night in a haunted house."

Sonia looked at him with her habitual interest. He was short and thick set with a three-cornered smile, which appealed to her.

"Did you see anything?" she asked.

"No. I cleared out before the show came on. Windy. After a bit, one can imagine anything."

It was then that Poke introduced a new note into the discussion by his own theory of the mysterious deaths at the Waxworks.

Sitting alone in the Gallery, Sonia preferred to forget his words. She resolutely drove them from her mind, while she began to settle down for the night. Her first action was to cross to the figure of Cardinal Wolsey and unceremoniously raise his heavy scarlet robe. From under its voluminous folds she drew out her cushion and attache case, which she had hidden earlier in the evening.

Mindful of the fact that it would grow chilly at dawn, she carried on her arm her thick white tennis coat. Slipping it on, she placed her cushion in the angle of the wall, and sat down to await developments.

The Gallery was far more mysterious now that the lights were out. At each end it seemed to stretch away into impenetrable black tunnels. But there was nothing uncanny about it, or about the figures, which were a tame and conventional collection of historical personages. Even the adjoining Hall of Horrors contained no horrors, only a selection of respectable-looking poisoners.

Sonia grinned cheerfully at the row of waxworks which was vis ible in the lamplight from the street. "Later on, if the office is right, you will assume unpleasant mannerisms to try to cheat me into believing you are alive. I warn you, old sports, you'll have your work cut out for you. And now I think I'll get better acquainted with you. Familiarity breeds contempt."

She went the round of the figures, greeting each with flippancy or criticism. Presently she returned to her corner and opened her notebook ready to record her impressions.

"Twelve o'clock. The first hour has passed almost too quickly. I've drawn a complete blank. Not a blessed thing to record. Not a vestige of reaction. The waxworks seem a commonplace lot, without a scrap of hypnotic force. In fact, they're altogether too matey."

Sonia had left her corner, to write her entry in the light which streamed through the window. Smoking was prohibited in the building, and, lest she should yield to temptation, she had left her cigarettes and matches behind her, on the office table.

At this stage she regretted the matches. A little extra light would be a boon. It was true she carried an electric torch, but she was saving it, in case of emergency.

It was a loan from young Wells. As they were leaving the office together he had spoken to her confidentially.

"Did you notice how Poke glared at you? Don't get up against him. He's a nasty piece of work. He's so mean he'd sell his mother's shroud for old rags. And he's a cruel little devil, too. He turned out his miserable pup to starve in the streets, rather than cough up for the licence."

Sonia grew hot with indignation.

"What he needs to cure his complaint is a strong dose of rat poison," she declared. "What became of the poor little dog?"

"Oh, he's all right. He was a matey chap, and he soon chummed up with a mongrel of his own class."

"You?" asked Sonia, her eyes suddenly soft.

"A mongrel, am I?" grinned Wells.

"Well, anyway, the pup will get a better Christmas than his first, when Poke went away and left him on the chain. We're both of us going to overeat and overdrink. You're on your own, too. Won't you join us?"

"I'd love to."

Although the evening was warm and muggy the invitation suffused Sonia with the spirit of Christmas. The shade of Dickens seemed to be hovering over the parade of the streets. A red-nosed Santa Claus presided over a spangled Christmas tree outside a toy shop. Windows were hung with tinselled balls and coloured paper festoons. Pedestrians, laden with parcels, called out seasonable greetings.

"Merry Christmas!"

Young Wells' three-cornered smile was his tribute to the joyous feeling of festival. His eyes were eager as he turned to Sonia.

"I've an idea. Don't wait until after the holidays to write up the Waxworks. Make it a Christmas Eve stunt and go there tonight."

"I will," declared Sonia.

It was then that he slipped the torch into her hand.

"I know you belong to the stronger sex," he said. "But even your nerve might crash. If it does, just flash this torch under the window. Stretch out your arm above your head, and the light will be seen from the street."

"And what will happen then?" asked Sonia.

"I shall knock up the miserable porter and let you out."

"But how will you see the light?"

"I shall be in the street."

"All night?"

"Yes. I'll sleep there." Young Wells grinned. "Understand," he added loftily, "that this is a matter of principle. I could not let any woman—even one so aged and unattractive as yourself—feel beyond the reach of help."

As he turned away, he cut into her thanks with a parting warning.

"Don't use the torch for light, or the juice may give out. It's about due for a new battery."

As Sonia looked at the torch, lying by her side, it seemed a link with young Wells. At this moment he was probably patrolling the street, a sturdy figure in an old tweed overcoat, with his cap pulled down over his eyes. As she tried to pick out his footsteps from among those of the other passersby it struck her that there was plenty of traffic, considering that it was past twelve o'clock.

"The witching hour of midnight is another lost illusion," she reflected. "Killed by night clubs. I suppose."

It was cheerful to know that so many citizens were abroad, to keep her company. Some optimists were still singing carols. She faintly heard the strains of "Good King Wenceslas." It was in a tranquil frame of mind that she unpacked her sandwiches and thermos.

"Merry Christmas to you all! And many of them."

The faces of the illuminated figures remained stolid, but she could almost swear that a low murmur of acknowledgement seemed to swell from the rest of her company—invisible in the darkness.

She spun out her meal to its limit, stifling her craving for a cigarette. Then, growing bored, she counted the visible waxworks, and tried to memorize them.

"Twenty-one, twenty-two. . . . Wolsey, Queen Elizabeth, Guy Fawkes, Napoleon ought to go on a diet. Ever heard of eighteen days, Nap? Poor old Julius Caesar looks as though he'd been sunbathing on the Lido. He's about due for the melting-pot."

In her eyes they were a second-rate set of dummies. The local theory that they could terrorize a human being to death or madness seemed a fantastic notion.

"No," concluded Sonia. "There's really more in Poke's bright idea."

Again she saw the office—sun-smitten from the big unshielded window faced south—with its blistered paint, faded wallpaper, ink-stained desks, typewriters, telephones, and a huge fire in the untidy grate. Young Wells smoked his big pipe, while the sub-editor—a ginger, pigheaded young man—laid down the law about the mystery deaths.

And then she heard Poke's toneless dead-man's voice.

"You may be right about the spiritualist. He died of fright but not of the waxworks. My belief is that he established contact with the spirit of his dead friend, the alderman, and he learned his real fate."

"What fate?" snapped the sub-editor.

"I believe that the alderman was murdered," replied Poke.

He clung to his point like a limpet in the face of all counter-arguments.

"The alderman had enemies," he said. "Nothing would be easier than for one of them to lie in wait for him. In the present circumstances, I could commit a murder in the Waxworks, and get away with it."

"How?" demanded young Wells.

"How? To begin with, the Gallery is a one-man show and the porter's a bonehead. Anyone could enter and leave the Gallery without his being wise to it."

"And the murder?" plugged on young Wells.

With a shudder Sonia remembered how Poke had glanced at his long knotted fingers.

"If I could not achieve my object by fright, which is the foolproof way," he replied, "I should try a little artistic strangulation."

"And leave your marks?"

"Not necessarily. Every expert knows that there are methods which show no trace."

Sonia fumbled in her bag for the cigarettes which were not there.

"Why did I let myself think of that, just now?" she thought. "Really too stupid."

As she reproached herself for her morbidity, she broke off to stare at the door which led to the Hall of Horrors.

When she had last looked at it, she could have sworn that it was tightly closed. . . . But now it gaped open by an inch.

She looked at the black cavity, recognising the first test of her nerves. Later, there would be others. She realised the fact that, within her cool, practical self, she carried a hysterical, neurotic passenger, who would doubtless give her a lot of trouble through officious suggestions and uncomfortable reminders.

She resolved to give her second self a taste of her quality, and so quell her at the start.

"That door was merely closed," she remarked, as, with a firm step she crossed to the Hall of Horrors and shut the door.

"One o'clock. I begin to realise that there is more in this than I thought. Perhaps I'm missing my sleep. But I'm keyed up and horribly expectant. Of what? I don't know. But I seem to be waiting for—something. I find myself listening—listening. The place is full of mysterious noises. I know they're my fancy. . . . And things appear to move. I can distinguish footsteps and whispers, as though those waxworks which I cannot see in the darkness are beginning to stir to life."

Sonia dropped her pencil at the sound of a low chuckle. It seemed to come from the end of the Gallery, which was blacked out by shadows.

As her imagination galloped away with her, she reproached herself sharply.

"Steady, don't be a fool. There must be a cloak-room here. That chuckle is the air escaping in a pipe—or something. I'm betrayed by my own ignorance of hydraulics."

In spite of her brave words she returned rather quickly to her corner.

With her back against the wall she felt less apprehensive. But she recognised her cowardice as an ominous sign.

She was desperately afraid of someone—or something—creeping up behind her and touching her.

"I've struck the bad patch," she told herself. "It will be worse at three o'clock and work up to a climax,. But when I make my entry, at three, I shall have reached the peak. After that every minute will be bringing the dawn nearer."

But of one fact she was ignorant. There would be no recorded impression at three o'clock.

Happily unconscious, she began to think of her copy. When she returned to the office—sunken-eyed—she would then rejoice over every symptom of groundless fear.

"It's a story all right," she gloated, looking at Hamlet. His gnarled, pallid features and dark, smouldering eyes were strangely familiar to her.

Suddenly she realised that he reminded her of Hubert Poke.

Against her will, her thoughts again turned to him. She told herself that he was exactly like a waxwork. His yellow face—symptomatic of heart trouble—had the same cheesy hue, and his eyes were like dull black glass. He wore dentures that were too large for him, and which forced his lips apart in a mirthless grin.

He always seemed to smile—even over the episode of the lift— which had been no joke.

It happened two days before. Sonia had rushed into the office in a state of molten excitement, because she had extracted an interview from a personage who had just received the Freedom of the City. This distinguished freeman had the reputation of shunning newspaper publicity, and Poke had tried his luck, only to be sent away with a flea in his ear.

At the back of her mind, Sonia knew that she had not fought level, for she was conscious of the effect of violet-blue eyes and a dimple upon a reserved but very human gentleman. But in her elation she had been rather blatant about her score.

She had transcribed her notes, rattling away at her typewriter in a tremendous hurry, because she had a dinner engagement. In the same breathless speed she had rushed towards the automatic lift.

She was just about to step into it when young Wells had leaped the length of the passage and dragged her back.

"Look where you're going," he shouted.

Sonia looked—and saw only the well of the shaft. The lift was not waiting in its accustomed place.

"Out of order," explained Wells before he turned to blast Hubert Poke, who stood by.

"You almighty chump, why didn't you grab Miss Fraser, instead of standing by like a stuck pig?"

At the time Sonia had vaguely remarked how Poke had stammered and sweated, and she accepted the fact that he had been petrified by shock and had lost his head.

Thinking about it in the Gallery, she realised for the first time that his inaction had been deliberate. She remembered the flame of terrible excitement in his eyes and his stretched, ghastly grin.

"He hates me," she thought. "It's my fault. I've been tactless and cocksure."

Then a flood of horror swept over her.

"But he wanted to see me crash. It's almost murder."

As she began to tremble, the jumpy passenger she carried reminded her of Poke's remark about the alderman.

"He had enemies."

Sonia shook away the suggestion angrily.

"My memory's uncanny," she thought. "I'm stimulated and all strung up. It must be the atmosphere. Perhaps there's some gas in the air that accounts for these brainstorms. It's hopeless to be so utterly unscientific. Poke would have made a better job of this."

She was back again to Hubert Poke. He had become an obsession.

Her head began to throb and a tiny gong started to beat in her temples. This time she recognised the signs without any mental ferment.

"Atmospherics. A storm's coming up. It might make things rather thrilling. I must concentrate on my story. Really, my luck's in."

She sat for some time, forcing herself to think of pleasant subjects—of arguments with young Wells and the tennis tournament. But there was always a point when her thoughts gave a twist and led her back to Poke.

Presently she grew cramped and got up to pace the illuminated aisle in front of the window. She tried again to talk to the waxworks, but this time it was not a success.

They seemed to have grown remote and secretive, as though they were removed to another plane, where they possessed a hidden life.

Suddenly she gave a faint scream. Someone—or something—had crept up behind her, for she felt the touch of cold fingers upon her arm.

"Two o'clock. They're only wax. They shall not frighten me. But they're trying to. One by one they're coming to life. . . . Charles the Second no longer looks like sourdough. He is beginning to leer at me. His eyes remind me of Hubert Poke."

Sonia stopped writing, to glance uneasily at the image of the Stuart monarch. His black velveteen suit appeared to have a richer pile. The swarthy curls which fell over his lace collar looked less like horsehair. There really seemed a gleam of amorous interest lurking at the back of his glass optics.

Absurdly, Sonia spoke to him in order to reassure herself.

"Did you touch me? At the first hint of a liberty, Charles Stuart, I'll smack your face. You'll learn a modern journalist has not the manners of an orange girl."

Instantly the satyr reverted to a dummy in a moth-eaten historical costume.

Sonia stood listening for young Wells' footsteps outside. She could not hear them, although the street now was perfectly still. She tried to picture him, propping up the opposite building, solid and immovable as the Rock of Gibraltar.

But it was no good. Doubts began to obtrude.

"I don't believe he's there. After all, why should he stay? He only pretended, just to give me confidence. He's gone."

She shrank back to her corner, drawing her tennis coat closer for warmth. It was growing colder, causing her to think of tempting things—of a hot water bottle and a steaming teapot.

Presently she realised that she was growing drowsy. Her lids felt as though weighted with lead, so that it required an effort to keep them open.

This was a complication she had not foreseen. Although she longed to drop off to sleep, she sternly resisted the temptation.

"No. It's not fair. I've set myself the job of recording a night spent to the Waxworks. It must be the genuine thing."

She blinked more vigorously, staring across to where Byron drooped like a sooty flamingo.

"Mercy, how he yearns! He reminds me of— No, I won't think of him. . . . I must keep awake. Bed blankets, pillows No."

Her head fell forward, and for a minute she dozed. In that space of time she had a vivid dream.

She thought that she was still in her corner in the Gallery, watching the dead alderman as he paced to and fro, before the window. She had never seen him so he conformed to her idea of an alderman – stout, pompous, and wearing the dark-blue, fur-trimmed robe of his office.

"He's got a face like a sleepy bear," she decided. "Nice old thing but brainless."

And then, suddenly, her tolerant derision turned to acute apprehension as she saw that he was being followed. A shape was stalking him as a cat stalks a bird.

Sonia tried to warn him of his peril but, after the fashion of nightmares, she found herself voiceless. Even as she struggled to scream, a grotesquely long arm shot out and monstrous fingers gripped the alderman's throat.

In the same moment she saw the face of the killer. It was Hubert Poke.

She awoke with a start, glad to find that it was but a dream. As she looked around her with dazed eyes, she saw a faint flicker of light. The mutter of very faint thunder, together with a patter of rain, told her that the storm had broken. It was still a long way off.

Then her heart gave a violent leap. One of the waxworks had come to life. She distinctly saw it move before it disappeared into the darkness at the end of the Gallery.

"My nerve's crashed," she thought. "That figure was only my fancy. I'm just like the others. Defeated by wax."

Instinctively, she paid the figures her homage. It was the cumulative effect of their grim company, with their simulated life and sinister associations, that had rushed her defences.

Although it was bitter to f ail, s he c omforted h erself w ith the reminder that she had enough copy for her article. She could even make capital out of her own capitulation to the force of suggestion. With a slight grimace she picked up her notebook. There would be no more on-the-spot impressions. And young Wells, if he was still there, would be grateful for the end of his vigil whatever the state of mind of the porter.

She groped in the darkness for her signal-lamp but her fingers only touched bare boards.

The torch had disappeared.

In a panic she dropped down on her knees and searched for yards around the spot where she was positive it had lain.

It was the instinct of self-preservation that caused her to give up her vain search.

"I'm in danger," she thought. "And I've no one to help now. I must see this through myself."

She pushed back her hair from a brow which had grown damp.

"There's a brain working against mine. When I was asleep someone—or something—stole my torch."

Something? The waxworks became distinct with terrible possibility as she stared at them. Some were merely blurred shapes—their faces opaque oblongs or ovals. But others—illuminated from the street—were beginning to reveal themselves in a new guise.

Queen Elizabeth the First, with peaked chin and fiery hair, seemed to regard her with intelligent malice. The countenance of Napoleon was heavy with brooding power, as though he were willing her to submit. Cardinal Wolsey held her with a glittering eye.

Sonia realised that she was letting herself be hypnotised by creatures of wax—so many pounds of candles moulded to human form.

"This is what happened to those others," she thought. "Nothing happened. But I'm afraid of them. I'm terribly afraid. There's only one thing to do. I must count them again."

She knew that she must find out whether her torch had been stolen through human agency; but she shrank from the experiment, not knowing which she feared more—a tangible enemy or the unknown.

As she began to count, the chilly air inside the building seemed to throb with each thud of her heart.

"Seventeen, eighteen." She was scarcely conscious of the numbers she murmured. "Twenty-two, twenty three."

She stopped. Twenty-three? If her tally were correct, there was an extra waxwork in the Gallery.

On top of the shock of the discovery came a blinding flash of light, which veined the sky with fire. It seemed to run down the figure of Joan of Arc like a flaming torch. By a freak of atmospherics, the storm, which had been a starved, whimpering affair of flicker and murmur, culminated in what was apparently a thunderbolt.

The explosion that followed was stunning but Sonia scarcely noticed it in her terror.

The unearthly violet glare had revealed to her a figure which she had previously overlooked.

It was seated in a chair, its hand supporting its peaked chin, and its pallid, clean-shaven features nearly hidden by a familiar broad-brimmed felt hat, which—together with the black cape—gave her the clue to the identity.

It was Hubert Poke.

Three o'clock.

Sonia heard it strike, as her memory began to reproduce, with horrible fidelity, every word of Poke's conversation on murder.

"Artistic strangulation." She pictured the cruel agony of life leaking bubble by bubble, gasp by gasp. It would be slow—for he had boasted of a method that left no tell-tale marks.

"Another death," she thought dully. "If it happens everyone will say that the Waxworks have killed me. What a story. . . . Only, I shall not write it up."

The tramp of feet rang out on the pavement below. It might have been the policeman on his beat but Sonia wanted to feel that young Wells was still faithful to his post.

She looked up at the window, set high in the wall, and, for a moment, was tempted to shout. But the idea was too desperate. If she failed to attract outside attention, she would seal her own fate, for Poke would be prompted to hasten her extinction.

"Awful to feel he's so near, and yet I cannot reach him," she thought. "It makes it so much worse."

She crouched there, starting and sweating at every faint sound in the darkness. The rain, which still pattered on the skylight, mimicked footsteps and whispers. She remembered her dream and the nightmare spring and clutch.

It was an omen. At any moment it would come. . .

Her fear jolted her brain. For the first time she had a glimmer of hope.

"I didn't see him before the flash because he looked exactly like one of the waxworks. Could I hide among them, too?" she wondered.

She knew that her white coat alone revealed her position to him. Holding her breath, she wriggled out of it, and hung it on the effigy of Charles II. She was now clad in black, and with her handkerchief scarf tied over her face—burglar-fashion—she hoped that she was invisible against the sable-draped walls.

Her knees shook as she crept from her shelter. When she had stolen a few yards, she stopped to listen. In the darkness, someone was astir. She heard a soft padding of feet, moving with the certainty of one who sees his goal.

Her coat glimmered in her deserted corner.

In a sudden panic, she increased her pace, straining her ears for other sounds. She had reached the far end of the Gallery, where no gleam from the window penetrated the gloom.

Blindfolded and muffled, she groped her way towards the alcoves that held the tableaux.

Suddenly she stopped, every nerve in her body quivering. She had heard a thud, like rubbered soles alighting after a spring.

"He knows now." Swift on the trail of her thought flashed another. "He will look for me. Oh, quick!"

She tried to move, but her muscles were bound, and she stood as though rooted to the spot, listening. It was impossible to locate the footsteps. They seemed to come from every quarter of the Gallery. Sometimes they sounded remote, but, whenever she drew a freer breath, a sudden creak of the boards close to where she stood made her heart leap.

At last she reached the limit of endurance. Unable to bear the suspense of waiting, she moved on.

Her pursuer followed her at a distance. He gained on her, but still withheld his spring. She had the feeling that he held her at the end of an invisible string.

"He's playing with me, like a cat with a mouse," she thought.

If he had seen her, he let her creep forward until the darkness was no longer absolute. There were gradations in its density so that she was able to recognise the first alcove. Straining her eyes, she could distinguish the outlines of the bed where the Virtuous Man made his triumphant exit from life, surrounded by a flock of his sorrowing family and their progeny.

Slipping inside the circle, she added one more mourner to the tableau.

The minutes passed, but nothing happened. There seemed no sound save the tiny gong beating inside her temples. Even the rain-drops had ceased to patter on the skylight.

Sonia began to find the silence more deadly than noise. It was like the lull before the storm. Question after question came rolling into her mind.

"Where is he? What will he do next? Why doesn't he strike a light?"

As though someone were listening-in to her thoughts, she suddenly heard a faint splutter as of an ignited match. Or it might have been the click of an exhausted electric torch.

With her back turned to the room, she could see no light. She heard the half-hour strike, with a faint wonder that she was still alive.

"What will have happened before the next quarter?" she asked.

Presently she began to feel the strain of her pose, which she held as rigidly as any artist's model. For the time—if her presence were not already detected—her life depended on her immobility.

As an overpowering weariness began to steal over her, a whisper stirred in her brain:

"The alderman was found dead on a bed."

The newspaper account had not specified which tableau had been the scene of the tragedy, but she could not remember another alcove that held a bed. As she stared at the white dimness of the quilt she seemed to see it blotched with a dark, sprawling form, writhing under the grip of long fingers.

To shut out the suggestion of her fancy, she closed her eyes. The cold, dead air in the alcove was sapping her exhausted vitality, so that once again she began to nod. She dozed as she stood, rocking to and fro on her feet.

Her surroundings grew shadowy. Sometimes she knew that she was in the alcove, but at others she strayed momentarily over strange borders. She was back in the summer, walking in a garden with young Wells. Roses and sunshine. . .

She awoke with a start at the sound of heavy breathing. It sounded close to her—almost by her side. The figure of a mourner kneeling by the bed seemed to change its posture slightly.

Instantly maddened thoughts began to flock and flutter wildly inside her brain.

"Who was it? Was it Hubert Poke? Would history be repeated? Was she doomed also to be strangled inside the alcove? Had Fate led her there?"

She waited, but nothing happened. Again she had the sensation of being played with by a master mind, dangled at the end of his invisible string.

Presently she was emboldened to steal from the alcove, to seek another shelter. But though she held on to the last flicker of her will, she had reached the limit of endurance. Worn out with the violence of her emotions and physically spent from the strain of long periods of standing, she staggered as she walked.

She blundered round the gallery, without any sense of direction, colliding blindly with the groups of waxwork figures. When she reached the window her knees shook under her and she sank to the ground—dropping immediately into a sleep of utter exhaustion.

She awoke with a start as the first grey gleam of dawn was stealing into the Gallery. It fell on the row of waxworks, imparting a sickly hue to their features, as though they were creatures stricken with plague.

It seemed to Sonia that they were waiting for her to wake. Their peaked faces were intelligent and their eyes held interest, as though they were keeping some secret.

She pushed back her hair, her brain still thick with clouded memories. Disconnected thoughts began to stir, to slide about. Then suddenly her mind cleared, and she sprang up staring at a figure wearing a familiar black cap.

Hubert Poke was also waiting for her to wake.

He sat in the same chair, and in the same posture, as when she had first seen him, in the flash of lightning. He looked as though he had never moved from his place—as though he could not move. His face had not the appearance of flesh.

As Sonia stared at him, with the feeling of a bird hypnotised by a snake, a doubt began to gather in her mind. Growing bolder, she crept closer to the figure.

It was a waxwork—a libellous representation of the actor Kean.

Her laugh rang joyously through the Gallery as she realised that she had passed a night of baseless terrors, cheated by the power of imagination. In her relief she turned impulsively to the waxworks.

"My congratulations," she said. "You are my masters."

They did not seem entirely satisfied by her homage, for they continued to watch her with an expression half benevolent and half sinister.

"Wait!" they seemed to say.

Sonia turned from them and opened her bag to get out her mirror and comb. There, among a jumble of notes, letters, lipsticks and powder compacts, she saw the electric torch.

"Of course!" she cried. "I remember now, I put it there. I was too windy to think properly. Well, I have my story. I'd better get my coat."

The Gallery seemed smaller in the returning light. As she approached Charles Stuart, who looked like an umpire in his white coat, she glanced down the far end of the room, where she had groped in its shadows before the pursuit of imaginary footsteps.

A waxwork was lying prone on the floor. For the second time she stood and gazed down upon a familiar black cape—a broad-brimmed conspirator's hat. Then she nerved herself to turn the figure so that its face was visible.

She gave a scream. There was no mistaking the glazed eyes and ghastly grin. She was looking down on the face of a dead man.

It was Hubert Poke.

The shock was too much for Sonia. She heard a singing in her ears, while a black mist gathered before her eyes. For the first time, in her life she fainted.

When she recovered consciousness she forced herself to kneel beside the body and cover it with its black cape. The pallid face resembled a death mask, which revealed only too plainly the lines of egotism and cruelty in which it had been moulded by a gross spirit.

Yet Sonia felt no repulsion—only pity. It was Christmas morning, and he was dead, while her own portion was life triumphant. Closing her eyes, she whispered a prayer of supplication for his warped soul.

Presently, as she grew calmer, her mind began to work on the problem of his presence. His motive seemed obvious. Not knowing that she had changed her plan he had concealed himself in the Gallery in order to poach her story.

"He was in the Hall of Horrors at first," she thought, remembering the opened door. "When he came out he hid at this end. We never saw each other, because of the waxworks between us, but we heard each other."

She realised that the sounds that had terrified her had not all been due to imagination, while it was her agency which had converted the room into a whispering gallery of strange murmurs and voices. The clue to the cause of death was revealed by his wrist watch, which had smashed when he fell. Its hands had stopped at three minutes to three, proving that the flash and explosion of the thunderbolt had been too much for his diseased heart—already overstrained by superstitious fears.

Sonia shuddered at a mental vision of Poke's face, distraught with terror and pulped by raw primal impulses, after a night spent in a madman's world of fantasy.

She turned to look at the waxworks. At last she understood what they seemed to say:

"But for Us, you would have met... at dawn."

"Your role shall be acknowledged, I promise you," she thought, as she opened her notebook.

"Eight o'clock. The Christmas bells are ringing and it is wonderful just to be alive. I'm through the night, and none the worse for the experience, although I cracked badly after three o'clock. A colleague who, unknown to me, was also concealed in the Gallery has met with a tragic fate caused, I am sure, by the force of suggestion. Although his death is due to heart-failure, the superstitious will certainly claim it to another victory for the Waxworks."

PASSENGERS

Just before the blow fell Edna felt unusually well and happy. Her holiday was over, her bill at the hotel was paid, and her suitcase lay on the station platform. For over an hour she had sat—the sun beating down on her uncovered head—feasting her eyes on the scenery.

Before her was a grass-green lake, sparkling with diamond reflections and backed with white-spiked mountains.

She had just spent a glorious three weeks rambling the mountains in congenial Anglo-American society, and it seemed strangely civilised to be wearing a skirt and silk stockings again after shorts and nailed boots. The rest of the crowd had returned yesterday, but she had chosen to stay one day longer, alone.

She was sorry to be leaving, partly because she was not going home, but merely "back." At these times she felt she paid a heavy price for her freedom as an attractive orphan of twenty-two with no relatives, clumps of friends, and a private income.

Suddenly the sun struck her. Owing to the altitude, the air was cool and bracing so that she had not realised the fierceness of its rays. She felt a violent pain at the back of her neck, followed by a rush of sick dizziness. As the white-capped mountains darkened and rocked she had a ghastly moment of panic.

"I'm going to be ill—alone—amongst strangers."

Then everything slipped away. . . . When she opened her eyes she was in the cool gloom of the primitive little waiting room, while a black-pinafored woman held a glass of raw spirit to her lips. People stared at her curiously and spoke to her, but she could not understand a word.

Luckily, she soon felt better and was able to reward her Good Samaritans. But, after they had left her, she had another bad minute when she wondered if she had been robbed while she was unconscious. Examination of her bag, however, proved that her tickets, passport, and money were untouched.

She was now in a fever of impatience to get away, for her experience had unnerved her. It had made her realise, for the first time in her life, the horror of helplessness far away from familiar things.

Suddenly the signal fell and a coil of smoke whirled around the bend of the rails. With a whistle and a roar the engines steamed into the little station.

The porter had difficulty in finding a place for Edna, for, although her seat was reserved, the carriage already held its quota of six. He appeared to be abjectly apologetic to a majestic lady in deep black, who plainly resented the newcomer.

The whistle shrilled and the engine began to throb slowly on its way back to England. Except the frontiers there was only one stop—Milan—before Basle, where Edna would change into the Calais express.

A family party—two large parents and a daughter of about twelve—sat on the same side of the carriage as herself. Opposite was a fair and beautiful girl in black and white, who appeared to have modelled herself on a film star, a typical British spinster and the lady who had opposed her intrusion.

Veiled and draped in heavy black, she was an overwhelming and formidable personality—essentially of the ruling class—with an arrogant beaked nose and fierce, proud eyes.

Presently the majestic lady received a visitor—a pallid man with dead eyes, a black spade beard, and glasses. As they carried on a low conversation Edna was amused to notice that the British spinster was straining her ears to listen. She also remarked that the black-clad lady looked in her direction as though in annoyance and made a low observation to her companion.

Sensing their hostility she closed her eyes and only knew when the man had left the compartment by the absence of guttural whispers. The motion rocked her to a light sleep.

Her torpid trance was broken by an official who poked his head through the door and shouted something to which the company, in general, was unresponsive. The British spinster, however, tapped Edna on the arm.

"You're English, aren't you?" she asked in a crisp, pleasant voice. "Tea is ready in the restaurant car. Coming?"

Edna's head was aching badly, so that she was glad to follow her guide into the corridor. As they passed the next compartment to theirs, they saw through the door a figure, covered with rugs, stretched out on one seat. Both head and forehead were bandaged, while a criss-cross of plaster strips concealed the features from brow to chin in a diagonal line.

The invalid was in the charge of the pallid, black bearded man who had just visited their carriage, and a nursing sister, who was dressed like a nun. Her face was hard and repellent, with a brutal mouth, so that it was difficult to connect her with the profession of nursing.

"How ghastly to be ill on a journey," shuddered Edna with a memory of her recent attack.

Her companion was able to tell her all about the invalid, for she was the type that collects information.

"Yes, a motor smash higher up the valley. Her face is terribly cut poor thing, and there's head injury, so they're rushing her to Milan for an operation. The doctor was telling the baroness about it just now."

She shouted the information over her shoulder as she led the way down the corridors, across the clanking connections, and into the crowded restaurant car. Wedging herself into a corner, she looked blissfully at the smutty tablecloth, the cakes of butter, and the cherry jam.

"Isn't this fun!" she cried.

The lady was nondescript—being middle aged, dowdy, and vaguely oatmeal in colouring; yet there was a sparkle in her faded blue eyes which suggested youth.

Edna learned that her compatriot was a Miss Winifred Bird, who had been English governess to a titled family for two years and was now going home on her first holiday. To her surprise this adult lady actually possessed living parents.

"Mummy and Daddy say they can talk of nothing else but my return," Miss Bird told her. "They're excited as children and so is Ruff. He's an old English sheepdog, not pure, but an appealing dog, and so devoted to me. He understands I'm coming home, but not when, so he meets every train. Mummy says he always comes back with his tail down, the picture of depression. They're both imagining his frantic joy the night I do come. And that's tomorrow."

Edna felt quite a lump in her throat at the thought of the reunion. It was the dog that really won her, for she got a clear picture of him—a shaggy mongrel, absurdly clownish, with amber eyes beaming under his wisps.

But she grew rather to like the old parents, too. Daddy was a parson—schoolmaster, who, when he retired at the age of sixty-five, began to learn Hebrew as a light holiday pastime.

"Are you going back after your holiday?" Edna asked.

"Yes, but not to my post." Miss Bird looked around her and then lowered her voice. "I'm coming back to give evidence in a murder trial. I'll mention no names, but I was governess to the very highest in the place. You've no idea of his power. What he says goes, and he hasn't got to speak, for a wink is enough. But, although he rules absolutely, there's a small Communist element in the town and their leader—a young man—accused the—my employer—of corruption. I'm afraid it was true. There was an awful scene at the castle and the—my employer—shot the young man. I saw it all."

"You've really seen a man killed?" gasped Edna. "How terrible."

"Terrible at the time, my dear, but afterwards it all turned to a thrilling adventure. Life's so interesting because things are always happening. Everyone wanted to hush it up and say it was suicide but, of course, I had to insist on being heard for the sake of justice. You've no idea how unpopular I was. The children threw stones at me in the street and shop people refused to serve me. Even the police were quite angry with me. And I'm sure the muddle about my seat was intentional."

"What muddle?" asked Edna.

"I booked my seat second class, but when I got to the train they said my place was already taken. But the baroness was kind and said I was to travel 'first' with her and she would make it right about my ticket. I felt awkward as she's related to the—my employer."

Edna gathered that the autocratic lady in black was the bareness and that she had annexed her own reservation for Miss Bird. By this time, however, she was growing tired of Miss Bird's confidences. After they had blundered back to their compartment she felt she must make a bid for silence.

"Do you mind if I don't talk?" she asked."My head is nearly splitting. I've just had a touch of sunstroke."

As she knew Miss Bird's curiosity had to be appeared she gave a brief account of her attack. While she did as she had the feeling that the baroness was listening to her story with concealed interest.

Miss Bird kindly supplied aspirin, which made Edna feel pleasantly drowsy.

Down, down. She drifted into sleep. Suddenly she gave a violent start and her heart began to leap as though she had just stepped into vacancy. Opening her eyes, she stared around her confusedly.

Miss Bird had disappeared.

She was astonished by her own pang of sudden loneliness. The baroness slept in her corner. As her nerves were still on edge, Edna had a nightmare impression that these people were not really human but a set of dummies.

The family party read different sections of the same newspaper. The father was big, polished and clean-shaven, even to his head. The mother had a straight fringe and her eyebrows appeared to be corked. The girl wore babyish socks but her expression was adult.

As they remained dumb and motionless as waxworks, Edna glanced at the beautiful blonde, only to be reminded of a model in a shop window.

Common sense told Edna that Miss Bird had probably gone to wash and would soon be back. She looked at her watch to time her absence. In five minutes she would be surely back, with her warm humanity, her curiosity, and her stories about family and home.

Five minutes passed, then ten, then fifteen. Still Miss Bird did not come back. When, after twenty minutes had passed, Edna chanced to look up at the rack, she received a nasty shock.

Miss Bird's suitcase was not there.

She could restrain her uneasiness no longer. As the baroness still slept she appealed to the other passengers. She was probably the world's worst linguist, but she made a brave effort in three of the languages of civilisation.

"*Ou est la dame?*"

"*Wo ist die dame?*"

"Where is the lady?"

She eked out her inquiries with pantomime, pointing to Miss Bird's empty place, while she raised her brows in exaggerated inquiry. But the passengers merely shrugged and shook their heads to show her that they did not understand.

Since no sign of intelligence gleamed on their blank faces, Edna decided to find out whether Miss Bird had changed her seat. But it seemed unlikely, in view of the fact that the train was so full, and she felt acutely worried as she worked her way down the shaking corridor—clinging to the rail, pushing past loiterers, and staring into every compartment.

Her quest reminded her of the hunt for the proverbial needle in the haystack. Although she visited every portion of the long train, including restaurant cars—where men were smoking and drinking—she could find no trace of Miss Bird. With a leaden sense of apprehension she returned to her own compartment.

The baroness still slept. Suddenly desperate, Edna leaned forward and shook her awake. As she did so, she heard a smothered gasp from the other passengers, as though she had committed some act of sacrilege.

The baroness opened her proud eyes in a glare of outraged majesty. But Edna was too overwrought to apologise.

"Where is the English lady?" she cried.

"What English lady?" asked the baroness, speaking without a trace of accent.

"Miss Bird. The one who sat here."

"I do not understand. That seat has not been occupied, ever."

Edna's head began to reel.

"Yes, yes," she insisted. "I talked to her. We had tea together."

"No." The baroness shook her head and spoke with slow emphasis. "You make a strange mistake. There has been no English lady here except you, yourself."

Feeling as though she was trapped in some bad dream, Edna sank weakly down in her seat, while the train rocked on its way, back to England. Slides of twilight scenery streamed past the window, but she saw only a rush of chaos.

Either they're all mad, or I'm mad, she thought. No Miss Bird! Did I dream her? No, she was as real as me, with her old parents and Ruff. O, heavens! It's ghastly to be so helpless. I must think.

Presently she sprang to her feet in a burst of nervous futility.

"I must do something."

Scarcely conscious of her actions, Edna began to make a second search through the train. But, this time, she was aware that she was an object of curiosity and amusement. In every carriage was a blur of faces.

As she entered the first class restaurant car she thought she heard an Oxford accent. Unable to locate it, she made a general appeal.

"Please, is there anyone English here?"

The spectacle of a pretty girl in distress brought two men to their feet, although one of them appeared to regard chivalry merely as a duty. He was tall, thin, and of academic appearance, which, in his case, was not deceptive, since he was a university professor of modern languages.

The other was younger and rather untidy, with rough hair and audacious blue eyes.

"An English lady, Miss Bird, has disappeared on the train," Edna declared, her voice shaking as she spoke. "They say... But that's absurd I'm frightened by it all. Something's wrong.... And I can't speak their miserable language—and—"

As her voice failed, she was conscious of a tall grey man, bald as a vulture, who stared at her with piercing eyes as though she was something on a microscope slide.

"Could you pull yourself together and make a concise statement?" asked the professor.

The chill in his voice was tonic to her nerves, bracing her to compress the situation into a few words. To her overwhelming relief the professor was impressed, for he looked grave.

"This must certainly be investigated," he said. "Will you show me where your compartment is?"

The frivolous youth joined them and, somehow, managed to infect Edna with a sense of comradeship as they fought their way through the crowded corridor.

"My name's Carr," he said. "Much too long for you to remember. Better call me 'John Michael Peter,' like everyone else. I'm an engineer and speak the lingo, too. Look on me as a second string."

Strong in the support of her compatriots, Edna felt certain of a happy outcome as she entered her own compartment. The baroness was talking to the doctor, who was paying her another visit, but she listened, with gracious condescension, to the professor's statement.

He appeared to be in his element as he held his official inquiry and questioned the passengers, in turn. She looked up at him with a smile and was unpleasantly surprised by his unresponsive face. Although she could not understand the language, it was easy to follow the proceedings by the negative shake of each person's head.

By degrees, her confidence began to cloud. The ticket collector was called into the carriage to add his contribution to the general confusion and noise. She glanced at Carr, but he only pulled down his mouth in a grimace.

Her heart sank and her head began to swim. It was inconceivable that all these people should lie—yet they appeared to be denying the existence of Miss Bird.

Presently the professor spoke to her coldly.

"You appear to have made a most extraordinary mistake. No one in this carriage—including the ticket collector—knows anything about the lady you say is missing."

"Are you telling me I invented her?" asked Edna wildly. "We had tea together."

"Then, will you describe her so that I can interview the tea waiters?"

To her horror, Edna remembered that she had barely glanced at Miss Bird. Most of the time she had kept her eyes closed because of her blinding headache.

"I'm afraid I can't tell you much," she faltered. "There was nothing about her to catch hold of. She's middle aged, and ordinary, and rather colourless ."

"Surely you know if she is tall or short, dark or fair?"

"No. But I remember she had blue eyes."

"What did she wear?" asked Carr with a flash of intuition.

"Tweed, I think. I didn't notice much because I've such a splitting headache."

"Exactly." The professor's tone was dry. "Cause and effect. The doctor tells me you've just had sun stroke."

Suddenly Edna saw her chance to convince him.

"How does the doctor know that?" she asked. "I only told that to Miss Bird. How could I tell anyone else when I only speak English?"

The professor seemed impressed, for he took off his glasses to polish them. But, as the doctor began to speak rapidly, his expression hardened to its former fixity.

"It appears you were taken ill on the station platform. The baroness was there and she told the doctor."

"It explains all," said the doctor, speaking English with a grating accent. "Your sunstroke has given you a delirium—a delusion. You went to sleep and you dreamed. Your Miss Bird is only your dream."

The worst of it was they made her doubt herself. The mass of cumulative evidence against her story was too overwhelming. Even the friendly Carr did not believe in Miss Bird.

"I once had concussion, after footer," he said Edna. "The bishop of London came into my room and did a music hall turn. He was as real as you. Suppose you play 'shut eye' for a bit. You'll wake up right as rain."

Edna wearily obeyed him. Once again she lay with closed eyes, listening to the clamour of the train. A long drawn howl, as though a damned soul were lamenting, and a succession of rattles, like gunfire, told her that they were passing through a tunnel.

Suppose Miss Bird's body was, even then, being thrown out of the carriage in which it lay concealed. She was the victim of some treacherous plot in spite of all the evidence from the other side. As Edna's mind began to work again she remembered a story she had read in a magazine which, to her mind, surpassed in sheer horror the most lurid of crime stories.

Two ladies arrived by night at a continental hotel on their way back from an Oriental tour. The daughter carefully noted the number of her mother's room before she went to her own. When she returned later she found no trace of her mother, while the room itself was transformed with different furniture and new wallpaper.

When she made inquiries, the entire staff from the manager downward assured her that she alone had come to the hotel. Her mother's name was not in the register. The cab driver and the porters at the railway terminus all supported the general conspiracy.

The mother had been blown out like a puff of smoke.

Of course, there was an explanation. In the daughter's absence the mother had died suddenly of plague, contracted in the east. The merest rumour of this would have kept millions of visitors away from the exhibition about to be held in the city. With one's important interests at stake a unit had to be sacrificed.

This story was declared authentic and Edna began to wonder whether Miss Bird's disappearance were not a parallel on a small scale. An unimportant foreigner dared to accuse a personage of murder. She would be chief witness at his trial. It followed that she must be suppressed—blown out, like the other lady, in a puff of smoke. In her case it would not involve a vast, complicated, and fantastic conspiracy, merely the collusion of a few interested persons.

Edna felt her temperature rising as though she were in a furnace. Everyone considered her slightly mad and found her action a funny spectacle. Mocking eyes followed her as she stormed the restaurant car.

The professor sat in interested conversation with the vulture-headed man while Carr listened. When he saw Edna he looked up with a slight frown.

"I must tell you something," she cried. "I've discovered that there's a conspiracy against Miss Bird. We've got to help her because she's English like ourselves. Do listen."

The professor heard her story in stony silence and then he raised his brows interrogatively to the man with the piercing eyes. He nodded agreement when the other made some rapid explanation.

"Will you take some advice, offered in a friendly spirit?" asked the professor, speaking to Edna as though to a fractious child. "This gentleman is a famous Russian alienist, and he is of the opinion that you may be, temporarily, very slightly deranged, as a result of your sunstroke."

"D'you mean mad?" cried Edna in horror. "Me?"

"Nothing to be frightened of, in the least," the professor assured her. "But, he is not quite happy about your safety since you are alone. If you cannot keep quiet he may think it necessary to send you to a nursing home at Milan in your own interests until he can communicate with your friends."

"He can't do that to me," screamed Edna as England suddenly seemed very far away. "I'm going home, I should resist."

"Violence would be most unwise. Don't you understand? You have only to keep calm, and everything will be all right."

The professor was not so inhuman as he appeared. He believed Edna to be a neurotic specimen who was telling lies from love of sensation.

He thought he was acting for the best, and had no idea of the hell of fear into which he plunged her. White to her lips, she staggered into the adjoining restaurant car, where she shrank into the farthest corner.

She dared not go back in her own compartment, because she was afraid of everyone there. The whole world seemed roped into a league against her sanity. Lighting a cigarette with trembling fingers, she tried to realise her position.

Suspicious of everyone, she imagined the alienist might be in league with the baroness, and, if she persisted in her charges, he would send her to a home in Milan.

Any opposition on her part would only be used as evidence against her, and she might be kept imprisoned until she really crashed under the strain. It would be some time before she was missed, as her friends would imagine that she was still abroad.

She knew that Miss Bird existed and that she had been tampered with; but her rescue presented a hopeless proposition. Utterly worn out and paralysed with fear, Edna slipped into the trough of lost hopes.

She closed her eyes wearily and let herself drift on the choppy current of the train's frantic rhythm.

She was recalled to reality by a friendly voice, and she looked up to see Carr smiling at her.

"I've been thinking over 'The Strange Disappearance of Miss Bird,' " he said. "If you like, I'll tell you how it could be done. But first—when you came on the train was there one nun next door to you or two?"

"One."

"And now there are two."

"I know. But the other might have been somewhere else in the train. There's such a jam in the corridors."

"Good," declared Carr triumphantly. "No one would be likely to notice them. Now, we'll assume your little lady has got up against the High Hat—and it's true about the feudal system being still in force in these remote places. So she's got to be bumped off. And what better way than on a railway journey?"

"Do you mean— they've thrown her on the rails in a tunnel?" asked Edna faintly.

"Lord, no. Her body would be found and awkward questions asked. What I meant was that a lot of valuable time will be wasted before it's proved she's missing. Her people will think she's missed a connection or is stopping for a few days in Paris. Even if they are influential and know the ropes the trail will be cold by the time they get busy."

"And they're old and helpless," said Edna.

"Bad luck. In any case, when they make inquiries locally they'll find themselves up against a conspiracy of silence . . . . This would be a natural matter of tradition and policy. But I believe the baroness, the doctor and the two nuns are the only people in the plot. All the other passengers are local folk who would back up the baroness as a matter of course. There's no doubt, though, there was dirty work at the crossroads over her reserved seat, so as to force her into the baroness's compartment, which is at the end of the train and next door to the doctor."

"But what's happened to her?" asked Edna faintly.

"My theory is that she's lying in the next compartment to yours, covered up and disguised with bandages and trimmings. You were an unwelcome interloper but, when you obligingly went to sleep, Miss Bird was asked to render some slight service to their invalid, and I'm sure she would go like a bird."

"Yes," nodded Edna. "I'm positive she would."

"There you are, then. Directly she entered, she was gripped and gagged by two of them while a third gave her an injection. When she was unconscious they bandaged her up roughly and stuck plasters all over her face to disguise it. Then the false patient, who was already dressed in uniform, would only have to put a veil over her bandages, which would look like the proper bands, and peel off her own strip to look the perfect nun."

"And—when they reach Milan?" asked Edna fearfully.

"I'm afraid the betting is she'll be taken in an ambulance to some lonely place near a river. But she'll know nothing of it. They'll keep her unconscious all the time."

Edna sprang to her feet.

"We must do something at once," she cried.

"Listen to me," Carr pulled her back to her seat. "All this is only my idea; because I was suspicious of the way the invalid is on view in order to show all is above board. If it was genuine illness I am sure they'd pull down the blind . . . . But, remember, it is impossible to prove it."

"But why? Why?"

"Because it may be a real patient. We can't insist on examining her bandages to see if they are wound on in correct surgical manner, or rip off her plasters to spy her face. We might start the wound bleeding and she might pass out. We can't risk years in quod for manslaughter."

Edna fought against his restraining arm, but he continued to hold her.

"Don't start anything mad," he said. "The truth is I can't forget your sunstroke. I just showed you how things *might* be done. But I'm like the old lady who saw a giraffe for the first time. I don't believe it."

The passengers for the first dinner began to stream into the car. Feeling that food would choke her, Edna was driven out into the corridor. When Carr spoke to her she turned on him in a fury.

"Go away. I hate you."

After an age-long struggle through two sections of the train where the connecting passages seemed clanking iron concertinas, in which she might be caught and pressed to death, she realised that she was near to her own compartment. The brainstorm, whose symptoms the alienist had detected, now swept over in full force, so that she lost her sense of identity and actually changed places with Miss Bird

She thought she was bound, gagged, helpless—unable to cry out or move a finger—surrounded with cruel enemies, awaiting a hideous end.

"I must find her," murmured Edna confusedly.

Her fingers were touching the handle when the door opened and the doctor came into the corridor. His face looked like white wax above the blotch of his black beard, and his eyes, magnified by his glasses, were dark, muddy pools.

"Is madame better?" he asked.

At the sight of him Edna grew afraid. She nodded and looked out at the shrieking darkness rushing past the window. While the sinister doctor stood but a yard away she managed her own seat.

Very soon her mental and physical distress fused so that she lost all sense of time or space but seemed outside her own body, lying on the rails, while the engine drove remorselessly over her head,. *Clankety-clankety-clank.* With every revolution of the wheels she felt a separate pang.

Her temperature rose until she was actually in a fever. Vivid pictures kept flickering before her eyes. Two old folks standing waiting in a lighted doorway. Ruff—blundering and eager eyed—waiting for the "young" mistress who would never come home.

They were getting near Milan. She could see scattered lights in the distance. In the conflicting reflections of the windows, walls and roofs appeared like quivering landscape and running water. She could hear movement in the next carriage. Luggage was lowered to the floor and voices called for service. The guard passed in the corridor, just as Carr came to the door.

"We're coming into Milan," he said.

"Milan!" As though the word were an electric needle stabbing a raw nerve Edna sprang to her feet, inflamed by a dynamic impulse. She acted with the blind delirium of fever. Ducking under the guard's arm, she pushed into the next compartment, and—before anyone could guess her purpose—dug her fingers under the plaster, tearing it from the invalid's face.

The guard gave a gasp of horror which sharpened into a whistle of surprise as the adhesive strip peeled off. Instead of raw gashed flesh he saw the skin of a middle-aged woman.

"Miss Bird," screamed Edna.

There followed a panic of noise and confusion, in which Edna felt herself pushed roughly on one side. At the same moment she went to bits, utterly exhausted by her supreme effort. Staggering back to her own seat she collapsed.

Shouts and sudden flashes of light told her that they were entering a large station, and she felt the jerk of the train as it stopped. The tumult in the next compartment seemed to increase. Then it died down. Other passengers entered her carriage. She heard the whistle of the engine and the slow clank of wheels as it steamed slowly on its way to Basle.

Very soon someone spoke to her, and she looked up into the eyes of an old and intimate friend who did not know her name.

"I say, you," said Carr. "Everything O.K., and I've had the time of my life. The guard was immense, and knew just what to do. The doctor and his little lot went like lambs. They know they'll only have to stand for a charge of attempted abduction, and though the baroness sailed out—no connection—she'll work it for them somehow. Wheels within wheels, you know."

Edna was indifferent to their fate, one way or the other.

"What happened to Miss Bird?" she asked.

"Responding to treatment, and all that. The alienist, who's a frightfully decent chap, is looking after her, and she'll soon be conscious. But she must stop at Basle and go on tomorrow. Will you break your journey to keep her company?"

"Will you be there, too?" He nodded. " Then I will."

Suddenly Edna felt wondrously happy. At the beginning of her journey she had been bored with life and her wasted youth, but the agony of Miss Bird's peril had brought some change which seemed to be actually chemical. Her body felt composed of brand new cells—each tingling with the joy of life.

There was so much happiness in the world. Tomorrow would see the happiest of reunions. The carriage was crowded with fresh passengers, all shouting, smiling, and gesticulating.

That night she slept like a log at Basle. When she entered the hotel restaurant the following morning, Miss Bird was taking *café complet* on the balcony which overhung the Rhine—green and sparkling in the sunlight. The little woman looked marvellously fresh, as though she had thriven on her experience.

"I'm just making up my story to tell them at home," she said. "Mummy will be thrilled."

"Do you think it wise to tell her?" asked Edna. "At her age it might be a shock."

As Carr entered the restaurant and looked eagerly in their direction, Miss Bird gave Edna the conspiratorial look of one school-girl to another.

"I'm not going to tell her that," she said. "No fear. She might forbid me travelling—and more things might happen abroad. No, I'm going to tell her all about your romance."

The night before the last expedition of her holiday Stella was oppressed by a sense of impending catastrophe. She looked at the noisy crowd of young people in the hotel lounge with a feeling of responsibility.

Ought she to warn them of their danger?

Her common sense told her that she had no facts to offer them, she probably was exaggerating the windy boasting of an egomaniac. Many young men had attacks of "Red rash", yet developed into normal, good citizens. It was mainly youth's recognition that the social system is not perfect.

Yet from the first Ivan Morgan gave her the impression of being an enemy to society. He reminded her of some mad machine, driven by gusts of class hatred, and he made no secret of his views.

Tired from her train journey and seated by herself in the lounge, she noticed at once that the slovenly young man with famished eyes and spikes of black hair was also an outsider. No one spoke to him or took the slightest notice of him. He slumped in his chair, his arms folded and his eyes scorching the face and figure of a beautiful blonde who was taking part in a hectic game of pool.

When Stella tried vainly to attract the attention of a waiter he crossed over to her side.

"Waste of time to ring." His voice grated unpleasantly. "Since the millionaires have condescended to honour this hotel with their patronage, ordinary visitors must wait on themselves or go without."

"Then it's an abominable scandal." Stella spoke sharply, for she wanted her coffee. "I shall complain to the agency when I get back. I've paid for service."

"Don't." Ivan made a dramatic gesture which revealed black-rimmed nails. "Don't blame the waiters. They're only the spineless victims of the rotten capitalist system which must be smashed if we want to build a brave new world."

Stella soon discovered that he could reel off that kind of speech without any encouragement, but she listened to him and even drew him out—partly because she was an intelligent girl who liked to study types of humanity and partly because she was sorry for him. When he learned that she had a job on the staff of a big London hotel, he claimed her sympathy as a fellow worker.

She soon grasped the facts of his grievance. The hotel was shut during the winter and was only full for six weeks in the summer; during the rest of the time it was run on a skeleton staff for the benefit of such tourists as took out-of-season holidays.

The village was miles away from a railway station but was an excellent centre from which to explore the numerous historic ruins—abbeys and chateaux—set amid wild and picturesque scenery. Probably for that reason a party of riotous young people in a fleet of luxury cars had suddenly swooped down for lunch and then—on impulse—had decided to make it their headquarters.

Coming in the dead season they proved a little gold mine to the proprietor and not unnaturally the staff became demoralized. Money flowed constantly into the bar and waiters reaped a rich harvest of tips. The handful of ordinary visitors went to the wall.

Stella, however, was swift to prove her mettle, for she forced a surly waiter to bring her coffee. While she drank it she smoked a cigarette and studied the crowd.

They seemed much alike—young, attractive, high-spirited, and strangers to any form of inhibition or restraint. Apparently unconscious of anyone outside their own circle, they behaved as though this particular hotel had been created for their pleasure and use. It was plain that they believed that they were roughing it in the wilds, and their joking remarks were so frank that Stella thought it was fortunate that the waiters could not understand English.

The proprietor, who was a linguist, merely shrugged and smiled at his cash register, but Ivan took up the cudgels for him and spurted venom as he harangued Stella.

"Look at that swilling mob of drunken swine. They know nothing. They don't know the meaning of hunger, or pain, or fear. They're stuffed with food instead of ideas. But if I were to hurl a bomb into their midst, they'd be nothing but bloody rags."

"You'd be blown up, too," Stella reminded him.

"What of it? Death's nothing. Life's nothing." His eyes smouldered. "But what a scoop. The heirs to millions all here together.

What a blow to strike at capitalism. The man who did that would be a hero."

"He'd be a murderer."

"No. An avenger. These millionaires are mass murderers. See that girl." He pointed to the beautiful blonde. "That's Mitzi Cross, heiress to sweated millions. She's a human being, like myself. Yet she doesn't know I'm made of flesh and blood, too. When we meet she doesn't see me. If I speak to her she doesn't hear. I hate her."

The boredom of her first evening was typical of the days to follow and it soon become plain to Stella that this special holiday was not a success. The millionaires—to use Ivan's collective title for sake of convenience—disorganised the hotel. They claimed the easiest chairs, monopolized the billiard table, exacted preferential treatment for meals and baths. Hot water ran tepid and the best dishes were declared "off."

They were chaperoned by a depressed elderly lady who remained mostly invisible, partly from rheumatism and partly from dread of making an acquaintance. This fear was unfounded, for the other guests usually retired to their own rooms for refuge. They were all of them quiet, pleasant people and included an American family, two English women school teachers, and several French and Belgian married couples.

As Stella was an attractive girl and used to attention, she grew rather bored and resentful. Ivan soon got on her nerves, especially when she discovered that her pity was wasted on a swollen self-conceit. After she had made it clear that free love was mud to her he left her alone.

All his attention was concentrated on the millionaires and in particular the heiress, Mitzi Cross. He devoured her with glittering eyes which missed no movement of her slim figure, and strained his ears to catch every word of her fluting high-pitched voice. When she laughed he shivered as though the sound touched an exposed nerve.

"I believe it's an inverted passion," thought Stella. "It's unhealthy."

But gradually she, too, became affected by the adverse conditions, both spiritual and climatic. Although the weather was bad she went on daily motor excursions because the hotel was so uncomfortable. The landscape looked savagely depressing, viewed through sheets of torrential rain, and she left the car only to stumble through melancholy ruins which smelt of mouldy damp.

Presently she began to sleep badly from lack of air and exercise. The village lay deep in a tree-lined valley, so that from her bedroom window she could see only a wall of sodden foliage. After her light was switched off she lay staring out at the gloom until she fell asleep, often to dream of *oubliettes* and medieval torture.

She had reached the point of deciding to cut her loss and return to England and was on her way to the bureau, when to her surprise a member of the millionaires' party asked her to play billiards with him.

Before the game was over she had not only shed her depression but was pledged to stay out her fortnight. The young man, whose name was Lewis Gough, had an interesting personality besides charm. She discovered that in spite of his father's wealth he was a keen worker and a clever chemist.

Her pleasure, however, was partly spoiled by the presence of Ivan, who sat and stared fixedly at Lewis and herself as thought they were a pair of performing fleas, hopping about for his ironic amusement. The next time she met him he cut her dead.

Although this extraordinary behaviour was a relief, since it rid her of his company, she experienced a sense of discomfort and also of unmerited guilt. Ivan's clap-trap speeches were usually ridiculous, but his silence got on her nerves. It changed him into the unknown — a figure of sinister and inscrutable menace.

But as gradually she was drawn into the outer ring of the charmed circle she thought about him less, even while he remained in the background of her consciousness.

Two days before the end of her holiday she had just returned from a motor trip with Lewis and was standing on the bridge over the river when she was startled by the sound of Ivan's harsh voice.

"Are you going to the caves tomorrow?"

"Yes," she replied, stressing her smile to show him that she was still friendly. "Are you?"

"What does that matter to you? I'm not your new friend — the millionaire."

"Oh, don't be silly. If you mean Mr. Gough, he's not a millionaire. And he probably works harder than you."

"Probably. But not between meals. . . I came to give you a warning. Don't go tomorrow."

Her heart gave a little leap.

"Why not?" she asked.

Ivan stared down at the swirl of the soupy rain swollen current and smiled darkly, as though he were dipped in the turgid depths of his imagination.

"These rich people feel secure," he said, "because they always herd in crowds. They're cowards who find safety in numbers. But suppose an—accident—happened tomorrow, they would be trapped in the bowels of the mountain."

"What could happen?"

"The light might be cut off. They're all at the mercy of some poor devil, but they'll never give one thought to him. Suppose he was one of us? They'd be left in pitchy darkness. And then—anything might happen."

As she listened Stella's imagination galloped away with her, so that she gasped with a sense of blind, choking horror, as though someone had crept behind her and smothered her in a black cloth. Before her common sense returned Ivan had turned away.

While she was dressing for dinner she was shocked to discover how shaken she was by the episode. Her fingers trembled and she hunted for garments after she had put them on. Presently she opened her suit-case and drew out her book of return tickets.

As she checked the stages of her journey home the fear coiled around her heart, raised its ugly head.

"Suppose these are never used. Suppose I don't go back."

Even while she told herself that Ivan's threats were ridiculous she knew that one thoughtless or irresponsible person could precipitate a catastrophe. Ivan was incapable of clear thought. His head was a clouded broth of revolutionary phrases. He talked glibly of death, but knew nothing of life.

They were at the mercy of a child—an idiot—a drunkard—who walked amid piles of gunpowder, flourishing a lighted taper.

Suddenly she decided to trust to her instinct and not go to the caves. It was lowering her flag of superstition, but in the circumstances the excursion would prove a penance instead of a pleasure.

After she made the decision she felt happy again. Dinner was quite a festive meal and she ordered a bottle of wine to mark the occasion. But afterward, as she looked around the lounge, to her dismay her sense of responsibility awoke.

Tonight some freak had prompted the millionaire to appear in full evening dress. Hitherto, as though to mark the difference between the other guests and themselves, they had not changed for dinner, appearing in the breeches and shorts of the daytime.

Although they were now far too ornate for the occasion they were exceedingly good to look at. The girls were like a swarm of brilliant butterflies, quivering with colour and life. Mitzi was alluring and exquisite in an amazing backless gown of black velvet; her nails and lips were vivid coral, and the loose waves of her silvery hair shimmered like moonlight.

"They have something which is beautiful," thought Stella. "They have youth."

She glanced anxiously at Ivan, who was glowering at Mitzi as he sprawled in one of the chairs which the millionaires had grown to regard as their especial property. Presently he was tackled by one of Mitzi's special young men whom everyone called "Pony."

This youth was the richest member of the party and incidentally not a favourite with Stella; he was spoilt, sophisticated, and brainless. His grin was confident as he spoke to Ivan.

"I say, Miss Cross wants her chair. Do you mind frightfully?"

"I do," snarled Ivan. "But if she's bought the chair she shall have it when she shows me the receipt."

The youth started, stared, and then turned away with a shrug.

"Was that necessary?" asked Stella, speaking to Ivan in a low, soothing voice. "Why do you let these people make you unhappy? Soon you'll never see them again. Forget them."

"I can't." His voice was choked with passion. "Look at them. Dancing, drinking, laughing. They are always laughing."

"And you're jealous because they laugh. You could laugh, too."

"I'm not a hyena nor yet a grinning ape . . . Look at that girl. You're a worker. Have you ever worn a dress like hers?"

"No, but I don't envy her. You and I have the luck because we have jobs, while these people are all on the dole. They must be so bored . . . Can't you realise you're above them? You have personality — power."

It was second nature with Stella to smooth rough places. Her hotel experience had taught her to regard dissatisfied guests as so many fractious children to be calmed. She fed Ivan with spoonfuls of grossest flattery through sheer force of habit.

It came to her as a shock of surprise when he swallowed her bait.

"You're right," he said. "I am above them. I'll show them."

"I can influence him," she thought as he watched him rise to his feet. She felt something of the thrill of the engine driver when he controls a runaway machine.

"I'm going to give her one last chance," said Ivan. "It is in her power to save the lot of them."

Still acting in the grand manner he crossed to Mitzi, made a low bow, and pointed in the direction of his empty chair.

Mitzi accepted the courtesy with quite a gracious nod and half a smile. But even as Stella drew a deep breath of relief the girl gingerly picked up the greasy cushion—against which Ivan's head had rested—and pitched it on the floor.

As it was not clean the action might have been a precaution to protect her frock. Besides, Mitzi was the kind of girl who threw things about. But Ivan construed it as a deadly insult.

His lips quivered with fury as he strode from the lounge. There was a burst of laughter as he went, but Stella shuddered, for she had seen his eyes.

She started at the sound of Lewis's voice.

"What's worrying you?"

"That young man!" she replied. "He's class-conscious and not quite normal. I feel he's dangerous. Miss Cross offended him just now. Could you persuade her to say something decent to him?"

"Wouldn't if I could. I know his type. Harmless. All the fellow wants is to be a hero and pose in the limelight. Come on. Dance, little lady, dance."

So Stella danced and tried to forget her fears. She told herself that it was hopeless to try to control the situation. In any case, it was not her business. In two days' time she would never see any of these people again. . . . Life went on.

On her way up to bed she met Ivan on the narrow staircase. He was carrying a suit-case and his face was white and his eyes glazed as though he had been drinking.

"Are you going away?" she asked.

"Yes," he replied thickly. "I've been kicked out of the hotel by the blasted millionaires"

"What do you mean?"

"I complained to the proprietor about their filthy behaviour. And he had the damned insolence to tell me to go . . . Me!"

The triumph of his laugh and the bravado of his swagger told Stella that the ultimate disaster had happened. He was now a martyr to his cause.

She tossed sleeplessly in bed, a prey to every kind of foreboding fancy, and when at last she dropped into a doze she had horrible nightmares of dark places. She was drowning in the darkness. Choked in the darkness. Crushed by the darkness. Sinking down into the bottomless gulfs of darkness.

It was a relief to wake up and see the rare sunlight streaming through her window and to remember that she was not going to the caves.

But all the same she could not shake off a sense of her own responsibility. During *café complet* she felt a pang whenever she looked around the restaurant. The young people were in the highest spirits and their shouts of laughter tore at her heart.

She told herself that they were going to their doom like sacrificial lambs. It was true that they were graceless, noisy lambs, but they were so unconscious of any overhanging fate. Their faces had the bloom of youth; some of the boys had only begun to shave; they were merely spoiled, reckless babes.

She alone was forewarned and had any influence over Ivan. At a critical moment she might prove the driver, able to control a mad machine. One word might mean all the difference between life and death. If she stayed safely at the hotel and later heard of some catastrophe in the caves she would never be able to forgive herself—or to forget.

Presently Lewis crossed to her table.

"Change your mind and come to the caves," he pleaded. "It is our last excursion together. Come for me."

As Stella looked at his clear eyes and the clean corners of his mouth she suddenly realised that he meant more to her than she had guessed. In that moment she changed her mind.

"All right," she said. "I'll go."

Although the rest of the party were in the highest spirits, Stella felt as though she were in the tumbrel on her way to the guillotine as the car tore through the sunlit countryside. When they arrived at the village, which was the starting point of their expedition, the little train was already waiting by the side of the road. But Mitzi and her crowd, with whoops of glee, rushed to get drinks at the hotel, outside which stood the usual painted iron tables and chairs.

Stella seated herself beside the two English school-teachers. One was tall and rather gloomily handsome; the other was a little, pale girl in glasses, with a vivid face and an astounding store of information.

"What are we waiting for?" complained the tall teacher.

"Those boys who are drinking," replied her little friend. "People like that spoil things for everyone."

Stella mentally agreed with her. Although Ivan was not on the train she held her breath with suspense, fearing every second to see him hurry down the street. But at last, to her joy, the train began slowly to move. It jolted through the town and then ran under a tunnel of shady trees. An amber river flowed beside the avenue, but gradually its water gleamed below them as the engine chugged up the hillside.

As they climbed higher and higher through the gaps in the rocks they had visions of the country spread out below like a painted map. The scarlet of poppies and yellow of mustard made bright splashes amid the multi-shades of green, while the shadows of racing clouds swept across in tremulous blue and purple patches.

The journey was short and soon the conductor came and took Stella's ticket. Thinking he had made a mistake she held it firmly as she explained that she wanted it for the return journey.

"*Pas de retour*," he said.

"Sounds ominous," laughed the little school mistress. "'No return.' He means we don't go back by train. We walk back inside the mountain to our starting point."

Although the explanation was sound Stella felt absurdly depressed by the incident, as though the conductor's words were prophetic. "No return." The phrase rang in her head as she got out of the train. The rest of the tourists were crowding to look over the lip of a Dantesque gorge at the source of the river, which foamed in a dark boil through the rocks far below.

Turning away with a shudder she followed her companions down a slippery path which zig-zagged along the base of the mountain until the entrance to the caves was reached.

She looked nervously around her as she passed through the turn-stile, dreading to see Ivan's white, sneering face. Although he was apparently not among the crowd of sightseers, his absence did not reassure her altogether.

"Perhaps he's already inside," she thought, "waiting."

In a kind of nightmare she entered the maze of passages and caves with which the mountain was honeycombed. From the beginning of the expedition her mind was so heavy with apprehension that she received but a confused impression of her surroundings. The marvels of the stalactites were lost upon her; she could only plod through cracks in the rocks, along galleries, and up and down endless steps. She was dimly aware of dripping walls, of corners of fantastic draperies, of what appeared to be guttering stone altar candles, but she could neither admire nor wonder. She could only endure.

"How far is it to the end?" she asked faintly.

"About two and a half miles," replied the little teacher.

The tourists straggled on in a long thin line like ants on march. Sometimes they clustered together in some chamber while the guide explained its formation, in three languages, which did not include English. Stella's brain was too dull to attempt to translate; she was only fretted by the repetition, although she recognised the standardized jokes by the bursts of laughter.

All the time she was acutely on the alert—waiting for some horror which might await them round the next bend. The shattering roar of an explosion—the rumbling avalanche of rocks sealing their tombs—the thick, choking blackness.

"Tired?" asked Lewis.

"Oh, no. But the air's rather thick, isn't it?"

"A bit dead probably. We're getting pretty deep in."

He put his hand through her arm to help her as they scrambled onward. The tourists went in pairs or single file along the narrow paths. Most of them were silent. Some were feeling the strain of the stagnant atmosphere and of climbing steps; some were bored; some were memorizing what they saw.

But there were others who were oblivious of their surroundings and carrying on as usual. These included Mitzi and her young men who, following precedent, regarded the mountain as their private property. They chased each other down the flights of steps with shouts and laughter, pushing aside the other tourists without ceremony.

Stella's feeling of oppression deepened as they got further inside the mountain. Sometimes when they walked over the tongues of rock they caught glimpses of a black river boiling down below.

At one point where it was wide and oily it was spanned by a bridge. The guide halted to name it the River Styx and to make jokes about hell in three different languages.

"Looks pretty foul," remarked Lewis. "I shouldn't care to swim in it. Would you?"

"I can't," Stella confessed. "It's awful, but somehow I never got the chance. I suppose I'm unique."

"No, you aren't. Mitzi can't swim either. She'll do any stunt in the air, but she's always had a dread of water. Some sort of complex."

The expedition had now become a test of endurance through cracks of rocks or stops in the caves during a ghastly period of explanation. Everything seemed calculated to draw out the agony. The guide had so many regulation jokes to be cracked; there were theatrical effects of coloured flares to be admired; musical chimes and echoes were evoked to heighten the effect of the grottoes.

Presently Stella noticed a man who was always running ahead of the party.

"He turns on the lights before we come and then goes back and switches them off again," explained the little teacher.

"I don't commend their economy," grumbled her tall friend. "If a light fused we should be left in the dark."

A memory stirred in Stella's brain. "Some poor devil. . . Suppose he was one of us." To stifle it she spoke to the little school-teacher.

"Are we near the end?"

"Yes," was the comforting reply. "But we've got to wait and have refreshments first."

The subterranean cafe reminded Stella of a foretaste of the infernal regions, with its waitresses and the members of the orchestra all in scarlet, and the weird, echoing music. Tortured by the delay, she was trying to swallow a cup of bitter black coffee when she suddenly saw Ivan looking down from an upper balcony.

Only his face was revealed by the red flare, so that he seemed to swim in space. The light accentuated its bony structure and the hollows of his eyes, making him resemble a corpse awaiting burial.

Like a spirit of evil he brooded in gloating triumph over the abyss. At last his enemies were in his power.

Stella could imagine the drunken dreams which flooded his brain. He would believe it to be a glorious deed to hurl a bomb into their midst. With one gesture entire nests of capitalists and blood suckers would be wiped out. The others who perished would be merely incidental to the sacrifice.

He would be a hero — and die a martyr's death. He would be photographed and paragraphed in the press. Beyond that his thoughts would not go.

"I must get to him. I must speak to him before it's too late."

As the thought flashed across Stella's mind he disappeared. She tried to scramble in his direction just as the little teacher called out to her that they were moving on again. Afraid to be lost in the ramifications of the caves, she had to turn and follow the party through other passages until they reached a wooden dock which was built over a stretch of black, still water. On it floated a huge, clumsy craft, rather like a barge.

"In a few minutes we shall be outside," explained the little teacher. "We just float down the river . . . Jump in. I wish people wouldn't push."

The tourists crowded forward while the boatmen helped them into the barge. They were packed together so closely that the boat seemed to sink down almost below the level of the water.

"We're not enough for two boats, so they're making one do," remarked the little teacher.

Stella could see nothing of her party because of the intervening heads, although she could judge the whereabouts of Mitzi, who was shouting to Pony to sit beside her. As he tried to rise the barge lurched perilously and everyone yelled to him to keep still.

But in that moment of shifting positions Stella had a glimpse of Ivan's white face and staring eyes. . . . They had taken death on board.

They began to slide slowly through the water, leaving the lighted dock for the semi-gloom of the tunnel. She could see its lofty, dripping roof as they crawled onward foot by foot. Each moment the light grew dimmer until it suddenly went out altogether.

The eclipse was greeted with laughter and faint screams of excitement.

"They always do this," said the little teacher. "We shall drift around the bend and then we shall see the daylight at the end of the tunnel, like blue fire."

Stella listened in an agony of terror. At last she realised why Ivan had withheld the bomb of which he talked. This was the opportunity for which he had waited. The darkness.

Each minute seemed to hold an eternity of dread. She could hear the trickling and glugging of water—the creaking of timber. And then—the catastrophe happened within three seconds. The barge rocked with a sickening lurch as someone rose to his feet. There were shouts of "Sit down," but almost in the same moment the boat keeled completely over and she felt herself slipping down through the water.

It was like her dream—a choking agony in the darkness. Pandemonium raged all around her as people fought and struggled, while a mad medley of limbs thrashed and kicked in every direction. Just as her fingers touched the slimy boards of the barge she felt a violent blow under her chin and dropped down into an abyss of blackness.

When she opened her eyes she was lying on the grass, staring up into a dazzling blur of light. Gradually the landscape stopped floating about like bits of a jigsaw puzzle and reassembled itself into definite shapes of trees, fields, and people. She saw the barge—now righted on the sunlit river—and heard excited voices and shouts of laughter.

Then she smiled into Lewis's concerned eyes.

"Am I drowned?" she asked.

"No, just a spot damp," was the reply. "You were knocked out in the scrum."

"Were any lives lost?" she whispered as she shuddered at the memory.

"Of course not. At one time things looked a bit ugly. People lost their heads because of the dark. But when the light came on we soon got things sorted out."

"But it might have been a tragedy. You see, I was right about Ivan. He was dangerous."

"But that chap didn't scuttle the boat," explained Lewis. "It was that fool, Pony, trying to cross to Mitzi. No, the Mad Mullah fished her up and now she's telling the world he's her hero. I told you all he wanted was the limelight. Look at him, lapping it all up."

As Stella followed his pointing finger she could hardly believe the evidence of her eyes. Shouting and laughing with excitement—Ivan was the central figure of his group. His thin cheeks were flushed and his fingers snapped as he spouted like a stump orator. One arm was thrown around Mitzi, who literally clung to him, for she was a girl who never did things by halves.

But later that evening, looking into the swirl at the soupy river, he made his confession to Stella.

"I did upset the barge. The other chap got up afterward. I gripped Mitzi. I meant to drag her down with me and hold her under until we were both drowned. . . But when she put her arms around my neck and cried out, I—I couldn't. Something got hold of me."

Stella understood. This youth who had walked and talked daily with death, for the first time had been gripped by the mighty force of life.

THE GILDED PUPIL

The essential part of this tale is that Ann Shelley was an Oxford M.A. Unfortunately, so many other young women had the same idea of going to college and getting a degree that she found it difficult to harness her qualifications with a job. Therefore, she considered herself lucky, when she was engaged as resident governess to Stella Williams, aged fifteen—the only child of a millionaire manufacturer.

It was not until her final interview with Stella's mother, in a sun room which was a smother of luxury, that she understood the exact nature of duties. Lady Williams—a beautiful porcelain person, with the brains of a butterfly—looked at her with appealing violet eyes.

"It's so difficult to explain, Miss Shelley. Of course, my husband considers education comes first, but what I want is someone to exercise an moral influence on Stella. She—she's not normal."

"Thymus gland?" hinted Ann.

"Oh, far worse. She won't wash."

Ann thought of the times she had been sent upstairs to remove a water mark, because she had overslept, or wanted to finish a thriller, and she began to laugh.

"That's normal, at her age," she explained. "Schoolgirls often skimp washing."

Lady Williams looked sceptical, but relieved. "The trouble began," she said, "when she was too old for a nurse. Nannie used to wash and dress her, like a baby. But she refuses to let her maid do anything but impersonal things, like clothes. It's her idea of independence. She's terribly clever and socialistic. She'll try to catch you out."

"That sounds stimulating," smiled Ann.

All the same, she was not impressed pleasantly by her new pupil, and her superior. Her sole recommendation to Ann's favour was her intelligence, which was far above the average.

On her first Saturday half holiday, Ann walked out to the grounds of Arlington Manor—the residence of the Earl of Blankshire—to visit her old governess, Miss West. It was a May day of exciting weather, with concealed lighting bursting through a white, windy sky. She thrilled with a sense of liberation, when she turned in to the road through the woods, where the opening beeches were an emerald filigree against the blue shadows of the undergrowth.

Miss West's cottage suggested a fairy tale, with its thatched roof and diamond-paned windows. It stood in a clearing and was surrounded by a small garden, then purple with clumps of irises.

Ann's knock was answered by the maid, Maggie—a strapping country girl. She showed the visitor into the bed-sitting room, where her mistress, who was crippled with rheumatism, was sitting up in bed.

Miss West was an old woman, for she had also been a governess to Ann's mother. Her mouth and chin had assumed the nutcracker of age, so that she looked rather like an old witch, with her black blazing eyes and snowy hair.

Her dominant quality was her vitality. Ann could still feel it playing on her, like a battery, as they exchanged greetings.

"I love your little house," she remarked later, when Maggie had brought in tea "But it's very lonely. Are you ever nervous?"

"Nervous of what?" asked Miss West. "There's nothing here to steal, and no money. Everyone knows that the earl is my banker."

This was her way of explaining that she was a penniless pensioner of the earl, whom she had taught in his nursery days.

"Every morning, someone comes down from the manor, with the day's supplies," she said. "At night a responsible person visits me for my orders and complaints. . . . Oh, you needn't look down your nose. The earl is in my debt. He is prolonging my life, at a trifling expense to himself, but I saved his life, when he was a child, at the risk of my own."

Her deep voice throbbed as she added, "I still feel there is nothing so precious as life."

Later, in that small bewitched room, Ann was to remember those words.

"Life's big things appeal most to me," she confessed. "Oxford was wonderful—every minute of it. And I'm just living for my marriage with Kenneth. I told you I was engaged. He's a doctor on a ship, and we'll have to wait. In between, I'm just marking time."

"You have the important job of moulding character," Miss West reminded her. "How does your gilded pupil progress?"

"She's a gilded pill!" Ann grimaced.

"Is Oxford responsible for your idea of humour?" asked Miss West, who had a grudge against a university education.

"No, it's the result of living in a millionaire's family. Please, may I come to see you, every Saturday afternoon? You make me feel recharged."

Although Miss West had acted like a mental tonic, Ann was conscious of a period of stagnation when she walked back through the wood. She taught in order to live, and had gone to see an old woman as recreation. Life was dull.

It might not have appeared so flat had she known that she was marked down already for a leading part in a sinister drama, and that she had been followed all the way to the cottage.

For the next few weeks, life continued to be monotonous for Ann, but it grew exciting for Stella, as gradually, she felt the pull of her governess' attraction. Ann had a charming appearance and definite personality. She made no attempt to rouse her pupil's personal pride by shock tactics, but relied on the contrast between her own manicured hands and the girl's neglected nails.

Presently she was able to report progress to the young ship's doctor.

"My three years at Oxford have not been wasted," she wrote. "The gilded pupil has begun to wash."

In her turn, she became fonder of Stella, especially when she discovered that the girl's aggressive manner was a screen for an inferiority complex.

"I always feel people hate me," she had confided to her governess one day. "I'm ashamed of having a millionaire father. He didn't make his money. Others make it for him. He ought to pay them a real spending income, and, automatically, increase the demand and create fresh employment."

Ann found these socialistic debates rather a trial of tact, but she enjoyed the hours of study. Stella was a genuine student, and always read up her subject beforehand so that lessons took somewhat the form of discussions and explanations. Ann was spared the drudgery of correcting French exercises and problems in algebra.

But her gain was someone else's loss. She had no idea how seriously she was restricting the activities of another in the plot.

Doris—the schoolroom maid—searched daily amid the fragments in the wastepaper basket for something which she had been ordered to procure. And she searched in vain.

When Stella's devotion to the bathroom was deepening to passion, she began to grow jealous of her governess' private hours.

"Do you go to the pictures on Saturday?" she asked.

"No, I visit an old witch, in a cottage in the wood."

"Take me with you."

"You'd be bored. It's my old governess."

"*Your* governess? I'd love to see her. Please."

Ann had to promise a vague "some day." Although she was sorry to disappoint Stella, she could not allow her to encroach on her precious liberty.

By this time, however, her time table was an established fact to the brains of the plot. Therefore, the next Saturday she visited Miss West she was followed by a new trailer.

She noticed him when she came out of the great gates of the millionaire's mansion, because he aroused a momentary sense of repugnance. He was fair and rather womanish in appearance, but his good looks were marred by a cruel red triangular mouth.

He kept pace with her on the opposite side of the street when she was going through the town, but she shook him off later on. Therefore it gave her quite a shock when she turned into the beech avenue—now a green tunnel—to hear his footsteps a little distance in the rear.

Although she was furious with herself, she hurried to reach the cottage, which was quite close. The door was opened before she could knock, because her arrival was the signal for Maggie's release. It was Ann herself who had suggested the extra leisure for the maid while she kept the old lady company.

Miss West, whose bed faced the window, greeted her with a question.

"When did you lose your admirer?"

"Who?" asked Ann, in surprise.

"I refer to the weedy boy, who always slouches past the minute after your knock."

"I've never noticed him. . . . But I thought I was followed here today by a specially unpleasant looking man."

"Hmm. We'd better assume that you were. . . . How much money have you in your bag?"

"More than I care to lose."

"Then leave all the notes with me. I'll get the manor folk to return them to you by registered post. . . . And remember, if the man attacks you on your way home, don't resist. Give him your bag—and run."

"You're arranging a cheerful programme for me," laughed Ann.

When nine struck, Miss West told her to go.

"Maggie is due now any minute," she told her, "and so is the housekeeper from the manor. Good bye—and don't forget it means 'God be with you.'"

Ann was not nervous, but when she walked down the garden path she could not help contrasting the dark green twilight of the woods with the sun-splashed beech avenue of the afternoon. Clumps of fox-gloves glimmered whitely through the gloom, and in the distance an owl hooted to his mate.

She passed close by the bushes where a man was hiding. He could have touched her had he put out his hand. She was his quarry, whom he had followed to the cottage, so he looked at her intently.

Her expensive bag promised a rich haul. Yet he let her go by and waited, instead, for someone who was of only incidental interest to the plot.

A few minutes later Miss West's maid, Maggie, charged down the avenue like a young elephant, for she was late. She had not a nerve in her body, and only three pence in her purse. As she passed the rhododendron thicket a shadow slipped out of it like an adder—a black object whirled round in the air—and Maggie fell down on the ground like a log. . . .

The mystery attack was a nine days' wonder, for bag snatching was unknown in the district. But while Maggie was recovering from slight concussion in the hospital, Ann had the unpleasant task of mental bludgeoning her pupil out of a "rave." After the weekly visit of the hairdresser, Stella appeared in the schoolroom with her hair cut and waved in the same fashion as Ann's.

"Like it?" she asked self-consciously.

"It's charming." Ann had to be tender with the inferiority complex. "But I liked your old style better. That was you. Don't copy me, Stella. I should never forgive myself if I robbed you of your individuality."

Stella wilted like a pimpernel in wet weather.

"I'm not going to have a crush on you," she declared. "Too definitely feeble. But we're friendly, aren't we? Let's have a sort of friend's charter, with a secret signature, when we write to each other. Like this." She scrawled a five-fingered star on a piece of paper and explained it eagerly. "My name."

Ann was aware that Doris, the school-room maid, was listening with a half grin, and she decided to nip the nonsense in the bud.

"You'll want a secret society next, you baby," she said, as she crumpled up the paper. "Now, suppose we call it a day and go to the pictures."

Stella especially enjoyed that afternoon's entertainment, because the film was about a kidnapped girl, and she was excited by the personal implication.

"If a kidnapper ever got me, I'd say 'Good luck' to him. He'd deserve it," she boasted, as they drove home. "They wouldn't decoy me into a taxi with a fake message."

Ann's private feeling was that Stella's intelligence was not likely to be tested, since she ran no possible risk. Lady Williams was nervous on the score of her valuable jewellery so the house was burglar-proof, with flood-lit grounds and every kind of electric alarm.

Besides this, Stella either went out in the car, driven by a trusted chauffeur, or took her walks with a pack of large dogs.

So it was rather a shock to Ann when the girl lowered her voice.

"I'll tell you a secret. They've already had a shot at me. They sent one of our own cars to the dancing class, but I noticed Hereford wasn't driving, so I wouldn't get in. I wouldn't tell them at home because of Mother."

Ann, who was still under the influence of the picture, was horrified.

"Stella," she cried, "I want you to promise me something. If ever you get a note signed by me take no notice of it."

"I promise. But if you signed it with our star, I'd know it was genuine. And if *you* were in danger nothing and no one would stop me from coming to your rescue."

"Single-handed, like the screen heroines who blunder into every trap?"

"Not me. I'll bring the police with me. . . . Isn't that our school-room maid coming down the drive? Isn't she gorgeous?"

Doris, transformed by a marina top and generous lipstick, minced past the car. She had had to dress smart because she was meeting a fashionable gentleman with a cruel red mouth.

When she saw him in the distance she anticipated his question by shaking her head.

"No good swearing at me," she told him. "I can't get what isn't there. But I've brought you something else."

She gave him a sheet of crumpled paper on which was the rough drawing of a star.

The next time Ann went to the cottage in the wood the door was opened by the new maid—an ice-cold, competent brunette, in immaculate livery. There was no doubt Coles was a domestic treasure, and a great improvement on Maggie, but Ann was repelled by the expression of her thin-lipped mouth.

"I don't like your new maid's face," she said to her old governess when Coles had carried out the tea table.

"Neither do I," remarked Miss West calmly. "She's far too good for my situation—yet she's no fool. My opinion is she's wanted by the police and has come here to hide. It's an ideal spot."

"But you won't keep her?"

"Why not? She's an excellent maid. There's no reason why I should not benefit by the special circumstances, if any. After all, it's only my suspicion."

"What about her references?"

"Superlative. Probably forged. The housekeeper hadn't time to inquire too closely. The place isn't popular after the attack on Maggie."

"But I don't like to think of you alone, at her mercy."

"Don't worry about me. She's been to the cupboard and found out it's bare. I've nothing to lose."

Ann realised the sense of Miss West's argument, especially as she was in constant touch with the Manor. Not long afterwards she wondered whether she had misjudged the woman, for she received a letter, by the next morning's post, which indicated that she was not altogether callous.

Its address was the cottage in the wood.

"Dear Madam," it ran, "Pardon the liberty of my writing to you, but I feel responsible for Miss West in case anything happens sudden to her and there's an inquest. I would be obliged if you would tell me is her heart bad and what to do in case of a sudden attack. I don't like to trouble her ladyship, as I am a stranger to her and Miss West bites my head off if I ask her. I could not ask you today because she is suspicious of whispering. Will you kindly drop me a line in return and oblige."

"Yours respectfully,"

"Marion Coles"

Ann hastily wrote the maid a brief note, saying that Miss West had good health—apart from the crippling rheumatism—but recommending a bottle of brandy, in case of emergency. She posted it and forgot the matter.

Meanwhile, Miss West was finding Coles' competency a pleasant change, after Maggie's slipshod methods. On the following Saturday, when she carried in her mistress' lunch, Miss West looked, with approval, at her spotless apron and muslin collar.

After she had finished her well-cooked cutlet and custard, she lay back and closed her eyes in order to be fresh for Ann's visit.

She had begun to doze when she heard the opening of the front door. Her visitor was before her usual time.

"Ann," she called.

Instead of her old pupil, a strange woman entered the bedroom. Her fashionably thin figure was defined by a tight black suit and a halo hat revealed a sharp rouged face.

As Miss West stared at her she gave a cry of recognition.

"Coles!"

The woman sneered at her.

"Here's two gentlemen come to see you," she announced.

As she spoke, two men, dressed with flashy smartness, sauntered into the room. One was blonde and handsome except for a red triangular mouth; the other had the small cunning eyes and low-set ears of an elementary criminal type.

"Go out of my room," ordered Miss West. "Coles, you are discharged."

The men only laughed as they advanced to the bed.

"We're only going to make you safer, old lady," said the fair man. "You might fall out of bed and hurt yourself. See?"

Miss West did not condescend to struggle while her feet and hands were secured with cords. Her wits told her that she would need to conserve every ounce of strength.

"Aren't you taking an unnecessary precaution with a bedridden woman?" she asked scornfully.

"Nothing's too good for you, sweetheart," the fair man told her.

"Why have you come here? My former maid has told you that there is nothing of value in my cottage."

"Nothing but you, beautiful."

"How dare you be insolent to me? Take off your hats in a lady's presence."

The men only laughed. They sat and smoked cigarettes in silence, until a knock on the front door made them spring to their feet.

"Let her in," ordered the ringleader.

Miss West strained at her cords as Coles went out of the room. Her black eyes glared with helpless fury when Ann entered and stood—horror-stricken—in the doorway.

"Don't dare touch her," she cried.

The men merely laughed again, as they seized the struggling girl, forced her down on a bedroom chair, and began to bind her ankles.

"Ann," commanded the old governess, "keep still. They're three to one. An elementary knowledge of arithmetic should tell you resistance is useless."

The pedantic old voice steadied Ann's nerves.

"Are you all right, Miss West?" she asked coolly.

"Quite comfortable, thanks."

"Good." Ann turned to the men. "What do you want?"

They did not answer but nodded to Coles, who placed a small table before Ann. With the deft movements of a well-trained maid she arranged stationery—stamped with Miss West's address—and writing materials.

Then the fair man explained the situation.

"The Williams' kid wot you teach is always pestering you to come here and see the old lady. Now, you're going to write her a nice little note, inviting her to tea this afternoon."

Ann's heart hammered as she realised that she had walked into a trap. The very simplicity of the scheme was its safeguard. She was the decoy bird. The kidnappers had only to install a spy in the Williams' household to study the habits of the governess.

Unfortunately she had led them to an ideal rendezvous—the cottage in the wood.

"No," she said.

The next second she shivered as something cold was pressed to her temple.

"We'll give you five minutes to make up your mind," said the fair man, glancing at the grandfather's clock. "Then we shoot."

Ann gritted her teeth. In that moment her reason told her that she was probably acting from false sentiment and a confused sense of values. But logic was of no avail. She could not betray her trust.

"No," she said again.

The second man crossed to the bed and pressed his revolver to Miss West's head.

"Her, too," he said.

Ann looked at her old governess in an agony, imploring her forgiveness.

"She's only fifteen," she said piteously, as though in excuse.

"And I'm an old woman," grunted Miss West. "Your reasoning is sound, but you forget someone younger than your pupil—your unborn son."

Ann's face quivered, but she shook her head. Then the old governess spoke with the rasp of authority to her voice:

"Ann, I'm ashamed of you! What is money compared with two valuable lives, not to mention those still to come? I understand these—gentlemen—do not wish to injure your pupil. They only want to collect ransom."

"That's right, lady," agreed the fair man. "We won't do her any harm. This will tell the old man all he'll want to know."

He laid down a typewritten demand note on the table and added a direction to Ann.

"When we're gone off with the kid, nip off to the old man as fast as you can go and give him this."

"With her legs tied to a chair?" asked the deep, sarcastic voice of the old woman.

"She's got her hands free, ain't she? Them knots will take some undoing, but it's up to her, ain't it?"

"True. No doubt she will manage to free herself . . . but suppose she writes this note and the young lady does not accept the invitation? What then?"

The fair man winked at his companion.

"Then you'll both be unlucky," he replied.

Ann listened in dull misery. She could not understand the drift of Miss West's questions. They only prolonged the agony. Both of them knew they could place no reliance on the promise of the kidnappers. The men looked a pair of merciless beasts.

If she wrote that note she would lure her poor little gilded pupil to her death.

She started as her governess spoke sharply to her.

"Ann, you've heard what these gentlemen have said." She added in bitter mockery of their speech, "They wouldn't never break their word. Write that note."

Ann could not believe her ears. Yet she could feel the whole force of her vitality playing on her like an electric battery. It reminded her of a former experience when she was a child. Her uncle, who paid for her education, was an Oxford don and he raised an objection against Miss West because she was unqualified.

In the end he consented to give his niece a viva-voce examination, on the result of which depended the governess' fate.

Ann passed the test triumphantly, but she always felt, privately, that Miss West supplied the right answers, as she sat staring at her pupil with hypnotic black eyes.

Now she knew that the old magic was at work again. Miss West was trying to tell her something without the aid of words.

Suddenly the knowledge came. Her old governess was playing for time. Probably she was expecting some male visitors from the Manor, as the earl and his sons often came to the cottage. What she, herself, had to do was to stave off the five-minute sentence of death by writing a note to Stella, which was hallmarked as a forgery so that the girl would not come.

As she hesitated she remembered that she had extracted a promise from her pupil to disregard any message. The question was, whether it would be obeyed, for she knew the strength of her fatal attraction, and that Stella was eager to visit the cottage.

Hoping for the best, she began to write disguising her handwriting by a backward slant.

"Dear Stella—"

With an oath the man snatched up the paper and threw it on the floor in a crumpled ball.

"None of them monkey tricks," he snarled. "We know your proper writing. And sign it with this."

Ann's hope died as the man produced the letter which she had written to Coles about Miss West's health and also Stella's rough drawing of a star. She was defeated by the evidence—a specimen of her handwriting—for which Doris, the schoolroom maid had searched in vain—and the secret signature.

"I—can't," she said, feebly pushing away the paper. Again the pistol was pressed to her head.

"Don't waste no time," echoed Miss West. "Ann, write."

There was a spark in the old woman's eye and the flash of wireless. Impelled to take up the pen, Ann wrote quickly, in a firm hand, and signed her note with a faithful copy of the star.

The men hung over her, watching every stroke and comparing the writing with Coles' letter.

"Don't put no dots," snarled the fair man, who plainly suspected a cipher, when Ann inserted a period.

He read the note again when it was finished and then passed it to his companion, who pointed to a word suspiciously. The old woman and the girl looked at each other in an agony of suspense as they waited for the blow to fall.

Then the fair man turned sharply to Miss West.

"Spell 'genwin,'" he commanded.

As she reeled off the correct spelling he glanced doubtfully at his companion, who nodded.

"O.K.," he said.

Miss West's grim face did not relax and Ann guessed the reason. She was nerving herself for the second ordeal of Coles' inspection.

Fortunately, however, the men did not want their female confederate's opinion. The job was done and they wanted to rush it forward to its next stage. The fair man sealed the note and whistled on his fingers.

Instantly the weedy youth who had followed Ann to the cottage appeared from behind a clump of laurels in the drive, wheeling a bicycle. He snatched the letter from Coles and scorched away round the bend of the road.

Ann slumped back in her chair, feeling unstrung in every fiber. Nothing remained but to wait—wait—and pray Stella would not come.

The time seemed to pass very slowly inside the room. The men smoked in silence until the carpet was littered with cigarette stubs and the air veiled with smoke. Miss West watched the clock as though she would galvanize the crawling minute hand.

"Don't come," agonized Ann. "Stella, don't come."

But absent treatment proved a failure, for Coles, who was hiding behind a curtain, gave a sudden hoot of triumph.

"The car's come."

"Push the girl to the front," commanded the fair man.

He helped to lift Ann's chair to the window so that she saw the Williams' Lanchester waiting in front of the cottage. Stella stood on the drive and the chauffeur, Hereford, was in the act of shutting the door. He sprang back to his seat, backed, saluted, and drove swiftly away.

Ann watched the car disappear with despairing eyes. She could not scream because fingers were gripping her windpipe, nearly choking her. But Stella could distinguish the pale blue blur of her frock behind the diamond-paned window and she waved her hand as she ran eagerly up the garden path.

Had Ann been normal she might have guessed the truth from Stella's reaction to the scene when she burst into the room. Instead of appearing surprised, she dashed to Ann and threw her arms around her.

"They didn't fool me," she whispered.

Then she began to fight like a boxing kangaroo, in order to create the necessary distraction, while the police car came round the bend of the drive.

The prelude to a successful raid was Mr. Williams' call for prompt action, when his daughter brought him Ann's note.

"It's her writing and our private star," she told him. "But—read it."

He glanced at the few lines and laughed.

"An impudent forgery," he said.

"No, it's an S.O.S. It looks like a second try for me."

After she had told her father about the first unsuccessful attempt to kidnap her, he realised the importance of nipping the gang's activities in the bud.

This seems the place to print the note, which was the alleged composition of an Oxford M.A.

Dear Stella: Miss West will be pleased if you will come to tea this afternoon. Don't waste no time and don't run no risks. Let Hereford drive you in the car. To prove this is genuine, I'm signing it with our star, same as you done, one day in the schoolroom. Yours,"
"ANN SHELLEY"

THE CELLAR

"There's a Invisible Man in our cellar," declared Baby Lamb—her big blue eyes round as moons. The new nursery-governess, Lesley Bishop, understood her fear, for as a child, she, too had been terrorized by the threat of the terrible occupant of the cellar, who—according to her nursemaid, would come up to her, if she cried.

"Don't believe it, darling," she said to Baby. "There's nothing in the cellar but coals. Who told you such a wicked lie?"

"Max."

Lesley was not surprised, for her second charge, Max, was a Boy Scout who never failed to do his good deed per day. He was a pale, skinny little shrimp, with the large eyes of a stranded angel and a contrast to the stout, prosperous-looking Baby.

"'Tisn't a lie," he persisted. "I've seen him. He's all black, and he's got no face, like the Invisible Man—"

"Who took you to see 'The Invisible Man'?" broke in Lesley.

"Rosa," volunteered Baby.

Rosa was the children's late nurse and Max had been devoted to her. Lesley guessed that he resented her as a usurper and tormented her out of revenge. During that afternoon's walk he had been in the championship class of young demons. She had grown so breathless while chasing him away from doorsteps—to prevent him from giving runaway knocks—that, presently, she weakly accepted his conditional surrender.

"I'll stop now, if you'll let me ring at the empty house."

As she nodded consent, she looked the most frightened child of the three. This was her first engagement and she was still in her teens. It was the darkest time of the year when the old town was shrouded by the mist from the river, which flowed through it.

And under the fog and the shadows, like the quivering outline of a shark in deep water, lurked the threat of a murder.

A series of crimes, believed to be the work of a homicidal maniac, had recently shocked the population. Although the tragedies were

104

confined to the poorer parts of the town, Lesley went through the ill-paved historic streets with her heart fluttering at every footstep behind her.

It was dark when they reached the sweep of the Crescent, where Captain Lamb, who was a widower, lived with his sister as temporary housekeeper. The houses were imposing stucco erections of Regency period. The Lambs lived in the middle, next door to Number 11—the empty house.

Amid the lighted semi-circle, it stood out as a wedge of darkness. Inside was absolute blackness. For a life-time, it had been unilluminated even by the flicker of a match or a thread of moonshine.

Max had not forgotten his bargain, and he rushed up the steps, followed by Lesley, who feared further rebellion. When he tugged at the old-fashioned chain there was a discordant jangle and a series of faint tinkles. The bell seemed to go on ringing further and further into the dark distances of the house, awakening the echoes. On and on—deeper and deeper. The sounds filled Lesley with the sense of having precipitated some calamity, and she tried to tug Max away from the door.

"No," he shouted, clinging to the railings. "Somebody's coming to answer the door. Listen."

"It's the Black Man from the cellar," whimpered Baby.

As Lesley struggled with Max, she thought that she, too, could hear padded footsteps, slithering over layers of dust. They seemed to be drawing nearer to the door. In another second, they would reach it. . . .

Smitten by sudden panic, she leaped the flight of steps in one bound, dragging the children with her, and hammered furiously for admission to their own house.

Lesley was dismayed when Captain Lamb himself opened the door. Although she liked him, she was in awe of him, as her employer.

"Just in time for tea," he said genially, herding the nursery-party into the drawing room.

Miss Lamb, who wore trousers, merely grinned at the intrusion. She was a typical John Bull, with a jolly red face and a crop of copper curls. The big room, modernised with metal furniture, was so light and cheerful, that Lesley forgot the creepy darkness outside. When she was fortified by tea and muffins, she began to apologise.

"I'm sorry I made that awful din. But we thought we heard someone in the empty house."

"Rats," explained the Captain. "No one could get inside that house, or out of it again."

"Not even through the roof? Or down the chimneys?"

"Certainly not. After the last murder, the police examined the premises thoroughly. You see, there was dust on the poor creature's clothing, which made them wonder whether the crime was committed in the empty house. But every lock and bolt on Number 11 was intact."

"What a relief. I hate to think of that blackness, only the other side of my bedroom wall, when I'm listening for Miss Lamb to come home."

When Miss Lamb looked at her in surprise, she flushed.

"It's a stupid habit I got when I was a child," she said. "My nurse left me alone in the house, and I was so frightened I couldn't sleep until I heard her come back."

"Well, you won't have to worry tomorrow," Miss Lamb told her. "I shall be away for the Golf Tournament, Miss Nightingale—who used to live here—is coming instead, and she asked to sleep in her old room. Sentiment, you know."

The Captain who had been watching Lesley's face closely, made a lightning decision.

"I'm going to sleep there while my sister is away," he announced. "And directly I'm back from the club, I'll give three knocks on the wall, so you won't have to strain your ears."

"Oh, thank you," murmured Lesley. "Where has Max gone?" she added, to change the subject, as the boy stole out of the room.

Baby, who was a natural news collector, began to broadcast.

"I 'spect he's ringing up Rosa on the basement phone. He is always calling her. He wants to frighten Miss Bishop away and get nasty Rosa back. I'll go and stop him."

After she had marched out, like a young policewoman, Miss Lamb began to gossip.

"You know, Miss Bishop, the police believe these crimes are the work of a local criminal lunatic. He strangled a woman, but they said he'd a missing gland, or something so he was imprisoned for life. Then he escaped and the murders broke out again. They can't find him, and they think some woman is hiding him, so they came here after Rosa. The horrible creature was attractive to women, and she was supposed to be a sweetheart."

"Did you know?" gasped Lesley.

"No, her testimonials were forged and I never took them up. Dashed careless. We discovered afterwards that she did an unclothed act in some low hall, and never had been in service."

"It was rum," broke in the Captain. "She couldn't hope to hide the man here, in a house full of people. Yet she must have had some object in coming—especially as she wanted to get back again, after we sacked her. She was a flashy creature but she petted Max, who fell for her."

Reminded of her charges, Lesley walked to the door, where she turned to speak to Captain Lamb.

"It shows Max wants love. He's missing his mother."

"That girl's got a nice nature," remarked the Captain to his sister, when Lesley had gone. "Pretty, too."

Miss Lamb lit a cigarette thoughtfully, for she wanted to return to her own flat, and it struck her that Lesley might be a solution to her problem.

Lesley, too, felt happier as she walked up the fine staircase. Since the gossip over drawing-room tea, she felt less of a stranger. She was also pleasantly conscious of the Captain's dawning interest.

Suddenly she was startled by piercing screams from above, as Baby, shrieking like a steam engine, dashed down the nursery stairs and hurled herself into Lesley's arms.

"The Black Man's in our nursery!" she wailed. "He's gone and left his awful hand behind him!"

"Nonsense!" said Lesley sharply. "Come back at once!"

Dragging the protesting child after her, she reached the landing, where Max, who was also screaming, pointed to the door.

Standing out with sinister distinctness on the cream-painted panels was the black print of an open hand.

Lesley was so startled by the unexpected sight that she almost yielded to panic. She felt a sudden weakness at her knees, and was about to grab the children and run, when, luckily her prestige was saved. Just in time she surprised a glint in Max's eyes.

Pouncing on him, before he could guess her purpose, she forced open one of his hands and revealed his palm which glistened with black lead.

"Silly," she said lightly. "You're too big to play with coals, like crawling babies."

He writhed under her ridicule, especially as Baby joined in the joke. Lesley had not only the satisfaction of putting two young angels to bed, but had received a valuable lesson in morale.

The incident had taught her the folly of fear since the Black Man in the cellar was nothing but smudges of lead.

That night, she awoke from a sound sleep to find that she was ravenously hungry. As she tossed and turned, she kept thinking of a cold chicken which had left the nursery supper-table, almost intact. Presently she decided that she was really entitled to it, so she determined to raid the larder.

There was a touch of stolen apples about the adventure which thrilled her as she stole out into the broad landing and crept down the stairs. Crossing the hall, she opened the small baize-covered door which led down to the kitchen regions. She switched on the lights as she went, so that there were no dark corners to avoid, or shadows riding the walls.

The basement had been modernised as far as possible with gleaming white enamel and electric labour-saving contrivances. Gleeful at the prospect of her feast, Lesley was crossing to the refrigerator when she was startled by a low rumbling sound, directly underneath her feet.

Someone was in the cellar.

Her heart began to race as she listened. She heard movements like those which had terrified her when she waited outside the empty house. There was a drag of slow footsteps, while heavy objects seemed to be rolled about. Then a door was shut with a dull thud.

As she stared with wide frightened eyes, she remembered the captain's explanation that the noises were due to rats. Besides, no intruder could get inside their safe burglar-proof house. She knew, too, that the slightest sounds were magnified at night.

"I'm worse than Baby," she thought. "I must conquer my miserable nerves or I'm not fit to look after children. . . I'll prove to myself there's no one in the cellar."

It took all her courage to open the small door in the passage. She remembered the black gaping hole in her grandmother's old house and the smell of cold, stale air rising from the vaults. But, to her relief, her groping fingers found an unexpected switch and she snapped on the electric light to reveal a narrow staircase and yellow-washed walls.

She stopped to listen but was reassured by the silence. Apparently her approach had scared the rats back to their holes. Growing more confident, she descended as far as the halfway turn, from whence she could see a section of the cellar.

Suddenly, a dark flicker—swift as the passage of a bat's wing—shot over the butter-hued plaster.

Lesley realised it, rather than saw it, as—shying like a racehorse at a flash of lightning—she bolted back up the stairs.

When she was in the kitchen again, the leisurely ticking of the grandfather's clock made her feel ashamed of herself. As her heart ceased to flutter, her reason assured her that the shadow might have been cast by herself, unless it was merely a trick of imagination.

"Back you go, you little fool," she said to herself.

When she had forced herself to venture down the stairs a step at a time, with a pause to listen, she was rewarded for her boldness by a prosaic explanation of the rumbling noise. She discovered that the cellar had been converted into a furnace-room, with a central furnace and bags of anthracite stacked around the walls. One of these had overbalanced, and now lay on the floor, the coals spilling from its mouth.

She guessed that she had been startled by its fall; and she laughed at her own cowardice as she scampered back to the kitchen—snatched some cheese and crackers—and finished her adventure with a schoolgirl feast in bed.

As usual, next morning, she was the first of the household to get up, for there was no regular domestic staff, at present. After the police exposure of Rosa, Miss Lamb had dismissed the other servants, for fear of collusion. It was Lesley's duty, therefore, to open the door to the temporary staff.

This morning, everyone, including the man who stoked the furnace, was so late that she thought she had better see if the stove were in danger of going out. Full of morning confidence, she ran down the cellar steps—to stand, at the entrance, frozen with bewilderment.

The sack—which she had left lying on the floor—had been restored to its original position, and all the coals were removed from the flagstones.

As she stared, a disturbing thought struggled through the ferment of her mind.

"Things don't move by themselves. Someone—"

She turned and fled. Unlocking the back door to the servants who were knocking for admission—she rushed upstairs to the nursery, to find fresh trouble awaiting her. The little angels of the previous night had reverted to type, and Baby was howling.

"Max is frightening me," she wailed. "He says he's been inside the empty house and it's full of lions and tigers and bears. And there's a great big tree growing up inside. And he says the Black Man lives there—"

Lesley had to go through the tiresome business of soothing Baby and scolding Max all over again. It was a relief to be called down to the morning-room, where Miss Lamb was reading the paper while she breakfasted.

"Another murder," she shouted. "Some wretched girl found strangled, early this morning, outside some low pub. But you won't feel nervous with Miss Nightingale. She's a bit of a dud, so just keep a tab on the servants — I've proved that food is being taken out of the house."

Lesley felt rather depressed after Miss Lamb's car had disappeared into the gloom. It was the darkest morning of the year, and the street lamps were still alight in the Crescent, which was shrouded in fog. Miss Nightingale, too, proved a bad exchange for the jovial sportswoman. She was elderly and faded, while her voice was ultra-refined. As she looked around the hall, she drooped like a weeping-willow.

"It's heartbreaking to come back to my old home as a stranger," she confided to Lesley. "It doesn't look the same place. It's so bare without any draperies. And all the rooms are changed. We had a beautiful double drawing-room on the first floor."

"I'm afraid it's been turned into two bedrooms," confessed Lesley. "I sleep in one, with the children, and the Captain is sleeping in the other, just for the present."

"But there's a connecting door," cried Miss Nightingale in a horrified voice. "Of course, you keep it locked."

"It probably is."

"How peculiar. . . Is there a key to my bedroom door?"

"I don't know, but we'll see."

When they reached the second floor, the key to Miss Nightingale's old room was missing. The fact distressed the lady so much that Lesley went in search of it. To her annoyance, she discovered that there had been a wholesale removal of keys—not only from the doors of the rooms, but from bureaus and drawers.

She guessed the culprit and pounced down on him.

"Max, where are those keys?" she demanded.

Instead of protesting his innocence, the boy proposed a bargain.

"If I tell you, will you go away, and let Rosa come back?"

"Certainly not."

"Then I won't tell you—never."

"Oh, Max," cried Lesley in distraction, "you're enough to make me cry."

To her surprise, he was genuinely startled and distressed.

"Not cry?" he asked. "But—you're big. . . . See here, I'll put them all back again. But you're not to look where I go."

"Mind you fit them in properly," Lesley warned him, as he stole away to his secret hoard.

As Miss Lamb had prophesied, Miss Nightingale proved only a figure-head, so Lesley had to grapple with housekeeping responsibilities, without any aid. It had one good result—she was too busy to worry over the incident of the coal sack, until she believed she had the clue to the mystery. While she was tidying the children's wardrobe, she discovered that one of Max's jersey suits was covered with dust and cobwebs.

"That boy's been up to some monkey-trick in the cellar," she concluded.

As the morning wore on, the fog thickened until the lights had to be kept burning permanently. Outside the windows was an opaque world of chaos and shadows. It was impossible to take the children out, so Max was left to his evil deeds while Baby entertained Miss Nightingale in the drawing room.

In the afternoon, the Captain—who had barely lunched at his club to avoid Miss Nightingale—returned.

"Not frightened?" he asked Lesley. "Don't get steamed up about anything—and let things rip. I'm sorry, but I've got to go to a reunion dinner at Burnley tonight. I'll leave early, but don't lie awake to listen for me. I'll give those three knocks."

His voice was unconcerned, but his eyes held such personal interest that he might have been making an assignation. Lesley felt so lonely after he had driven off through the fog, that she went round the house, in order to see whether Max had restored the keys to their rightful places.

When she reached the captain's room, she had rather a disagreeable shock. As she crossed to the connecting door, she noticed a speck of oil on the key.

Miss Nightingale's insinuation and the captain's ardent gaze combined to give rise to an ugly suspicion.

"So that's the idea," she thought angrily. "Don't flatter yourself, my gentleman. This key's coming in my side of the door."

But before she could remove it, she repented.

"It's an insult to think that about him," she decided. "If he notices the key is gone, he'll think me a nasty-minded little prig. Probably Max has been up to one of his little jobs."

When she went to the drawing room for afternoon tea, she found that Baby had managed, as usual, to collect news.

"Miss Nightingale was a beautiful girl," she said, "and she had a beautiful young man. She's got their pictures. Show them to Miss Bishop, please, darling."

The term of endearment showed that Baby was enslaved by Miss Nightingale's past attraction. Lesley was not surprised at the fact when she saw the old and faded photographs inside a limp leather case. One depicted a young girl of rare beauty, while the other showed a handsome youth with a delicate face.

Miss Nightingale explained them with an apologetic cough.

"Me at eighteen. It missed my colouring, which people used to praise. I was very fair, with golden hair."

"It's enchanting," cried Lesley. Then she glanced at the other photograph and added, "I expect you had a wonderful time when you lived here?"

"You would consider it dull," replied Miss Nightingale primly. "I never went out alone. Ladies were ladies then."

Somehow Lesley received the impression that, many years ago, the house had held a prisoner.

"What would you like for supper?" she asked, to banish the beautiful ghost of Miss Nightingale's lost youth.

"A dry biscuit, please." Miss Nightingale's voice almost died from refinement. "And some very weak whisky-and-water."

When Lesley reached the basement, she found that the servants had left. It was Max who informed her of the fact.

"Daddy will be mad," he said gleefully. "He ordered them to sleep in, tonight, so you wouldn't be frightened. Because of the murder, you know."

"Run upstairs and turn on the bath," Lesley ordered.

She shot the bolt of the backdoor, since the key proved unexpectedly stiff from damp, and put up the chain for extra safety. But, she felt so bored and lonely that she spun out the children's bath, for the sake of their company. When at last she had dumped them in their beds, she lingered over her own supper until her conscience reproached her with neglect of Miss Nightingale.

Lesley found her sitting over her bedroom fire, while she smoked a cigarette with a guilty air. Her curlers were covered with a pale-blue boudoir cap and she wore an attractive dressing-gown.

"Come in and talk," she invited gaily.

It was obvious that Miss Nightingale was unaccustomed to spirits, for it took so little to flush her cheek and untie her tongue. After preliminary confidences about her health and toilette, she broke into the romantic tragedy of her youth.

"You saw Eric's photograph, this afternoon. He was the only son of General Hurley and they lived in the house that's empty now. We fell in love—but there were terrible scenes. The General thought we were mud, because we had been in trade, and Pa's pride was mortified, so they kept me a prisoner to keep me from meeting Eric. Then the General took Eric, who was delicate, to the Riviera, and he died there of a broken heart. The General never came back and the house has been empty to this day."

"Have you ever been inside?" asked Lesley.

"I was once in the hall. It was crowded with stuffed animals which the General had shot—lions, tigers, and bears—and there was an enormous family tree painted on the wall. . . . Oh, those terrible children are screaming again."

"Lions, tigers, bears. An enormous tree." The words swam in Lesley's head as she dashed down the stairs to her bedroom. The children were clinging together in very well-acted terror, as they screamed, "The Black Man's been here."

But they did not find their slave in her usual pliant mood. She hurried them back to bed and refused to glance at the smudged fingerprints on the connecting door.

"'Tisn't me," wailed Max. "Look at my clean hands."

"Yes, you remembered to wash them, this time," snapped Lesley.

She scolded them partly because she was distracted with a sudden memory. Max had given an accurate description of the hall of the empty house when he frightened Baby that morning.

"He couldn't have known," she assured herself. "No one knows, except Miss Nightingale. Unless—he's got inside."

The idea was so horrible that she was driven upstairs to ask the prim spinster an incredible question.

"Is there a secret way leading from this house to the empty one?"

To her dismay, Miss Nightingale smiled triumphantly.

"Yes," she declared, "there is . . . we cheated them . . . he used to come to me secretly by night."

"How?" whispered Lesley.

"He was studying to be a mining engineer, and he made a hole between the two cellars. It led through to the back of the boot cupboard in our cellar."

"Does anyone else know of this way?" she asked fearfully.

"No one but our housemaid, who was our go-between with notes, and she's been dead for years. I had to pay her hush money. Not long ago, her daughter, Rosa, tried to blackmail me, but I was too wise. I told her no one would believe such a fantastic old tale, and I dared her to tell it. She never did, of course."

As Lesley listened, her heart seemed to turn over; she had believed so confidently in their burglar-proof security, while all the time they had been linked directly with the dreaded empty house—and any horror that might lurk within. The cellar was their danger-spot.

"Good night," she said quickly. "Oh—do you lock your door at night?"

"Always, with a gentleman in the house," was the prim reply.

It was a tonic reminder that the Captain would be home soon, which sustained Lesley as she rushed down to the basement, as though pursued by fiends. When she had turned the key of the cellar door, she felt safe again. But although she walked quietly upstairs, she was careful to smash up the sequence of her thoughts.

While she was responsible for the children's safety, it was criminal to indulge in neurotic speculation. Following Miss Nightingale's example, she locked her own door and undressed quickly, keeping her mind on safe subjects. As she lay in bed, listening for the Captain's step in the passage in the corridor, she told herself that her only worry now was the Captain's meals, and she would soon discover his tastes. That was how people fell in love—living in the same house.

Relaxed in delicious warmth, she must have dozed for she was startled awake by three welcome knocks on the other side of the bedroom wall.

The Captain had not forgotten the signal. She smiled into the darkness at this proof that he had been thinking of her.

She was just dropping off to sleep when she heard the faint ringing of the telephone in the library below. She locked her door noiselessly and stole down to the library. Expecting a wrong number, the shock was greater when she heard the Captain's voice.

"That you, Miss Bishop? I'm hung up with the car, but I'll soon be back."

He was in a hurry, for he rang off before she could grasp the fact that, although he was speaking to her, he was actually miles away. . . .

Her first thought was for the children. She must return to them immediately. Almost incoherent with terror, she rang up the exchange and gasped into the receiver.

"Police. Police. Send them here. We're in terrible danger. Murder."

Her hands shook so violently that she could scarcely unlatch the front door in readiness for the police. She only knew that, since the maniac was in the adjoining room to hers, she must fetch the children and seek sanctuary with Miss Nightingale.

But, even on her flight back, that wild hope died. She realised that the maniac would be listening for movements, and that, in order to escape, they must be swift and silent as shadows. While she might depend on Max, Baby was too heavy to be carried and while she would wreck everything by screaming, if she were aroused from sleep.

There was nothing to be done but wait and pray for the police to come. Almost dead to sensation, she stood in the middle of her room, while her eyes darted alternately from door to door. And then, for the first time, she noticed the smudged hand on the panels of the communicating door.

No child had left that mark.

Baby was snoring like a little porpoise, so she covered her with a light shawl, in a vain effort to hide her. Max slept in a little cubbyhole, adjoining her room, so he was safer from attack. But even while she stooped over the bed, she thought she heard a board creak behind her, and she swung round, expecting to see a crouching black form, with no face.

Presently the strain of trying to keep both doors under observation at once proved intolerable. She had the feeling that if she took her eyes away from one door, he would steal her, unawares, and she cracked under her ghastly expectation of that sudden bound.

"I must see him," she thought, as she tip-toed to the door which led into the corridor and locked it silently.

The minutes crawled away as she faced the connecting door. It was added agony to remember that she had been given her chance to remove the key to her side of the door. She had thrown her safety away, merely to make a futile gesture.

She knew he must come that way, because of the oiled key. Silence had always been his safeguard, for none of his victims had screamed. The fact that he had fooled her with the Captain's signal proved that he had listened-in.

"He thinks the Captain is away for the night," thought Lesley with sudden clarity of mind. "But he thinks the servants are sleeping here. He is waiting for everyone to be asleep, before he creeps in to me."

Then her strained ears seemed to catch the faintest sounds from below. She did not know whether she imagined them, or if a car had stopped in the road, and the front door creaked open.

In the same minute, she heard another sound — the turning of a key in the lock of the connecting door.

She knew then that the police might capture their man, but they would be too late to prevent another crime. In her terror, she had forgotten to tell them where to find her. While they were cautiously exploring the ground floor, her neck would be broken in that gorilla-grip. She had read that the victims had died almost instantaneously. Even if they located her screams before she was silenced, they would not come until life was extinct.

She was past all help. At the knowledge, her brain jammed, and she stood and stared at the door. There was the sound of a click — and then another — as though the key was turning round and round in the lock. But she knew that he would come, and she remained with her eyes fixed on the door — waiting. A long time passed, while she heard shouts on the other side of the wall, and the sounds of a struggle. Yet she did not move.

She knew the door would open, and eventually it did — but it was a man in uniform who entered.

"Are you all right?" he asked anxiously.

To her surprise, she realised that she was still alive.

"Yes," she muttered.

He saw that she was still dazed, and he patted her arm.

"We've got him," he said. "Nothing to be frightened of now."

As she listened, her jammed brain began to work again, so that she realised the source of the miracle. It was Max, who had mistaken two nearly identical keys. The maniac had oiled the key of the back door — for silent excursions — and the boy had fitted it into the lock of the connecting door.

DON'T DREAM ON MIDSUMMER'S EVE

"**W**hat would happen to Puck if I had been killed?"

This was the first thought which flashed across Merle's brain after her crash. It was the agonized question of the bread-winner, for her small nephew—Puck—was entirely dependent on herself.

The accident was not the fault of the motorist, since she had crossed the road against the lights. She had been mooning back to work, down the scented gloom of the lime avenue. It was June 23rd, Midsummer's Eve, and someone had told her that a dream on that special night, always came true. . .

Even as she smiled at the fancy, she was conscious of a shattering shock, followed by a black out; and then she opened her eyes, to find herself lying on the pavement, while an elderly man with a kindly face, bent anxiously over her.

"Oh, I'm sorry," she cried. "Have I hurt the car?"

"The question is—has the car hurt you?" he asked.

To his relief, although bruised and shaken, she was miraculously intact. She rose unsteadily to her feet, and was beginning to fumble for her powderpuff, when he spoke to her.

"You had better let me drive you home."

As she was on her way to work it seemed wiser to give the address of the doctor, for whom she acted as secretary-dispenser. To her dismay, there was an appreciable pause before she could remember it. In the end, however, her brain began to function again, and not long afterwards, the car stopped before the right door.

Dr. Perry lived in a large, old-fashioned house, at the end of the ancient city which was dominated by grey cathedral towers. Nearly every street was lined with limes, or chestnuts, which formed cool tunnels during the summer heat. A slow green river flowed slowly through the town, which had been half-asleep for the last two hundred years.

Merle loved every stone of it, but this evening, it seemed doubly precious, because she had so nearly lost it. When the motorist had driven away, she entered the house, by the private way of the dispensary, and threw herself down into a deep leather chair.

The sun had been beating down on the glass roof all the afternoon, so the place was warm as a conservatory. It was very quiet, for Mrs. Stock—the housekeeper—was in the kitchen and the doctor was out at a case in the country. He was only beginning to build up a practice, and there were no appointments for the evening.

As she sat in the twilight, smelling the familiar druggy odour, blending with the scent of the jessamine screen over the windows, Merle grew cold to realise the risk to which she had exposed Puck by her criminal carelessness. Although the gentleman had an imposing string of names, his nickname was apt, since he was rather like a mischievous elf.

He was the kind of child to whose appeal most women are vulnerable—delicate, affectionate, clever, and a champion trouble-maker. Merle was especially sentimental and apprehensive over him, because he was her sole salvage from an unhappy past.

She had endured a little hell of proxy suffering during her twin-sister, Mavis's disastrous marriage to Lewis Gore. Unfortunately, her brother-in-law's conduct offered no loop hole for legal redress. His mean bullying nature was not manifested in acts of violence, just as—although he soaked continually—no one had ever seen him drunk. . . But he contrived to drain his young wife of her joy and vitality, so that, at the first illness, she flickered out of life, leaving her baby boy in Merle's care.

At first, Merle was too stunned with grief, and too worried about the future to appreciate her legacy. It took nearly all that remained of her small capital to finance Lewis and clear him out of the country. Since he had gone, however, she could hardly believe in her present happiness and peace.

She often told herself that she had everything—Puck, her work, her home, and loyal service, for Puck's nurse looked after the bungalow. Lately too, a new element had come into her life, for she was conscious of the doctor's growing interest in herself. He was a kindly, practical man, and she was growing very fond of him.

As usual, she considered Puck's interests first, and she came to the conclusion that, besides the benefit of a resident physician, the young domestic tyrant needed masculine authority.

She had drifted off into a light sleep—for the warm gloom acted as a soporific—through which she could hear faintly the cooing of pigeons and the ticking of the grandfather's clock. Presently she opened her eyes and forced herself to rise. The movement made her feel so queer and dizzy that she knew that further work was out of the question.

"I'll mix myself a draught, to quiet my nerves," she decided. "And then I'll rest a bit, before I go home."

To her dismay, she found that she lurched against the furniture when she crossed over to the shelves. Her head was spinning like a weather-cock in a high wind, while the floor heaved like the deck of a steamer during a Channel crossing. Half-blinded by a mist which drifted before her eyes, she managed to measure and mix a sedative.

As she raised it to her lips, she felt suddenly too sick to drink it. Laying it down again, she groped her way from the dispensary into the cool cavern of the big dining-room, where she flopped down in an easy chair.

Closing her eyes, she listened to the distant sounds of Mrs. Stock moving about the kitchen, until she was aroused by the creaking of the door.

Jumping up in a panic, she stared, in incredulous horror, at her brother-in-law, Lewis Gore.

He was tall and enormously stout, with a head too small for his bulk. His light cold eyes—set in deep pouches—glittered like white glass, as he nodded in casual greeting.

"Hello, Merle."

She forced herself to speak.

"When did you come back, Lewis?"

"I landed yesterday. I've come back to collect my boy. I am taking him back to Borneo."

"Borneo?" she echoed, scarcely able to believe her ears. "But Lewis, he is so wee and delicate. He could never stand the heat."

"He'll get used to it. The kids there don't play. They just sit about and sweat. Very healthy, on the whole."

"No. Lewis, I can't let him go. You don't understand. I've had all the trouble in the world just to rear him. . . . If you want money—"

"Money?" He laughed thickly. "My dear girl, I've not come back to hold out my hat. I've married a rich widow, with rubber plantations, out there. You can send in your bill for his keep. It can't be much for bread-and-gravy."

The mean speech, which flattened out two years of sacrifice into a thin spread of pap, was typical of his mentality, but Merle barely heard it. Her head was throbbing like a dynamo as she thought of Puck. He had to be tempted to eat, even in an English imitation heatwave, while he grew languid and limp as a wax candle.

It was torture to picture him—bewildered, unhappy, ill-torn from his devoted slaves and handed over to callous strangers. She knew he could never survive the change from his own little kingdom to a damp tropical exile.

"You can't do it," she cried with sudden fierceness, which was foreign to her nature. "I won't let you. It would be murder. Murder."

As her voice rose, the door slipped open a few inches, and the long horse-face of the housekeeper appeared in the aperture.

"Was any-one hollering 'murder'?" she asked.

Merle was too agitated to do more than shake her head, but her brother-in-law growled an order of dismissal.

"Clear out."

After another long suspicious gaze at the girl's quivering face, Mrs. Stock went away, banging the door to register protest.

As though the noise caused her jammed brain to vibrate, a wild plan suddenly flashed through Merle's head. When her brother-in-law dropped into the empty chair and spoke in the amicable tone that paved the way for a customary request, she agreed with him, in token of defeat.

"That's settled then," remarked Lewis.

"I'll collect him some time this evening."

"I'll have him ready," she told him.

"Well, then, what about a quick drink?"

"I'm sure the doctor would offer you one. I'll get it at once."

As she walked slowly toward the door her decision was made. She intended to take Puck away immediately and hide him in some quiet place until Lewis had gone abroad again.

Only, since every minute's start was of importance to her to get away, it was necessary first to take steps to prevent his father from coming to the bungalow that evening. Lewis must be doped, so that he would sleep for a few hours in the safe haven of the doctor's dining room. It was evident that no meal was going to be laid there that night, for the doctor would return too late for dinner.

Lewis' back was turned toward her as she crept to the sideboard and snatched up the whisky decanter, so he did not see her go into the dispensary.

Her heart bumped furiously when she crossed over to the slab where she had left the sedative which she had mixed for herself. The specks of light, which kept flashing across her eyes, blinded her vision but as the powder was already dissolved in the glass, she had only to fill it up with whisky.

"Lucky I had it all ready," she thought, as she carried it back to the dining room.

Her brother-in-law remained seated and appeared to be already at home, as though in anticipation of his enforced visit.

"It's neat," she told him tremulously.

"That's right." He nodded approvingly. "Never waste good water."

She gave him the tumbler, and she saw him drain it as she reached the door. He sank back and the chair hid him from view; but she heard a satisfied grunt and a creaking of springs, as though he were settling himself more comfortably.

"I must wait a few minutes, just to see if it is going to take effect," she told herself.

Her heart was hammering with impatience, for she was in a fever to get back to Puck. In spite of recurrent fits of giddiness she paced the room, unable to keep still. As she paused by the dispensing-slab, she took up the bottle she had left standing there.

Suddenly her vision cleared, so that she read the label clearly. Unable to credit what she saw, she stood, staring at it in frozen horror.

Instead of a sedative, she had just given her brother-in-law a fatal dose of virulent poison.

She clutched her throat to strangle her screams, as she realised her position. She felt sure she would be under suspicion of committing a crime, since the principal factors—motive and opportunity—could be proved. Everyone knew about her devotion to her small nephew and also her hatred of his father.

Further, there would be the evidence of the housekeeper, who disliked her intensely, and who had overheard a dispute, which included the incriminating word "Murder." Who would believe her story that she had killed him with poison which she had mixed, in error, for herself?

"I must do something," she thought desperately.

Then she shook her head hopelessly. Calling for help would be useless. The doctor was away, and the hostile housekeeper would only complicate her trouble. Besides, she knew that it was too late to attempt to administer antidotes.

Her brother-in-law must have died almost immediately—and in agony. As she remembered the creaking springs of the chair, which heralded the first spasm she crashed completely and dropped down into darkness. . .

It seemed to her that she had been falling for years, yet still she went on sinking. Deeper and deeper, while the blackness thickened around her. . . All at once, she became conscious of faint sounds in the void, which reminded her of homely things—the cooing of pigeons and the ticking of a clock. She smelt a familiar odour compounded of jessamine and drugs, as she opened her eyes.

She was sitting in the same chair in the dispensary, as when she had felt herself growing drowsy. Her hat and bag lay beside her, just where she had thrown them after she had first entered. In front of her was a calendar, which displayed the date.

It was Midsummer's Eve. And she had been asleep.

The compensation of an evil dream is the relief of waking up. Although she was still feeling the effects of her crash, Merle laughed joyously.

"Lewis went to Australia," she said. "And he couldn't fascinate anyone—let alone rich widows . . . Except my poor Mavis, and she was spellbound. But I know where the Borneo part came from, I was staring at that."

A journal, dealing with tropical disease lay open on the table, displaying the word "BORNEO," in heavy type above an article.

In spite of her happiness, some of the horror of her dream remained. She felt apprehensive and feverishly anxious to see Puck and know that all was well with him. Ramming on her hat, she hurried from the dispensary. She ran most of the way home, so that when she reached the bungalow, she was in a state of utter exhaustion.

Mrs. Megan Thomas broke off her song—for like most Welsh people, she was a tireless vocalist—when she opened the door.

"Oh, my Heavenly Father," she gasped. "What's happened to you?"

"I was knocked down by a car," gasped Merle. "How's Puck?"

"Lively as a flea."

"Thank heaven. . . Anyone called about him?"

"Of course not. . . Now you drink this, and off to bed with you, my lady."

As she was unaccustomed to sedatives, Merle was practically drunk when Mrs. Thomas undressed her, and tucked her up. She lay through the night in a heavy dreamless sleep, and awoke carefree and refreshed.

As she lay and listened to the cheerful sounds of an awakening world, she watched the curtains blowing into her room, and the green flicker of a beech tree shaking against a windy blue sky. It was a day when it was good to be alive. She heard the milk-cart on the road and the welcome rattle of china from the kitchen, while she waited for the reassurance of a child's voice, to tell her that the angels had not called for Puck during the night.

It came almost instantly—the protesting squeal of a young autocrat disturbed in mischief. The next minute, the door was burst open and Puck rushed into the room and hurled himself on her bed.

To an unenlightened eye, he might appear an ordinary small boy in a thin vest and under pants; but when he hooked his arms around her neck, Merle knew that she held the World's Wonder.

He was followed by Mrs. Thomas with the tea tray.

"What did you have for breakfast?" Merle asked him, knowing his passion for important words.

"Partridges," he replied promptly.

"Porridge," explained Mrs. Thomas. "You don't eat partridge in summer, Puck."

"But it's winter today," he assured them, glancing out of the corners of his almond-shaped blue eyes. "I made it 'fair and frosty.'"

"He's been playing with the barometer again," groaned Merle, feeling that she need not have worried about angel visitations. "Have you broken it again, Puck?"

"Not much," he replied virtuously. "Not nearly so much as I did last time."

Mrs. Thomas and Merle smiled at each other when their young lord and master had scampered from the room to find the puppy whom he really adored.

"Fancy sending him out to Borneo," said Merle. "I had a ghastly dream about his father yesterday."

Mrs. Thomas listened to Merle's dream with a creditable show of interest; but at its end, she sniffed with disgust.

"Pity you only dreamed. . . . Why, what's the matter now?"

To her consternation Merle had grown suddenly pale, while her eyes were dark with horror.

"Oh, Megan," she cried. "I've just thought of something terrible. Suppose it wasn't a dream? Suppose I really did poison him?"

"Oh, don't be daft," snapped Mrs. Thomas. "Did you give him rat poison?"

"Of course not."

"Then he's still crawling round in your dream. Only vermin killer would make his sort curl up properly."

But Merle refused to be comforted. Her hands shook so violently that Mrs. Thomas had to take her cup from her, as she went on speaking.

"You see, when I woke up in the dispensary, I was so confused that I took it for granted I'd been asleep, I never looked around . . . But I remember now, that I must have fainted when I found out what I'd done. Suppose I was just coming to after a faint, instead of waking up?"

Mrs. Thomas tried to scold or laugh her out of her morbid fancy, without success; in the end, she decided to humour her.

"If you bumped off Puck's pa," she reasoned, "you must have left the corpse lying about. We know that housekeeper is a slummock but even she wouldn't overlook a nasty trifle like that. . . I'm going to ring her up and ask her if she found anything out of its place."

Merle held her breath with suspense, while she listened to Mrs. Thomas's voice in the hall, where the telephone was installed. Her heart pounded when the woman returned to the bedroom.

"The housekeeper says you left your bag behind you."

"Oh, the blessed relief," cried Merle, laughing to keep back her tears. "What a fool I've been."

She left the bungalow in a gay mood that matched the sunshine. As she walked down the avenues, every garden was fragrant with roses. The river sparkled in the light as she leaned over the parapet of the old bridge and looked down at the slow current.She was swinging away with it, when a voice brought her back to earth.

"Morning. Merle. Day-dreaming?"

She looked up into the ruddy cheerful face of Captain Cliff. He was the club gossip, and, as usual, he had plenty of amusing tales for her entertainment. Presently, however, his expression grew graver and he lowered his voice.

"By the way," he said. "I heard that precious scoundrel—your brother-in-law, Gore—was back in town. I hope, for your sake, it's not true."

As Merle listened, she felt in the grip of a nightmare.

"No," she protested vehemently. "It's not true."

"Good. Some chap fancied he recognised him. I'm glad. It's no secret that you hate him like rat-poison, is it?"

The Captain strolled away, chuckling, while Merle gazed at his receding back, as though she beheld the Angel of Doom.

"It's no secret that you hate him." The words echoed in her brain as she began to run toward the doctor's house. It was like the Voice of the Town, condemning her with corroborative evidence, only—she had not murdered him. It was a dream, from which she was not yet fully awakened.

When she reached the familiar door, it took an effort to ring the bell. While she waited for the housekeeper to come, she reminded herself of the reassuring telephone call. All the same, she moistened her lips nervously when at last the door was opened.

No policeman stood in the entrance—only the slatternly figure of Mrs. Stock.

"The doctor's gone away for the morning," she said in a surly voice. "He says put off all appointments till the afternoon. And he wasn't back until nearly midnight. But I suppose he knows his business best."

"He certainly does, Mrs. Stock."

Merle's voice was firm, to hide the fact that she was vaguely worried by the unexpected absence. As she crossed the hall, instead of entering the dispensary, she nerved herself to open the door of the dining room.

Her first glance showed her that the big chair was empty. No huge distorted body lay stiffened there in its death agony. There was nothing worse than dead flowers in the vases and the usual signs of the housekeeper's neglect.

She started at the sound of Mrs. Stock's voice.

"Your bag's in the dispensary, if that's what you are looking for." Convicted of trespass, Merle returned to her own domain of the dispensary, where indignation drove out every other emotion. It was only too obvious that Mrs. Stock had taken advantage of the doctor's absence to slack shamefully.

"She's not so much as shown it a duster," thought Merle furiously. "Her number's up, as far as I'm concerned. And she knows it. That is why she looks so venomous."

Although a note in the doctor's handwriting was lying on a table, she did not open it at once. After telephoning the few patients who had appointments, she decided that she must restore some order before she could work. The waste-paper basket was stuffed to overflowing and had evidently been used as a communal dump for the rubbish from the living rooms.

As she picked it up, with the intention of carrying it out to the kitchen, she noticed some fragments of glass lying amid the dead flowers from the dining room.

Her heart dropped a beat, as she scooped them up to examine them. They were parts of a broken tumbler, to which a smear of sediment still adhered.

Her dream was true. She had given poison to her brother-in-law.

Feeling as though she had been sandbagged, she looked around her dully. By now, Lewis Gore's death was known, for someone had discovered the body and removed it. The most likely person was the doctor, who would do his utmost to protect her. It was even possible that his absence was connected with her interests.

The thought of his championship was her one ray of light. There was a wan smile on her lips as she opened his note, but it stiffened to a grimace of horror as she read it.

"I've just seen your brother-in-law. He spun me a lie about taking Puck out to Borneo, but I soon got wise to it. He wanted to be bought off again, and it was merely a threat to raise his price. . . . Now, you'll be furious with me, but I knew he would only go on bleeding you, so I wrote him a final check. (I'll tell you how you can repay me, when I come back). In return, I have his stamped agreement, appointing you Puck's guardian and renouncing all claim. I am taking it up to Somerset House to get it stamped."

The letter made the tragedy doubly grim, by reason of its irony. It was torment for Merle to reflect that Lewis had already signed away his claim to the boy when he called yesterday. He was telling lies to try and get something extra out of her.

For some time, she sat, stunned by the blow. The telephone bell rang but she did not stir from her chair. Presently she roused herself to speculate on her future.

She could not see any ray of hope for herself. Her fate would be hanging, or imprisonment for life. What jury would believe her story of a mistake, in view of the fact that the bottle was plainly labelled, and that she was accustomed to dispense drugs?

But her own fate was nothing compared with Puck's future. By the deed, now in process of being stamped at Somerset House, she was appointed his legal guardian. And she had failed him utterly. It appalled her to imagine what would become of him—penniless and left to strangers.

Even if the doctor took charge of him, for her sake—and she only assumed his affection for herself—it was natural that he would marry some other woman, later on.

In that dark hour Merle had to admit that she and Mrs. Thomas had spoiled Puck, even although, in their opinion, he redeemed their fondness by a hundred ways, just by being himself—the most adorable small boy in the universe.

But this practical hypothetical woman—the doctor's future wife—would probably resent him as a usurper and pack him off to boarding school. On the other hand, if no one accepted his responsibility he would be sent to some institution, which would be worse.

And she could do nothing to help him—for she was going to be hanged.

The idea was so fantastic and monstrous that her mind slipped away on another journey. Although her brain was too blurred for clear thought, it was apparent even to her, that, since the doctor knew nothing of the tragedy, there remained only Mrs. Stock who could have made the discovery. Remembering her dilatory habits, it was likely that she found the distorted body in the chair only a little time before Merle had appeared on the scene.

In her employer's absence she would notify the police, who has evidently removed the body to the mortuary. There could be no other explanation of the empty chair. Yet as Merle thought of the housekeeper's grim silence when she opened the door, and her denial of any unusual incident, over the telephone, she had the helpless feeling of being ambushed.

If she were already connected with the tragedy why had no official appeared to take her evidence? And why were the fragments of glass in the waste-paper basket? She always understood that—in a case of sudden death—nothing on the scene was allowed to be moved.

For a moment she wondered whether Mrs. Stock had smashed the tumbler herself, only to reject the idea immediately. Lewis must have swept it off the table in his death agony. But the mere fact that the pieces had been piled on top of the dispensary rubbish basket, where she could not fail to see them, seemed to indicate an attempt to trap her.

She knew that if she yielded to her impulse, she was bound to incriminate herself. For Puck's sake, she wanted desperately to hide the bits. . . Yes the first thing the police would look for would be the medium by which the poison was administered and they must have seen the broken glass already.

Perhaps they were in a conspiracy with Mrs. Stock to watch her own reaction. Although the dispensary was empty, she felt the unseen presence of a company of spies. Eyes were everywhere—looking at her through holes in the ceiling and chinks in the wall.

As time passed and nothing happened, she felt that she was being subjected deliberately to the torture of suspense—waiting for the inevitable knock on the door and the footstep in the hall. They wanted to break down her resistance, in advance. Yet she could do nothing else but wait. . . .

Wait. Listening to the ticking of the clock—to the buzz of a fly on the window-pane—to the throbbing of her own heart. . .

"It must be a dream," she told herself.

If she hung on to this certainty, she might wake up and find herself in the warm gloom of the twilit dispensary, where she dozed last night.

Only—this was reality. She was wide-awake and the sun was shining on the trees outside. This was today—and she was powerless to recall the past.

Suddenly, her heart gave a mighty leap. Her fingers gripped the arm of her chair, as she heard footsteps outside the room. The door was opened, but she did not turn round. She had reached the limit of sensation when nothing mattered any more.

"Merle."

It was the doctor's voice, tense with anxiety.

"Are you all right?" he asked. "Mrs. Thomas has just been telling me about your accident."

"Perfectly," she told him.

"Did you get my note?"

"Yes."

"Isn't it fine news about Puck? Aren't you thrilled?"

"Yes. It's marvellous."

The doctor was in a state of jubilant excitement and he accepted Merle's lack of enthusiasm as the result of her smash. He went on talking eagerly and rapidly, while she watched his face without grasping the meaning of his words.

Suddenly a chance sentence galvanized her to life.

"Lewis confessed he tried to touch you for money first. But he said you gave him a drink and then walked out on him. So then he came to me."

"When did you see him?" asked Merle.

"Oh, lateish. I had to get the lawyer to draw up the document, after hours. Oh, by the way, I ran Lewis up to London, with me, this morning, to clear him out of your way. I. . . What's the matter?"

In her relief, Merle broke down completely.

"Then he's alive. I didn't poison him," she cried.

As she sobbed out her story, the doctor's face, too, worked with emotion.

"You might have drunk that poison yourself. That's the part I can't get over," he said. "It was just touch-and-go that you are alive today."

"But he drank it—and he's alive, too," said Merle. "I can't understand it all. I always thought you told me that potassium cyanide is a deadly poison."

"So it is. For heaven's sake don't try to find out for yourself. . . . But the poisonous effect of the cyanide is due to a great extent to the fact that it reacts with the acid normally secreted in the process of digestion by the stomach to form a highly poisonous partial compound which is instantly absorbed. . . . Now your brother-in-law suffers from chronic alcoholic gastritis—a form of dyspepsia in which the stomach fails to secrete acid. So like Rasputin—whom they tried to kill, in vain, by the same poison—he was immune."

THE HOLIDAY

Nearly everyone in the small block of old-fashioned mansion flats seemed to be going on holiday, with the exception of Charles Bevan. For the past eight months, he had been lying in a background-floor flat, which looked out into the well of the courtyard. He disliked reading, so had nothing to do but listen to the rush of bathwater down the pipes, from six o'clock in the morning, and to watch the lights appear in the opposite building until the final eclipse.

The walls were so thick that he could not hear voices or footsteps of the other tenants. He had few visitors, and depended mainly on the society of the porter—Tory—and his wife, who looked after him. That was his life.

In the circumstances, it was hardly surprising that his energy had corroded to mental irritation, his ambition had turned to poison, and all hope had soured and died. On this particular hot August morning he had sunk to a stage when he doubted not only the doctor's assurance of his ultimate recovery—but his own power to endure. . . .

At the top of the building, Janet Lewis—the girl in the fifth floor flat—was going on holiday. She didn't want to go, but as there was a lull in her typing commissions, it seemed prudent to take advantage of the chance, for reasons of health.

Her suitcase was packed and lay on the floor; inside the tradesman's lift was placed a note to Mrs. Tory, who shopped for her, asking her to send up no more provisions until further notice. Before she left, she was finishing an article intended for a woman's journal, which contained hints on holiday preparations.

As she typed it she checked its points for her own benefit.

"Turn off the gas, water, and electricity at the mains." She would do this just before she left.

"Make provisions for pets." She had none, for lack of room.

"Dispose of all perishable food." While she thought of it, she would crumble up the remains of the loaf for the birds.

Plate in hand, she unlocked her front door and ran up the last flight of stairs to the roof. It was hot weather and she gazed down at the forest of chimneys pricking through the smoky haze, she suddenly realised that she was stale and overworked.

In spite of her youth, she had known the horrors of poverty, as a result of which she had begun a Twenty Years' Plan. This involved continuous work to secure an annuity at the age of forty, when she would live in a cottage in the country and grow her own spinach.

Although she was sacrificing everything to her purpose—leisure, exercise, and amusement—she remained surprisingly healthy and attractive, with fresh colouring that complemented the dash of red in her brown hair. She was too busy to worry or question, while her flat, which consisted of two rooms—a living room and a kitchen, with a hall which held the usual offices—seemed a luxury apartment to her.

But as she looked down at the city for the first time, she welcomed the prospect of a holiday, when she would be free to wander, according to her whim and without a single plan.

Next door to the mansion flats, the cashier of a small branch bank was thinking also of his holiday. He had booked rooms at Eastbourne and was due to meet his wife and young family at Victoria station in half an hour. Anticipating his emancipation, he was wearing grey flannel bags and he sported in his button hole an orange carnation from his garden.

There remained only two minutes to closing time, so he looked up with a slight frown, at the entrance of a late comer.

The man walked up to the counter, but instead of a check, he presented a revolver.

Even as he realised he was being held up, the cashier rushed at the bandit. The next second, he lay crumpled up on the floor with a bullet in his brain.

The bandit worked swiftly, but even as he packed his bag, the alarm was raised. He reached the door just in time to see his partner scorch away in the car, either to save his own skin or to draw the pursuit. Panic-stricken, he darted into the entrance hall of the mansion flats and tore up flight after flight of stairs, until he reached the haven of an open door.

A minute later, Janet ran down from the roof and entered her flat. The first thing she saw was a leather bag on the floor of the hall. She was wondering where it came from, when someone behind her sprang on her and gripped her throat.

"One squeal, and you're dead," he whispered. "I've just killed a man."

Too stunned with shock to feel fear, she realised the strength of his position. He could shoot her and be invulnerable to reprisal, since the law could not hang him twice.

She was beginning to choke, when she heard the sound of heavy footsteps ringing out on the stone stairs.

They stopped on the fifth floor landing and then someone hammered on her door.

"Open the door," the killer whispered fiercely.

As he spoke, she felt a ring of metal against her back. Flinching from the contact, she drew back the catch of the lock with trembling fingers.

The porter and a policeman stood outside; both were out of breath and appeared hot. She looked at Tory with beseeching eyes as he mopped his face. Although she could touch him, she was divided from him by a gulf she could not bridge.

"Did you hear anyone pass this way?" asked the policeman.

Her unwelcome guest stood behind her where he was screened from view, but she felt the increased pressure of the metallic ring. It was a hint whose nature she could neither mistake nor ignore.

"No," she replied quickly.

"Has your door been open?"

"No."

As she spoke, a hope flared up that they would insist on searching her flat, but Tory crushed it immediately by a suggestion.

"We'd better try the roof, to satisfy you."

Once again Janet was left alone with the man. He took no notice of her, but looked around him with intent eyes which missed no detail.

"Yours?" he asked, kicking the suitcase aside. "Are you going away?"

"Yes," she replied.

"How long?"

"A fortnight."

"Do your friends know?"

"Yes."

She answered mechanically, for she was listening for the sound of footsteps coming down from the roof. It was a cheering reflection that the man was only waiting for the chance of a safe getaway. She was wondering how long he would linger in the building and whether he would force her to act as his scout, when he snatched her note to Mrs. Tory off the lift.

She swallowed her indignation as he tore it open and read it.

"Does the woman send up all your food?" he asked.

"Yes," she replied.

"Don't you ever go out?"

"Yes, sometimes, when—"

"Shut up."

The threat of his revolver made her realised that Tory and the policeman were returning from the roof. They tramped across her landing, passed her door, and went down the stairs.

When they reached the hall, Tory had the satisfaction of reminding the policeman that he was right.

"I told you he couldn't be here. All the flats are kept locked and there's nowhere he could hide."

He was still very pleased with himself when he entered the ground-floor back flat, to give his gentleman a second-hand thrill. His idea was to cheer up the invalid, so he was taken aback by the glum misery of Bevan's face, as he interrupted the tale.

"He came in all right. I heard him on the stairs, but I didn't give it a thought. Even if I had. . . . Amusing, isn't it? On the spot and able to do nothing, while some decent chap is sent West, and his murderer gets away with it. I'm a valuable member of society."

"Now, sir," protested Tory. "You'll soon be all right again. The doctor says—"

"Don't quote the comedian. It's his daily joke. . . Of course, it's obvious what happened. The man went up to the roof and came down by the fire escape to the back entrance, while you were on the tiles. He's well away by now. . . . Will you tell Mrs. Tory not to trouble to send me in lunch. Thank her very much."

When Tory repeated the message to his wife, her jolly face grew grave.

"I don't like it," she objected. "He's too polite. If only he'd buck up and swear."

The bandit experienced the terror of a cornered rat. Since he had been followed to the flat, he felt sure that the building would be kept under observation.

He reasoned that the police would count on his being starved into submission in the event of his having found some hiding place on the premises. Therefore, if he remained in this girl's room for a definite period, their suspicions would be destroyed and they would call off any guard.

The girl would not be missed at her place of business for the duration of her holiday, while supplies of food would arrive daily. The fact that she did not go out would not be noticed unless a deliberate watch was set upon her movements. In this case, there would be nothing to attract attention, since apparently she would be carrying on her usual routine.

The flaw seemed to lie in her holiday arrangements. He knew it was useless to question her about these, since she would lie, but he counted on the fact that anyone who was puzzled at her non-arrival, would ring up the flat when he could impel her to reassure them.

Fortunately for his conspiracy, the telephone, speaking tube, and tradesman's lift were all in the kitchen where he could control them. Success depended on whether he had the nerve to lie low and sit tight. Spinning a coin for luck, he tore up Janet's note to Mrs. Tory, countermanding supplies.

"Listen, you," he said. "You're not going away. I'm staying here —and you've got to stay, too. You've only one chance. Keep quiet."

Too terrified to protest, Janet stared at him with dull wonder that he should look so average and normal. He did not resemble the gangsters of the screen, neither did he use their slang. Hard-eyed and tight lipped, with smooth hair, there was nothing to distinguish him from any keen young businessman.

Yet, in spite of her fear, she found it impossible to believe in such an amazing situation.

"It can't last," she told herself. "Someone is bound to come to the flat—Tory or the postman. I must make them suspect something is wrong."

Her hope rising at a sudden inspiration, she ventured to speak to the bandit.

"I think I had better send a message for extra supplies. I don't eat much and you won't like my food. I don't have meat."

His sneer at her flimsy ruse shrivelled any expectation of success. He did not even trouble to reply, but asked a sudden question.

"Has the porter a master key of the flats?"

"Yes, in case of fire," she told him.

"Well, if he uses it, for any reason, he's a dead man. That goes for anyone who tries to come in. And the next bullet will be yours."

He went to the door, locked it, and put the key in his pocket, thus formally making her his prisoner.

She was too stunned to protest. His last speech had reminded her of the hideous truth that he had just killed a harmless citizen in cold blood and that any unsuspecting person who entered her flat would meet with the same fate.

It would be an invitation to be murdered, if she incited Tory to come to her rescue, unless she could smuggle through a note to him, telling him the facts. If he communicated with the police, she knew that they would devise a means to draw the man's fire and take him by surprise.

But, pending such information, she must do her utmost to keep the porter—or anyone else—away.

"Directly I've a chance, I'll write to Tory," she decided. "I don't suppose he'll let me get near the lift—but I can throw it out of my window."

As though he were playing into her hands, the man went into the living room and wheeled out the divan, which served as her bed, by night, and a couch, by day.

"I'm sleeping in the kitchen," he told her. "There'll be no monkey business with the lift. You stay in the other room."

Even as her heart lightened at the prospect of privacy, he went into the living room and jerked the pictures from the walls. Wrenching out the long nails, he drove them through the frame of the window, so that it was impossible to open it. Then he came close to her and stared into her eyes.

"It's a noisy business to try and break glass," he said. "I don't advise you to try. I shall hear you . . . And now, listen I don't like you. I don't want you, here. Keep out of my sight. Don't speak to me. If you call out or try to attract attention, I'll shoot you like a rabbit . . . And this is to show you I mean it."

His fist shot out and she fell to the floor.

Her holiday had begun.

When the man had gone back to the kitchen, Janet sat in the living room and tried to think. Although she felt mentally bruised, and her cheek was beginning to swell, in one way, she was vaguely relieved by the man's attack. It expunged the human element from the situation and made him seem almost disembodied, like a destructive force of indiscriminate and universal hatred.

As she lit a cigarette to soothe her nerves, he reappeared at the door.

"So you smoke," he muttered. "Fags, too."

He snatched up the packet of cigarettes as he nodded at the typewriter.

"Carry on as usual with that," he commanded.

The incident made her realise the cunning of his imagination, which foresaw every possible pitfall. In the determination to avoid any discrepancy, he had refrained from smoking until he had learned her own habits.

He meant to shield himself with her identity. It was fortunate for her sanity that she was allowed occupation. In accordance with her principle of never refusing work, she had accepted some heavy monotonous matter, which was poorly paid, but which she was privileged to deliver in instalments.

She now set herself to the task of clearing it off in bulk. As she tapped away, her thoughts circled around her imprisonment. She could see no shred of hope anywhere. The other tenants of the fifth floor were away on holiday, and no one could possibly miss her, or know of her predicament.

When she set out to complete her Twenty Years' Plan, she had isolated herself rather too well. All wires were cut, while signals were worse than useless.

"I could keep flashing the light, when it is dark," she told herself. "But whoever noticed it would only tell Tory and send him up. Sherlock Holmes is the only person who could help me now."

Presently, when Tory whistled up the tube—as a preliminary to winding up the lift with her supplies—the bandit ordered her into the kitchen.

"Thank you, Tory," she said faintly.

"Have you got a cold, miss?" he called up. "Your voice sounds rather queer."

As the bandit flourished his revolver, she forced herself to speak brightly.

"No, thanks, Tory. I feel splendid."

Then the lift was wound down, empty, and her brief interlude of intercourse with the world was ended.

"Is this all?" snarled the man, as he looked at the small supply of wholemeal bread, butter, and egg and salad.

"I warned you," she told him.

"Then take this."

As he handed her the lettuce and fruit as her portion, she managed to pluck up her spirit.

"I'd better smash the window and let you shoot me," she told him. "It's quicker than starvation."

She could not know that the man's calculations were seriously upset by the food shortage. While her own rations were sparrow's food to him and he did not scruple about reducing her to a state of semi-starvation, he did not want to lose his official voice, whose function was to quell any outside suspicion. Therefore, he was relieved by her suggestion to order a tin of biscuits.

"I always have one in stock," she told him. "The last one is practically finished."

When he had tested the truth of her words by finding the empty container in the cupboard, he allowed her to whistle down the tube to Tory, who was not pleased with the request.

"Won't tomorrow do, miss?" he asked.

"No, today, please," she told him. "I'm terribly hungry."

"Very good, miss."

As he expected, his wife was annoyed at the prospect of having to go out again when she had finished her day's shopping.

"Give me a man to do for every time," she declared. "If she can't remember she shouldn't order in penny numbers. She can wait till tomorrow."

Tory, as usual, saved the situation with a suggestion.

"There's Mr. Bevan's new tin, not opened. He never eats now with his tea. You can get in another tin for him by the time he asks for them again—if he ever does."

In spite of the calendar, that day was the longest in the year to Janet, but at last it came to an end. As she dozed—fully dressed—in an armchair, she kept reminding herself of her identity, and also that there was a time limit to her ordeal.

"I'm Janet Lewis", she told herself. "Something has happened to me—but it will pass. In three weeks' time he'll be gone and I shall be here. I'll still be Janet Lewis."

During the hideous days that followed the fifth-floor flat was not a dwelling, but a temporary shelter where two alien personalities shared an intolerable situation. Except for unavoidable contacts, they kept apart. Sometimes the man gave her an order in a penetrating whisper, but otherwise they remained silent.

Janet grew pale and thin from semi-starvation, but she suffered most from the enclosed atmosphere. In spite of the relief of an almost continuous wind which whistled down her chimney, the air grew daily thicker and fouler, so that she had to deny herself the consolation of smoking. She made cups of tea over the gas ring in her room, when she forced herself to nibble biscuits, but all appetite for food had deserted her.

As she tapped away at her machine, she lost all sense of place and felt suspended in a curious dimension outside space, even while she was enclosed within the walls of her flat. She could hear people pass by her door and see them cross the courtyard, yet she was cut off from all intercourse with humanity.

Sometimes she wondered whether Tory would remark about her closed window, but he never appeared to look up. In any case, it was almost screened from observation by the high coping of the small balcony in front.

Besides—she did not want him to notice any unusual feature— lest it should prove his death warrant.

Although she welcomed the end of every day, as one stage nearer release, the nights were even worse, when she sat, in her clothes and dozed, starting awake at every creak in the divan in the kitchen. The man too scarcely slept, for he was strung up to a state of nervous expectancy which exceeded her own, and which kept him continually on guard.

Through the day he lay on the divan, smoking and counting his piles of new notes; but while he was obsessed by his fortune, his main object was to get away in safety. He always turned on the wireless to get the news, in case of a police S.O.S.; and he strained his ears for the movements of the porter and other tenants, in order to get a clue to their time-table.

Although he ate Janet's daily rations, after his first outburst, he seemed indifferent to food. At night, he removed only his boots and slept with one eye open—his revolver beside him, ready for instant flight.

Being shut up with him was about as safe as sharing a confined space with an infernal machine, but Janet endured because of her confidence of the end.

One hot, muggy night, however, when she was panting for fresh air, this certainty of release was replaced by a new and ghastly dread. Suddenly she remembered a picture she had seen at a cinema, when a gangster shot the doctor and nurse who had rendered him a service, in order to secure their silence.

For the first time she asked herself the question: "What will my own fate be?"

Meanwhile, the occupants of the fifth floor flat were not the only sufferers. Bevan, too, was feeling the heat acutely and was more than usually depressed. In his morbid position he seemed to assume responsibility for the fact that the criminal who had shot the bank cashier was still at liberty. He feverishly searched numerous papers for news of his capture and practically ceased to eat.

One afternoon, however, he staggered Tory by a request for biscuits with his tea.

"I'm afraid you've finished your tin," he said. "The missus will slip out and get you some in two minutes."

"It doesn't matter, thanks," Bevan's voice was listless. "It's very quiet," he added. "I suppose everyone on this side of the building is away?"

"All but the young lady up there."

Glad to change the subject, Tory pointed to a window set high in the side of the wall.

"She sits typing all day," he told Bevan. "She's so set in her ways, you could put a clock by her, for all she's young and pretty. My missus shops for her, too, as she doesn't get out much."

"Sounds unhealthy," yawned Bevan, who had lost all interest in young and pretty girls.

Life went on somehow in the fifth-floor flat. Every morning, Janet told herself: "This can't last another day," but the hours crawled on until she was forced with the torment of another night, with its question of haunting suspense.

"What will my fate be?"

A week passed, every day of which left its mark upon her. She lost all personal pride and stopped looking in the mirror. Because of her shrinking dread of passing through the kitchen in order to reach the hall, she did the minimum of washing.

Whenever she typed, her thoughts winged on strange journeys. Gradually she became a kind of split personality, when she carried on conversation with herself, semi-delirious from strain and hunger, she listened to a girl of twenty—her own age—who reproached a woman of forty.

"You're a selfish introvert, you've never considered me. I've never been to dances. I've had no time to make friends. I've had to slave for you. . . Why couldn't you wait till you were fifty-five to get your cottage in the country?"

The voice droned on in unison with an imprisoned fly which buzzed maddeningly over the window pane. But in the lucid interlude which followed Janet admitted the truth of her ravings. She had wasted her youth and was losing the present for the future.

In this connection, she remembered with a pang that Tory had told her of a bed-ridden young man on the ground floor, to whom she could have lent books, in token of sympathy. Now, as though in punishment, it was her turn to feel completely cut off from the world.

On the eighth morning the bandit returned from the hall, completely altered in appearance. He was cleanly shaved, his hair shone, and his coat was well brushed. He looked like a smart young business man, except for the revolver with which he drove her into the kitchen.

"Whistle down to the porter," he commanded. "Tell him to stop sending food, as you are going away on your holiday."

Too excited to think clearly, Janet rushed to the tube and delivered the message to Tory.

"Will you want a taxi?" he called up.

"No, thank you," she replied, obedient to the shake of the bandit's head.

"Then, a pleasant time, miss," said Tory. "If you should want me for anything, I'll be over in the back block, after eleven, as I'm showing some people a flat."

Janet noticed the sudden glint of the bandit's eye and realised that, unconsciously, Tory had revealed the exact time when the entrance hall would be unwatched.

The next half hour was an agony of suspense, when hope struggled with fear of her fate. Suddenly the man glanced at his watch, and —laying his revolver on the table—came towards her.

"If this was a picture, I should seize it and hold him up," she thought wildly.

Even while she was trying to nerve herself for the attempt, the man threw a double coil of laundry cord around her and the back of the chair on which she was sitting, pinioning her to her seat. Too terrified to cry out, she struggled silently and vainly, while he bound her wrists together and fastened her legs to the rungs.

She told herself that if he meant to leave her gagged and bound in a locked flat, her end would be so terrible that she had better scream, and so ensure the swift mercy of a bullet. But, on the other hand, there was a glimmer of hope that he might send information to the porter which would lead to her release once he was safely away

It was taking a desperate chance, for she had noticed no scruple or sign of ordinary humanity in the bandit; yet the passion for life was so overpowering that she resolved to remain silent.

As the man folded a strip of linen into a pad, there was an unexpected interruption. A loud scrape and rattle against the outside wall of the building was followed by the appearance of the top of a ladder against the kitchen window.

"The cleaner," gasped Janet.

With an oath the man pushed her towards the window.

"Tell him to go away," he ordered.

His back was turned to the door, so that he was unable to gauge the significance of the psychological moment of distraction. But even as Janet remembered that the window cleaner was not yet due, she realised that the noise of the ladder had covered the silent entrance of Tory with two policemen.

With the fury of a tidal bore, they rushed at the bandit. Unarmed and taken completely by surprise, he fought like a maniac but, after a period of noise and confusion, he was overcome and handcuffed.

After the police had tramped away in triumph with their prisoner, Tory stayed behind to release Janet. Now that her ordeal was ended she had become hysterical and she overwhelmed him with blessings and thanks.

"How did you know about me?" she asked, when she had grown calmer.

"I didn't," he told her. "It was Mr. Bevan, the gentleman in the ground-floor flat. He fixed everything up. . . . If you are all right now, I must go down and tell him everything went off according to plan."

"I'm coming, too," said Janet. "I must thank him."

She drew out her pocket mirror and then gave a scream.

"Is this me?" she gasped. "You'd better go down without me. I won't be long."

When Tory opened the door of the ground-floor flat to her, ten minutes later, it was evident that Bevan also had prepared for a reception. He looked gorgeous as a sultan in a new dark purple dressing gown, while his thin face wore an unaccustomed grin.

"Don't tell me who you are," he called out, before Janet could speak. "You're the Six O'Clock Bath. I've known you for eight months. You're punctual to the dot. And you're cold."

"How could you tell that?" gasped Janet.

"Because no steam ever issued from the overflow. I knew the exact point in this antiquated plumbing where to expect to see you. And since a cold morning bath is a Spartan habit which, once acquired, is not lightly or wantonly abandoned. I noticed the fact when your water stopped running down the pipe."

"I had to give it up," explained Janet. "You see, the bath is in—"

"In the kitchen," finished Bevan. "I knew that, from the arrangement of my own flat. At first, of course, I paid no attention to your lapse, as it was obvious that you were either ill or away. But when Tory told me that you were still in residence, I grew reflective."

Suddenly Janet began to feel hungry.

"He ate all my food," she said piteously.

"That's why you are going to have lunch with me at once. Mrs Tory has kindly promised to arrange it."

Tory caught his wink and beamed at the new development. While he hurried away to tell his wife, Bevan went on with his explanation.

"As, providentially, I had nothing to do but lie still and puzzle it out. I came to the conclusion that you might be entertaining an uninvited visitor in your kitchen. I remembered the scare over the bank bandit, and as he was still at large, I thought I might connect the two. After that the significant silence pointed to the threat of a bullet."

Janet forgot to shudder as she gazed at Bevan with shining eyes.

"I can never thank you," she told him. "It was marvellous of you."

"Oh, that part of it was elementary," he told her lightly. "The difficult bits were, first, to prevent the gallant Tory from using his master key on his lonesome, and then to sell the idea of a surprise visit to the police. . . . By the way, you appear to have the remains of an old-fashioned black eye."

"Yes. He knocked me down."

"Good luck for you. He might have been amorous. . . . When I'm up again—and that will be very soon—we must go to the pictures together and see a gangster film, to criticise its technique."

"No," shuddered Janet. "It will bring it all back."

"Now, don't be sorry for yourself. I know it's Satan rebuking sin, but we're both alive—and that should be enough for us. You've been jolted out of your rut, and I—"

He lowered his voice as he added: "You'll never know what this has meant to me. I had lost my faith. Everything seemed a futile mess and waste . . . But now I know why I had to lie like a log for eight months, and listen to water rushing down the pipes. It was because I had to miss the Six O'Clock Bath . . . You."

LIGHTNING STRIKES TWICE

The temperature was so high in the city that someone tried to fry an egg on the pavement.

The baked air was stagnant and reeked of petrol. The traffic shrieked in competition with the din of a pneumatic road-drill. Yet Hermione Heath, the young film actress, drew a breath of rapture as she gazed at the squalid street.

She had just left the Old Bailey where she had been on trial for murder.

"No," she protested, as her agent beckoned to a waiting taxi. "I want to walk. I want to feel free."

"And you want to escape the cameras, don't you?" he asked. "Directly the press men find out we've fooled them, they'll be swarming back through this alley."

Hermione—it was not her real name, but she had grown used to being called by it—leaped instantly into the cab.

"This seems all queer and wrong somehow," she said in a troubled voice, as her agent drew down the blinds. "You've always tried to get me publicity."

"Not this kind of publicity, my dear."

"You mean—."

As he did not reply, she nerved herself to ask another question.

"Will this affect my career?"

"I'll tell you that later," he replied. "There's a clause in your contract which covers this—kind of thing. That will let them out, if they want to get rid of you."

"Why should they? I've been proved innocent."

"Yes, you've been very lucky."

"Lucky?" Her voice broke. "I wouldn't wish my worst enemy my luck. But I mustn't talk about it. I must forget."

In spite of her determination, as she sat back in her corner, with closed eyes, her mind was flooded by unhappy memories. She had been a victim of the most damning circumstantial evidence that fate could contrive against an innocent person. Thoughtless words and unfortunate incidents had dovetailed together to lend ominous significance to her discovery of the body of the murdered financier.

She had gone gaily to his West End flat, expecting to lend a cocktail party. Instead, she found her host lying on the floor, shot through the heart.

The shock was so severe that she was instantly panic-stricken, when she incriminated herself with every possible indiscretion. After she had left her blood-stained finger prints to testify against her and further advertised her identity by dropping some personal property, she ran away. Later, she was numbed to a state of mental collapse when her memory could not function properly . . . She had endured weeks of torturous suspense. She had lost all hope. She had gone through hell.

Today, she was free. And now — in the first flush of liberty — she faced a new threat, the ruin of her career.

Although she was only a starlet, she was rising steadily in her profession. It absorbed her to the exclusion of other interests, so that she could not contemplate life apart from the studio.

"If I'm going to be thrown out," she said, "they might as well hang me and call it a day."

"Keep your chin up," advised her agent.

Luckily, there was no further call on her fortitude. When they reached the offices of the film company, the personage who controlled Hermione's destiny received her with a smile and extended hands.

"This is splendid to see you again," he said. "Now don't begin to cry. I want to discuss your new picture."

After this promising beginning, he broke the news that, although she could not play lead, he might use her in a minor part, but her chance would come later, if she justified his confidence.

"Best to let some of the mud settle," he said. "We must consider the susceptibilities of the public. That chap was such a stinking character."

Although the counsel for the defence had demonstrated the slight nature of Hermione's acquaintance with the murdered financier, she knew that it was impolitic to protest. She was forced to "eat crow", while the chief laid down the law.

"In future, no wild parties, no car offences, no more shady friends. We may have to sell you again to the public. Remember, even the smell of a second scandal would finish you. And now what about taking a real holiday out of the public gaze?"

"Switzerland is quiet in the summer," suggested the agent.

"Fix it . . . Good-bye, my dear."

Although she was dismissed, Hermione lingered to ask a question.

"You do believe I'm innocent?"

"Of course . . . only don't do it again."

His words rang in her ears, making her unduly sensitive to the congratulations of her friends.

The next afternoon, when she boarded the Continental express at Victoria, she felt acutely self-conscious because her departure was so purposely inconspicuous.

The first week slipped quickly and happily away. After her long ordeal, she was grateful merely to be alive amid such beauty and peace. No one recognised her or asked for her autograph. Most of the guests at her hotel were drifters—stopping for only a night or a two.

Wearing shorts and dark sunglasses, she spent her time alone— either climbing steep wooded heights to reach an "aussicht," or a river. Presently, the solitude which had been so healing to her shattered nerves, began to lose its benefit. With restored bodily health, her mind began to work again.

"Don't do it again."

The sentence rang in her ears as she went over and over the wretched business of her trial, until the injustice of her position, scared her sense of rectitude. It seemed to her that, even on this holiday with her enforced anonymity, she was still being penalized for a crime she had not committed.

It was as though she had been struck by lightning—unexpected, unmerited, unexplained.

"Why should it have happened to me?" she asked herself. "I've done nothing to deserve this."

She had grown so used to regarding herself as invisible, that it came as a surprise when she realised that one person had guessed her identity. Their first meeting took place on a mountain-railway. At first, she barely noticed the red-haired young man, with bare knobby Scotch knees, who sat on the opposite seat of her carriage.

She was gazing at the range of great snowy mountains glittering against a deep blue sky, when the young man spoke to her.

"Aren't   you   Hermione   Heath?" She hesitated, as she did not wish to be pestered by a fan, but before she could reply, the young man went on.

"I was furious with you over your trial. You mucked up every-thing as though you were working in with the cops to give them a case in the bag. Surely you know the elementary rules on finding a corpse?"

"No," gasped Hermione. "W-what are they?"

"First touch nothing. Second, ring the police. Haven't you read any detective thrillers?"

"No."

"Then my Heaven have mercy on your soul. You almost deserve all you got. I write them. And what's the good of me trying to educate the public when you deliberately work for a conviction?"

His abuse was incense to Hermione and exhilarated her more than the challenge of the snowy mountains. Here, at least, was someone who recognised her for what she really was, a blundering fool but innocent.

Hermione answered his questions with real relief. In spite of his blunt words, his hazel eyes held sympathy and understanding.

"What's your real name?"

"Amy Barker."

"Hermione wins with me. My name is Andrew Mackintosh. It ought to register—but it won't. I'm staying at your hotel, although you've not noticed me."

"I've noticed no one. I've kept thinking of—"

"I knew. You kept thinking of poor little Hermione Heath. You've got to forget the little fool. . . . Don't you hate your face?"

"Should I?" Her voice was startled. "What's wrong with it?"

"Definitely nothing. But I know I should get dead sick of mine splashed all over the screen."

"I don't. I'm clear on that point anyway. Film acting is under my skin and it's also my big gamble. I spent my last shilling in dramatic training. It's mighty important for me to cash in on it."

"I understand. In fact, this holiday must put you together again. But it won't, unless you forget everything. . . . Suppose we stick around together?"

During a week of perfect weather which followed their first meeting, they spent most of their time in the open air. With the object of giving her no time to think, Andrew ruthlessly took the pampered starlet for stiff mountain scrambles. He made her eat plain picnic lunches, perched on a boulder beside some roiling glacier-fed river.

"You get to know a person better in one day spent in the country than if you met her in drawing rooms for a year," he explained.

His exact word was "matey"—but he looked at her with the eyes of a lover.

He did not let her relax until his last afternoon, when they made a tour of the lake in the little steamer.

Hermione watched the shores with the sensation of being in a happy dream. There were fantastic houses and gardens where late crimson roses shed their petals and strangely remote people drank tea in the dense shade of chestnuts.

Chateaux with pointed towers and flights of stone steps leading down to deep peacock-blue water; cream-and-coal villas, spun about with delicately wrought-iron verandas and flights of filigree stairs which spiralled from balcony to balcony.

Presently the residences were spaced at longer distances as they reached a desolate area of reeds and bushes, where the river flowed swiftly into the lake. Near its outlet stood a small, white-shuttered villa, apparently encircled by a thick girdle of closely clipped shrubs, which overhung the water.

"It's like a house built of toy bricks," exclaimed Hermione. "And the green stuff is like artificial moss. It fascinates me, I can't imagine anyone living there."

"I expect it's a week-end residence," exclaimed Andrew. "Most of these places are shut."

On the second-class deck two women were also talking of the villa.

"That belongs to a rich businessman," one informed her companion in rapid French. "He manufactures chocolate. Or it might be watches. That's his '*nid d'amour.*' Always a lady. He is very attentive, you understand."

Although she could not hear, at that moment Hermione suddenly shivered, as though a brain-wave had touched her dormant memory of the murdered London financier.

"Don't look like that," said Andrew sharply.

"I can't help it," she confessed. "I'm afraid of the past. But I am more afraid of the future. That terrible thing happened to me in one second—just by opening a door. It can happen again."

"It can't. By the law of averages, it is impossible. Lightning never strikes the same place twice."

"That's not true. I remember reading about a woman who had just won a prize in a sweep and the account said that she had also held a winning ticket in the previous draw. When you consider the millions of tickets that seems impossible. But it happened. . . Andrew, why did this happen to me?"

"Perhaps to test you," he replied. "If we had only soft, pleasant experiences, we should degenerate to spiritual slugs. These tough breaks develop initiative, resource, courage."

"But all I did was to crash. I'm ashamed. I'm so used to being directed—told to do this or that. . . . Oh. Andrew, I'm going to miss you."

That evening, she went with him to the station. While they waited for the train, she looked so unhappy that he tried to cheer her.

"I shall be at Victoria to meet you soon. We're not going to let this drop, are we?"

"I shall count the days."

"Good." His face grew suddenly grave. "Hermione, I've been thinking about what you said this afternoon. I want you to promise me that if you are ever in a fix, like the last, you will fade away at once. Scram—disappear into the blue and leave no traces behind."

"I promise. But of course, it won't happen again."

"No. You got me rattled by suggesting it. You see, you couldn't risk a second show-up."

"No, I should be finished in films."

"Much worse than that. A repetition of the first affair might be regarded as proof of homicidal mania. I'm frightening you, but you frightened me first. So remember this. You've brains inside your head, not pulp. Use them—and don't crash again."

She missed him even more than she feared. It was difficult to force enthusiasm for the beauty which surrounded her now that the human element was lacking. The mountains were beginning to assume the aspect of prison walls, when her holiday came to a premature end.

The circumstances were exhilarating, for London came on the hotel telephone just as she was finishing her coffee on the veranda. "London" proved to be her agent, who told her that production was to begin immediately on the picture which had been shelved owing to her trial. The choice of lead lay between another promising young actress and herself.

"I must be frank," he warned her. "Clara's their best bet. No scandal about her. But give them all you've got and they're bound to admit it's your part. Come by tonight's express as you won't have to change. I'll meet you at Victoria and take you out to the studio for the test. Don't let me down, or it will be a walkover for Clara."

When he rang off, Hermione felt dizzy with excitement. She rushed about, making arrangements for her departure, but there was little to do. After every detail had been discussed, there stretched before her most of the morning and all the afternoon.

"I've got to walk, or I shall blow up," she thought.

She decided to take the steamer to the town at the end of the lake and then walk on to the first village, where she would await its arrival on its homeward trip.

When she reached the little medieval town, she loitered over her lunch, but, in her impatience, the hands of her watch seemed to crawl. It was a relief to set off along the lake promenade, lined with small chestnut trees beginning to brown. She walked quickly and got to the village, to find the quay deserted. The steamer was not due for some time, so she began to explore.

It interested her to see the backs of the houses, or rather, their entrances. Many were impressive, with glass corridors or covered courtyards leading to the front doors. Their gardens, too, were beautiful, with vivid emerald grass and brilliant flowers.

While she was admiring a border of dahlias in the garden of a villa, named *"Mon Asile"* an Alsatian dog watched her through the green and gilt railings. Having decided that she had no design on the family security, he butted the gate open with his head and made it plain to her that she might take him for a walk.

"No, my lad," she told him, shaking her head. "You're pedigree, by the look of you. I'm taking no chances. Someone might think I was enticing you away."

As he continued to plead, she weakly compromised by throwing her stick for him to retrieve. Apparently he could not get too much of this game, which lasted for several hectic minutes, but he behaved like a gentleman when, at last, she took her property from him and ordered him not to follow.

Leaving him sitting obediently inside his own garden, she swung along the deserted shore road. On one side was a twelve-foot wall, topped with the trees of an estate—on the other, the sheet of sunlit water. Her objective was the river, which was boiling out in a greenish-white streak over the sapphire lake.

Presently she reached the unreal little villa, encircled with shrubs, which had impressed her with such a sense of artifice.

"It's either hollow inside and stuffed with shavings," she told herself, "or it's a block of solid plaster. No, I'm wrong. They've got a telephone there—and it's ringing like mad. Why doesn't someone answer it?"

The sound of the bell continued to whirr in her ears as she picked her way down a path between willows and rank undergrowth, in order to reach the river. Soon, however, the track came to an end amid a stretch of reedy swamp, with gaps of water, so that she was forced to turn back.

To her surprise, the telephone bell was still ringing when she came again to the white villa. It was obvious that no one was in the house and she marvelled at the patience, or laxity, of the exchange. She lingered to gaze at the shuttered windows, when, suddenly, she heard the piteous wail of an animal.

"Oh, dear," she cried in dismay. "They've left a cat locked in and it's only Monday today. It'll be there for days. . . . What on earth can I do? I can't break in. It's against the law."

Although the unanswered telephone stressed the fact that the villa was deserted, she rang the bell and knocked loudly upon the door. No one came, but she did not expect admission. Only the cat scented rescue, for its mewing sounded closer, while she could hear it scratching the panels.

It was against every humanitarian scruple to leave an animal to starve to death, yet the position seemed hopeless to Hermione. A glance at her watch told her that she had time, but little to spare.

At that moment, to add to her worry, a further complication ensured. She felt a tug at her stick and turned to see the Alsatian dog waiting expectantly in the road. He had trailed her from *"Mon Asile,"* and now—with insane optimism—had chosen this moment to ask her for another game.

"You keep out of this," she said, surrendering her stick to keep him quiet. "Oh, I wish I could get in."

In desperation and without the faintest hope of forcing an entry, she turned the handle of the door. To her intense surprise it was neither bolted nor locked. While she was pushing it open, a small grey-and-white cat shot through the aperture and dashed into the road, evidently bound for his home in the village.

Hermione remained on the step gazing before her. Instead of a darkened interior, she saw a gleaming black-and-white marble hall, with glossy buttercup walls and yellow rugs. The light streamed in through the door of the salon, which was just beyond. Only a section of it was visible, revealing the telephone on the floor.

She was compelled by strong curiosity to peep in at the salon. She reminded herself that not a soul was near. Closing the front door to keep out the dog she approached the salon.

It was full of sunshine, while the walls and ceiling were mottled with dancing water reflections from the lake. The unshuttered windows were hung with ice-blue satin curtains, patterned with white roses—the gilt Empire furniture was covered with royal blue-and-white striped brocade. Everything was gay and brilliant—with the exception of a man's body, lying outstretched on the carpet.

She stared at it with a feeling of terrible familiarity. This seemed a coloured and almost cheerful version of her recent grim experience. A sunny room, instead of the dark stuffy flat—a debonair corpse, in place of the other horror with his gross body and distorted face.

The dead man was slim and elegant with silver hair and black eyebrows. He wore a cream tussore suit with a brown silk shirt and socks. A tangerine carnation was in his buttonhole and a monocle had fallen from his eye. There were signs of a struggle, but on his mouth was the ghost of a smile—protesting and surprised—as though his visitor had gone rather too far beyond the limit of good taste.

Hermione stared—petrified by the sight of blood oozing from a wound in his heart. At that moment, her dominant sensation was incredulity, although—in itself—the happening was not altogether improbable. Any dissolute person, who plays also with souls, may run the risk of violent death, while it follows logically, that someone must discover his body. The amazing element centred in the fact that she—Hermione Heath—should be the victim of an extraordinary and almost impossible coincidence.

Lighting *had* struck the same place twice.

As she realised it, she felt about to be overwhelmed by an avalanche of terror which would sweep away her wits, as in the first catastrophe. But even while she trembled on the brink of panic, she remembered Andrew.

He had warned her that she must not risk a second scandal and he had told her what she must do. She must touch nothing and go away immediately.

Merely to think of him strengthened her with the knowledge of invisible comradeship. She lost the sense of being overwhelmed by Fate's betrayal as she regained mastery over her nerves. Checking an impulse to stop the maddening ringing of the telephone, she hurried from the room.

Just as she reached the vestibule, she heard a ring, followed by a double knock upon the front door.

The desperation of the crisis cleared her brain, so that she guessed what had happened. The bell had been ringing for some time and the exchange operator, when she realised that something was out of order, had rung up the police station.

The man who had been sent to investigate the mystery must not find her in the house. She glanced at the closed windows of the salon and decided that the official might enter while she was trying to open one of them. The white marble staircase was nearer, so she sped noiselessly over the thick black carpet up to the shuttered gloom of the landing.

Trembling violently, she waited for him to make the discovery... Then suddenly the shrilling of the bell was cut off as the official talked to the police station.

She strained her ears to listen. Fortunately, he did not speak in a patois, so that she was able to understand the drift of his statement.

"Herr Silbermann shot in his summer residence. The disorder indicates murder. Come at once to watch the house from the outside, so that no one can leave it. The miscreant may be hiding. No, I cannot search yet, lest someone should slip out, while I am upstairs. Here, I can guard the front door as well as the body. Stop anyone you meet on the road who is running, or hurrying, or agitated, or who is at all suspicious."

Hermione bit her lip and clenched her hands. She was caught in a trap... But there might be a way out. There must be one. She thought she remembered a spidery iron stair way that spiralled from the top veranda down to the garden. If she could descend unseen, she might hide in the shrubbery until the relief police reached the villa—and then choose the psychological moment to make a dash for the quay.

Holding herself in dread lest a board should creak, she opened a door. Her heart sunk at the darkness within. If the upper storey were still closed, it would be difficult to unshutter a window with out betraying her presence by a noise. But she had to go on. As her eyes grew accustomed to the darkness, she groped her way safely through a bathroom, to the principal bedroom.

To her joy, the windows were open, so that it, too, swam with sunshine and water reflections. Drawing aside an orchid-pink satin curtain, she stole cautiously out.

In that moment of exposure, she felt certain that someone must see her from the lake. It was possible, too, that the spiral stairs were visible from a corner of the salon, where the policeman guarded the body. But although she knew that she was incriminating herself more deeply with every action, she crept down the steps and reached the ground.

Without giving herself time to falter, she dived underneath the nearest shrub. If she could crawl under its shelter to the left of the villa, she could reach the road without having to pass the open front door.

At first, however, the task seemed impossible. It was difficult to make any progress through the dense mass of interlacing twigs. She was stifled by heat and lack of air and almost choked by layers of dust and rubbish. To test her endurance still further was the additional fear of making any sound.

Inch by inch, foot by foot, she dragged herself through the hedge until she reached a shrub behind which she could crouch while she waited. It was then she glanced at her watch and realised that she could catch the steamer only by making a sprint.

It was the last boat back to the town where she was staying. If she lost it, she would also lose the express back to England and her chance of making a test for the new picture. Any attempt to hire a car in the village would attract attention to her presence as a stranger when the least publicity would be fatal. No one had seen her come—and no one must see her go, except in impeccable circumstances.

Even as the thoughts were whirling through her mind, she noticed that the dog was nosing among the bushes, as though he were on her trail. He was bound to find her and give away the secret of her hiding place.

But his presence made no difference now except to precipitate the crisis. Circumstances forced her out into the open to make a dash for the steamer. On her way she was bound to be stopped and questioned by the police. The passport, which—in accordance with the regulations of her regional ticket—she carried always with her, would be examined and her identity revealed.

Unless she could think of some expedient whereby she could run without attracting attention, it was indeed the end of Hermione Heath.

In that moment she knew that she was being tested. Her whole future depended on her own initiative and brains. No one could direct her now. Andrew's phrase, "a spiritual slug," stung her memory as she wrestled with the psychological aspect of the situation.

Just as the dog leaped toward her in joyful welcome, the inspiration came.

"The dog. If I saw a man running in the street, I should turn and stare. But I should take no notice of a man running with a dog."

Leaping over the low parapet of the garden, she snatched up her stick where the Alsatian had dropped it and held it out in invitation to him to follow. She had two bits of luck: she was still wearing shorts with a sleeveless jersey—and the road curved just beyond the villa, so that anyone around the bend could not see the point where she began her run.

Shouting encouragement to the delighted dog, she raced at top speed, while snatches of "The Charge of the Light Brigade" floated through her mind. 'Shot and shell.'

Two men, wearing dark caped uniforms and peaked caps, cycled toward her. "Boldly they rode." She was passing them. They did not stop her, but they might be following her. She dared not turn her head to find out, but dashed on. "Into the jaws of death."

Another policeman—this time, on foot—came around the next corner. He looked keenly at her and she heard him stop, as though to look after her. "Into the gates of hell . . . On . . . On . . ."

She had run herself nearly to the point of collapse. Her heart was leaping—her lungs felt punctured—when, suddenly, she saw below her the quay and the little steamer. The gangway was on the point of being hauled away, but she dashed across it just in time.

The paddles churned the water and the boat steamed away. Hot and panting, Hermione stood on deck and watched the shore glide past her. The Alsatian was trotting back to *"Mon Asile"* and his dinner. Under the trees, people drank afternoon tea.

A sense of deep relief enfolded her. She knew that she was safe. It was as though she had prescience of a day in the near future, when she was to read in her paper a Continental item which stated that the police had arrested the murderer of the late Herr Silbermann.

Even then, in the villa of the deceased, the policeman was questioning his colleagues.

"You met no one on the road?"

"No one," was the reply. "Only the priest on his bicycle and a kennel maid exercising a hound."

THE ROYAL VISIT

Viva Richards had one of her hunches about the royal visit to Tudor Green, and, as usual, she managed to infect her policeman husband with her own foreboding.

No one could understand the secret of her influence over him. Besides being an Oxford Boxing Blue, he had a trained mind, while she was small, nervy, and as full of superstitions as an old wife.

But for all that, she had her big husband by the short hairs.

It was grilling weather toward the end of August, so that he was glad to get off the baked pavements of High Street into the cool of his home. Viva—looking like a high school girl in her tight dark-blue frock, with white collar and cuffs—had tea waiting for him on the daisied lawn at the back of the cottage.

She flew at him, kissed him, rescued the dish of plums from the wasps, poured him out a glass of tea and then looked at him with dark, tragic eyes.

"Bread and butter always tastes of grass out-of-doors," she said mournfully. She added in the same breath, "Hugo, I'm so unhappy about the Royal Visit."

Constable Richards groaned, for he was sick of the subject. He considered that the residents of Tudor Green had swollen heads and had lost their sense of proportion over the civic honour. Besides, the affair was only small beer—a rushed visit of under half an hour. The prince was actually scheduled to fulfil an important engagement at a large industrial city, but with unselfish good nature had consented to break his journey to lay the foundation stone of the new hospital.

"I'm unhappy, too," Richards informed his wife. "I have to be on duty. But I can't see why you're mourning."

"Because—Hugo, I know there's going to be a terrible tragedy."

He ran his finger uneasily round the inside of his collar, as though it had suddenly grown unbearably tight. Although he always laughed at Viva's presentiments, he had noticed that there was usually a logical origin in a tangible fact behind her tangled fancies and intuitions.

"What makes you think that, my child?" he asked.

"I'm not sure. One can never be certain, for warnings are such shadowy things. But I think it's this burglary at Sir Anthony Kite's."

He laughed indulgently, for it was obvious that, this time, she had strayed too far from any connecting sequence.

"It's queer," she went on. "I feel it must be leading up to something." Then her voice changed to professional interest. "Do you expect to make an arrest?" she asked.

"No, to you. There's not a clue. And the stolen notes are all old ones, so we can't trace their numbers."

Both he and his superior—Sergeant Belch—were annoyed by the affair, for burglaries were practically unknown in Tudor Green, while the special circumstances made it appear an outrage. Sir Anthony Kite, who was a well-known London ear specialist, had retired to live in the little old-world town, but, owing to his persistent interest in his profession, he saw local patients at his private residence, besides giving his services to the hospital and clinic.

It was really a gesture of benevolence to the community, so that he was both bewildered and hurt when he came downstairs, on the preceding morning, to find that his study had been entered, through the French window.

Apparently, the burglar had either been disturbed or in a panic, for he had roughly forced a drawer in the desk and grabbed its entire contents, which included private papers and records, besides Treasury notes to the value of fifty-two pounds.

Viva noticed her husband's frown and changed the subject.

"Mrs. Greenwood-Gore has a Union Jack dress for the ceremony. Red, blue and white. It positively shouts loyalty. It sounds pretty grim, but she carries it off. She is so lovely."

She could afford to be generous in view of her husband's antipathy for the local beauty and social leader of Tudor Green.

"Why don't you like her, Hugo? She's always gracious to you," she reminded him.

"She's gracious enough to talk to me, but she rarely takes the trouble to listen to what I have to say. Because I'm a policeman, I suppose. . . Well, I must toddle back to the station."

Viva walked with him to the front gate, where they lingered to get the effect of the decorations on High Street. They were on a lavish scale and presented a regal spectacle of fluttering scarlet and gleaming gold.

Even as they admired them, a cloud passed before the sun, so that the bright colours were suddenly dimmed, while the gilded crown turned dull, as though tarnished by the poisoned breath of anarchy.

Richards felt Viva's sudden shiver and knew that she was reading an omen of evil in the eclipse.

In spite of the heat, he hurried back to his work. Notwithstanding his common sense, he felt vaguely apprehensive, as though he, too, had prescience of certain seemingly disconnected events which were already beginning to fit themselves into a dark and abominable conspiracy.

When he reached the station, he found his superior officer, Sergeant Belcher, listening with the grim expression which betrayed opposition, to Colonel Clarence Block. . . . The Sergeant was not only a popular local sportsman, but a native of the place, and he instinctively distrusted a newcomer to the district.

Colonel Block suffered from that handicap police will concentrate on making handicap, but, against precedent, he had forced his way to the top, through sheer pressure of wealth and a plus-personality. Consequently he had crashed the position of Chairman of the Reception Committee, on the occasion of the Royal Visit, to the annoyance of the Mayor, who was a dignified silver-haired lawyer of long pedigree.

The Sergeant addressed Richards with a sceptical grin.

"Extra work for you, Richards. The Colonel's got the wind up about this Royal Visit."

The support of Viva's presentiment came from such an unexpected quarter that it stunned Richards to silence. He could only stare as Block began to explain.

"I've made myself personally responsible for the safety of His Highness, so I'm insisting on extra precautions. I've just carried my meeting, in the teeth of strong opposition. Now I want the co-operation of the police."

"I can't see what there is to worry about in a loyal little town like ours," objected the Sergeant.

"Then you can't see further than your nose. Don't you realise that the Prince is going to a big industrial centre, with a strong Communist element? Of course, the police will concentrate on making it safe for him. . . . But if a mad dog escapes their round-up, if he has any sense, he will come to our little show where he'll have the chance of a lifetime."

"Hmmm . . . What do you propose?"

"I'm going to have all the Territorials on the ground, so as to crowd out the general public. And I'm going to limit strictly the number of those present in the enclosure for the ceremony."

"All right for your friends, Colonel, but rough on the townspeople who've spent their money on decorations."

"They can line the route. And you needn't talk of my friends. They'll soon be my enemies, for I'm going to boil down the list of invitations to the bone. But my back is broad and I'm used to taking hard knocks."

Constable Richards looked at him. He noticed the strong-featured face, the bull-neck, the aggressive lips, the dark blood-shot eyes, the coarse hairs which covered his hands — and decided that his claim to resistance was no idle boast.

The Colonel continued to lay down the law.

"There is to be no broadcasting. No photographers and no pressmen, except the local rag. And no planes are to fly over the ground."

"Then you had better speak to your son, Colonel."

Block scowled as he walked the door.

"If that young cub of mine breaks the regulations," he said, "I'll make a point of being on the bench to give him the maximum sentence."

The Sergeant grinned at Richards as the door slammed, for the strained relations between Block and his only son were common knowledge.

"Too gentle for this world," he remarked. "The angels must be calling him. There's the telephone. Take the call, Richards, and if it's Sir Anthony again, I'm not in."

Richards grinned, for the ear specialist had been continually ringing up the station, to inquire if the police were on the track of his burglar. On this occasion, however, and to Richards' astonishment, he had some news for them.

"My case book has just been returned to me by post," he said in his dry, clearly articulated voice. "Apparently the perverted person who stole it has some muddled idea of making a gesture."

"But it's very satisfactory," remarked Richards heartily. "The loss of confidential documents must be the worst part to a professional man."

"I'm glad I've raised your spirits. . . . But my fifty-two pounds were not returned."

"I'll be round now to examine the postal wrapper."

"I have already done so. The only deduction from the postmark is that the criminal is spending my money in London."

Constable Richards rang off, wiping his brow. His only consolation was that, at long last, he could go home to Viva.

When he walked home, in the greenish dusk, he chose the back way beside a small brown river, shaded with hedges, which flowed through part of the town. Even here, his luck was out, for instead of avoiding people, he ran into Mrs. Flora Greenwood-Gore.

A flawless blonde—ageless and childless—she was the wife of an important man. Even the prejudiced Richards had to admit her beauty as he looked at her perfect complexion and violet eyes. He noticed that she was wearing a frock printed with poppies and cornflowers on a white ground, before she drew his attention to it.

"My royal reception dress. My husband says the colours are too daring."

"They've done more than dare. They've hit me in the eye," said Richards.

As she was not married to him, there was no reason for Mrs. Greenwood-Gore to smile at his joke. She went on talking in her habitual monologue.

"Oh, by the way, a man we knew in the Transvaal has just flown over to see me. I had to go out, so I sent him over to your wife, as he met her uncle at the Cape. I'll ring up when I get home and you can send him over . . . ."

She passed on, leaving Richards indignant at her autocratic manner.

When he reached the small cream-washed building which held all he loved most, the French windows of the drawing-room were open and the light fell on a patch of vivid green grass. As he lingered, he could tell, by the halting sound of voices, that both Viva and her visitor were finding it difficult to sustain a conversation.

He plunged to the rescue, when Viva gratefully introduced him to the South African. He was a dried-up man with a nasal voice and no entertainment value, so that Richards was justified in not realising his supreme importance in the development of future events.

There was nothing to tell him that had that specific man not called that evening, the course of history would have been changed.

To make amends for his next stiffness, he produced whisky, which presently unloosed the stranger's tongue. Even then, he was not a success, for he annoyed the Richards family by tactless praise of Mrs. Greenwood-Gore.

"Loveliest woman I've ever met. They were big people in Jo'burg, but she hadn't a scrap of side. Always the same to everyone. And she's not altered a bit. I do admire the way she puts it over."

"She certainly throws her weight about," said Viva coldly.

The stranger glanced at her quickly and then a change came over his expression. For the first time, Richards really understood what is meant by a poker face.

"Are you folk keen on flying?" he asked.

"Not me," replied Richards. "A policeman has to stand on his famous flat feet."

"Only way to get about. The drawback is the engine noise. You see, my job is in a cyanide works at Jo'burg, where the din is chronic. All the workers wear these."

He scooped out of his pocket a couple of curiously shaped rubber plugs and tossed them down on the mantel shelf.

"Never without them. Always wear these flying. . . . Isn't that the 'phone?"

"I'll go," cried Viva joyously.

The South African's face lit up when she returned from the hall with her message.

"Mrs. Greenwood-Gore is waiting for you."

He was as eager to go as they were to speed his parting. The instant he had gone, Richards dropped heavily down in his shabby Varsity chair, which he had brought down from Oxford.

"The end of a perfect day," he sighed. Then he glanced at the mantel shelf and added. "That darned fool has left his gadgets behind. Well he can fetch them himself. I'm not going to turn out again even to save the whole of the Empire."

His ill-temper and Viva's nerves were partly due to atmospherics for during the night they were disturbed by a flickering sky and the mutter of distant thunder. In the morning it was pouring with rain and all day a succession of storms kept rolling up over the hills.

As though the electric weather affected the general temper, the final meeting of the Reception Committee was an explosive affair. Colonel Block read out his revised list of those persons privileged to attend the ceremony, regardless of angry mutters of protests from those who were disappointed.

He was supported in his tactics by Admiral Steel—one of the oldest residents who was virulently anti-Communist.

The Vicar arose to make a protest.

"I am sure we all appreciate your difficulties and your courage in tackling them," he said to the Colonel. "But there is one person who should be present. Surely you could squeeze in Miss Spenser?"

There was a hum of approval for the little spinster was a devoted parish worker and a zealous member of the Primrose League.

"It would break her heart to be left out," cautioned the Vicar. "She has all the portraits of the Royal Family in her parlour. The memory of the occasion would remain with her always. Besides, in view of her deafness, she is deprived of so much amusement."

He looked for support towards Flora Greenwood-Gore, whose fair face wore its habitual expression—serene yet remote—as though she dwelt on another plane. When she smiled and bowed her head, the applause grew so vigorous that the Colonel had to give way.

"All right, since you insist, she shall have her ticket. And while we're on the subject, I have a special announcement to make. There will be no admission without a ticket. It doesn't matter who the individual or what the circumstances."

"I second the measure," approved the Mayor. "It would take time to check a list at the entrance. In view of the rush, everything must go off without a hitch."

Unfortunately, after the concession, the meeting was marred by another incident. The Admiral — who was so staunch a supporter of home interests that he had not left Tudor Green for years — rose on his gouty feet.

"I have been informed," he said, "that the Presentation silver trowel and mallet to be used at the ceremony were not supplied locally. In my opinion, it is scandalous to spend one penny of the ratepayers' subscriptions out of the town."

"It was considered necessary," explained the Mayor soothingly, "to avoid suspicion of favouritism."

"In any case," interrupted Col. Block, "the expense will be carried by me, as my contribution. I'm entitled to choose my own firm, aren't I? I don't truckle to local graft."

After that implicit insult, it took all the Mayor's diplomacy to prevent the meeting from degenerating into a dog-fight. At its conclusion, the Colonel made a final arbitrary announcement.

"The invitations will not be sent by post. They must be applied for, personally, at my house. I shall initial them myself and hand them to the rightful persons."

Miss Spenser lost no time in applying for her precious card. She enjoyed the experience as a little social occasion, for she met others who were at the Colonel's imposing mansion on the same errand. While they waited, they were invited into the dining room for refreshments and the spirit of the house was hospitable and friendly.

It was fortunate that she had a taste of pleasure, because within five minutes of leaving she was the victim of a disagreeable incident. She went home by the short cut, a paved passage running between the garden walls of some large houses. In its darkest part, a youth rushed past her, snatched her bag and ran off with it.

She went immediately to the Police Station, to report her loss.

"Luckily, there was only a little money in it," she told Sergeant Belcher. "A trifle over four shillings. But my card case and latch-key were inside. I shall get the lock changed instantly, but I do hope my cards will not be used for an improper purpose."

Then she gave a cry of dismay.

"Oh, dear, oh dear. My card of admission was there too. I get another. The Colonel warned me not to lose it. He will be so angry with me."

"Did you get a view of the young man?" asked the Sergeant.

"The merest glimpse as he rushed under the lamp. Of course, I could not be certain, but I thought he looked like young Block. Only that is too ridiculous."

"Well," remarked the Sergeant after the distressed lady had gone, "it seems one of two things. Either the Dictator is so annoyed at being crossed over Miss Spenser's ticket that he arranged to have it pinched—or else the son did it on his own. He's been left out of the show and he may be planning some fool revenge on his dad."

Constable Richards went home in a disturbed frame of mind. He kept asking himself a question. Could there be any connection between the loss of Sir Anthony's fifty-two pounds and Miss Spenser's fifty-two pence?

If such were the case, there might indeed be some foundation for Viva's miserable hunch. But although he thought until he was stupid, the two thefts remained poles apart and he could conjecture no point of fusion.

He did not tell Viva about the incident until the next morning. She made no comment, but he was dismayed to notice her pale face as she poured coffee.

Constable Richards found the light duty, which was his lot at Tudor Green, an arduous test of endurance. Of course, he told himself that he was worried solely about his wife and he watched the clock—or rather, his wrist—until he was able to get back to the cottage.

He was glad to find his father-in-law, Dr. Buck, having tea with Viva. He was a brisk, sensible man, with a tight pink clean-shaven face, and he would certainly disclaim the responsibility for his temperamental daughter.

On this occasion, however, his gossip had done nothing to relieve her symptoms, for her small face was pinched with anxiety.

"Have you heard about the Admiral, Hugo?" she asked.

"No," replied Richards. "What about him?"

"He's fractured his leg. Daddy has just been called in to him. He fell down his front steps."

"Rather early in the day for that."

"No," said the doctor," he was quite sober. The steps were greased. I nearly slipped on them myself."

"Who could have done it, Hugo?" asked Viva.

Richards tried to hide his uneasiness.

"Some silly practical joke," he declared. "But I'm off duty now and I want my tea. . . ."

Although he refused to discuss the incident, he followed his father-in-law to the front gate.

"You might send over a bromide for Viva," he said. "She's got a case of the jim-jams."

"Even I have diagnosed them," remarked the doctor dryly. "I'll let you have a draught."

The sedative did its work, for Viva had no warning dream to relate on the following morning. The sun was shining from a clear blue sky and she felt cheerfully normal. During the morning she remembered that she had not even tried on the new frock which had been bought for the ceremony. It required to be shortened, and she grew so interested in her appearance that she had not time for apprehension.

She was dressed and seated at the luncheon table when Richards entered the room.

"Aren't you cutting it rather fine?" she asked.

Then she noticed that he had made no comment on her new finery, although he was usually responsive.

"What's the matter?" she asked.

"Nothing," he replied with forced lightness. "Bad show for Flora Greenwood-Gore. That's all. She's going to miss the fun."

"You mean—she won't be at the ceremony? Why?"

"Got a telegram early this morning saying her mother was dying and asking her to come immediately. Her husband is away so she wired him where she'd gone before she left. He rang up the old folks to find out exactly what was wrong . . . and nothing was."

He stopped speaking, and gazed at his wife in consternation. She sat motionless, her fork poised in the air, while she stared fixedly at him as though her wits had deserted her.

"What's the matter?" he asked sharply. "Say something, but don't look like that."

"*Dear Brutus*," she murmured.

"My dearest girl, it sounded as though you said 'Brutus'. Or am I imagining things?"

"No, I said it. Hugo, don't you remember Barrie's play where a lot of ill-assorted people were invited to a house because they had something in common?"

"Yes. But—"

"Don't you see? Someone has prevented Miss Spenser, the Admiral, and now Mrs. Greenwood-Gore from coming to the ceremony. There's an object behind it—and I'm terribly afraid. What have those three people got in common? What?"

Although he was six feet of stodge, Constable Richards felt himself beaten by his wife's hunch. He became conscious of something secret and diabolical creeping in the darkness, like a slow train of gunpowder eating its way to the explosion.

He glanced at the clock distractedly.

"If you are right," he said, "we've got to find it out in double quick time. We must be in our places in fifteen minutes."

"I know. Think, Hugo."

"It beats me. I could find points of resemblance between the Admiral and Miss Spenser. They are both elderly and rheumatic and amateur gardeners and Primrose Leaguers and deaf. It's Mrs. Greenwood-Gore that's the complication. She has everything they haven't got."

The telephone bell began to ring, but he shook his head impatiently.

"Shut up," he muttered.

"Answer it," commanded Viva suddenly. "I feel it may be important."

Obediently, he took the receiver off the hook. He was so strung up to a pitch of nerves that he wanted to swear at the sound of Mrs.

Greenwood-Gore's voice at the end of the line. She was furious over her grievance, and insisted on telling him what he already knew, in spite of his efforts to interrupt her.

"I've rung up the Police Station," she said, "but I can get no responsible person. They say the Sergeant has left for the ceremony. So I appeal to you. You must find out who sent that telegram and prosecute the person."

"I'm not sure a practical joke is within our province," he told her.

"Thank you. Now I have your promise. I feel satisfied."

"I'm afraid you didn't hear. I said it's not within our scope—" "I hope so, too. Good-bye."

Constable Richards rang off and stared at his wife as though he could not believe his ears.

"Viva," he shouted, "I've got it. I know now what they have in common. . . . They are all deaf."

Viva shook her head.

"Not Mrs. Greenwood-Gore," she protested.

"But she is. . . . That South African chap— Yes, that's the idea."

Dashing across to the mantel shelf, Richards began to turn over the ornaments.

"Where are his gadgets?" he panted.

She instantly picked up a vase, turned it upside down and shook out the plugs.

"Why do you want them?" she asked.

"Because I want to make myself deaf. It seems to me that there's going to be a planned disturbance at the ceremony—probably some noise. That's why they've eliminated all the deaf people. They might not react to the distraction—whatever it is . . . Well, they'll have *me* now."

"What will you do?"

"Just act on the spur of the moment. Come along. The car's outside."

The great moment was at hand. The cheers grew louder as the Prince entered the enclosure. He was accompanied by the Mayor and Mayoress, who had met the Royal train at the station, and he wore the rosebud which had been presented by their grandson.

Colonel Block, as Chairman of the Reception Committee, bowed himself forward with a few words of welcome to superintend the laying of the foundation stone. There was no time for speeches and the short ceremony was soon over. Having done his part, the Prince glanced at his watch and then smiled at the company with his customary charm.

At that moment, there was an unexpected commotion. With a threatening snarl, which grew louder every second, an airplane swooped down out of the clouds and dived lower and lower over the ground, while the roar of its engine increased. Instantly, every head was turned in its direction while every face looked upwards.

There were two exceptions to the general company of sky-gazers. Constable Richards heard a deadened noise, but the sound reached him a fractional period later than the rest of the crowd. It was in this interval that he, alone, saw what was about to happen.

Colonel Block whipped a knife out of the handle of the silver trowel, as though it were a sword-stick and poised it, ready to stab the Prince in the back.

The blow never fell. While the company, including the Prince, were still engrossed by the antics of the aviator, who was flying in dangerously low circles, Constable Richards and the other constable had gripped their prisoner and run him out of the enclosure, with the minimum of commotion.

The incident passed with such despatch that afterwards, no one could claim truthfully to be an eyewitness of the outrage. . . . The Prince laughed and hurried back to his car. There was a second outburst of cheers along the return route to the station. Soon afterward he was back in the Royal train, only conscious of an amusing break in the boredom of a municipal ceremony.

That evening, at the cottage, there was a festive meal when Constable Richards returned—full of importance—after the excitement of the proceedings at the Police Station.

"The Blocks," he explained to his wife, "are paid agents of the Wrecker Gang, whose aim it is to upset the peace and security of the world. Father and son worked together, hand in glove. The feud was a dodge to throw dust in our eyes."

"Of course, they were going to be very well paid for bumping off royalty. The son did all the active part. He stole Sir Anthony's case-book and Miss Spenser's bag and he greased the Admiral's door-steps. As you saw, he did the flying stunt for which his father was going to inflict a heavy penalty, according to plan."

"That was a smart idea," remarked Viva. "If you watch a crowd when a plane flies low overhead, I defy you to find anyone who does not look up instinctively."

"Exactly. Block's part was to strike instantly in the confusion and then to slip the knife back, before the murder was spotted. When it was discovered, it would be difficult to associate him with the crime, as they all had an equal chance."

"But wouldn't the knife be traced to him, as he ordered the trowel?"

"He would probably have taken it away during the uproar. Remember, there were no brainy C.I.D. men present, to take command and order everyone to be searched and all that. I don't see why anyone would suspect the trowel. And if it were found, he would probably be able to prove delivery of an innocuous duplicate and swear to substitution on the part of persons unknown, in order to frame him."

"But when did you get on to the idea that Mrs. Greenwood-Gore was deaf?" asked Viva.

"When she began to guess at what I was saying on the telephone. I wonder why we never spotted it before that she was deaf. It explains why she goes on talking and never seems to listen. Sheer bluff. My own idea is that she is much older than anyone knows and like many beautiful women she can't stick the thought of age or infirmity. You remember how the South African talked about her putting over 'something.' That chap knew."

"Well, it's all very clever of you, darling," said Viva. "But don't forget, Block had to steal Sir Anthony's case-book, to find out all the cases of deafness in the district!"

"What of it?" asked her husband.

"Well—wasn't that my *hunch?*"

"**L**ook," said Mary. "There are the lights of Mabel's house." "They're cheerful," she said to John. "Shan't be sorry to get back to a home-fire myself."

The young people were tired from trudging along the semi-obliterated moorland road, as well as disheartened by an unsuccessful quest. All the afternoon they had been searching for Mary's lost dog, Dopey. Yet, although it was growing dark, with a biting wind and a scurry of snowflakes, Mary stopped to gaze up at the lighted windows of "The Chestnuts."

"Could you find anything more hopelessly commonplace than that house?" she asked. "And the mayor isn't a bit like a Great Lover, with his red face and his bawdy jokes. But he's been faithful to one woman, John. I want our love to be like that."

John pressed the hand tucked through his arm, to show that he understood. As they stood in the keen blue twilight they were a well matched pair—endowed with health, good looks, and youth—and fit pioneers for the new world which held their future.

In spite of the fact that "The Chestnuts" was within the municipal radius and had main water and electricity, its position was both exposed and lonely. It was the last impost of the town, for beyond it stretched the moor—now practically deserted because of the snow. On the other side of it was a half mile of road, dimly lit with widely spaced lamp posts, which linked it up with the residential suburbs of Pooksmoor.

Although it was the most romantic dwelling in the district—and a monument to a lover's fidelity—its appearance was prosaic. Solidly built of grey stone, with a short drive of red gravel and a belt of laurels to screen its lawn from the road. It looked exactly what it was designed to be—a prosperous middle class residence.

Over thirty years ago the mayor of the town had built it for the girl he was going to marry. Just before their wedding, however, she had died from undiagnosed appendicitis and was buried in her wedding dress.

The mayor never lived in the house, but he had kept it exactly as it was, as a shrine to her memory. With the exception of silver plate and jewelry—which might attract burglars—he arranged all her wedding presents about the rooms. Nothing was changed nor allowed to deteriorate from disuse. A woman cleaned and aired it regularly, but no one else was allowed to enter it.

This was the mayor's private sanctuary, which he visited regularly so that passers-by were used to seeing its lighted windows and hearing the music from the wireless. But, although he remained unmarried, he did not behave as though his life were blighted. He found occasional consolation in liquor and always kept whisky on the premises. A telephone, too, was installed so that he could be informed of any business or municipal development that might arise during his absence from his office.

As the lovers lingered on the snowy road the music ceased and the upper windows were plunged into the darkness. Shortly afterward the lower lights were switched off and they heard the slam of the front door. Then the mayor crunched down the drive and pushed open the gate. He was a huge, bull-necked man, athletic still in spite of his overweight. His face was red and his walk not quite steady, but his smile beamed genuine welcome.

"Still courting?" he shouted. "When are you young people going to do your duty?"

"We're going to be married in the new year," Mary told him.

"Directly afterward we're sailing to Canada," added John.

"So you're getting used to snow, eh? But you mustn't go on the moor alone, Mary, until this confounded Convict 193 has been caught."

"Isn't he a nuisance?" she agreed. "John won't let me stir without him. Our farm's in a very lonely part, so I must get used to taking risks. I'm not afraid."

"This chap's a human tiger," remarked the mayor, "leaving behind him a trail of victims."

"Only last night I was betting the governor of the prison that he'd slip through their fingers. He's got his belly full of food, and clothes no one can identify. All he needs is cash to make a getaway."

Then he wrinkled his brow.

"I'd a queer notion, just now," he said. "I wondered if he has used this place. He's hidden somewhere this bitter spell."

"Too near the town, sir," objected John. "Besides, isn't it burglar-proof?"

"Technically only. He could easily pick one of these old fashioned locks. And tonight the whisky was either underproof or someone had watered it. Maybe I'm losing my grip. I've half a mind to come out to Canada with you."

"The town couldn't spare you, sir."

"That's right. The town made me, so I must stick to the town. Besides, I couldn't leave this."

He jerked his thumb toward "The Chestnuts." Then because his whisky had made him sentimental, he retold them the story with which they were familiar.

"I was about your age, John, when I bought this house. It was the last word in modern improvements then. Mabel was proud of it. We went up to London together to buy our furniture and she was in most days, arranging things and finishing the twiddly-bits. We used to sit here in the evenings. We would turn on the lights and put a record on the gramophone and pretend we were married. All the family life I ever had. You know how it ended."

"What was she like?" asked Mary softly.

"She was a real woman. You're the nearest to her I've met. But my girl was a lady and wore white petticoats with lace frills."

The mayor grimaced at Mary's dark blue trousers and leather coat, as he made two vague semi-circles with his hands.

"Mabel came out here and here," he explained. "But her waist was only twenty inches. She'd the sweetest temper, but she was the boss. If she lived, there would be no more wet lodge nights for me."

Suddenly Mary dared to say what was in her mind.

"Mr. Mayor, I know it sounds precious, but Mabel is a real person to me. She's been a sort of inspiration, when people make love sound cheap, with their silly jokes. I never pass here without thinking of her. Before I go to Canada may I go over her house alone? Indeed, it's not idle curiosity."

There was a long pause before the mayor spoke in a choked voice.

"Nobody has ever gone there except me and the woman who cleans. but—yes. I'm going up to London for a couple of days and you shall have my key."

He lowered his voice to a hoarse whisper as he placed the Yale key in her hand.

"I could have sold the house time and time again," he confided. "But I kept it empty. It's all fancy, of course, but when I sit there, in her drawing room and look at her photograph, I don't feel quite so lonely. You listen to me, both of you. It may sound funny talk from an old chap that gets tight, but—love is the only thing that counts."

He glanced at his watch and added in a matter-of-fact manner: "I'm expecting my car. Can I give you a lift back?"

They refused his offer from an instinctive feeling that he wanted to be alone. As they watched his Rolls-Royce drive off amid a whirl of snowflakes, John spoke to Mary.

"Poor old chap. He's rich—and we've not even begun to be poor—but we've everything."

"Except Dopey," Mary reminded him.

While Dopey possessed all the endearing canine qualities, he had one grave fault: he was gripped periodically by a pioneer spirit which caused him to forsake home and family, in search of a new empire.

It was true that hitherto he had always returned—thin and hungry and ready to admit that, in spite of all its faults, the old country home was best. But this time his return was so long overdue that Mary had almost given up hope.

When she reached home that evening she ran into the house, calling out her usual question, "Has Dopey come back?"

"Not yet," her mother told her. "But he will."

She spent another broken night, listening for his return. Every time she awoke she strained her ears for the sound of his bark, and once she went downstairs and opened the front door in the hope of finding him outside.

The next afternoon the baker knocked at the door.

"Dog still missing?" he asked. "Wonder if it was him I heard this morning when I was doing my round on the moor. I fancied there was a sort of whining coming from the old shepherd's hut."

"Thanks, but I've heard so many of these tales. Dopey seems to have been everywhere except at his home."

But when he had gone she told herself that, in spite of so many false rumours, this latest story might be actual fact. If Dopey had crawled to the hut and was lying there, starved and exhausted, she was leaving him to die.

At least she could endure the suspense no longer. John was away at a market and there was no one she could ask to accompany her. Besides, the hut was about a mile out on the moor and not much daylight remained.

From the moment she pulled on her snow boots she began a relentless race with time. Soon she was running past the select residences of the suburb. The houses with their snow-capped roofs and white muffled gardens looked snug and comfortable in contrast with the leaden sky and the drift of flakes which powdered her hair and blew into her eyes.

She was almost blinded when she reached the stretch of lonely road which led to "The Chestnuts." On one side was the high stone wall of Pooksmoor park and on the other flowed the cold grey slide of the river.

The present gripped her and her mind was possessed only by Dopey and his need. She scarcely noticed the mile. The moor rose in a long, gruelling climb and when the summit was reached it dipped down again to a deep fold in the landscape.

It was a relief to jog down the hill, holding her side, until she reached the slatey trickle of a small river at the bottom. It looked bitterly cold, for icicles formed a stiff fringe dropping from the arch of the bridge, but she had grown so hot that her hair was plastered in damp rings on her brow.

On the other side, the moor rose in a steeper slope, like a white wall. Once again she toiled upward, impelled by thoughts of her dog and repeating his name foolishly, as though it were a spell.

"Dopey, Dopey—"

Suddenly there was a break in the clouds and the sky grew lighter. To her joy, she realised that the storm was about to clear. As she climbed higher she could see the stone pile of the ruined hut standing out against the skyline.

Without a thought of personal peril she left the tracks and plowed over snowy mounds of heather, calling the dog's name.

There was no answering bark or whine to encourage her. Appalled by the silence and dreading what she might discover inside, she forced herself to enter the aperture of the ruin.

At first it was almost a relief to find the place empty. At least Dopey had not starved to death in the cold. The next moment she awoke from her dream of hope to the dull ache of yet another disappointment.

"I might have known it," she thought bitterly. "Just some of the baker's fun. The sooner I get back the better."

For the first time she remembered that an escaped convict was somewhere at large and that the light was fading rapidly. She was about to reach the road again when she chanced to look across the white wilderness, stretching deeper into the heart of the moor.

On the opposite rise, silhouetted blackly against the sky, was the figure of a man.

Although he was a considerable distance away, he stood out clearly, magnified by atmospheric conditions. There was something so menacing about the solitary shape—brooding over the waste— that her heart began to flutter with fear.

"It might be any harmless country man," she told herself. "It need not be the convict."

As she watched him, the man suddenly disappeared from view, as though he had dropped down to the ground. It was an ominous development, for it seemed to signify that he knew he was being observed. In that case, it was certain that she, in her turn, was visible to him.

As she strained her eyes she distinguished something dark moving over the white surface of the opposite slope. There appeared to be no doubt that the man was running in an effort to overtake her.

If it were really a race between them, he was bound to win in spite of her long start. She was already tired from her sprint against time. Even if she could outdistance him on the moor, which was chiefly downhill, there remained the long stretch of lonely road between the stone wall and the river.

Although it seemed madness to forsake the road and run the risk of being lost, just when dusk was falling, she decided to drop down into a gully and chance her luck in reaching the bottom without a broken limb. Running some way down the slope, so that she, too, might be lost to view, she turned to the left and plowed over the snow until she reached the steep side of a cleft.

In her excitement she lost all sense of danger, as she slipped recklessly down the almost vertical incline—rolling, bumping, sliding. More than once she came perilously near to breaking her neck, but she always managed to save herself from disaster, up to the moment when her heels slid under her and she shot headlong into a narrow lane.

She scrambled to her feet, to find that she was miraculously intact. The moor now rose high above her, shielding her from observation. Although she sank up to her knees in drifted snow, she knew that she would cut off two-thirds of the distance covered by the winding moorland road.

The next twenty minutes were a test of strenuous endurance. Every muscle, nerve and sinew was strained to its utmost as she plowed a way through the choked gully. Presently, to her joy, the surface grew better as the lane began to wind upward, until she saw the chimneys of Mabel's house.

Soon afterward she reached the tradesmen's entrance at the back, where she stopped to consider her next step. Although she hoped the man had given her up as lost quarry, she had to be certain that she had shaken him off. Keeping in the shadow of the garden wall, she crept forward until she was able to peer around the corner.

To her horror she saw the back of a man. He was crouched on a spot from where he could watch the house, the moorland road, and the approach to town. Although he was dressed in ordinary country clothes, waterproof and tweed cap—there was such a suggestion of vulpine cunning in his pose that she knew instinctively that he was Convict 193.

Suddenly she remembered that the mayor had given her a key to the house. Fortunately it was buttoned up inside an inner pocket of her leather coat and had not been shaken out by her fall. Opening the back gate with utmost caution, and stooping until she was bent nearly double, she worked her way around the side of the house until she reached the front door.

The key turned easily in the lock and she slipped into the hall, taking care to shut the door with the minimum of sound.

Before she shut out the dying daylight, she had seen the outline of the telephone on the hall table. Groping through the darkness, she rang up the exchange.

"Police station," she whispered.

Her call was put through without delay. Breathless with haste, she gasped out her story. To her dismay the official at the other end of the wire appeared maddeningly sceptical and was concerned chiefly in repeating her statement to ensure accuracy. At the end he told her to hold the line while he was reporting the matter and left her in an agony of suspense.

When he returned his manner was different and showed that he had changed from a machine to a human being.

"There's nothing to worry about," he assured her. "We have the matter in hand. Police cars are already on their way to "The Chestnuts". And we've got through to the prison. Now what about you, miss? Are you safe?"

"Perfectly safe," she replied. "He doesn't know I'm here. Besides, how could I get inside a locked house? He couldn't suspect I had a key."

"Is there any room where you can lock yourself in?" he asked.

"I shouldn't think so. The house has been empty for years and the locks must be rusty."

"Try them at once. If you can't find a key that turns, hide yourself at the top of the house. And, mind you, don't show a light or make any noise."

After the man had rung off, the darkness did not seem quite so secure to Mary.

She groped her way to the nearest door, but, as she had expected, the key was rusted in the lock. She tried two others, with the same result. Then something seemed to stir behind her in the darkness, as suddenly she remembered the mayor's remarks about the vulnerability of the house.

At the thought of all the unshuttered windows on the ground floor, a gust of fear shook her, as a terrier worries a rat. With an instinctive craving for reassurance, she stole back to the telephone and gave John's number to the exchange.

As a matter of fact he was expecting her to ring him up. He had just returned home and was unlacing his boots when he heard the bell. Stumbling across to the instrument, directly he recognised her voice, he broke in excitedly.

"Isn't it great about old Dopey?"

"Dopey?" she repeated dully.

"What? Don't you know he's come back? Where are you?"

"Mabel's house . . . I've been chased by the convict. He's outside now—watching the road for me."

John's face paled as he listened to her breathless tale. It seemed to him that there remained one chance only to save her and that was to put up a desperate bluff. She must attempt to confuse the criminal and make him suspect a trap, in order to gain those priceless minutes of respite before the arrival of the police.

While he hesitated, he was goaded on to action by the merciless logic of the situation. The convict was still uncaptured mainly because he had left no witness in a fit state to give information about him. He had broken in, robbed and beaten up his victims, leaving them unconscious and in several cases on the point of death; but by the time the crime was discovered he had travelled miles from the scene. It was certain that Mary would not be spared the fate of those others.

The muscles throbbed in his cheeks as he cleared his throat.

"Mary," he said thickly, "I want you to snap on all the lights in the house. At once."

He heard her gasp in dismay.

"The police told me to hide in the dark."

"That's no good. You must trust me. Your only chance is to fool him. Turn on the wireless, too. Make him think the mayor's in the house."

"I—I dare not. It's just telling him I'm here."

"Mary—he knows that already."

Again he heard the faint wail of dismay which told him that she realised her peril.

"All right," she said faintly. "I will. I only hope you are right."

"That's my brave girl. I'm coming to you now."

As he rang off, Mary felt desolate and abandoned to her fate. She was alone in a strange hostile darkness, while outside stretched the menace of the twilight moor. Sure that she was signing her own death warrant, she switched on the nearest light.

Immediately she found herself transported back into another world of more than thirty years ago. The hall was a formal polished place which faintly reproached her for a breach of decorum in entering unannounced. Its floor was composed of alternate black-and-white marble flags, covered with red-and-blue Turkey rugs. There was a massive mahogany hall stand, while a big carved bear from Switzerland held out a salver for her visiting card.

In spite of her panic she was sustained by a strong sense of unreality which made her feel that she must be exploring a house in a dream. It was almost with a throb of anticipation that she opened two other doors and switched on the lights. The dining room with its suite upholstered in dull purple leather and its gilded walls must have been a daring departure from convention.

As she gazed at it Mary could almost imagine that she was accompanied by an invisible hostess who was proud to do the honours of her house. Then the present returned in a rush of fear. John had said "all the lights."

In a panic, she darted up the first flight of stairs, which—like the square landing at the top—was carpeted with thick blue Axminster. Panting like a hunted fugitive, she left behind her a betraying trail of light.

Out of the darkness flashed the grandeur of the spare room, with its walnut suite and amber satin bedspread and curtains. Then Mary was arrested by what was evidently Mabel's room. The carpet had a mauve ground—covered with pink roses—and the furniture was French.

When she entered the drawing room she felt that she had reached Mabel's own domain. This was where she used to sit with her lover and dream of the future. Soft lights, low music, and all around her, accumulated treasures. She felt safe there, since it was impossible that it could be the scene of outrage or crime.

Mary was struck by the fact that everything was arranged as though the mistress of the house was still in residence. A copy of *Punch* lay on the divan, beside a piece of drawn-thread work, stretched on a frame. On a small table was a big box of chocolates, tied with a festive yellow ribbon. The clock kept perfect time, while the calendar in its silver frame was up to date with the month.

An enlarged photograph of Mabel hung above the mantelpiece. She was a pretty girl with a good crop of hair piled high on her head in a profusion of rolled curls. Her eyes were maternally kind, her lips sweet yet firm, while from her full bust and rounded chin it was easy to see that she indulged a weakness for cream-puffs.

Underneath the photograph was placed a vase of Neapolitan violets which perfumed the air.

Gazing at the portrait, Mary lost all sense of peril as she thought of the woman who had planned this room. Unlike a modern girl, she had never earned a penny. Marriage was her natural goal. And now, when she ought to be fussing over her grandchildren, she was only a memory kept ever green by the mayor's devotion—expressed in a house.

Suddenly remembering John's instruction, Mary turned on the wireless and the strains of a Mayfair hotel orchestra flooded the air. Up in London fashionable folk were dancing at their tea. It was impossible to realise the fact as she examined the relics of Mabel's last visit to her house. The linen of the needlework was yellow and the chocolates looked like fawn wax.

The copy of *Punch*—then the current number—was dated January the third, 1961. Seated on the divan, Mary began to turn its pages. Soon she lost all sense of her surroundings in her enjoyment of the jokes, so that she never heard footsteps—muffled by the thick pile of the carpet—which were mounting the stairs.

A smile was still on her lips when she looked up at the sound of the opening door.

While the police were dashing along the snowy roads, and while John was letting out his motorcycle in an effort to overtake them, the convict stood staring up at Mabel's house. He had ceased to watch the moor, for he knew now that she would not come that way.

There was nothing in his appearance to suggest his prison association, while his description—issued by the police over the air—might have been that of any listener. Unfortunately it was not possible to establish what he wore. His first escapade was an attack on a lonely house, where he stocked himself with food and clothing; but as the maltreated tenant was still unconscious in a hospital, no one knew what was missing from his wardrobe.

Pursuing the same tactics of cunning and cruelty, Convict 193 had reached the fringe of civilisation. He could walk through the streets of Pooksmoor by night and reach the railway station unchallenged, since he had no blemish or peculiarity to betray him; but he still lacked the money to pay his fare. Once he was in London, he could get in touch with his gang and get the benefit of their resources.

Therefore his need of money was urgent and desperate; and when he saw Mary's outline against the sky his hopes flamed high. He knew that no woman in her senses would walk for pleasure on the moor in the present circumstances. The conclusion was that she was a cottager who was venturing to the town to buy household stores. In that case she would have a purse, which was as good as his.

This time, however, it was essential not only to silence her for good but to conceal her body so that it would not be discovered until after his train had arrived at the London terminus.

When he failed to overtake her on the moor he thought at first that she had doubled on her track and returned to some cottage tucked away in a pocket of the waste; but during the last few minutes her disappearance was no longer a mystery.

He knew exactly where she had gone—just as he knew that she was inside the lonely house. . . .

He was about to steal around to the back, to force a window, when suddenly he was arrested by a flood of light from the ground floor. One after another the windows became glowing frames of illumination. Then—muted by the screen of glass—the faint sound of music became audible.

Growling like an animal baffled by guardian bars when on the spring, he cursed his luck. In spite of telephone wires and curtained windows, he believed this house to be temporarily empty. Two nights before, emboldened by its darkness, he had forced entry, but only to find a completely bare larder.

All he had gained was a lodging for the night and a tot of whisky. On this occasion he had left no traces of his visit and had craftily filled up the bottle of spirits with water.

Now all the evidence pointed to occupation. The woman could not be alone. If she were hiding from him she would not betray her secret by flashing him a signal.

Suddenly he scented a plot. She had been sent out on the moor on purpose to lure him to this place. Inside was a posse of warders from the prison waiting to seize him directly he ventured near.

For several minutes he lingered, staring up at the windows in the hope of solving the mystery. As the time passed and nothing further happened, he began to reject the possibility of a planned capture. The fact that he had not been rearrested was proof that his movements were unknown. Certainly the police would not expect to find him so near the town.

The explanation was that the woman did not know that she had been followed and was turning on the lights in the normal way. Meanwhile he had to get money. The chances were that woman might have some, either on her person or hidden in the house.

Creeping around to the back of the house, he peered through every window in turn. Kitchen, scullery, and larders—all were dark and silent. There was no evidence of the servants such as the importance of the house would entail.

He decided to pick the old fashioned lock of the side door through which he had made his previous entrance. Although it was an elementary operation for his talents, some skill and patience were needed. Engrossed by his task, he never noticed when the police closed in on him from two sides.

John, when he arrived on the scene a few minutes later, dashed upstairs in search of Mary. He expected to find her badly shaken by her ordeal, but to his great relief he burst open the drawing room door to find her smiling over a copy of *Punch*.

"They've got him," he shouted.

"Thank God you had the courage to turn on the lights."

"I was a bit scared," she confessed.

He felt her shudder in his arms, but the next minute here face grew radiant with happiness.

"O, John," she cried, "I've just remembered something marvellous. I didn't realise it at the time, but when I rang you up you told me that Dopey has come home."

CAGED

When the wind was in a certain quarter Kathy could hear the roaring of the lions in Lord Hammersmith's private zoo.

The sound was faint and fitful—little more than an ominous mutter in the distance. She strained her ears to catch it, for she welcomed it even as a sleepless person greets the first cock-crow. To her also it was symbol of hope—telling her that no night could last forever.

Some time, somewhere, another day would dawn.

Alan—who was superintendent of his uncle's collection of wild animals—was there in the darkness, localised by that snarling cough which throbbed like a nerve in the air. It linked them together in a wireless wave. So long as he was in her life some glimmer of happiness remained.

Yet when she listened to the steady blast of snores from the other bed she had to admit the truth. Like the caged lions, she, too, was behind bars. While her second husband—Hector Mint—lived she could never be free.

As she lay sleepless she wondered whether she were being punished for her youthful folly during her first year in college at Oxford. She had grasped life too adventurously and too greedily. Impatient of the future she had eloped with a fellow under graduate.

While she was an orphan, with no one to consider over her marriage, her husband came of a poorish family that resented the wreck of his academic prospects. Therefore, when they flouted authority, they were left to face the consequences alone.

They took them on the chin, gaily and recklessly. They snaffled odd jobs, loved a little, starved a little, and laughed through everything. Una was born without christening mugs or press announcements and was accepted as part of the joke. Eventually, just as Dick was beginning to shape as a promising freelance journalist, he was killed in a road smash.

In order to provide a home for Una, Kathy started a guest house, which was foredoomed to failure through lack of capital. As she tried to do the work of a staff she was on the verge of complete collapse when Hector Mint arrived with his offer of a home.

She had known him at Oxford where he was a figure of civic importance whom she regarded as a sort of benevolent uncle. It was not until she married him that she realised the dark jungle of his heart. She discovered that she had always been his secret obsession and that his mind was twisted with jealousy of her first husband.

From the first Kathy had been completely honest with Mint. She made it plain that Una's welfare was her chief consideration, but in return for it she tried to fulfil her part of the bargain cheerfully and generously. She refused to regard herself as a martyr, for her joyous and elastic spirit persisted. So long as the sun burst through the clouds, or one daisy cropped up in the lawn, she could smile and keep her chin up.

Like her mother, Una could take punishment—and there was plenty of a mean kind for her to take. Although her stepfather provided her with a technically good home, she never had pocket money, parties, presents, or pets.

Fortunately she was a vigorous, fearless child-possessed of a special radiance—probably the heritage of her light-hearted birth. As Kathy thought of her she tried to forget the snores as they rose in an elephantine trumpet from the other bed.

"I've kept Una," she reminded herself. "I didn't have to lose her to an orphanage. She's worth it all."

She came down to breakfast in a jubilant mood. There was a rare treat in store for Una and herself as Lord Hammersmith had invited them to visit his zoo that morning.

As she seated herself she noticed that Una was struggling to eat her porridge without sugar, in token of punishment. Although she boiled inwardly, she never fought Una's battles, as she felt it was better for the child's happiness not to poison the atmosphere with constant quarrels which could do no good.

"Been bad again?" she remarked cheerfully. "Little silly. Well, sailors don't care, do they? I won't have sugar either. If we are too fat the lions may want to make a meal of us. I heard them roaring in the night. That means fine weather."

"They kept me awake," complained her husband. "That zoo's a scandal. It's a rich man's hobby, or it would be made illegal. It's a source of danger to the district. Eventually one of the wild beasts is bound to escape."

"Escape." The word echoed in Kathy's mind as she gazed at Mint. He was a big burly man with a broad florid face and grizzled curly hair which grew low on his forehead. Twinkling blue eyes gave him a misleading air of geniality which tempered an imposing personality. He looked a model householder and British taxpayer as he read the newspaper and ate the conventional breakfast of bacon and eggs.

Kathy suppressed a sigh. When nature was so lavish, life would be beautiful. If only one had freedom to enjoy it then she thought of Alan, whom she was going to see within a few hours—and the smile returned to her lips.

As though he could read her thoughts, Mint spoke.

"Lucky for that young Easter that his line is zoology. He's his uncle's heir on condition that he carries on the zoo. He's made for life, if he does not run about with women. Hammersmith would never stand for a scandal."

His words sounded so suspiciously like a warning that Kathy wondered whether Mint were also jealous of Alan. She thought she had concealed this new love of hers which was so different from that first selfish rapture of youth. Then she had wanted to take and share—but now she gave her heart without thought or hope of return.

"No woman who cared for him would let him ruin his life for her,," she said.

"You should know how it works out."
As her husband's eyes drilled her face in an effort to interpret its expression. Una broke the silence.

"Molly Dean's daddy has bought her a lovely big Alsatian dog. May I have a dog, Minty?"

"What did you call me?" asked her stepfather.

"'Daddy.' . . . Can I have a dog, Daddy? It needn't be a rich Alsatian. I could find a poor little hungry puppy and bring it home."

"If you do it will be drowned at once. Animals are dirty and unhealthy. I won't have one in my house."

Una stared at her stepfather with puzzled eyes, as though unable to credit such brutality, but she made no attempt to press her claim.

At that moment Kathy saw red. Biting her lips to control her anger, she snatched up the newspaper and began to read it mechanically. Mint wiped his mouth and rose from his chair with a jocular warning.

"Keep your eye on Una. There have been ugly accidents at zoos. Remember the lady of Riga who went for a ride on a tiger?"

Kathy drove the car over to Lord Hammersmith's estate by way of lanes and secondary roads, so as to enjoy the beauty of the countryside.

When they reached the lodge gates of Lord Hammersmith's park Alan was waiting for them on the road. Their greetings were formal—the conventional meeting of any casual young man on his best behaviour and a married lady who was chaperoned by her small daughter. But no social code could disguise the revealing light in his eyes or the glow in her face.

"Lions first," commanded Una. "I love cats."

The lions lived in semi-natural quarters. At the back of their huge cages were low openings leading to the dens scooped in the sides of a ravine which was guarded with spiked bars. When they reached it all the animals had withdrawn to the gloom of their lairs, with the exception of one majestic lion who lay close to the bars of the outer cage, blinking in the sunlight.

"May I speak to him?" asked Una eagerly.

As she ran toward the lion house where the keeper was standing, Alan lowered his voice.

"What's the matter with her?" he asked. "Has she been crying?"

Kathy's heart sank at this further proof of a visible change in Una.

"No," she replied, trying to speak lightly. "Una doesn't cry. She's a tough guy and can take it. But there was a spot of bother at breakfast. She wants a dog."

"I'll give her one."

"No. My husband wouldn't let her keep it."

"Why not?"

"I suppose he doesn't like animals."

His lips tightened as he looked down at her. It seemed to him that she had shrunk since their last meeting—flyweight instead of featherweight. Her dark hair, which she wore in a long, curling bob framed a pale face, now too small for her grey-blue Irish eyes.

"I wish she were mine," he said impulsively.

She knew that he was really thinking of herself. The same instinctive feeling told her that both she and Una could be safe and happy in Alan's care. As she felt herself slipping out to deep waters she floundered desperately back to the shallows.

"You don't know your luck," she assured him. "Una's like me at her age, and I was a little devil on wheels. I was—"

She broke off as Alan gripped her wrist.

"Don't speak or move," he said in a low, strained voice.

Looking up, she saw that he was staring at the lion house. The keeper, too, was gazing in the same direction. Their eyes were fixed on Una.

She had slipped her hand between the bars and was scratching the lion between his eyes.

That moment seemed to draw itself out to an eternity. Everyone stood as though petrified. The landscape appeared frozen to flat dead shades of blue and green—the trees ceased to wave in the breeze. Kathy felt that the scene could not be real, but that they were all confined inside some incredible painting.

Then Una withdrew her hand—and the spell which bound them was snapped. The lion, who had been blinking benevolently, became aware of his audiences. Turning his head he broke out into a shattering roar as Una scampered back to her mother.

"Cats like being tickled," she explained nonchalantly.

"Yes," agreed Kathy faintly. "But the animals are very shy and nervous. Don't touch them again or you will frighten them."

"O, poor little things." Una's voice was compassionate. "I guess I seem terrible to them 'cause I've got boots to kick with and they've only go bare feet."

"Go and see the sea lions feed," suggested Alan.

As Una dashed away with the keeper, Kathy spoke to Alan.

"Is that a savage lion?"

"No," replied Alan. "Jupiter's on the tame side. He will let both me and the keeper stroke him. But he wouldn't let a stranger take a liberty."

"He never touched Una."

"I know. I'm still knocked sideways. The whole thing is incredible. . . . I suppose it was her complete confidence. She must have a natural power over animals. I saw the whole thing. She slipped her hand in between the bars so quietly that she was rubbing him before he realised that it was there. He liked her touch, so he kept quiet. But if we'd startled him there would have been a ghastly accident. As it was I expected every second to see him snap her arm off."

"Don't. It was all my fault. I should have watched her. I was warned."

Reaction had set in as she began to feel the effect of her recent shock. While she fought her emotion, Alan's self-control suddenly slipped like a sandbank undermined by the suction of flood water.

"Darling," he said roughly, "you must leave that man. Don't pretend anymore. I know it's hell. He's eating you up. You and Una must come with me."

She pushed him away as he tried to take her in his arms.

"No," she said. "My husband would not divorce me, so we could not get married. The scandal would finish you. I won't let another man ruin his prospects for me."

"I have my profession. I can get a job."

"A job? So did Dick. And he lost it again. Over and over. O, my dear, you don't know what it means."

To save Alan from his own generous impulse, she tried to appear hard and calculating.

"It's a matter of finance, baby. I'm twenty-six, but I'm far older than you in experience. I've been through all this before. I can't risk poverty again, for Una's sake. When I married again I deliberately chose security in her interests. We must not meet again. It's not fair to you."

She shuddered involuntarily at a familiar trumpet from the elephant house—reminding her of duty.

"It's not fair, either, to my husband," she said firmly, staring miserably at a huge leaden statue of Pan, playing inaudible pipes to a greened unicorn. "I made a bargain—and I must keep it."

"You're mad," protested Alan. "You can't go on with it."

"Hush. . . . Here's Lord Hammersmith."

In other circumstances Kathy would have shrunk from the ordeal of meeting the formidable uncle. The peer wore a disreputable hat—burred with a tangerine rosebud in his buttonhole. His features—verging on the nutcracker—were beakily aristocratic and his eyes arrogant. Kathy received the impression that if his family honour were threatened he would cheerfully feed the source of danger to the lions.

When he heard of Una's escapade he did not conceal his anger.

"Sheer negligence," he fumed. "Suppose this child's arm had to be amputated. There would have been an outcry in the press and fools would have howled for a beautiful creature to be destroyed, when he only obeyed his natural instinct."

"So did Una," said Kathy. "She really loves animals."

"Hmm. She certainly has the magic touch. I must meet this hypnotic young lady."

As they neared the sea lion's pool Una ran up with a request.

"I've seen the lions. Now I want to see the unicorns."

Kathy was thrilled to remark how Una's radiance gradually melted Lord Hammersmith's resentment. He made the rounds with his visitors and at the end of the tour invited them to stay to lunch.

She declined the invitation for herself, but consented to let Una stay.

"Please send her home when she's demoralized the whole zoo," she said. "I can drive myself back."

After Lord Hammersmith made it clear to his nephew that his duties would not permit him to act as deputy chauffeur to their guest, he did Kathy the honour of acting as her personal escort to the lodge.

"When will you pay us another visit?" he asked.

"Not for a long time," she replied. "I don't like zoos."

"I agree." His worldly old eyes approved her. "They can be dangerous."

She resented the meaning in his voice.

"There is no danger here for me," she said proudly. "Especially when all the poor animals are confined in cages."

"Unhappily, caged animals have been known to escape," remarked Lord Hammersmith grimly.

Kathy drove home recklessly, her eyes blind to the beauty of the apple blossom in cottage gardens and the hedges powdered white with may. After she had garaged the car she approached the solid grey stone house slowly and reluctantly. The slam of the front door as it closed behind her reminded her of the clang of iron bars.

Once again she was caged. The hall was dark after the sunshine as the blind was drawn over the stained glass window. She was about to go up to her bedroom when she was arrested by an unusual noise.

It was a cross between a rattle and a gasp and sounded somewhat as though a kettle was boiling over. As it appeared to come from her husband's study, she hurried to the door and flung it open.

Mint was slumped back in his chair, fighting for breath. His face was grey and dripped with sweat—his mouth gaped open like a gasping fish.

"He's dying."

As the thought flashed through Kathy's brain she rushed into the dining room and snatched up the whisky decanter. Supporting her husband's head, she managed to dribble some of the spirit down his throat, drop by drop. It was a slow business, for most of it slopped down his neck, but gradually his heart began to respond to treatment.

After he regained consciousness he recovered rapidly from his fainting fit. By the time the doctor arrived he was almost normal, although his face was still a bad colour. Feeling limp and shaken after her second shock, Kathy left the men together, at her husband's request, and went into the drawing room.

The reek of the whisky was still in her nostrils as, for the first time, she was able to realise the situation, together with its possibilities.

"If I had stayed for lunch—"

She dared not dwell on the consequences lest she should be compelled to admit the horror of her own regret. As she tried to wrench the thought from her mind, Mint entered the room.

"What did the doctor say?" she asked.

"The verdict is satisfactory," he replied. "My condition is static. I have the family heart. I thought I had escaped. It was an unpleasant experience, but I've had my warning."

"I thought your family were all long-lived."

"That is true. We have iron constitutions, but we suffer from valvular disease. It is chiefly dangerous in case of ignorance. When one knows one's vulnerable, one is naturally careful to avoid violent exertion or shock. All my father's family lived to be ninety or more."

It was in vain that Kathy struggled to force her concern and show a decent interest. She knew that she could not speak naturally when she thought of the years that stretched ahead. Years and years of dissension and misery. As though he guessed her thoughts, her husband probed her face with his bright little blue eyes.

"If you had not come in at this minute you would be a widow," he reminded her.

Suddenly she found courage to make an appeal.

"Hector," she said, "you say you owe your life to me. I am going to ask for something in return for it. A very little thing."

"What?"

"A dog for Una."

"Certainly not. You couldn't have done less than you did without being a murderess. Are you going to use a normal instinct as a bargain basis?"

"No . . . . but, Hector, if we are to have a long life together it won't be worth living if we cannot put more happiness into it. I must be to blame too. Will you tell me where I have failed you?"

Mint's smile was acid.

"You failed me before you married me," he replied. "You cared more for that wretched youth's little finger than for my whole body. You can't undo the past."

The following days were charged with misery for Kathy. She knew that if she were to avoid an inevitable crash her future meetings with Alan must be mere casual encounters, in the presence of others. Such a ban meant that loss of much of her remaining happiness. She suffered as acutely from the sudden deprivation as a drug addict from the abrupt cessation of his source of supply.

Although she tried to appear bright for Una's sake, she felt like a butterfly trying to soar with sodden wings. To add to her depression the weather changed overnight. A downpour of rain was followed by damp days.

Her spirits had sunk to zero on one unusually dark day when the sky was covered with layers of black clouds. The weather was so unnatural and the atmosphere of the house so repressive that she felt almost suicidal as she glanced at the paper. Its headlines announced the verdict on a woman who was on trial for poisoning her husband. It found her "Guilty"—but owing to the brutality of the man, recommended her to mercy.

Kathy found herself hoping that the woman would get off scot-free. She mooned about in a kind of bad dream where she was only partially conscious of her surroundings. When she paid her morning visit to the kitchen she displayed none of her usual warm humanity which her husband criticised as lack of dignity. As a rule she took an interest in the maids' remarks, but that day she scarcely heard what they said.

She was also blind to the signs of suppressed excitement in Una during teatime. The child's face was flushed and her eyes were bright with defiant exultation.

Kathy started nervously when the telephone bell rang in the hall.

"Expecting a call?" asked Mint.

"No," she replied indifferently.

A minute later the parlour maid appeared to tell her that she was wanted "on the phone." She almost ran from the room, her heart leaping in anticipation. Directly she recognised Alan's voice it seemed to her, in her strung-up condition, to be a prelude to disaster. She felt certain that he was about to rush over and force an issue with Mint.

"That you, Kathy?" He spoke breathlessly, as though he shared her excitement. "I'm coming over. At once."

"No," she cried, "you must not come. I don't want you. I—"

"But it's urgent. I've something to tell you."

He rang off before she could protest further. As she laid down the receiver she looked up to see her husband standing beside her.

"Who was that?" he asked.

"Alan Easter. He says he's coming over."

"And you tried to stop him. Why? Your manner was most odd. Almost vehement. One would think he had designs on our valuables. Is there anything in this house that he covets?"

"Yes," she replied recklessly. "Una."

"Really? Only Una? When this young man arrives I must have a little enlightening chat with him."

She read the threat underlying his jocose voice. When Alan came, he meant to provoke a distressing scene. Indifferent to the drizzle, she rushed from the house and walked up and down the sodden red gravel and squelching lawn.

"I must warn him," she thought. "I must send him away."

As she pushed open the heavy front gate, to see whether the car was in sight, she heard footsteps behind her. She turned to see the parlour maid who was holding a newspaper over her head to protect her starched frills from the rain.

"Please, madam," she said primly. "Cook wants to know what you've done with the joint?"

"Joint?" repeated Kathy blankly. "Why?"

"It's gone, madam. The whole of it—ribs and sirloin together. And Cook wants to know what's for dinner."

The last sentence recalled Kathy to her domestic responsibility. Her husband was a heavy eater and she knew that there would be pandemonium if an inadequate meal were provided.

She must ring up the butcher and arrange for an express delivery, she said. "Perhaps I had better drive over myself. I'll speak to her."

Directly she opened the front door she became aware that her husband had been informed already of the mystery. He seemed to be holding a kind of furious investigation in the hall where the staff was collected. Una was hiding behind the cook and appeared terrified by his questions.

Kathy flew to her defence.

"Don't be silly, Hector," she said, trying to speak lightly. "Why have you picked on poor Una? She's not responsible for everything that goes wrong. A stray dog must have stolen it."

"Dogs don't open refrigerators," stormed Mint. "Una, did you steal the joint? Now—no lies."

Kathy stared at the child incredulously. To her dismay Una's face was scarlet and her lids drooped to hide her guilty eyes.

"Yes," she admitted in a shaky voice. "I took it for my dog."

As they stared at her she burst into tears.

"I don't care," she sobbed. "He's my dog. I found him. I saw him from the staircase window crawling over the back garden. He's all muddy, but he's a lovely big Alsatian when he's clean. I took the joint out to him—and he was so glad."

"Where is he?" shouted Mint.

"In the woodshed. I brought him a pan of water and some straw and I left him in the dark. He's asleep and you're not to disturb him. He's too tired."

Mint's face was livid with rage as he snatched a heavy stick from the hall stand.

"I'll soon have him out," he said to Una. "I warned you I'd have no dog here."

Kathy caught his arm as he strode toward the side door.

"For pity's sake, let the poor creature rest," she said. "Tomorrow we can decide what to do with it."

Without speaking he flung her aside and went out of the house. As Una rushed after him the cook caught her up in her arms where she struggled in a passion of anger and grief. The other well-trained maids looked on in an uncomfortable silence which was broken by the parlour maid.

"Excuse me, madam, there's a car in the drive. Shall I say 'not at home'?"

Looking up, Kathy saw Alan standing at the open front door. He seemed an answer to prayer as she ran toward him. I'm and panted out her tale. He was quick to catch its drift, for he broke into her explanation.

"A big dog? Where?"

"The woodshed in the back garden. That way."

He shouted to her as he sprinted around the side of the house.

"Everyone stay indoors."

Kathy returned to the drawing room and dropped limply down on the divan. For the present she had forgotten the complications of the situation. She merely accepted the fact that her troubles were over because Alan was there. . . .

Suddenly she opened her eyes at the sound of a long-drawn howl in the distance.

It was followed by silence. As she waited—listening—her scalp tightened and her temples grew cold. Then the room seemed to break apart and the fragments to whirl around her. Sometimes she knew she was staring at the cream wall paper—at others, her surroundings were blacked out.

After a long while she became conscious of Alan kneeling beside her and chafing her hands.

"Did you hear?" he whispered.

She nodded.

"Yes, I know. It was a wolf. Is Hector dead?"

"Dead from shock. It never mauled him. I was at his heels and I saw the whole thing. It sprang, but he collapsed first. I called it off at once but he was dead. . . . Was his heart weak?"

"Yes."

In imagination Kathy reconstructed the grim tragedy. The big bully, bursting into the shed to drive out an exhausted, starving dog, only to be confronted by a nightmare vision; green eyes glowing like points of fire through the gloom and a dark shape reared up to spring.

Then she vaguely realised that Alan was speaking.

"The wolf escaped from our zoo some days ago. I was away on the Continent and knew nothing about it until I returned today. I came out to warn you about it, for I was afraid it might be a shock if I told you over the wire. But I suppose you heard the rumours?"

"No. . . . Yes," answered Kathy." I remember now the maids were excited over something this morning, but I didn't listen."

She broke off with a faint scream.

"Where's Una?"

"In the kitchen with Cook," Alan told her. "I've just been talking to her."

"She might have been killed," shuddered Kathy. "She went in to that wolf. She thought he was an Alsatian dog. Why didn't he attack her?"

"Because he was gorged with meat, besides being exhausted. He probably was glad to be back in shelter. He's used to captivity."

"He sprang at Hector. Yet he never touched her."

Her eyes were awed as though she glimpsed a miracle. Although he did not share her exaltation, Alan felt he could not drag her down to a commonplace level.

"Do you remember how Una stroked the lion?" he asked. "She has a certain quality which wins the instinctive confidence of animals. She is fearless and she loves them. They know that. All the same"—his voice sank to a mutter—"I'm thankful she threw Pluto the joint first."

Then he rose to his feet.

"I must ring up the zoo and have the motor lorry sent out with his cage," he said. "My uncle will be glad there was no tragedy. Pluto is an unusually fine specimen and he would have been upset if I had been forced to shoot him."

"No tragedy?" Kathy's eyes reproached him. "You forget—Hector is dead."

As they looked at each other in silence Una burst into the room. She was transformed with her old radiance which lit up her whole face. Her cheeks were flushed—her eyes beamed with happiness.

"Cook says Minty's dead," she cried joyously. "I can have a puppy now."

Before Kathy could protest Alan took the child in his arms.

"Why should we be hypocrites?" he asked. "We can learn from Una. She sees only the truth. You are free."

BLACKOUT

The blackout over London was nearly absolute. When Christina drew aside the window curtains of the sitting room, at first she could distinguish nothing. It was as though a wall had been built up outside the glass. As her eyes grew accustomed to the darkness she saw the dimmed lights of traffic and glowworm gleams speckling the pavement, cast by the electric torches of invisible pedestrians. Her nerves were somewhat frayed, owing to lack of sleep. She went to bed late because she was afraid of a recurrent nightmare. It was always the same dream. She found herself walking down an unknown road, in absolute darkness—with the knowledge that she had a long distance to go. Suddenly she felt herself gripped by invisible hands—when the horror always shook her awake.

She was furious over this leakage of energy at a time when she needed all her reserves of strength. Recently she had the honour of a personal interview with Mr. T.P. Fry—a younger member of the firm which owned the factory. It took place in his private room, when the august man explained the facts.

"Every country in war time," he said, "is subject to the abuse of sabotage. The scum of a nation will always seize its chance to profit. To protect our interests in the factory we have organised some of our most trusted workers as counter-espionage agents."

Christina thrilled as she listened, although his next sentence conveyed a warning.

"The work requires courage and discretion. You remain anonymous and—in your own interests—you must not try to make contacts. You should take extra precautions against accidents inside the factory and not go out in the blackout, if you can avoid it. You may be followed by malcontents. . . . No extra pay—but I hope there will be a bonus at the end of the war."

After the minimum of reflection, Christina volunteered for the special service. Instead of dull routine, she felt elevated to something in the John Buchan tradition. At first, although she was especially zealous in the prevention of carelessness, she made no exposures.

But—as though her vigilance had been marked as inconvenient to the cause of sabotage, a few days previously she had been nearly the victim of an accident.

One of the girls had turned faint, and, in the general rush to help her, Christina had been pushed up against a machine. . . . For a terrible moment her heart felt iced, before a worker switched off the mechanism.

When she went over the incident she felt doubtful about one of the Good Samaritans who had dragged her to safety. Meta Rosenburg was a thin, attractive brunette, slant-eyed and overpainted.

Christina shared the expenses of a flat with Ida Brown—a plump, reliable girl. That evening she was looking around at the comfort of the room with its fire and softly glowing lights when the telephone bell began to ring. As she went to answer it a warning sense reminded her that ambushes were always prepared by fake invitations. Primed by her intuition, she was scarcely surprised to hear Meta's deep, husky voice at the other end of the line.

"I'm throwing a sherry party. Come over."

"No thanks," she replied, "I don't drink."

"But you must come. Montrose is here. He wants to know you."

Christina's heart beat faster, for—like all the girls at the factory—she was attracted by Montrose. He held an important position and was tall and handsome. There was also a legend about him that he had been an air ace before a smash which took a mysterious toll but thoughtfully left no visible marks.

Before Christina could protest Meta rang off.

"You shouldn't keep on saying 'no,'" advised Ida Brown, who always listened to telephone conversations. "Snap out of it. Go to this sherry party."

"I don't know where she lives."

"I'll look her up in the telephone book."

"Thanks . . . I will."

Christina told herself that it was important to reassure Ida, lest—in perfect innocence—she might start the first fatal whisper. In reality, however, it was the thought of Montrose's handsome face which lured her out into the blackout.

She put on an ice-blue frock and made up her face with delicate care. While she was slipping on a near white coat, Ida came into the bedroom to tell her the number of her bus.

"I've written down the address and put it in your gas mask carrier," she explained. "You get off at the terminus."

Her journey was reduced to such a simple and effortless proposition that she felt ashamed of her former hesitation. But as she stood in the doorway of the entrance hall of the mansions, waiting to accustom her eyes to the darkness, a man nearly knocked her down.

Both laughed at the encounter, but she felt exactly as though she had bumped into the invisible man. It was with a return of her old inhibition that she snailed along the pavement.

She reached her starting point, only to realise the handicap of her poor eyesight. Other people boarded the vehicles while she remained on the pavement, running from bus to bus as fresh ones drew up at the half. Unable to see their numbers, she always left it too late and boarded them, to be told by the conductor, "Full up."

She was thinking rather desperately of Montrose when someone flashed a torch over the face of the crowd. It cursed him as one man, although—as the bus was stationary—there was no risk of an accident. Christina blinked at the tiny search-light with a sense that her identity had been revealed. Her mind flooded with morbid wonder as to whether Ida were in league with Meta to lure her into a trap.

Her turn had come at last. She felt herself borne upwards to the step on a human surge and then pressed forward into a darkened interior.

"Where's the empty seat?" she appealed. "I can't see a thing."

Helpful hands passed her along the aisle and drew her down on a seat beside a stout woman who smelt strongly of cloves.

"There you are, lady."

With the comfortable sensation of being enclosed in the safety of an ark—tossing on a stormy sea—she felt the bus move onward. From now on the driver would have the headache. She was merely a fare—his responsibility.

They journeyed on through the black blanket, occasionally stopping with a back-breaking jerk to avoid some too optimistic pedestrian. Presently, as the stout lady continued to overlap her, Christina felt as though she were slowly smothered by a feather bed. Her chance of release came when a semi-visible young man who sat on the opposite side—level with their seat—leaned across the side.

"Change places with me, Mother," he urged. "I want to sit by my young lady."

"Right you are, duck," consented the lady.

Christina waited for the exchange to be made before she spoke softly to her slimmer neighbour.

"I'm afraid I must break it to you. I'm not your friend."

"I know," said the young man. "I had to take a chance on you. I saw your face when someone flashed a torch. I knew I could trust you."

Although his voice was uneven—either pitched to a crack or blurred to thickness—his accent was educated and inspired her with confidence.

"What do you mean?" she asked distantly.

"When I tell you, you'll think me mad," he said.

"I do already. . . . Or drunk."

"Not drunk. No, I'm drugged. . . . Like a fool, I had a drink with a man. He's following me on this bus. . . . But you must see who you are backing—and use discretion."

Before she could protest he lit a cigarette. In the flame of the match she saw a face which was too charming and delicate for a man. Its oval shape—combined with fair hair and large blue eyes—suggested some universal younger brothers who needed cuddling and protection.

"I seem to know your face," she said. "Are you at Fry's munition factory?"

"Yes," he replied eagerly. "I'm a draughtman there. You've probably seen me in the canteen."

Then he lowered his voice to a whisper.

"Are you one of us?" he asked.

She scented a trap in time to avoid it.

"Yes, I work there," she said coldly.

"Then you are in this, too. . . . Listen carefully. I've a letter here. It's desperately important. Secret service. I got involved—never mind how. . . . You must take it to Bengal Avenue, sixth house on the left. It's the second stop. The man is waiting to pounce on me when I leave the bus. But he won't suspect you."

Christina grew wretchedly uncomfortable as she listened. If she had not been enrolled for confidential service at the factory she would have been immune to suggestion. Now, however, she was susceptible, because she admitted to herself that the young man's story could be true. Stolen documents, espionage, secret agents—these were the phantasy of peace but the commonplace of war.

She struggled desperately to get free of the coils.

"Don't talk like a film," she said. "I can't swallow that melodramatic stuff from a stranger."

"But you dare not refuse." The young man's voice was stern. "It is not for myself. It is for England. . . . Do you remember the address?"

"Of course not. I don't need it."

Heedless of her refusal, he tore a leaf from his notebook, and after scrawling on it stuffed it inside her gas mask carrier.

"That's enough to remind you," he said, blinking his eyes. "My head's beginning to buzz. Thank heaven I lasted long enough to contact you. Look. That man—by the door. He's waiting for me."

The vehicle was too dimly lit to distinguish faces, but straining her eyes in the gloom, Christina saw a tall man whose hard felt hat was jammed over his eyes. He was strap hanging near the door; but as the bus slackened speed he stepped out on to the platform. As he was above average height, he had to stoop slightly to scrutinize the passengers who were getting off at the stage. This crouching posture gave him an appearance of tense vigilance which made the girl think of a jungle beast on the hunt.

"I'll call the the conductor," she whispered to the young man.

The words roused him out of his lethargy.

"For heaven' sake, no," he implored. "Don't start anything like that. The chap would plug him—and then us. We haven't got a chance in the dark. It's up to you. You—must—"

Suddenly his head jerked forward and then drooped, while his eyes closed. As she listened to his heavy breathing, Christina wondered what she ought to do. Self interest, as well as common sense, told her to keep out of the mess and continue on her way to the sherry party. On the other hand, in a remote lighted corner of her brain, was a reminder that Meta's invitation might be a trap. In such a case this mission—which involved her in no danger—might be a providential intervention.

There was a third consideration which outweighed the others. The youth had spoken the truth when he said that she dared not accept the responsibility of inaction, if there was the slightest chance to prevent some vital leakage.

"Your friend's having a nap," grinned the conductor as he came up the aisle.

"Not mine," she said quickly.

As she disclaimed him, the man in the felt hat was swift to seize his chance.

"That's all right, mate," he said to the conductor. "My pal and I will see him home. He's had one over the eight."

This dramatic fulfillment of the young man's fears spurred Christina to immediate action. She dared not extract the secret document from the young man's gas mask carrier, lest she should fumble and attract the attention of the nearest passenger. Such an action might look like an attempt to rob a drunken man. Snatching up the young man's gas mask carrier from the seat—in exchange for her own—she groped her way to the door, where she waited for the next stop.

Fortunately the conductor did not remember her usual stop, since in the blackout one girl looked much like another. He lowered her down on the pavement as though she were a precious consignment. Then she heard the ping of his bell and the bus rolled on its way.

In contrast with the subdued lighting of the vehicle, the surrounding blackness seemed pitch black as the depths of a coal mine; but after flicking her torch about she discovered the name "Bengal Avenue," printed on the corner of a wall. The bus had dropped her on the lefthand side of the road, so she had only to walk straight ahead.

It was also a very lonely locality, for as she followed long stretches of stone wall, partially revealed by light of her torch, she met no one, she heard no footsteps—no voices—no hoot of passing car.

"Every one might be dead," she thought.

For the sake of morale she told herself that there was light and life inside each blacked out exterior. Civilisation still functioned, for she had only to ring at a door to get in touch with humanity again. Probably, if she cared to deliver her document personally at the sixth house—instead of dropping it into the letter box—she would meet with a welcome.

"I suppose he lives here with his family," she thought.

In order to settle the point she scraped his identification card from a pocket of the carrier—fishing out two Yale latchkeys to get hold of it.

"Why two?" she wondered.

She knew the reason—or thought she did—after she had read the particulars about the young man in the bus, by the light of her torch. She discovered that his name was "Ivor Thomas" and that he lived in a north London suburb. Apparently No. 6 was an accommodation address, or belonged to a close friend, since he appeared to possess its key as well as his own.

She plodded on doggedly through the darkness, although she was beginning to wish she were not pledged to the adventure. At the back of her mind was a feeling of apprehension, while she was also teased by a sense of familiarity.

"I know this place," she thought. "But when have I been here before?"

The answer crashed from the depths of her inner consciousness. This was her nightmare. There was the same long, endless road—the utter blackness—the total loneliness. It only lacked the horror of gripping hands.

But those came later—in the dream.

She began to run—the fixity of her purpose propelling her on instead of turning back. It was panic flight which burned itself out, for when she was forced to stop her heart was leaping as much from exertion as fright. She had reached No. 6, which was also named "Elephant House" and had two roughly carved elephants surmounting its gateposts to demonstrate its claim to the title.

With the feeling that her ordeal was nearly over—for her run back to the bus stop would seem much shorter—she pushed open the heavy gate. As she groped her way up the drive the small dancing light of her torch revealed a general appearance of desertion and neglect. The front door steps were dirty and the brass knocker had not been cleaned recently.

It was no surprise, therefore, to find that the slit to the letter box was blocked.

"I must unload this darn document," she decided. "It's too jolly risky to carry it around with me."

Once again she hooked up the two Yale keys, one of which fitted the lock. It turned easily as she pushed open the door and stepped inside into that total darkness.

The precaution of shutting herself in, after she had slipped the key back in the carrier, was a test of her courage; but it was not until she felt secure from outside observation that she flashed her light around.

The next second she suppressed a scream as she stepped backward in an instinctive movement to save herself from being trampled underfoot. Towering above her—from the wall—was the head of an enormous bull elephant with gleaming tusks and upraised trunk. It dominated the most extraordinary hall she had ever seen.

It was screened with fretted woodwork and hung with the stuffed heads of wild beasts, as well as weapons.

"What a bloody place," she murmured. "The home of Anglo-Indians, I should think. Wonder if the sahibs are at home."

Flashing her torch, first low and then high, he saw a dusty Indian carpet—partially covered with drugget—and a flight of stairs leading to a landing on which was posed a black marble statue. Beyond was a shorter flight of steps, the top of which was wiped out by shadows.

"Hullo. Anyone there?"

Christina's hail was weak and tremulous, revealing that she was afraid of the empty house.

There was no answer to her call. Feeling that she had fulfilled her duty in England, she listened to the warning voice which told her to get out of the house and rush back to safety.

"Run—run."

She was about to place the document on a carved teak table when she noticed that she had torn a corner of the envelope in her extraction of the keys from the carrier. As she stared at the flimsy paper she was assailed by doubt. It looked so unofficial that she told herself that she must see the contents before she left it.

Feeling guilty of crime, she ripped open the envelope—to reveal what she had dreaded to find—tracings.

They confirmed her suspicion. Ivor Thomas was a rat who was stealing the factory's secrets. The men in the bus were trailing him; but to save himself from being caught with the evidence, he had fooled them and tricked her into taking it to his hiding place.

Slipping the document into her coat pocket, she was about to rush from the house when she was startled by a noise from above. It was a heavy thud, as though a statue had crashed down from its pedestal. With a recollection of the figure on the landing, she flashed her torch upwards.

What she saw drained the blood from her heart. . . . A stiff, white shapeless bundle—like a corpse—was rolling down the stairs.

At that moment she understood the hypnotic force of shock. She wanted to flee, but her muscles were locked so that she could not stir, although the thing was drawing nearer to her. Bumping from step to step, it reached the landing, where it lay—formless, without face or limbs, muffled in its burial clothes.

As she stood and stared, suddenly Christina thought she detected a quiver in the object. . . Goaded by the elemental duty to make certain whether life was really extinct, she began to mount the stairs.

Kneeling beside the human parcel, she wrenched away a fold of linen and exposed the shriveled, sunburnt face of an elderly woman with an arrogant nose. Her brave old eyes smouldered in token of an unbroken spirit as Christina first tore away the scarf over her mouth and then dragged from her blackened lips the pad with which she had been gagged.

The woman drew a deep breath, gasping like a fish.

"Thank heaven I'm a nose-breather," she gasped. "I was choking. I heard you call—and I managed to make it under my own steam."

"Who are you?" asked Christina.

"Miss Monteagle. This house belongs to my brother—the general. We were in Cornwall when war broke out and we stayed on. I came up to see the house. . . . I was attacked by thugs. Two of them." Her face grew suddenly tense as she added, "I can hear them in the cellars. Get help at once."

"But I can't leave you—"

"Quick. No time to loosen knots. If you can't make it, hide. Watch your chance to escape. . . . Cover my face."

Although Christina lacked Miss Monteagle's uncanny faculty of hearing, she realised the urgency. After winding the corner of the sheet around the elder woman's head she rushed down the stairs. The hall was clear, but before she could reach the door a series of knocks on the wood told her that Ivor Thomas was outside.

She was caught between two fires. The thugs had heard the summons and the sound of their footsteps in the distance was audible to her. Desperately flashing her torch around, she darted behind the velvet curtain which muffled a door—praying the while that the men would not come that way.

Her petition was mercifully granted, for the men entered through a low door at the rear. Although she could see nothing, Christina guessed that they carried a lamp from the faint glow which sprayed around the corner of the portiere. Then she heard the catch withdrawn and someone entered the house.

"Has the girl left the plans?" asked Ivor Thomas—his voice cracking with excitement.

Without waiting for a reply, he dashed to the letter box.

"Hell, it's nailed up," he complained.

"Sure, we had to pick an empty house," growled one of the men. "What's this about a girl?"

It was no satisfaction to Christina to learn that her suspicions were confirmed, since she was trapped and unable to save the plans. As Thomas told his story, she realised that he was cowed by the other men and eager to justify his action.

"The girl will come back when she finds the key," he assured them. "She fell for it all right. Besides, it worked. The dicks had to let me go. The laugh was on them."

"Did they follow you?" asked a new voice.

"Hell, no. Why? They found nothing on me."

As she listened, Christina noticed the difference between the voices of the two men. One was gruff and fierce, but the other frightened her more, because of its flat, inhuman quality. It was as though a dead man spoke from the grave.

She trembled violently as this second man made a discovery.

"I can see the marks of high heels in the dust. That girl has been here. Look around."

Even as Christina realised the horror of the situation, Miss Monteagle came into action. Risking a broken neck, she flexed her muscles in a supreme effort to distract attention. The men in the hall heard a thud from the upper darkness—outside the radius of their lamp—followed by the gruesome spectacle of a corpselike object rolling down the stairs.

As Thomas gave a high, thin scream, like a trapped rabbit, Christina realised her signal to escape. Not daring to creep toward the entrance, lest a man should turn his head, she leaped lightly over the thick pile of the carpet. Drawing back the catch of the lock, she slipped through the gap and drew the door softly to—fearing to shut it.

Once she was outside, she began to run, her high heels turning perilously on the slippery drive. She lost precious time in opening the heavy gate and barely reached the road before the sound of heavy footsteps in the distance told her that she was being followed.

Maddened by terror, she rushed on wildly, praying for help; but the road was as deserted as before. There was no welcome torchlight advertising an A.R.P. warden on his round—no resident returning to his home. It was useless to scream—hopeless to hide in a garden; she knew that the glimmer of her white coat was visible and that if she tore it off her ice-blue frock would betray her.

Realising that capture was inevitable, she determined that the men should not get the drawings; and since she could be tortured into revelation of their hiding place, she must put them in a safe place.

Suddenly she remembered that—on her way to Elephant House—she had passed a pillar box. Running blindly and keeping to the outside edge of the pavement, she collided with it before she saw it. The crash of the impact winded her completely, but before she collapsed she managed to push the envelope through the slit.

Then she felt herself gripped by unseen hands, in ghastly fulfillment of her nightmare.

After an interlude of strain and semi-suffocation, when—blinded by a coat over her head, she had been bumped along through the darkness—she realised that she was back in the hall of Elephant House. She looked around her fearfully, hardly daring to glance at a white shape doubled up at the foot of the stairs, because of its hideously unnatural posture.

With the exception of Thomas, the men had concealed their faces with dark scarves, while their eyes gleamed through slits in the material; but she recognised their tones.

It was the dead voice that spoke to her.

"Where is that envelope? If you don't talk, I can make you."

"O, I'll talk," she said with faint triumph. "I posted it in the pillar box."

"Very clever," he sneered. "You may like to hear you've killed a man by that master stroke."

"Who? How?"

"The postman. . . If we force the box it might attract attention. We will let him unlock it for us and then make sure he won't talk."

Christina stared at him in horror.

"It's all my fault. My fault."

She sat thinking, thinking—until her brain ceased to function. She had grown dead to emotion when she was startled back to life by the sound of knocking at the front door. It was so loud and persistent that the dead voice whispered a command.

"Gag the girl. Open the door, Thomas, and stall."

Nearly choked by the handkerchief which was roughly forced down her throat, Christina was dragged back into the shadow. She heard the door being opened a few inches and then Meta Rosenburg's voice.

"Where's Christina Forbes?" she demanded.

"Never heard of her," replied Ivor Thomas.

"You will. . . . The police are here. Come on, boys."

At the sound of a shot, Christina closed her eyes. She kept them closed throughout the sensational fight which followed and did not open them until her gag was removed by her rescuing hero—Montrose.

Later in the evening she sat in Meta's flat. Montrose was there as well as Miss Monteagle, who smoked a cigar and drank most of the sherry. The postman had already finished his round in safety, after having delivered an unstamped envelope to the detectives from the munition factory.

"Sorry my diversion failed to let you get clear away," remarked the sporting lady to Christina. "You made a hell of a noise. I'll never take you stalking. . . . Lucky I didn't break my neck. I've broken every other bone hunting, but I'm reserving that for my last fence."

"You were wonderful," Christina assured her, although her eyes spoke to Montrose.

"Want to know how the masterminds found you?" cut in Meta. "Thomas left your gas mask behind in the bus, since he was bound to be searched. He reckoned that when the conductor found it and took it to lost property there would be nothing to connect it with him. But an A.R.P. warden was on the bus and he spotted it and looked at your identification card. He's a bright local lad—and knows me by sight—so when he found an envelope with my address on it, it seemed a good excuse to bring it around, as my flat was near."

As she stopped to refill the glasses, Montrose finished the tale.

"Meta got rattled, as you hadn't turned up, while your gas mask proved you were on the bus. Fortunately, we discovered a scrap of paper stuck in your carrier with 'Bengal 6' scrawled on it. That gave us the idea where you'd got out."

"It's wonderful," repeated Christina, still looking at Montrose. "The funny part is, I suspected Meta, when really she is one of us."

Meta burst out laughing.

"Us?" she repeated. "You're too nice to be a mug. That sabotage-espionage is T.P's bright stunt to make the girls careful with the machinery. I know, because he's a relative of mine. Of course, the firm employs trained detectives."

"O!" Christina's mouth drooped with disappointment. "It was such a thrill to feel part of the war."

"Never mind," said Miss Monteagle. "I'm dated, so I can afford to spout Kipling, although I can't say I'm quoting word for word. . .

Two things greater than all things are,
The first is love and the second is war,
And since we know not what war may prove—

Intercepting the message flashing between Christina and Montrose, her bass voice softened to the tones of a girl who had vanished into the past as she finished the quotation:

Heart of my heart, let us speak of love.

"So this is a pothole," gasped Iris.

She was sunken below sun-level in a vast cavern of rock, chill with damp and earthy odours. Only the dimmest light filtered through a small hole in the roof—from which trickled a shrunken waterfall. But although she was muddy, breathless, and soaked to the skin, she felt the special thrill which accompanies achievement.

"Pothole?" repeated her companion scornfully. "What d'you mean? We're only in the daylight shaft. This is where the pothole begins. I'll show you."

The young engineer gripped her arm and they stumbled together across the slimed floor, following up the course of the streamlet from the fall until it disappeared down a wide fissure in the rocks.

"At the bottom of that fall is an eternal pothole which is pitch dark," Courage explained. "It will lead you down to another, and so on, down and down, until the stream disappears down a crack too narrow to follow it—or until the ropes give out—or until any old thing happens."

"And you mean to tell me you go down horrible holes like that for pleasure?" asked Iris incredulously. "It seems to me a specially morbid and debased way of committing suicide."

Courage laughed.

"Potholing is a bug, like any other philia," he said. "You have it or you haven't."

He knew that it was hopeless to try to explain to her the magnetism in the sound of that chuckling water which was an elusive thread, leading down to hidden treasure. Here, in Pothole Land— the Cumberland Dales—a vast region of subterranean wonderland had been already explored. Huge stalactite caverns, lakes streams and more than two miles of connecting passages.

But there remained still the lure of finding some new entry down some insignificant hole which might drop down hundreds of feet in one sheer swoop. There was also the eternal hope of the pioneer—to be first to stumble on some new enchanted territory.

Even then, it might be lying under his feet—waiting for him to discover it. Voices called to him from the halls of darkness.

Although he was a keen Alpinist and rarely missed a holiday in Switzerland, the joys of mountain-climbing lacked this thrill of exploration. As he strained his eyes to look at Iris through the gloom, he longed to share his secret passion with her. He had known her for less than a fortnight yet already she seemed so vital to his happiness that his mind shied at the prospect of a future apart from her.

She had been tramping the Fells without a hat and her face was very brown, making a piquant contrast with her fair hair. Essentially a modern girl with a mechanical mind, she was employed at an aircraft factory and had the hard muscles and the unself-conscious camaraderie of one accustomed to work with men.

Lately Courage had wished that her blue eyes were not so friendly and impersonal.

"Don't you ever climb?" he asked.

"Definitely no," she replied. "I've no head for heights. Something goes funny inside me. I fly, of course, but that's different. My job is on the ground and I feel safer there. . . . Let's get out of this tomb."

Although Courage remained below, to steady the rope ladder, she found its ascent both a tricky and humiliating performance. Whenever her shoe slipped on the narrow five-inch tread, she upset the precarious balance and either swayed under the fall or bruised herself against the rock.

It was a relief to get into the open air which was cooled by the spray from the Pharisee (Fairy) Fall. The great cascade foamed like a pillar of smoke down into the gorge, whose sides—emerald green with soaked ferns and vegetation—were hung with small trees, rowans, bird-cherries, and birch. After plunging into a deep pool at its bottom, it rushed down into the valley in a small river.

In spite of its present volume, it had shrunk so far below its normal flow that it sealed no longer the mouth to the pothole. Courage explained the situation to Iris when he rejoined her.

"It's about eight years since it's been possible to get near the pothole," he said. "A chap called Riley discovered it, but he had to give up for lack of ropes."

The climb up the gorge was heavy going, which left no surplus breath for conversation as they toiled out of the cool and shadowed radius of the spray. When they reached the path again, the sun beat down on them from a cloudless sky. The turf was scorched and the hills blurred by a thick blue soupy atmosphere, as though the heat had become visible.

"Today's going to be a real scorcher," panted Iris as she caught her heel in a crack in the baked earth. "Don't you wish it would rain?"

"I should say not," replied Courage. "I'm praying for this blessed drought to last. It's the chance of a lifetime to explore the Pharisee Pot again. There's still too much overflow from the fall."

"Are you really going down that awful drop into the dark? You must be crazy."

"Call it 'potty.' Yes, it's all fixed. Riley—the chap who did it before—young Collier and myself."

"Young Collier? That precious youth? I don't believe it."

"Oh, he's got guts all right, in spite of his pretty face. I sup-pose as you're a native, you've a down on him because his old man is living in your squire's ancestral hall."

"I'm not that sort of mouldy snob. No, my grouch is this: When Granny rented her cottage from his father, the conveyance covered adequate water rights. Now we're dry as a bone, while he's built a swimming pool. It doesn't make sense. I believe he's poaching our spring."

"That's a dangerous charge," Courage reminded her. "Can you prove it?"

"How can I? Gran is helpless. If she tried to pump any of Collier's men, or approached the local surveyor, he'd get to hear of it and then he wouldn't renew her lease. It would break her up to leave her beloved hovel."

"Well, don't be hasty. Water is a very tricky thing. This drought may have caused your spring to break out somewhere else. I'm an engineer, so I know something about it."

"And all I know is this: I've got to go to old hat in my hand, to beg for some water. Gosh, what a prospect for any girl of spirit.

They parted at a hurdle-gate at the union of two tracks. One led up to the Hall—a fine Elizabethan mansion, now the property of Sir Henry Collier, late of the Baltic Pool. For the past fortnight, Courage had been a guest at this house, so naturally was prejudiced in favor of the genial and hospitable host.

The other path wound down to a whitewashed cottage, rented by Iris' grandmother—an active, independent lady of sixty-two. It was only an accident to her leg which caused her to accept the services of her grandchild, who had given up her own holiday to look after her.

The sacrifice had proved to be not altogether a loss for she had met Courage, but the continuance of the drought was gradually getting her down. It had lasted now for weeks. First, the flowers had to be sacrificed—a hopeful collection of buds. Then the daily bath was replaced by a piecemeal wash in a basin. After that, vegetables had to take their chance, while most of them lost out. Now it had become a problem how to ration the drinking water to include the fowls and dog.

With the end of her holiday in sight, Iris was worried about the future. It was only the thought of her grandmother's disability which forced her to turn out in the afternoon heat and eat humble pie.

After the glare of the unprotected falls, it was a relief to walk under the shade of the lime avenue which led up to the Hall. She noticed enviously the vivid green of the lawn in front of the house and the beautiful flower beds. On her way, she also passed the new swimming pool which was lined with turquoise tiles.

She told herself that it held sufficient water to preserve the cottage garden for the duration of the drought. Her young lips were stern as she glanced contemptuously at two slim forms in bathing suits, stretched out on the grass. One was young Collier—a youth with a handsome slack face; the other was an exotic girl from London, whose skin was painted to get the same effect as the suntanned Iris.

There was no sign of Courage—a fact which disconcerted her, since she had counted on his moral support. Sir Henry Collier, however, was lounging in a deck-chair on the terrace.

He was a pleasant-faced, well preserved man in the fifties, with wavy silvery hair and a double chin. In his early struggling days he had been a thin, acid young man, full of snap and drive, and although prosperity had mellowed him, there was still a glint in his eye which hinted of the original wire structure under his genial overweight.

He welcomed Iris with the cordiality of a host to an honoured guest. Feeling slightly awkward, as though he had placed her in a false position, she refused his offers of varied refreshment.

"Really not, thank you," she persisted. "I only came to tell you that we've practically no water."

"No drinking water?" asked Sir Henry.

"Yes, we have that, but—"

"Then you must consider yourself lucky, when you think of the drought."

"I know. . . . But I have to walk a quarter of a mile to the village to get water for domestic purpose. Our garden is dying on us. Please, could you spare us a little of your surplus?"

"I don't know what you mean. If I had any surplus, my tennis courts would not be ruined."

"But that swimming pool—!"

"Oh, my dear young lady, don't look at me with such accusing eyes. I built that pool as a storage tank, in case of fire. Indirectly, it benefits you, for we could run a pipe down to the cottage."

He stopped, as though waiting for the gratitude she could not force. She felt beaten down and incapable of making a further stand as he went on talking.

"You can't blame me for the drought. It was an Act of God. It has dried up one of my best wells, but I am only too thankful for what is left. You must keep your chin up. I've always been on pleasant terms with your grandmother and I should be sorry to lose her for a more sporting tenant who would take the rough with the smooth. And don't forget it was I who put in the bathroom for her—not the old squire."

"Yes, that was kind. There is no water in the pipes, but it looks very nice."

"And so do you—very fit and charming from all your extra excercise. I walked ten miles a day, to and from work, when I was young. Are you sure you won't have tea."

"No, thank you." Her voice was bitter. "I only want water."

He took the request seriously and rang for a glass of ice water— Iris decided that it was impossible to impress such a man.

That evening Courage met her as she was toiling up the path from the village. She wore breeches and looked hot and limp as she carried two slopping pails of water.

"Where were you this afternoon?" she asked reproachfully, as he took the buckets from her.

"Out on a private prowl," he told her. "How did you get on with Collier?"

"I didn't. I got out. All he did was to hint that I couldn't take it. Well, I'm not sporting and I still believe he has pinched our spring."

Courage frowned thoughtfully.

"Even if he has," he said, "litigation over water rights is the very mischief. If you prove your claim—and experts usually differ—Collier could hardly take it for a friendly gesture. Directly your grandmother's lease was up, she'd be outside on her ear. So how's it going to help you?"

"I know, but I'm bothered about the future. This will happen every drought, and Gran can't carry water."

"Oh, buck up." Collier may have a change of heart. Any way, this heat is bound to crack soon with thunder. . . . That's why we are having a shot at the Pharisee Pot tomorrow.

"Tell me all about it. Do you go much deeper than that horrible black drop?"

"Deeper?" Courage laughed jubilantly. "That's only the entrance hall, with 'Welcome' on the mat. When we're down that, we come to a filthy crawl over the bed of a stream—which should be dry if it knows what's expected of it—along a passage which is nothing but a drain out to a main chamber. Then comes the clinking long drop which Riley couldn't tackle. I hope to be able to report its exact length and what's at the bottom of it tomorrow."

"Any—any danger?"

"Practically none. We're all experienced climbers. You've got to be very fit for potholing—and you've got to be slim or you'd stick. If you think of joining us, don't wear your crinoline. Of course, we've got to check up on ropes, food, lights and so on. If they are O.K. we shall be O.K., too, except for—"

"Go on," she told him.

"Well, if a storm broke up in the hills, we might get our feet wet."

Iris said nothing. Her eyes were wide with terror as she pictured the sudden rush of flood-water down the valley, as she had seen it once before. She saw it thunder over the Pharisee Fall, rushing down the holes and cracks at its base—flooding underground passages—filling every chamber.

"What's the matter?" asked Courage.

"I'm afraid." Her voice was low and husky. "Don't go. For my sake."

He shook his head.

"You're putting me on the spot," he said. "I don't want you to be worried over me. I would rather make you happy. But honestly, you don't know what this chance is to a potholer. Besides, there is no risk. We shall phone up to the hills, to get the weather report before we start."

"All right." Iris forced herself to speak in the voice familiar to all in the aircraft factory, where she claimed equality with men. "Good luck."

Iris was not the only person to sleep badly that night, for the heat was oppressive. She kept getting out of bed to watch from her window, in the hope of seeing a flicker of lightning as herald of a thunderstorm. Her prayers were not granted, for after a short sleep, she awoke to another cloudless sky, from which all colour was drained.

"Do you smell rain?" she asked, when she carried the morning tea in to her grandmother.

The small, alert lady who was already knitting in bed, so as to waste no time, looked at her over steel-rimmed spectacles.

"You insolent child. I'm not a witch doctor," she protested. "Besides, any fool must know this heat will break in a storm. Probably tomorrow. I'm afraid it will skin the face off the garden, but it will get right down to the roots, thank God."

"Good. We want another dry day. Some boys are going down the Pharisee Pothole."

"That's fine news. Good lads."

No lack of sporting spirit there—but Iris failed to feel responsive to the local passion. Although every domestic task—complicated by lack of water —seemed drudgery, she tried to forget her apprehension in a drive of furious energy.

Directly after lunch, she changed into shorts in order to fetch their daily ration of water. Just as she was about to start, she saw Sir Henry Collier sauntering down the hillside. He looked so aggres-sively cool and freshly-tubbed in his suit of tropical silk that she felt she could not endure to walk to the village in his company. She was loitering by the gate when he called out to her.

"The climbing party went off in fine spirits. They showed sense in not waiting. It's looking rather dark and heavy up the Pass. But no one can say our young men are deficient in grit."

Although his remark was not intended to be personal, Iris was stung to reprisal.

"You showed me your beautiful garden yesterday," she said sweetly. "Would you like to see what is left of ours? We have enough seeded nasturtiums to keep us in pickles all the winter."

As he was not the man to ignore a challenge, he followed her to the back of the cottage. They passed under a pergola, covered with withered rows, and then Iris, who was leading, gave a cry.

"Do you see what I see? Water?"

Overflowing from a tank at the end of the garden, where the spring was piped, a great pool was spreading out over the baked earth which could not absorb it.

"You've left the tap on," said Sir Henry reproachfully.

"But the tank takes a whole day to fill. The water dribbles in, drop by drop. . . . No, something's happened to the spring."

At the implication of her words his face turned suddenly grey.

"Come and see," he said hoarsely.

He spoken to the air for she had already rushed through the gate and was running up the hillside. He followed her, bursting through clumps of burned heather, whose tough roots noosed his feet and held him back, until he reached the spot where she stood.

At first, she was too breathless to speak as she pointed to a stream-let which was half-concealed by fronds of bracken.

"It's the normal-flow," she panted. "There must be rain in the hills."

The terror in her eyes leaped to his.

"Those lads," he gasped. "I'll ring up the rescue club. . . But it will be too late."

"Too late."

The words rang in Iris' ears as she rushed madly up the Pass, like one bereft of her senses.

The boulders on either side of the track blocked her view of the valley, but as she reached the gorge she became aware that she should have heard the roar of the little swollen river, dashing over its stony bed. Stopping for a moment to strain her ears, she caught—something—so faint that it was a vibration, rather than actual sound—as though a telephone were ringing in the last house of a long row.

It was thunder up in the hills.

Mercifully, it was very far away....

Rushing round the bend, she was able, at last, to see the Pharisee Fall through its screen of trees. To her amazement, it was still pouring down in a steady white column, with no visible increase in volume.

She stood, scarcely able to credit the evidence of her eyes, while a wild hope flared up in her heart. Some miracle of nature had intervened—a landslip or fall of boulder higher up—which had either dammed the flood or diverted its course.

There was no time to lose in speculation. Reckless of danger, she plunged down the steep side of the gorge, snatching at such frail holds as ferns and wild strawberry runners as she slid down muddy slopes and mucky rocks. Often she only saved herself from pitching headlong to the bottom of the gulf by catching at the branches of a wild cherry or birch.

Her luck held, for her last jump was blind, so that she landed with a crash amid the boulders of the stream. As she got up again, her first thought was for the torch, which she had snatched from the hall table in her rush through the cottage.

To her great relief, it was unbroken—to match her bones. Slipping it inside the neck of her pullover for safety, she scrambled over the exposed rocks until she reached the entrance to the pothole.

Without giving herself time to think, she gripped the rope ladder and began to lower herself with frantic haste—only to meet with disaster. In skipping rungs—to descend more quickly—she lost her footing and hung suspended by her hands. As she swayed to and fro the motion accelerated and she spun giddily round, like a fly dangling at the end of a spider's thread.

She realised that she was missing the ballast provided by Courage on her previous descent, when he had stood below to steady the ladder. Now, in her struggle to regain her footing, she kicked wildly against the rock, only to crash back under the fall. Fortunately, her palms were hard, to match her muscles, and she managed to lower herself until her toes scraped the insecure rungs again.

Lower and lower she dropped. The light grew dimmer as damp dungeon odours arose from the vault below and she found herself on the rocky floor of the daylight chamber. Shuddering in anticipation of what was to come, she flashed on her torch and guided herself, by the trickle of water, across the dark shaft.

All she could see was a ghastly drop—like the shaft of an elevator, enclosed by walls of dripping rock—and an insecure-looking rope ladder dangling sheer down into the blackness.

At first, she lingered to shout, in the faint hope that the climbing party might be on its way up, but she only awoke a mutilated echo which was plainly out of practice. Time was racing on, while up in the hills, the flood was piling itself up against its barrier, lapping higher every minute. Sooner or later water must find its level.

She gripped the rope ladder with one hand and dropped backwards into the shaft. The strain on her arm was terrific, but it was momentary. The next instant she stuffed her precious torch into her pullover, releasing both hands for use.

At first, she felt the demoralizing swaying movement, growing gradually stronger with every lurch, like the swing of the pendulum. One moment she banged against the rock and the next she hung under the spray of the fall. Then her feet found a hold on the ladder and the immediate crisis was past.

Afraid to hurry, lest she upset her balance, she crabbed downwards, rung by rung. As she did so, she began to lose her grip on reality. The darkness was so dense and muffling that it fulfilled the function of a drug, deadening her to the threat of vertigo. When, presently, her foot landed on rock again, she was only vaguely surprised that the descent had been accomplished so quickly.

She was about to step off the ladder when a warning signal was flashed from her brain. Still gripping the rope with one hand, she fumbled for her torch. . . . Its light revealed a narrow shelf of cliff on which she was perched, while below was the darkness of the shaft.

Her heart leaped at the thought of the fate she had just escaped. Both palms and forehead were clammy as she continued her descent.

The incident had shaken her nerve severely, but she had to go on. Down—down. Deeper—deeper. One, two… ten … twenty, until she lost count.

Once again she felt her foot bumping on a rough surface. This time she had reached the bottom of the shaft in reality and was standing in a cave. Only a section was visible in the light of her torch, but she received a dim impression of stalactites, like bunches of candles or carrots. Then she followed the course of the stream which oozed down the slope and disappeared into the underground passage of which Courage had spoken.

"The filthy crawl," she quoted in a high unfamiliar voice. "Then comes the clinking long drop. Nobody knows how far down it goes or what's at the bottom. That's the fun. At the end, we all break our necks, to make it a real success. . . But we've found another pot. Cheers—and mind your head."

She was able to crawl on her hands and knees along the bed of the underground stream for only a few yards. Very soon she was forced by the lowness of the roof to lie full length and drag herself along over the slimy trickle. She was scratched and bruised by grit, while the strain of her posture grew intolerable, but far worse than pain or exhaustion was the knowledge that she had to return the same way that she had come.

"Every terrible thing has to be done again," she thought. "I'm not even halfway. There's still the unfathomed drop to come."

In a way, her fear of the next, ordeal was merciful, for it prevented her from accepting a suggestion so horrible that her mind instinctively rejected it whenever it tried to drift into her brain.

It was the thought that even a slight fall of rock could seal her inside a living tomb.

She was gasping for breath and aching in every muscle when she crawled out of the passage. Her knees shook violently when she got up and her head began to swim. Flashing her light around, she got a confused impression of dripping, disrupted cliff and riven rock, murmurous with echoes and the chuckles of imprisoned waters.

The streamlet led her inexorably to the lip of a cracked precipice, down which dangled a jaunty rope ladder.

As she looked at it, she felt another wave of faintness surge over her and knew that Nature had beaten her. If she attempted to climb down that ladder, her fingers would surely lose their grip and she would drop down into the gulf. To persevere was merely to commit suicide.

"I must make them hear," she thought desperately.

She put all her strength into her screams. Again and again. . . Then from the depths arose an answering shout.

"Hel-lo!" It was Courage's voice. "What's up?"

"Flood!" she yelled. "Rain in the hills!"

She heard him shouting to the others, awakening a confusion of cross-current echoes. Then he called to her directly.

"Go back at once."

In spite of the command, she knew that she must rest, to gain strength for the crawl along the drain. She was still crouched on the rocky floor when Courage came up the ladder, like a steeplejack.

"Here, drink this," he said in a strangely stern voice.

She swallowed the brandy and then struggled to her feet.

"I can start now," she said.

As she followed him down the passage, a thought passed through her mind.

"At this moment, I am here in this ghastly place. Where shall I be in an hour's time? And—how?"

An hour later, she was curled up in a big chair in the cottage drawing room, while her grandmother lay upon a couch near her. She felt tired but pleasantly relaxed after the rare luxury of a hot bath, even although the water which gushed from the tap was coloured coffee-brown. A teapot was on the table and she smoked a cigarette as she watched the grand spectacle of a thunderstorm sweeping the Fells.

The clock ticked, her grandmother knitted, the ginger cat washed her face. In that scene of domestic comfort it was difficult to believe in her recent experience. It seemed incredible that she could have sustained such an ordeal and emerged with only cuts and bruises

Already its memory was growing blurred, owing to her acute mental tension at the time, and parts of it were altogether forgotten. Looking back on her return journey, it seemed concentrated into a test of overstrained endurance and forced effort; when will, nerve,

and muscle were teamed in one frantic drive to cheat the enemy—
Time. They were racing the flood, so they could not stop to relax
or rest. Once when they jammed in the terrible confinement of the
underground passage, Courage cursed them impartially, but it was
the very fury of his abuse which galvanized their limp muscles into
new life.

They got out of the pothole only just in time. They could hear the
distant roar of rushing water as they were climbing out of the daylight shaft, and they had to scramble for their lives to reach the sides
of the gorge.

As she was dragging herself up by the trees, Iris turned just in
time to see the white pillar of the Pharisee Fall spread out suddenly
in a broad brown fan as the flooded river foamed over its lip.

Afterwards there had been the comedy of their meeting with the
rescue club, when she had been overwhelmed with congratulations.
At the time she thought it was recognition of her feat, but learned
later that it was only local jubilation over the discovery of a new pot.

"You can't satisfy some folk," said her grandmother, breaking
the current of her thoughts. "Looks as if someone hadn't got wet
enough for his liking."

Looking up as a fork of lightning veined the sky, Iris saw Courage
coming through sheets of torrential rain. He looked excited and
happy as he waved his hand. A minute later he burst into the room
in front of the little maid who was trying to admit him.

"I've brought the doings," he said, crossing to the old lady's
couch. "A new lease of the cottage for your lifetime, with adequate
water provision and a special emergency clause, in case of drought.
It's rough, but it covers everything and it's signed and witnessed.
It comes from Sir Henry Collier as a mark of appreciation for your
granddaughter's heroism in saving his son's life."

Old Mrs. Holtby looked at the young man.

"I'll thank you later," she said. "First I want to hear the real story."

"Very well," he agreed. "The truth is this: I did a little private sur-
veying yesterday afternoon, after which I engaged a young man to
dig at a certain spot which seemed indicated. Result—I found that
Collier had played a mean trick on you. A stirrup-pipe had been
inserted, which reduced the flow from your spring by one-half. The
drought did the rest of the mischief."

"I knew it," cried Iris.

"At the time I couldn't decide what to do," went on Courage. "As I explained to you, I couldn't see you would be better off if you fought a claim. So I told the young man to cover everything up and say nothing for the present. He was very hot over the business, so it is evident he decided to take the law into his own hands and remove the stirrup-pipe. That was the explanation of the increased flow from your spring."

"Does Sir Henry know everything?" asked Iris

"Yes. I came out into the open. I also explained fully the providential nature of the incident. . . . You see, we rang up that place in the hills and from what they have told us, the storm did not really break until you were well underground. If there had not been this false warning, nothing and no one could have saved us from being drowned."

He stopped and looked wistfully at Iris.

"Here's your prize," he said, giving her the lease.

Her face grew radiant.

"It's wonderful," she said. "Gran will love you for this."

Suddenly Courage saw his chance to propose in the presence of a friendly third party.

"I want her to love me—as a grandson," he said boldly.

Mrs. Holtby's eyes twinkled as she went on with her knitting.

"Iris," she said. "I'm doing very well. I've just had an offer. If you will co-operate with me, I am inclined to accept it."

THE BABY HEIR

When Annabel was nervy—she would look at Wotherspoon about twenty times a day and murmur "How many people would like to kill you, angel?"

And about twenty times a day she declared with a determined thrust of her jaw, "But Belly won't let them."

"Belly" was the unrefined version of her poetical name decreed by Baby Wotherspoon. He had a heavy-handed way of dealing with human prejudices and destinies. It did not disturb him that his birth had upset a score of financial interests.

His millionaire father was a member of a large family. He liked none of them sufficiently for preferential treatment, but he was clannish and believed that money should not pass to strangers. Consequently, he had willed his wealth equally among charities and his relatives.

Under this scheme, no one could be wealthy, but the inheritance was highly acceptable. Therefore when old "Baby" Wotherspoon's third wife died in presenting him with a ten pound son, the event was a family calamity.

There was a mighty battle for John Jasper's infant life, as he had contracted heart trouble in his sensational journey to this world,

Among the nurses, Annabel worked at top strength to keep him alive, so it was not astonishing that the millionaire offered her the job of permanent nurse to the important heir. By that time, Annabel had become the abject slave of John Jasper, so she accepted the trust.

Annabel had no illusions about her job. The remuneration was high, but she knew it could not compensate her for the sacrifice of her youth and liberty. She was also attractive and vivid—red-haired, with beautiful colouring and sharp features; yet her charm had to be wasted while she was exiled in Sir Simon "Baby" Wotherspoon's house—"Four Winds," in the bleak and lonely north.

As the most important relative, Sir Simon had been selected the baby's guardian. He was a retired Harley Street specialist and was responsible for John Jasper's health—an arrangement which did not interfere with his writing of a medical manual—while young Wotherspoon paid the expense of his establishment.

At first Annabel was stimulated by the solitude and the stretch of open landscape. There were only two habitations in an extensive area—"Four Winds" and the cottage of Professor Deane. A ribbon of lane wound from the York road up to Sir Simon's house, continued for half a mile to the professor's home and then ended.

"Four Winds" was rather like a fortress, enclosed within a ten foot wall, with two entrances. In front of it, there was a rolling view of fields divided by stone walls. Behind it lay the moor. The back gate led out to a rough path which sloped down to a steep gully through which flowed a swift mountain stream. This was spanned by a plank bridge and then the track rose up to the Deanes' cottage.

The professor and his wife, Judith, always used this short cut across the moor when they visited Sir Simon. Every evening they arrived after dinner for a game of bridge with Sir Simon and his secretary—young Fish Baker. It was the sole social engagement and one from which Annabel was escused.

The house was not large and was practically divided between Sir Simon and the nursery. The work was done by a married couple—the Limes—while Annabel had a long-faced girl called Horsington as a nursery-maid.

In spite of her loneliness, she was not attracted to their only neighbours. The professor was a sapless, dreary man whom Annabel regarded as a still-life; his wife, on the other hand, seemed driven on by a gale of mental and physical energy. She was thin, dark, and possessed a red-lipped, long-lashed beauty. During the day she always wore shorts or slacks, but in the evening she languished in rest-gowns of glamorous Hollywood tradition.

Annabel suspected that she was interested only in men and resented her as competition, for she never failed to grab her job.

"It's an appalling life for any girl," she declared. "You will become mental. No one can remain normal in this shattering loneliness."

"I'm married," Judith gave a triumphant laugh. "That makes all the difference. . . When I heard you were coming, I was afraid we might develop a triangular situation. It would have been ghastly if my husband had fallen for you."

Annabel had to bite back her true opinion of the professor's power of fascination.

"I can't imagine your husband falling in love," she said.

"Neither could I. I was one of his students. Wasn't it gloriously romantic?"

Annabel liked the secretary no better than the Deanes. Fish-Baker had a small pursed mouth and a snobbish sense of social values.

The first night she was at "Four Winds," Sir Simon visited her nursery.

"I want you to know exactly what you are taking on," he said. "This baby is a power in the financial world and not altogether a welcome one. In arranging for his future, his father altered his policy in respects which tangled up other interests. There are people who would gladly see this child dead."

"O, Sir Simon," gasped Annabel. "Can you tell me of special precautions to take?"

"Certainly. They may sound theatrical, but this is the melodramatic situation. To begin with, you cannot rule out the possibility of poison—in case of the fifth column operating in the kitchen. You must prepare his food and taste everything before you give it to him."

"Of course."

"Then there is the risk of kidnapping. He must never be left alone. It is not necessary to take him outside the house. He can get good moorland air from his veranda."

That interview was the prelude to a strange withdrawn life for Annabel. Her world was enclosed within four walls and her interests focused on John Jasper—his weight, his diet, his temperature, and all that was his. She slept in his room, had her meals in the day nursery, and only left him in the charge of Horsington while she took her daily walk on the moor.

October passed with a shrill wind which scoured the moor and bleached the heather to the semblance of a tossing dun sea. The change in the landscape paired with a corresponding difference in Annabel. She slept badly, lost her appetite and her colour, and suffered from nerves.

The truth was that Annabel was weighed down by a guilty secret. She was a skilled nurse, trained in orthodox methods; but now that she was facing a crisis, she had allowed her instinct to triumph over her professional experience. Experiment had proved that Baby Wotherspoon throve only in defiance of the laws of health.

He could digest any food he fancied, while he threw up his proper nourishment. A breath of pure mountain air was enough to make him sneeze—and a cold was a menace to his heart. Even his personal taste was peculiar, for he preferred the advertisement-photographs of motor cars to the pictures of Snow White & Co. on the white walls of his nursery.

It cost Annabel a terrible pang to outrage her code. But she had taken an oath that John Jasper should live and flourish to the confusion of his foes.

She had the sensation of living on the crust over an active volcano, for she knew that Sir Simon would dismiss her without a character, if he discovered her disobedience. But it was not the thought of her professional peril which appalled her.

She dared not face the chance that she might be parted from Baby Wotherspoon because she was certain that she—and she alone—could rear him to boyhood.

The October winds screamed themselves into silence and November—grey and sullen—set in with sheets of steady rain. The weather was depressing to a normal person, while it appalled Annabel as a direct menace to the baby's health. To shield him from the peril of the raw air, she turned the nursery into a fortress from which even Horsington was excluded and she alone remained on guard—to the exclusion of her own daily exercise.

Fortunately, Sir Simon was of set habits, so she was able to open the windows in readiness for his bi-daily visits; but she lived in constant fear of spies who might report the ban on ventilation. In her extremity, she sank to the deception of making a dummy bundle and placing it in the perambulator on the veranda.

Owing to the constant strain on her resources, she had forgotten Sir Simon's warning about treachery. It was the professor's wife who recalled to her the danger of fifth column activity. One afternoon Judith Deane managed to storm the nursery and sink bonelessly down on a rug.

"Warm," she said appreciatively. "Glad you're not a bleak, anti-septic nurse. I adore a run."

"Then you're lucky." Necessity drove Annabel to lie. "The win-dows are shut while I get up the temperature."

Looking slender and attractive in black slacks and a blue-green pullover, Judith stared at the baby. She merely saw an overweight infant with a tendency to baldness. Annabel—who was also watch-ing him—considered him a cherub, with adorable dimples in his hands and an enchanting chuckle. With the exception of his beloved "Belly," he addressed everyone as "That." His other word was "no."

He grinned at Judith's ultra-scarlet lips—clutched his nose tightly with both hands as though to keep it safe—and declared "No."

"I agree," said Judith. "It's 'no' every time. . . . Did I ever tell you, Nurse, that I was a swell at biology? I was the professor's star turn. Well, speaking from a scientific angle, it is a crime to keep this child alive. He's far from being a one hundred per cent specimen and he's stopping the survival of better lives."

Annabel controlled her fury by a laugh.

"You're talking high and don't mean one word," she said.

"Of course not. Perhaps I mean something else. . . . A lot of people would like to see this child out of the way."

"Murder him? O, no, no."

"Kidnap him. He'd fetch a heavy ransom. His estate could stand the shock."

"But that would be murder. He couldn't live without me. The shock would be too much for his poor little heart."

"Then I'll give you a hint. On the first of December the trustees will pay their visit of inspection. They are relatives who have been cheated out of their expectations. Wouldn't it be an ideal time for one of them to arrange for the baby to be stolen, while he is here with the rest? He'd have a foolproof alibi."

"They'd find it impossible to kidnap John Jasper with me in charge of him. Besides, Sir Simon would also be on guard."

"But he's a relative, too." Judith's voice was loaded with mean-ing. "Do Harley Street specialists make enormous fortunes? Their expenses must be staggering. . . . O, by the way, one of the crowd is a real stinker. You can pick him out at a glance. I'm saying no more."

Although Annabel tried to ignore Judith's warning as the invention of a neurotic woman, some of its poison remained. When she lay awake at night, her mind throbbed with feverish suspicions. She began to wonder whether the lonely house had not been chosen by Sir Simon to facilitate a kidnapping plot. Horsington, too, was a queer, silent creature. There was some mystery about her, for Annabel sensed that she resented her menial position. Although she tried to appear uneducated, she had once quoted from a literary classic, in an unguarded moment.

Annabel began to wonder if anyone in "Four Winds" could be trusted.

Above all, loomed the ordeal of the trustees' visit. As the date drew near, the wind veered to the north and the weather became bitterly cold. Apart from the increased menace to John Jasper's chest, Annabel was grateful when a first scurry of white flakes shook from a leaden sky. Actually, the snow would prove her ally, if it kept the trustees away.

"They won't be able to make it, if we're snowbound," she remarked hopefully to the secretary, the day before the official visit.

Fish-Baker glanced out at the white waste of moor and grimaced.

"It's only drifted to any depth on the moor. It would have to lie a jolly sight deeper to keep them away. The York road will be clear and they can jam the lane in good cars. Under the hat, there's a carrot dangling in front of their noses."

"What do you mean?"

"None of them would lose their trustee-fee. Without betraying a confidence, I can tell you the figure is definitely stiff. The old bloke was so keen on protecting our young boss that he put all the family to check up on Simon. Hence these periodic inspections. I prefer to call them 'suspicions'."

"Isn't one of them rather a swine?" she asked.

"O, you mean Reginald. Definitely. Been in the army once—and quod twice."

Suddenly, as though some connections of ideas had been established in his mind, his eyes grew shrewd.

"If you ever think about easy money," he said in a low voice, "you've only to make a contact. Nothing to do—merely relax your vigilance."

Annabel's face flamed with fury; but before she could speak, Fish-Baker began to laugh.

"Only testing your loyalty. It's in my book of words—'Suspect the nurse.' By the way, old Simon asks me to tell you the arrangements for tomorrow. The trustees will have lunch directly after arrival—inspect the heir—and go back after tea. Horsington will be wanted to help with the meals. And there'll be another guest. Sir Donald Frost is coming to examine young Wotherspoon."

Sir Donald Frost. The name sang in her head. He was the nurses' pole star—young, good looking, in the first flight and still rising. As a probationer, she had waited in hospital corridors, merely to see him pass.

But now her jubilation was mixed with fear lest her unorthodox methods might be exposed. She went to bed praying for snow, snow, and more snow, to keep the invaders away.

She awoke to a white blanket spread over the countryside, but the weather conditions were not bad enough for the trustees' meeting to be cancelled. The party, however, had evidently not realised the full difficulty of their passage through the blocked lane; but they arrived eventually in three powerful cars with chains.

Even in the nursery, Annabel could hear the noise of their voices and laughter as Sir Simon greeted them. Lunch was very late and proved a protracted meal, for there followed a long and nerve-racking period of waiting. Annabel had to strain her ears for the sound of footsteps coming up the stairs, so that she could rush to open the windows of the nursery.

To add to her worry, John Jasper was beginning to display an ominous interest in the snow. For the first time in her experience, he asked to be taken outside. Apparently he wanted to go skiing, tobogganing, and all the other dashing things, for he grew very cross at being thwarted. When he cried, he roared and bellowed, so he had to be appeased, lest he should strain his heart.

Annabel was near the limit of her resources when—as the grey daylight began to fade—the nursery was invaded by the relatives. At first she saw them as a prosperous hostile crowd, among which she picked out Sir Donald. His face was thinner and his figure a trifle more important, but he was no less handsome. His black hair shone as though burnished, when he bent over the baby's case-sheet, produced by Sir Simon.

"Nurse," he said in his fruity voice. "We are ready." With a feeling of desperation Annabel wheeled forward her precious charge. He became instantly the centre of a circle, while Sir Simon presented him formally to the trustees. Sir Donald concentrated on his examination—the relatives stared at the baby—and Annabel watched their faces.

Suddenly Annabel noticed an unnatural element—sheer gloating cruelty in the eyes of a vulture-faced man with red-lined cheeks. He caught Fish-Baker's attention and winked at him. As the secretary winked back, Annabel recalled his remark about "easy money!"

Instantly her suspicions flared up again. Fish-Baker might not be a perfect fool but he could be a perfect tool and used as a pawn in another's game. As the possibility of collusion flashed across her mind, the sinister Reginald—"Major" no longer—spoke to Baby Wotherspoon in a jocular vein.

"You may not know it, old boy, but you keep a damn good cellar. You do yourself proud. Simon, old boy, what about going down-stairs for another spot?"

His sneering tone hinted that Sir Simon was taking advantage of his preferential position. To ease an awkward situation, Sir Donald began to congratulate Sir Simon on the baby's progress.

"His health shows an all-round improvement. Best of all, his heart is beginning to compensate. You've done excellently, Nurse."

As a medical man, Sir Donald recognised the helper to whom the credit was due; as a critic of feminine beauty, his smile approved an unusually attractive girl. Thrilled by his look as well as by his praise, his words rang in Annabel's head after the relatives had gone out of the nursery.

As she mechanically closed the windows, John Jasper was reminded of his thwarted desire for winter sports.

"No," he yelled, meaning "snow." "No."

Suddenly Annabel had an inspiration. Opening her store-cupboard, she rolled out a huge bale of cotton wool from which she made pneumonia-jackets.

Unrolling a few yards, she spread them over the carpet.

"Come and play with Belly in the nice warm snow," she invited.

The experiment proved a great success, for the baby soon shouted with laughter. Engrossed in her game, Annabel did not hear Sir Donald's quiet, professional tread as he returned to the nursery.

"What are you doing with that dangerous stuff?" he asked in a horrified voice.

Flushed with stooping, Annabel looked up into his disapproving face. Her lips trembled as she began to explain the incident. Instead of making any comment, he glanced around the room.

"You've got the window closed," he remarked. "What's the temperature?"

After reading the thermometer he crossed to the window and threw it open. His face set in a professional mask, he asked another question:

"Do you smoke?"

"Yes," she confessed. "I couldn't survive without my daily dozen cigarettes."

"You will have to, in future, with all this inflammable stuff about."

"Oh, but I take no risks. I—"

"You must consider the baby's safety before your nerves. Remember—no smoking."

Directly she was left with the baby. Annabel closed the window, but she did not latch it—in readiness for future emergency. Her mind was a turmoil of emotions as she raged against the embargo on smoking. Cut off from social life, she depended on tobacco as an essential nerve tonic. As she grew calmer, however, she was chilled by a menace which dwarfed her personal grievance.

Sir Donald had stormed her fortress when her weak spots were exposed. He evidently considered her untrustworthy—and there were bound to be unpleasant repercussions.

While the party downstairs lingered over their tea, the short winter twilight deepened into darkness. Annabel rang the bell but no one answered its summons. Before she went to find Horsington, she looked around the nursery to make sure that everything was safe and in order.

The fire was screened, the window closed, and John Jasper was taking a nap in his day bed.

She met Horsington in the hall and told her to sit with the baby

While she lingered in the hall in the hope that Sir Donald might come out of the drawing room, she heard a scream from above. Dashing upstairs, she collided with Horsington on the landing.

"Baby's gone," she answered. "There's a ladder at the window."

Stunned with shock, Annabel staggered into the nursery. She stared first at the empty day bed and then at the ladder head before she crossed to the window. As she looked down at the illuminated snow she saw footprints leading down to the front gate.

Horsington rushed down the back stairs and threw open the landing window. Tearing after her, Annabel stared down on the strip of path lighted by the back lobby lamp.

It revealed only a white, unbroken surface.

Suddenly Annabel realised that Horsington was speaking to her in an insistent tone. It suggested the necessity for speed.

"Will you tell the master? Or shall I?"

With an effort Annabel wrenched herself out of her frozen trance of horror. Feeling that the situation was too monstrous to be real, she went down to the drawing room and blurted out her tale. Although she was dimly aware of a storm of excitement breaking all around her, she answered Sir Simon's questions with unnatural calm. It was not until the others had rushed outside, leaving her alone, that she awoke to the shock of realisation.

Baby Wotherspoon had been kidnapped.

With a professional horror of hysterics, she pressed her hands to her lips, forcing back her screams. Rushing blindly up the stairs, she ran into the nursery, where the sight of the empty bed made her break down utterly. Unable to endure it, she went down to the back stairs landing and stood by the open window. Above her the stars glittered in the black sheet of the sky—below, stretched the blank white path. Then she laid her head down on the sill and tried to stifle her sobs.

For the second time, Sir Donald stole on her unawares.

"Well," he said, speaking in a matter-of-fact voice, "it's a planned job. The ladder had been placed under the window in readiness, for it was covered with snow. The footprints led down to the front gate. From there, the kidnapper must have gone by car down the lane to the York road. There are only the marks of car tires there, while there are no prints of any kind in the lane that goes on to the cottage."

"What is Sir Simon doing?" asked Annabel dully.

"Hitting the trail, in the hope of catching up. But that stout man insisted that the cars should be searched first, in case the child was packed into the luggage boot. He argued that they were all under suspicion until proved innocent."

"No," said Annabel. "I'm the only one to blame. I should never have left him. I didn't latch the window after you."

"After me?"

"Yes. I disobeyed all Sir Simon's orders. He didn't bring the baby on. It was all my work—my instinct. I found out that the ordinary rules did not apply to him. He made his own rules, bless him. But if I hadn't kept him happy, he would have been too bored to go on living. I had to stimulate his brain or it would have degenerated. . . . Do you understand?"

"Yes. Perfectly."

"But what's the good of it all now? He can't live without me. Nobody will know how I loved him from the very first. He was such a darling little John Bull, with all the odds against him, poor fat mite. But he hung on. I'll never forgive myself. I've just taken a vow never to marry or have a child—because I let him down."

"Steady on. Have a cigarette?"

Sir Donald put the cigarette between her shaking lips, lit it—and then threw the match through the open window.

The next second, he gave a shout. Underneath their eyes, the snowy path was on fire.

It blazed fiercely for about a minute, sweeping downward in a line before it died, revealing dark pits in the snow.

Instantly Sir Donald realised the explanation of the phenomenon.

"The kidnapper's trail," he said in an excited voice. "He covered it with cotton wool. We must follow it up. Quick."

Although she wore thin, white shoes to match her overall, Annabel rushed after him down to the lobby. Outside, the path which led to the moor was scored with the impression of boots when they kicked aside the rags of charred wool. The roll had lasted until outside the radius of the light—when, having served its purpose, it came to an end.

Treading in Sir Donald's footsteps, like the page in the carol, Annabel followed the beam of his torch as it picked up the trail. It led them down to the bridge across the gully and then over the moor, up to the Deanes' cottage.

"O, no," cried Annabel. "We've gone wrong. It couldn't be them. They've nothing to gain."

"Come on," insisted Sir Donald. "I'm going to rush them."

After hammering upon the cottage door, he pushed it open and went into the empty hall.

"I've come for the child," he shouted. "Thanks for the trail."

As they waited, he touched Annabel's arm and pointed to the pads of melting snow which still lay on the dark blue carpet. Then Judith came out of a room, holding a bundle in her arms. Her eyes flashed defiance and her lips were a scarlet line in her ghastly face.

"I did it. You know why. My husband knows nothing."

Sir Donald took no notice of her. Instead, he turned to Annabel and pushed her toward the door.

"We must get him back at once," he said. "You'd better take him"

As Annabel looked with anguish into Baby Wotherspoon's poor blue face, his rigid limbs suddenly relaxed as though he recognised the touch of his beloved's protecting arms.

"He knows me," she said.

Together they crashed across the snowy moor back to "Four Winds" where Sir Donald issued another order.

"Carry on. You know what to do. I'm going back to the cottage. I want a chat with that charming couple—just for the records."

When he returned to the nursery, Annabel sat before the fire, feeding John Jasper who sipped milk and brandy with real appreciation.

"You darling little boozer," murmured Annabel, adoring him with her eyes, before she spoke to Sir Donald. "What happened? I still can't believe it of them."

"Naturally," he agreed. "While everyone suspected the relatives, no one remembered the charities who were equally disappointed by the baby's birth. They were—and are—above suspicion. But the professor had been building his hopes on taking control of the new Wotherspoon's former will. Apparently the disappointment turned him slightly mental. He planned the kidnapping—taking advantage of the trustees' meeting and the snow—and he forced his wife to play her part."

"Forced her?" repeated Annabel incredulously.

"Yes, he may look meek, but he's a dominant partner. I knew her when she was a beautiful, brilliant student. I was shocked by the change in her."

"But how did they steal John Jasper?"

"Inside work. Real fifth column. Horsington is Deane's daughter by his first marriage. Directly it was dark, she stole through the front door, followed the path which was already beaten in the snow by the visitors, as far as the gate, and from there struck out toward the ladder. She placed it outside the window and then returned to the house, still keeping in her tracks. Fortunately for her, you played into her hands by asking her to watch the baby. Otherwise she would have made her chance. As it was, she gagged the baby, placed him in the veranda—in a perambulator underneath a dummy bundle—opened the window, and then screamed."

"He was there—all the time?" gasped Annabel.

"Yes. No one would waste time in searching the room with a ladder stuck outside an open window. Directly she got rid of you and she guessed that everyone would be safely outside at the front of the house, she threw the roll of cotton-wool down the back stairs and followed herself with the baby. The professor and his wife were already on the moor by the back gate, waiting for her to signal with a light. They rushed up to the lobby, where one of them grabbed the baby while the other drew out the roll of cotton-wool behind them as they went down the path, covering up their footprints. . . . A most ingenious dodge, for in the dim lamplight the deception was perfect. It looked a soft, unbroken surface."

"But they knew they must be found out."

"Why? They planned to remove the cotton-wool before it was discovered. Once they had established their alibi-trail on the lane or the short cut, their footprints would be accounted for in the normal way, for they would make them coming across for their nightly bridge."

"What were they going to do with my baby?" asked Annabel in a low voice.

"I'm afraid they counted on his dying from shock," replied Sir Donald. "Anyway, they meant to park him in the snow all night and bring up his body in the morning. Their story would be that they found it on their doorstep."

"Friends."

"I agree. Of course, the professor took the detached scientific view—divorced from humanity. One life against millions, you know. . . . Sir Simon will suggest that they leave the country. By the way, he wants to unload young Wotherspoon on me. I live by the sea on the south coast, which will suit him better. I must ask him to choose his own nurse."

As though in answer to his question, John Jasper looked drowsily up at the face bending over him and spoke in recognition of his beloved.

"Belly."

WHITE CAP

When Tessa Leigh washed her hair, one June evening, she invoked the issue of life or death... On the surface, it seemed merely a matter of a trivial change of habit. Instead of going bareheaded to work, she had to wear a cap.

The reason was that her thick, wavy hair became unruly if she exposed it to the open air too soon after a shampoo.

The turban was made from a white Angora scarf and was ornamented with a lucky brooch of green-and-white enamel in the shape of a sprig of white heather. Inside the band was stitched a laundry-tape marked with her name in red thread.

It was a glorious morning when disdaining the trams—she set out to walk to in the Peninsular Dye-Stuffs Corporation, where she was employed as a stenographer. The industrial town was built upon selling moorland whose natural beauty had been destroyed; but the Council had acquired a range of hills—the Steepes—as its lungs and playground. About 1,000 feet in height, they were dominated by the mountain-peak—the Spike—which rose another 3,000 feet into the air.

Tessa walked with the rapid ease of youth, swinging the suitcase which held her holiday-kit. From time to time she looked up at the Spike—sharply outlined against a cloudless blue sky. It helped her forget the smoking chimneys of the factories and also to calm her spirit—for all was not well either with her work or her love.

She had only herself to blame for her heart-trouble. No one at the Peninsular could understand why she had been taken in by the cheap glamour of Clement Dodd. She was attractive, athletic, and possessed of a sweet yet strong character. Fearlessly outspoken, she had deep sympathy with the under-dog and always rushed in to champion any victim of injustice.

As she approached the majestic, pillared entrance to the factory, she felt a reluctance to enter which was becoming a familiar sensation.

She knew that she was not the only employee to feel that suddenly sinking heart and lagging foot, in spite of the fact that old John Aspinall—who founded the Peninsular Works—had striven to make it a model factory. He had arranged for the health, comfort and recreation of his workers. There were extensive grounds, a swimming pool, an excellent canteen, and various athletic clubs.

These good things remained after his death when his son—Young John—went to the U.S.A. to study American methods, leaving his brother to direct the corporation. Brother Eustace was a lazy, inefficient man who was content to sink to the status of a puppet-government after Miss Ratcliffe had bought a controlling interest in the Peninsular.

She was a wealthy, keen-witted woman with a lust for power. Soured by lack of social sovereignty through her failure to marry a titled husband, she strove to become a power in commerce. Part of her policy was to use the brains and experience of the men employed by the Peninsular. While she was professing interest in them, her keen brain was mincing up their suggestions and theories until they emerged as facts—for which she took all the credit.

Unfortunately the process was accompanied by corresponding human wastage, when gradually the atmosphere became poisoned because employees feared for their jobs. Most of the small-fry were too insignificant to be vulnerable, but Tessa stood out from the bulk of the stenographer-staff, because of an unlucky incident.

The Peninsular ran a rifle club in connection with the municipal shooting-range. One day, Miss Ratcliffe visited them and gave what practically amounted to a demonstration in marksmanship. Tessa, who was also an expert, welcomed her only as a worthy opponent and challenged her in a match which she won by a narrow margin.

"Bad show," commented her friends. "After this, she will have her knife in you."

In addition to anxiety for her job, Tessa was beginning to fear that Miss Ratcliffe was developing her specialized interest in Clement Dodd. As chief accountant of the finance department, he frequently visited her office, although he denied any personal element to Tessa.

Tessa's frown deepened as she passed through the gates and entered the grounds—gay with lilac and laburnum. Although it was the half-holiday, the model factory repelled her like a prison. As she gazed wistfully up at the soaring Spike, she suddenly saw a bird circling over the rocky summit.

"Don," she called to a tall stooping man with grey hair and a classical profile. "Don, do you see what I see?"

He shaded his eyes with a shaking white hand.

"It must be an unusually large bird to be visible at this distance," Donovan remarked. "Can it be an eagle?"

"Of course it's an eagle," cried Tessa exultantly. "Oh, isn't he a real king of birds? So free and splendid. I've a passion for eagles. The sight of one in captivity makes me see red."

The old man did not respond to her interest for he was gazing eagerly at an imperative black car which had just driven up to the main entrance. As a majestic blonde ascended the steps, he glanced at the clock tower.

"Miss Ratcliffe sets us an example in punctuality," he remarked. "In confidence, I have an appointment with her. My poor wife has resented the overtime I have given to the corporation. The fact is I was staying late to work out a system of reorganisation for several of the departments, to submit to Miss Ratcliffe... Now I believe I am going to reap my reward. My letter states that the subject of the interview is important clerical changes."

As she looked at his flushed triumphant face, Tessa had a sudden pang of misgiving. Originally a schoolmaster, Don was a man of superior education. For the sake of a delicate wife and daughter, he had commercialized his scientific knowledge in the Peninsular Laboratory. He was extremely proud of his intellectual family and his cultured surroundings, where every book and picture was the result of selective taste.

"Don't count on it," she warned him. "Everyone knows that Ratcliffe is a rat."

A short girl, with a dark fringe and an important air looked at her sharply as she hurried past. She had chosen an unfortunate moment for her remark, since the energetic damsel was Miss Ratcliffe's secretary. Donovan, too, was visibly distressed by her imprudence.

But Tessa smiled at him and entered the great hall to clock in.

A young man came forward to meet Tessa as though he had been watching for her arrival. Ted Lockwood made no secret of his feeling for her. It was one of Nature's mysteries why she had rejected him for Clement, since he was so suited to be her opposite number. She had a mechanical mind, so could appreciate the fact that he was a clever engineer. Like her, he was a fine athlete, while he seasoned his sound qualities with a sense of humour.

"Will madame lunch with me?"

"Sorry, Ted," replied Tessa. "I'm eating with Clem. Have you seen him around?"

"In the sick-bay. He's got a hangover and Matron's fussing over him. If a woman wants to be maternal, it beats me why she doesn't marry and set up her own outfit."

"Meaning me?" asked Tessa with customary bluntness.

"Yes, Tessa." Lockwood's face was grim with resolution. "Why won't you face the facts? The most successful marriages are founded on mutual interests—and you and I have the same tastes. How will you make out with an artistic bloke like Dodd?"

"Oh, not again, Ted," pleaded Tessa wearily.

She had no further chance to brood for she always worked at high pressure. As the subject of the dictation was technical matter which exacted her entire attention, she welcomed a break, in order to freshen herself with a wash. The men's and women's cloak rooms were built off a central domed hall with a white marble drinking-fountain, which was a popular meeting-place.

When she entered it, a group of employees was talking in excited undertones as they gathered around Clement Dodd. He was a tall slim-waisted youth who would have made a pretty girl but for the rough lips. He spoke with a stressed Oxford accent, while his manner to women of all ages was that of a courtier.

"Heard the latest casualty?" he asked Tessa. "Poor old Don's got the K.O."

As Tessa stared at him in dismay, he lit a cigarette.

"Afraid he asked for it," he said casually. "Too big for his boots. That line does not appeal to our lady-boss."

"It's a real tragedy," exclaimed a woman who dyed her grey hair. "He was nearly due to retire. Now he'll lose his pension. What will become of him?"

"Hush," whispered a typist. "He's coming in."

His head held high, the old scientist approached the group. He cleared his throat before he made an announcement after the fashion of a headmaster addressing his school.

"I have just resigned my position. I have never been happy in a non-scholastic atmosphere. Now I shall hope to resume my academic career. I wish to take this opportunity to thank you for your loyal support and co-operation."

Although his lips quivered, he managed to make a grand exit.

As she watched him, Tessa grew suddenly hot and giddy.

"It's cruel—hateful—abominable—" she stormed. "That horrible woman has thrown him out just to save his pension."

"Cool off, you young volcano."

Tessa felt herself pushed down on a chair. Although she recognised Lockwood's voice, she barely saw him through a shifting mist. She gulped down the glass of water which he drew for her, and then gave him a grateful grin.

"O.K.?" he asked. "What was the matter? You went first red and then white."

"Temper," she replied frankly. "Only it's a bit more than that. Just before I left Canada, I was in an air crash. Since then, if I get too steamed up, I have a blackout. The doctor told me I'd grow out of it very soon, but he warned me not to get excited."

"What's it like?"

"Foul—and frightening. Everything turns black and I drop into a sort of sleep. The doctor explained that sleep was my salvation, but it scares me because when I wake up, I can remember nothing. I go right out."

The rest of the morning dragged itself out. Worried about Don, she forgot to concentrate on her work with the result that she had the greatest difficulty in reading back her outlines. As she was typing her notes, she noticed that Miss James—Ratcliffe's secretary—had entered the room and was whispering to the supervisor.

Although she vaguely expected it, her heart knocked at the summons.

"Miss Leigh. Please report at once to Miss Ratcliffe."

Seated at her desk, Miss Ratcliffe looked a model of impersonal administrative—correct to form and polished in every detail. Her dark suit was perfectly built and her silver-blonde wave faultless.

"Miss Leigh?" Her voice was languid. "Ah yes, I am sorry that your services will not be required after today. You will receive a week's wages in lieu of notice. This is no reflection on your work—but we have to reduce the staff."

"But Miss Ratcliffe," gasped Tessa, "there must be some mistake. My speeds are the highest in the office and—"

"This is not a personal matter."

"But it is personal." With characteristic courage, Tessa dared to interrupt the tyrant. "If it were not, I should be expected to work out my notice. I have a right to know the reason."

"The reason is this," she said. "You have been disloyal."

With a guilty recollection of unguarded remarks, Tessa could not deny the charge. Instead she sank her pride to make an appeal.

"I don't want to inflict a sob-story on you, but I really need this work. I came over here from Canada when my parents died and I have no friends in England. Jobs are so scarce at present. Will you give me a second chance? I promise you I'll do better in future."

Miss Ratcliffe looked at her with cold impersonal eyes as she touched her bell.

"My decision is final," she said.

As Miss James hustled into the office and opened the door pointedly, Tessa had a sudden vision of the eagle beating his great wings over the mountain top. The memory flooded over h er, fi lling her with a wave of power.

She realised that she, too, was free and able to meet Ratcliffe on equal ground.

"You are a cruel, petty woman," she said. "The most junior typist has more right in the Peninsular than you have. You've bought your power—not earned it. And instead of using it, you abuse it. When worthwhile people are dying every day, it is a crime for you to be alive."

She was conscious of passers-by in the corridor who paused to look into the office before Miss James pushed her outside and shut the door.

On her way to the cashier's office, she met Don in the corridor—stooping like a defeated man.

"The Gestapo's got me too, Don. I'm sacked."

"I'm deeply grieved," he told her. "But your conscience is clear, while I have something to regret. . . . When, I first had the news of my—my resignation, I was so stunned that—in trying to save myself—I threw someone to the lions. That hurts most." He added regretfully with a lapse of his grand manner, "Besides, it did me no good."

As the admission sank in, fitting the circumstances of her own dismissal, Tessa felt that she had been struck by the hand of a friend.

"You," she muttered as she turned away.

The second shock made her feel numbed to reality. After she was paid off, she went to the cloak room and, mechanically, changed into white slacks and a rose-red pullover. Her hair was beginning to get bushy, so she drew her white cap over it, in an instinctive desire to look her best when she met Clement.

She waited for Clement for a long time in the canteen, but he did not appear. Presently she accepted the disappointment with dreary fatalism. Too overwrought to eat, she went out of the Peninsular grounds. All she wanted was to escape to the Steepes and climb the rough ascent to the Spike, to stand on the mountain-top and meet the healing friction of the wind.

Owing to its precipitous quarried sides, the Steepes were accessible from the town by a small funicular which carried patrons up the face of the cliff. The girl at the turnstile who collected the tickets was a local character. Abnormally sharp although she looked a child, her mop of red hair had gained her the obvious title of "Ginger."

"Does it bring you luck?" she asked as her quick eyes noticed the white heather brooch on Tessa's cap.

"You may have the lot at bargain-price," Tessa told her bitterly.

On the summit of the Steepes stretched a wide level expanse of threadbare turf where a cafeteria, as well as chairs and tables were provided for the community. The bulk of the holiday-makers used to congregate there, eating, drinking, reading, and playing games, but it was deserted that afternoon owing to a circus performance in the town.

Tessa struck off along a narrow path which wound, like a pale green ribbon, amid clumps of whinberry and stems of uncurled branches. Farther off, on the left, the ground sloped down to the rifle range.

She threw herself down on the heather. She wanted the consolation of contact with primeval things. With a springy cushion of twigs supporting her head, she gazed up into the clear blue sky, when she noticed the flicker of wings.

Again the eagle was circling around the summit of the Spike, reminding her of her impulse to climb to the mountain-top. It was a long, rough walk, for the steep track zigzagged continually across natural obstacles of bog and rock. Even the optimistic guidebook stated that two and a half hours were required for the ascent.

Springing to her feet, she had a clear view of the patch leading to the rifle range. Two figures—pressed closely together—stood upon the slope. Even at that distance, it was impossible to mistake the sunlit shimmer of the woman's silvery blond hair or the slack grace of her companion.

As she watched them, Dodd threw his arms around Miss Ratcliffe and bent his head, as though seeking her lips. . . . At the sight, the blood rushed to Tessa's head. Again she felt the blast of furnace heat while a wheel seemed to spin remorselessly inside her brain.

Recognising the terrifying symptoms which heralded a temporary extinction, she fought with all her strength to resist them, but while she was struggling, a rush of darkness swept over her like a black rocket. As she fell—face downward—on the heather in her last moment of consciousness, she noticed the watch on her outstretched wrist.

It was three o'clock.

It was four o'clock. Tessa stared at her watch with frightened eyes. Only an instant before it was three. A whole hour had been rubbed out of her life. . .

She pressed her fingers to her eyes as the memory of Clem's treachery overwhelmed her. The knowledge made her feel not only miserable, but cheap and ashamed, so that her dominant instinct was to hide. Soon the holiday-maker's would be spreading fanwise over the lower slopes of the Steepes.

Shrinking from the ordeal of meeting someone from the Peninsular Factory, she rose stiffly and looked around for her cap. To her annoyance, she could not see it and after pulling apart the nearest clumps of heather, she had to give up the search. Stampeded by the sound of distant voices, she ran over the rough until she reached a slippery bank of turf which dropped sheer to a narrow ledge above a worked-out quarry.

A perilous climb along the rocky rim brought her to a shallow depression in the hillside which offered her sanctuary. When she leaned back in the hollow, she seemed perched upon a lip of some bottomless abyss. For a long time she lay there—watching the pageant of clouds which rolled past like a stormy sea.

When she forced herself to look at her watch, she grimaced.

"Gosh, it's late. Well—I've got to face people again."

In spite of this resolution, she made a circle to avoid passing the crowd around the cafeteria. She could not understand the force of the instinct which warned her to remain hidden.

As she clicked through the OUT turnstile, she noticed that Ginger was staring at her. The scrutiny alarmed her vaguely for it revived her dormant dread of her lost hour.

"Where did I go?" she questioned. "What have I done? Do I show the marks of it in my face? Why does that girl stare at me? Oh, dear heart, I wish Ted was with me."

Now that her infatuation for Clement had been shrivelled by the knowledge of his treachery, her heart turned instinctively towards Lockwood. On the homeward journey, while she sat upon the hard wooden seats of the tram and watched long lines of mean houses slide past, the lines of Kipling's poem swam into her mind.

The thousandth man will stand by your side

To the gallows-foot—and after.

She lodged in a comfortable house which belonged to a florist. It welcomed her like a haven, that evening. The flowers had never looked so beautiful in the sunset glow when she walked through the garden. The shabby dark green sitting room was cool and a meal was spread on the table, so that she had only to make her tea from the electric-kettle.

She was feeling refreshed and stimulated when her landlady entered the room to remove her tray.

"What news," she clucked. "Is it really true she's been murdered?"

"Who?" asked Tessa, with a pang of foreboding.

"Your Miss Ratcliffe, of course. It's all over the town that she's been shot dead."

As Tessa stared blindly at her landlady, the scrape of the gate made the woman glance through the window.

"It's Mr. Lockwood," she announced. "I'll go let him in."

"I knew he'd come, I knew he'd come," Tessa told herself.

As he entered, she turned away and stood with clenched fists and locked jaw, fighting for self-control. She heard his step beside her but he did not speak until they were alone.

"Tessa. . . Darling."

The new tenderness of his tone broke down her defences. Clinging to him, she pressed her face against his shoulder.

"We mustn't waste time," he said. "A copper will soon be here to question you. First of all, remember I'm with you, whatever you've done . . . Did you kill her?"

Her face grew suddenly white as he repeated his question with stiff lips.

"Did I kill her? I don't know. . . . Tell me, has my cap been found?"

"Why?"

"Because it's gone. I had a blackout. I can't remember anything. . . . But my cap might tell me where I went."

Lockwood's face grew grim as he heard her incoherent story.

"I know you are innocent," he told her. "But this is not exactly a watertight yarn. Keep off it as much as you can. Don't lie, let the police find for themselves."

"But why are they coming to me?"

In her turn, Tessa listened to his account of the tragedy. A member of the rifle-club had found Ratcliffe's body lying in the rough beyond the targets, about four-thirty. She had been shot through the heart at close range. The doctor estimated the death as between three and four—but probably about three-thirty. As Tessa's rifle was found lying near, the police had made inquiries about her at Peninsular Works, when they had learned about her dismissal and her subsequent threats.

He had just finished his story when the garden gate scraped again.

"It's the detective-bloke," Lockwood warned Tessa. "Don't forget I'm standing by. . . ."

Inspector Pont reminded Tessa of an uncle who grew prize dahlias. He was big and dark, with sleepy brown eyes which revealed nothing of his mental process.

Tessa met him with the desperate courage of one mounting the scaffold.

"I am Tessa Leigh. I am prepared to sign a statement."

"Not so fast," said the inspector. "You'll be warned when I'm ready for that. I want to know if you remember making any of these remarks about the deceased?"

As Tessa read the typewritten paper he handed her, her face flamed.

"Only one person could have told you these things," she said. "That's Clement Dodd. . . . Yes, I did say them. All of them—and more. They are true. She was a cowardly tyrant for she hit people who could not hit back. Cruelty or injustice always make me see red."

"The turnstile girl at the Steepes has told me you were up there from between three and six." Pont said. "What were you doing during that time?"

"Walking," replied Tessa.

"Where?"

"I don't know. . . It's no good asking me. I've been in an air crash which has affected my memory. I was terribly upset . . . But I walked."

"Did you lose your cap during your walk? The turnstile girl tells me you were wearing one when you clicked-in, but that you were bareheaded when you returned."

"That's right. But I don't know where I lost it. I tell you—I don't know."

"I'd like a description of it."

After the inspector had entered the particulars in his notebook he turned towards the door. Lockwood noticed the glint in his eyes when he spoke to Tessa.

"That cap's got to be found. I'll have flyers out tomorrow. Meantime, a notice goes up on the station-board. I don't expect any results tonight, but hold yourself ready to come and identify it."

Directly the door closed, Lockwood held Tessa tightly in his arms.
"I'm standing by you," he said. "We'll wait together."

She was not comforted because she knew that he too was feeling the same strain of suspense. She felt his start when the telephone bell began to ring in the hall.

"I'll take it," he said quickly.

When he returned, his smile was unnaturally broad.

"We're going for a joy-ride," he told her. "My bus is parked outside."

The journey to the police station had a nightmarish quality. The line of smoke-grimed houses seemed to flash by so that Tessa—who was dreading the end of the ride—bit her lip when the car stopped under the blue lamp. Still in an evil dream, she stumbled into a tiled hall, where an open door gave her a clear view into a room.

Standing by the glare of an unshaded electric bulb, Clement Dodd was smoking a cigarette. He appeared entirely at his ease until he saw Tessa. His face grew red and he turned his back to avoid meet-ing her eyes.

"This way," said a constable.

Supported by the pressure of Lockwood's arm, Tessa followed the man into another office where Inspector Pont was seated before a table littered with official papers.

"Yours?" he asked, holding out a white Angora cap for her inspec-tion. She glanced mechanically at her name printed inside the band and nodded ascent, before she realised that he was smiling at her.

"My congratulations," he said. "This cap was brought in by two hikers—strangers to the district—who chanced to see the notice on the board. They say they picked it up among the rocks on the top of the Spike, soon after four this afternoon. As the official time for the ascent is two-and-one-half hours and the deceased was alive at three, according to medical evidence, it stands to reason that you could not have committed the murder and afterwards climbed the mountain, all within an hour."

As she listened, Tessa's head reeled for she realised that the story was full of holes. Before she could protest, Lockwood grabbed her arm.

"Miss Leigh's our champion athlete," he told the Inspector. "Thanks very much. I'll run her home now."

"I may ring you later," remarked the Inspector. "I am going to chat with another party. If you're interested, you could take your time going out."

Tessa understood the reason for his wink when they reached the hall, for after the detective entered the room where Clement Dodd was waiting, he left the door slightly ajar.

"There's just one point I want cleared up, Dodd," he said in a loud, cheerful voice. "It's common knowledge that two articles were found on the scene of the crime. One — a rifle — has been identified as the property of a stenographer — Tessa Leigh. The other article has still to be identified."

"But her name's inside the band," Clement spoke quickly and confidently. "Besides, everyone knows her white-heather brooch."

"I was referring to a pencil stamped with PENINSULAR," remarked the Inspector. "The cap you describe was picked up at the top of the Spike at four o'clock this afternoon."

"That's a damned lie. I saw it — "

"You saw it?" prompted the Inspector as Dodd broke off abruptly. "Go on. Now that Miss Leigh has a perfect alibi, I must go further into your own movements."

He shut the door and Lockwood dragged Tessa outside to the car.

As they reached the front door of Tessa's lodging, they heard the telephone bell ringing in the hall, when, once again, he rushed to receive the call.

When he rang off, his face was beaming.

"Dodd's confessed to the crime," he said. "The Inspector said he was in such a state of nerves after he made that slip that he cracked directly they got to work on him. It appears that old Donovan — when he was ratting for Ratcliffe — found out that Dodd had been embezzling money from the accounts. He told Ratcliffe and she taxed Dodd.

"As usual, she pretended that she alone had been so clever as to discover the fraud, so he reasoned that if he bumped her off, no one would know. I am assuming old Don blew the gaff from something he said to me. Dodd admitted that he got Ratcliffe to come with him to the range, to talk it over, so it was a cold-blooded crime."

As she listened, Tessa felt almost light-hearted with relief.

"Oh, it's wonderful to know I never killed her. And I'm glad Don didn't give me away. It was Clem he threw to the lions. . . I was feeling that I could trust no one. And then—you walked with me to the gallows-foot. And after—"

Lockwood began to laugh as he interrupted her.

"I've some good news for you. It didn't matter before. Nothing mattered then but you. . . But Eustace has asked Doddy to carry on until young John returns from America. Looks as if the good times are coming back to the Peninsular. . . . But what's the girl frowning about now?"

"My cap," replied Tessa. "If it had been found near the body, I should be convinced that I had killed her. I should have confessed to it—and Clem would not have been brought into it. That should have pleased him . . . But how did that cap got on the top of the Spike? I passed out between three and four. Besides, no one on earth could have made the climb in that time."

"No one on earth," said Lockwood. "But what about someone in the air? There's a simple and natural explanation. My hunch is that Dodd saw you asleep after he shot Ratcliffe—in that white rig you'd be conspicuous on the heather—so he stole your cap and placed it beside the rifle, to frame you. That's why he crashed so badly. Nothing rattles a liar as much as to be disbelieved when he is telling the truth, and he knew it was inside the range. There was no wind, but probably it stirred a bit in the breeze.

"Enter Mr. Eagle. He sees something white and fiery moving on the heather. He swoops down on it, soars up again, realises he's been not here fooled and drops it again in disgust. . . By the luck of the air currents, it fell at the top of the mountain instead of the lower slopes. You owe your perfect alibi to your friend—the Eagle."

THE FIRST DAY

Vivien heard the clock strike seven, but she dreaded to open her eyes. Last night she had gone to bed, as usual, in her small room overlooking the courtyard, at the Hotel Monopol. She knew that when she forced her lids apart, she would see the same familiar surroundings—the dark polished wood, the crimson-patterned wall-paper, the veneered walnut suite, the lemon-chrome curtains. . . . But she knew, too, that she would awake in another world.

During the hours of darkness, the old life of carefree security had passed away, leaving her stranded in a new Dimension—where she would shrink from shadows and where no locked door could bar out the enemy.

It was her first day in the underground "V" Army.

Until recently, the war had not invaded her orbit and instinct warned her to remain aloof. She rarely listened to the radio or read newspapers. As the Squeeze gradually tightened, she closed her ears to rumours, since it was wiser to live one day at a time and concentrate on her job of running the hotel.

In spite of Anglo-American birth, she was in a privileged position, for her maternal grandmother was the sister of old Fritz Steiner, who owned the Monopol. Orphaned in babyhood, she had lived in Austria for most of her life. The only time she stayed in England with her father's brother—an Oxford don—the academic atmosphere had not proved congenial. Consequently, when war broke out, she chose to remain in Austria with her friends.

In appearance, she was a hundred percent. Aryan, with pale gold hair, worn in a long page-boy bob—and flax-blue eyes. Always cheerful—with a smile for the most difficult patron—she was also briskly efficient and an ideal hotel-worker. She made no secret of her nationality, and only laughed good-naturedly when either of her countries was attacked.

"Oh, we're not quite so bad as that," she would say. "Don't forget I'm half-British and the other half is American."

They always shared her joke, for— since the exact relationship was forgotten—to them she was always old Steiner's granddaughter.

Although she never mentioned it, she thought of the "V" Army as a sort of super-race apart from ordinary life. It was not until she met a certain hotel guest—who called himself "Vanderpant"—that she realised that girls like herself were somehow finding the courage to chalk up "V" signs, listen-in to *verboten* radios and even to commit acts of sabotage.

John Vanderpant was presumably engaged in business, and he often stayed for a night at the Monopol in the course of his travels. During their brief meetings their relationship was that of hotel manageress and patron; but she was drawn instinctively to him, and she was sure that he felt a similar attraction.

Through thinking constantly of him and watching him unobtrusively, her intuition bridged the gulf between them, so that it was no surprise, one evening, when he took the fateful first step which could place him in the power of the Gestapo. They were sitting together in the deserted lounge, drinking coffee and smoking, when he touched the "initial" brooch pinned at the neck of her gown.

"What does this 'V' mean to you?" he asked.

" 'V' for 'Vivien,' " she replied. Then she lowered her voice. "What does it mean to you? You can trust me. I'm English, too."

"*Too?*" he repeated with his acquired Continental grimace. "Well, since you've guessed my dark secret, call up your Gestapo."

When they had finished laughing at the absurd suggestion, he began to tell her about the "V" organisation.

"Think of it as a trunk with branches and twigs. The Gestapo are all out to discover the twigs, because they might be 'persuaded ' to reveal identity of the branches. So the hang-out of a twig is a very hush-hush affair and is changed constantly. When we want to contact him, we use our Intelligence—ordinary people of all grades— who pass on our messages. You see, it would be too risky for me to try the direct approach. I might be already under suspicion, and my work is too important for me to be liquidated before I've had a run for my money."

"What is your work?" she asked.

"I rake in new recruits. Great sport. If I slip up in 'sizing up' my man or woman, I can be handed over on a plate to the police. I get a terrific kick out of it."

"Don't," she shuddered."That's not funny. . . . Have you come here to try and contact anyone in this hotel? "

"Yes. You."

While she was still gasping with horror, he explained. "You are ideally placed to receive messages and pass them on, with all the comings and goings at the bureau. No one would suspect old Steiner's granddaughter."

She listened in incredulous dismay. His words had shattered her sense of security by suggesting her inclusion in the ranks of those heroic girls who seemed to be made of different clay from herself. As she looked around the lounge—at the mirrors, the palms, the show-cases—the idea seemed both monstrous and fantastic while she was safe in this warm, well-lit place of shoddy splendour. . . . She thought of the concentration camp and shuddered again. . . .

"No, no. I *couldn't*. I'm afraid."

"Good." His voice sounded relieved. "I've tried to recruit you and I've failed. Perhaps I'm glad to fail."

"Do you despise me?"

"Definitely no," he assured her. "A timid recruit is a positive danger. You can't force these things. When It grips you, you won't be able to resist It. It'll be part of you."

She looked into his shining eyes with a faint pang of jealousy. She felt that she had been offered something big and worth while— and she had rejected it.

"What do you get out of life?" she asked.

"Excitement."

"No happiness? Won't there ever be a woman? "

"No. *Verboten*."

"Not even a woman who worked with you and shared your danger? "

"No." Then suddenly he smiled. "Who knows? One day, perhaps, when all this is over, there may be a cottage in the country or a flat in town. Whichever she prefers. Some day. . ."

Some day. . . . After that, it was only a question of time before her first day. . . . She opened her eyes, jumped out of bed, and began to dress. Her face in the mirror looked unchanged as she put on the rouge and lipstick which, together with a tight, black satin gown and high-heeled shoes, marked her official status; but her fingers shook and her throat felt dry.

All the joy and exultation of the night before had oozed away while she slept. As she remembered John's hint about a weak link, she began to question her own quality and to wonder whether her decision had been "Dutch courage." There had been a wedding celebration at the Monopol the preceding evening, and as old Steiner's representative she could not refuse to join in the toasts.

"Perhaps it was those drinks," she thought. "I'm not used to so many. I must catch John before he goes and ask him for time. I'm *not* backing out. All I want is time—time to get steady and used to the idea." She felt relieved by her decision, although she was oppressed by a sense of urgency. John was due to leave the hotel early and she might have missed him. In her impatience, the lift could not take her quickly enough down to the ground-floor, and directly she reached the lounge she ran across to the bureau.

"Has Fifty-two checked out yet?" she asked.

"No," replied the clerk, glancing at the clock. "He's cutting it fine. I know my lord made a night of it, for I had the joy of letting him in. You must pardon my indiscretion if he is a friend of yours."

"Every patron is a friend of the hotel, Georg," she told him.

As she looked at the youth, she realised his secret hostility bred from a sense of grievance. He was rather like a Kewpie, with very light curly hair, slanting eyes and a broad, permanent smile. Unfortunately, he was not so good-natured as he appeared, while he was too slack to be. entrusted with authority.

Her other helper—Edda—was older than herself, but she too could not be allowed much contact with the guests, because of bad manners and a disagree-able personality. Although she was pure Nazi, she was dark and pallid, with mean, pinched lips. Not only was she envious of Vivien's blonde colouring, but she was also jealous of her position as old Steiner's official granddaughter.

Her insolence usually took the form of sardonic servility. That morning she carried Vivien's coffee and dry roll to the desk and laid it beside her with a stressed "Service." As she did so, John entered the lounge. His hat was on and he carried his coat and suit-case.

Because she knew that both her assistants were watching her, Vivien felt her face flush.

"Give me Fifty-two's bill, Georg," she said sharply.

As she crossed the lounge, she noticed a change in John, as if he too were fundamentally altered during the night. His lips were stern, and he looked at her indifferently as though she were a stranger. Taking the account from her, he glanced at the total with a shrug— as though to indicate he was stung—before he spoke in a peremptory whisper.

"Something broke, last night. I'm going hell-for-leather to contact someone. . . . This item is wrong, Fraulein. . . . *Listen.* At noon today a man will tap by a showcase. Pass him and whisper, 'To-night at eight, one hundred and three, Postgasse.' He's six foot, very fair, blue eyes, blond hair with shaven sides, well dressed, scar over his eye."

While he was murmuring the description, he opened his note-case, thrust some dirty notes into her hand—and dashed through the revolving doors. Her chance of reprieve was gone.

"Who's after him?" asked Edda.

"Not me."

Vivien felt too laden with heavy responsibility to snub the girl for her implied suggestion. John had accepted her as a new recruit to the "V" Army and had given her a definite job. The lives of others might depend on whether she kept a cool nerve and a clear head; yet her brain whirled when she tried to memorize the simple address.

In her confusion, she took up her cup so carelessly that the coffee slopped into her saucer and her roll fell to the carpet. Georg scooped it up and returned it to her with a low bow.

"There's this consolation—it can't fall butter-down," he remarked.

"Soon, there will be butter for all," said Edda. "You are nervous this morning, Fraulein. Didn't you sleep well? You should when your stomach is full and your conscience clear."

Vivien ignored the remark and hurried away, eager to escape from Edda's malicious gaze. She always worked at high pressure, but that morning she was grateful for the shortcomings of a skeleton staff. While she was engaged with the floor housekeeper and the chef, she forgot the ordeal ahead of her; but in her constant visits to the bureau—which was the nerve-centre of the hotel—she was conscious of Georg and Edda as potential spies.

When she looked around her, her chief emotion was incredulity. The familiar place appeared as it did yesterday, before she took the border-line step which removed her into another world. Old Steiner had a genius for hotel administration and she was a talented executive, so between them—and in spite of the prevailing economic conditions conditions—the Monopol still reflected some of its former high standard.

Vivien loved it as the only home she could remember. The mere threat of parting from it gave her a pang. As the morning wore on, the tension of waiting grew almost unbearable. She longed for noon, even while she dreaded the passing of every minute.

"First time I've seen *you* watch the clock," remarked Georg. "He's a lucky fellow."

"That's not funny, Georg," she said coldly. "We are here to work."

"Pardon, Fraulein," broke in Edda gleefully, "but you have made a grave mistake in the menu. We have not served this sauce for years. It needs a lot of butter."

Vivien bit her lip as she pencilled the correction.

"I've gone to bits," she told herself. "What can they think of me?"

She was aroused by the sound of a sharp tapping upon glass. Looking up, she noticed a tall heavily-built man who was rapping impatiently upon a showcase to attract attention. She was glancing at him indifferently—since showcases were Edda's business —-when, suddenly, her heart gave a leap as she recognised John's description of the anonymous agent.

This man had a fair skin which was florid and red-veined, ice-cold blue eyes, and closely-shaven hair under his smart hat. She searched for the distinctive scar and found it when he turned his head—a smallish, red, angry crisscross under his left eye.

It must be X, she thought.

Then she glanced at the clock for confirmation and discovered that the time was nine minutes to twelve. She told herself that either the clock was slow or the agent was too early; but the discrepancy was a bad jolt and made her hesitate to contact him.

The tapping grew so insistent that it goaded her from the safety of her base.

If I make a mistake, she thought desperately, I'm for it. He'll ask questions. Questions about the address and who gave it to me. All sorts of questions. How can I explain it away with Georg and Edda listening?

Before she could solve her problem, she had reached the show-case. The man pointed to a cigar, grunted and flicked a coin down upon the glass. As she swept it up, she realised that lives might depend on the message and whispered rapidly —

"Tonight at eight, one hundred and three, Postgasse."

Then she waited. Nothing blew up. Indeed the man's reaction was so unusual as to justify her soaring confidence. Instead of staring blankly and asking her to repeat her words, he eyed her keenly and then turned nonchalantly in the direction of the restaurant.

She returned to the bureau with a springing step. Now that her message was delivered, she felt that she had exaggerated the risk. John would not entrust a dangerous commission to an untried recruit. It was merely as a matter of form that she asked Georg a question.

"Is that man staying at the hotel for the night?"

"Yes," replied Georg, "I booked him in while you were upstairs with the boss. He's got Eighty-eight."

"Good. Did you get top price?"

"Unfortunately, no. I could tell he was Prussian and naturally he must have our best suite."

As she was reflecting on the excellence of the agent's disguise, he strolled into the lounge, to get an aperitif. His hat was now removed, revealing a completely-shaven scalp.

"Blond hair." The words slipped back into her memory, awakening a dormant suspicion. She watched the man throw back his drink and then—in an effort to allay her subconscious worry—she began to look through a pile of papers.

Presently she heard a faint drumming and glanced up to discover its cause. The carpet beside the showcase had worn so threadbare that it had been cut away to reveal the parquet flooring. Upon this strip of waxed board, a man was doing a sort of elementary tap-dance, as though to register impatience.

He was signalling with his feet.

As she grasped the fact, she realised that this was the agent she had been told to expect. He was tall and very fair, with bright blue eyes. Although his head was partially shaven, the hair on top was flaxen, while over one eye was a livid white scar.

She looked at the clock and saw that it was on the stroke of twelve.

It was the worst moment of her life. She had made a ghastly blunder, even if it were no fault of hers. The mistake was due to the fact that fate—in a freakish mood—had contrived the same description to cover two men. Staring at him with horrified eyes, as though she had condemned him to death, she realised that not he alone, but other victims, would pay the penalty of her error.

The crisis sharpened her wits. She knew that it was impossible for her to slip away, in order to warn the agent at one hundred and three Postgasse. The entire management of the hotel depended upon herself, so that such unprecedented action would focus on her the limelight she must avoid. Probably, too, she would be followed and so give the whole show away. As she knew no telephone number to ring, the only chance to save the "twig" was through the blond stranger.

After first glancing swiftly around, she caught his eye and—daring greatly—made the Victory sign with her fingers.

" Are you the gentleman who booked a room over the phone?" she asked in her high official voice. "I'm terribly sorry but there has been a blunder. I forgot to reserve it. Georg, who has Eighty-eight?"

" Herr von Ringner," replied the clerk.

As she stared at the agent, willing him to understand, she felt the flash of his response.

"Oh, bad luck," he said with a shrug. "I left it to a pal to ring you up about it. Did he leave any message for me?"

"No, Fraulein," broke in Georg. "The calls have been only for our clients. There has been nothing for this gentleman."

"On the contrary," Vivien informed him, "I took the message myself, when you were not in the lounge."

"If there is one, it will be here," declared Edda, almost snatching at the memoranda slips in her eagerness to prove that Vivien had made another slip.

Instantly Vivien removed it from the girl's grasp.

"Allow me to know my own business while you attend to yours," she said.

Her brain worked feverishly while her fingers rustled the pile of flimsies. She believed that the "V" agent understood that von Ringner had received the information which was meant for him, but that was a minor point. The essential was to give it also to him and in such a manner as to awaken no curiosity or suspicion in Georg or Edda.

Suddenly she took a bold step.

"I've found it," she said, removing a slip from the bottom of the papers and reading it aloud. "It says, 'To-night at eight, one hundred and three, Postgasse.' Your friend wants you to ring him. Here it is. You might forget the address."

The man glanced at the slip, on which was scrawled "Ring Laundry" and folded it and placed it in his note-case.

"Won't you have another room?" asked Vivien, as he turned to go. "We have some very good ones vacant. Georg—"

"No thanks," cut in the agent.

When he had gone through the revolving door, she shrugged her shoulders.

"Nothing but the best will suit His Highness. Who does he think he is?"

"Maybe he has a lady," sniggered Georg.

She was grateful for Georg's characteristic suggestion because it was proof of a normal atmosphere. She had carried through a daring bluff in the presence of her assistants—and it had sounded so like ordinary routine business that she doubted whether either could remember the message or the address.

During the hours when luncheon was being served, she had no time to think of anything besides work.

But during the slack hour after luncheon, when she was back in the bureau, she had too much time to think and realise her position.

She had saved the others at the price of her own safety.

After the Gestapo had raided the deserted one hundred and three, Postgasse, they would inevitably demand an explanation from herself. They would not believe her protestations of ignorance or any fairy-tale about a message given to her by an anonymous stranger.

To them, she would be merely a girl who knew something—and who must be persuaded to talk.

When the lounge was beginning to fill with afternoon patrons, she noticed a girl who was greedily sucking up raspberry sirop at one of the small tables. Her short fur coat, the tilt of her veiled hat and the way she crossed her legs were all familiar, but she could not place her immediately. She frowned—because it was her boast never to forget a face; but within a few seconds, her professional prestige was restored.

She recognised the girl as the daughter of a well-to-do business man and—incidentally —a minx. She was fond of sweets and had patronised the Monopol Café regularly, until recently. Presumably her absence was caused by illness, for her full cheeks were pale and her little dark eyes no longer shone with vitality.

Vivien noticed also the nervous twitch of one eyelid as she approached the girl.

"You've deserted us," she said reproachfully. "Why? Is the sirop better somewhere else?"

"Oh, *no*," the girl assured her. "It's divine. I've missed it terribly. But I've been away in—in a holiday camp."

The explanation was overheard by Edda who commented on it when she returned to the bureau.

"That little fool is learning sense," she whispered spitefully to Vivien. "Holiday camp? The Greeks have a name for it: concentration camp."

The blood seemed to drain from Vivien's heart as she listened.

"What did she do?" she asked.

"Nothing, so to say. She was having a drink with a pick-up when the Gestapo pulled him in and her as well. It took time to persuade them that she didn't know the man from Adam, but they let her go. She was lucky."

"*Lucky?*"

"Naturally. It is bad policy for the Gestapo to admit mistakes. They were rather rough with her, trying to make her talk—but of course, she has forgotten all that."

Only yesterday, Vivien would have heard such a tale in silence and then tried to forget it, with all the other things which must not be remembered. Since then, a gulf had been crossed and this story was her own—with one ominous difference. The girl was innocent of intrigue while she was deeply involved.

Their fates would be the same. She shuddered as she thought of "rough treatment" and wondered whether she could endure protracted pain. Her chief dread was that an admission might be wrung from her when she was in a dazed condition. Then she realised that Edda was speaking.

"What a fool to pick up a stranger. You and I, Fraulein, are too wise. We know that the hotel is packed with Gestapo agents posing as business men. Sometimes I wonder if your brooch keeps them guessing. Of course, here we know it is your initial."

The words made her realise that while she was facing the gravest peril, there might be worse to follow—the bitterness of betrayal by someone very dear. Suddenly she could endure the confinement of the lounge no longer.

"Carry on, Edda," she said. "I'm going out."

Too overwrought to wait for the lift, she ran up to the first floor. Old Steiner was his own best patron, for he occupied a vast apartment, furnished with stuffy Victorian splendour. He was bed-ridden, but, in spite of his age, his vast bulk had not shrunken.

"I'm going to the shops, darling," Vivien told him. "Can I get anything for you? "

"No, my dear," he replied, "but you can do something for me." He pointed to her initial brooch. "Don't wear that again. Didn't you know it is the Victory sign?"

Vivien had never seen his jovial face so grave. Suddenly, the sour atmosphere of the sealed room swept over her. She felt on the verge of fainting as the spark of suspicion, smouldering in her brain since she had heard Edda's story, now flared up in distrust of John.

She remembered that she had accepted him without credentials, other than his alleged British birth. That claim might be false, and even were it genuine, nationality excludes no one from the ranks of traitors. As a matter of cold fact, she had been attracted to him so strongly that she had walked voluntarily into his net.

"I must get away at once," she told herself in a panic.

She kissed her great-uncle fondly and when she reached the door, she looked back at him, wondering whether she would see him again. Then she rang for the lift which jerked her up to her room.

Without a plan and not daring to pause for reflection, she rammed on her hat and dragged on her coat. Then she ran downstairs, hurried through the lounge, and passed through the door out of the Monopol.

When she was in the street, she boarded the first tram-car. She did not know its destination, but when the conductor came to collect her fare, she had the presence of mind to say "All the way."

It will take me somewhere out, she thought. I must think. I must *think*.

In a half-comatose state — which was the aftermath of her brain-storm — she gazed through the dirty glass at the parks, the avenues, the groups of statuary and fountains. Presently they rolled over stony streets out to the country.

As she looked at rows of stacked foliage, blackened by frost, she suddenly thought of old Steiner, because he was especially fond of trees.

For the first time, she realised that lie might pay the penalty of her disappearance.

They won't believe he knows nothing, she thought. I must go back at once.

Because she was going to her doom, the return journey seemed much shorter.

It was while they were waiting for the traffic signals to change coloured that something happened — something as hideously unnatural as an evil dream, where a friend turns suddenly into an enemy. Suddenly she saw John in the street, standing on the pavement-kerb. Acting on impulse, she jumped from the car and ran towards him. Apparently, he recognised her for he half waved to her before he hailed a taxi and was driven away.

He can't look me in the eyes, she thought bitterly. Well, that's told me all I want to know.

When she entered the Monopol, she was dead to sensation. Sustained by courage bred of force of habit, she smiled and chatted to acquaintances on her way through the lounge. Afterwards, she put on her overall, as usual, and helped the chef in his preparations for the dinner.

Again she watched the clock as the hands left the numeral eight and began to travel imperceptibly around the dial. When they reached the half-hour, she knew that at any moment, she might be interrogated.

But although she expected a summons, when it came, it took her by surprise. She was listening with unfeigned interest to a stout man's account of his triplets and looking at the snaps of three super-babies, when the waiter touched her arm.

"Pardon, Fraulein," he said. "A gentleman wishes to speak to you in the lounge."

Her heart leaped and then seemed to stop as she forced herself to walk out of the restaurant. When she entered the lounge, it was nearly deserted, so that the first person she saw was the Prussian, von Ringner.

"You asked for me," she said with desperate courage.

His smiling eyes menaced her with the terror of a cat playing with its prey.

"Fraulein," he asked softly, "who gave you that message for me? "

She moistened her lips to utter, for the first time, the lie that must be repeated while her endurance availed, or to the end.

"I don't know. I never saw him before."

His smile broadened as he patted her shoulder.

"Wise girl," he said, "you know when to forget. Good. I will buy you something pretty."

Snapping his fingers at Edda, who produced a withered bunch of Neapolitan violets from the flower-stall, he presented them to Vivien clicked his heels, and marched out of the lounge.

She stood staring after him in dazed wonder as she fastened the violets to her dress. While she was fumbling with them, John passed through the revolving doors and walked towards the girls. He was the picture of a smart and larky business man as he greeted her with a familiar grin.

"I see you've been decorated. Who's my rival? Well, I've had a successful day. What about a drink?"

As Vivien walked beside him to a table in a distant corner, he spoke to her in an undertone.

"Never run after me again in the street. It might give a wrong impression and attract unwelcome attention to yourself. I'm not safe to know intimately."

"You cut me," she reproached him.

"You? Never. I only want to protect you. But I gather, from the violets, that your gentleman friend approved your discretion? "

"Yes. I can't understand it. John, I made a terrible blunder."

"I know and it's all been taken care of. Our Mr. X reported it to me. It was stinking luck—the sort of thing which would only happen once in a hundred times."

"Was the nice second man Mr. X?"

"Of course. We don't mention names. He tumbled to your bluff and called the tea-party off. He told me you were like an old-timer. Nice work."

As his eyes approved her, she thrilled to his praise.

"The snag was this," went on John, "it put you on the spot. Von Ringner would know that no girl would dare to play a practical joke on him and he would make it his business to find out who was behind you. I couldn't stand for that. . . . I've been on the job all day, saving you. My hat, *what* a day! "

"What happened?"

"Nothing much. Von Ringner and company turned up at one-o-three, Postgasse, on the stroke of eight. They found it dark and shut-up. A man stood in the doorway expecting them. He pushed a parcel into von Ringner,'s hand, whispered what it was, and then cleared off."

"Wasn't he followed?"

"Definitely no. Von Ringner loves his stomach; and the black market penalties are stringent. You see, I fixed up a pleasant and natural solution of the mystery. *Food.* Food—the one subject about which no questions are asked."

John tossed off his drink and laughed again.

"He'll look on it as a bribe—necessarily anonymous. He'll probably connect it with the next person to hint at preferential treatment. But nothing will be said. Some other blighter will get the credit for my day's hard labour. . . and *how.* Every hour of the day. I've bought, I've begged, I've borrowed.—I've even stolen. Nothing too small to swell the main amount. You must bribe handsomely or not at all."

"What was it?" asked Vivien.

"*Butter.*"

As their laughter rang out, she looked at him with shining eyes.

"What a thrill it is," she whispered. "And you and I are in it together."

Turning to a guest who drew near, as though to share the joke, she pointed to a vile caricature of an Englishman in an illustrated paper.

"Mr. Vanderpant was showing me this funny picture," she said. "But he won't believe me when I tell him I'm English."

Then the man joined in their laughter; but the eyes of both John and Vivien were dreamy. He was thinking of the future. Some day . . . and she was hearing faint far-away thuds, all beating in time together.

A vast underground army was marching on to victory.

YOU'LL BE SURPRISED

"**S**urprise," murmured Celia as she touched the latch-key in her coat pocket.

The contact gave her a throb of delight because it anticipated the moment when she would go out of the wind and rain, into the warmth and light of home. She was rushing into her future, all unconscious of peril—a peril against which she had been duly warned. . . .

This warning had been following her during her ten months' theatrical tour of America, tracking her faithfully but doomed always to be one stage behind. Even at that moment it was drawing nearer to her and approaching its journey's end—when it would be too late.

The railway terminus was not calculated to raise dim spirits. It was vast, ill lit, and minus the bustle and excitement of travel which had animated it during the day. But if the platforms were deserted, the refreshment buffet was crowded with passengers, surging to the counter to be served. Celia's arm was jolted and her coffee slopped into her saucer, but she continued to smile at the young man beside her.

"Is this strange stuff English tea?" he asked.

"That old crack," groaned Celia. "Typical of your mentality. You know jolly well it is coffee."

It was customary for the young American—Don Sherwood—and Celia to insult each other consistently.

It had cost Don an effort to ask his first personal question, for he knew nothing about Celia.

"Are you married?"

"Gosh, no. I share a flat with my twin sister—Cherry. You've got to be a twin yourself to know how close you are to each other. She's my other half. When she got married, even Jas couldn't maul up things between us. . . ."

"Have you wired her you're coming?" asked Don.

"That would spoil everything. It's a tradition in our family never to write or phone."

"Sounds risky to me. How d'you know your sister will be home?"

"I know because Jas—her husband—has a government job in London."

"If I were fond of any one, I wouldn't like to go without news of her for ten months," said the young man.

"Actually, it's never been so long before," she said. "But I know Cherry is all right because we're identical twins. There's a current of sympathy between us and if she were ill or in trouble, I should feel miserable."

"I suppose we must say good-bye."

Celia's hazel eyes were soft as she looked at Don's clear-cut features—his firm lips and well shaped head—as though to preserve a memory. In his turn, he gazed fondly at her—a ginger haired girl, hatless, and wearing her first fur coat. . .

A coat which within the next ninety minutes would be connected with an episode of unimaginable horror.

"I have a reservation at a hotel," Don told her. "My first commission will be to see madame safely home."

As the taxi bore them through the curtain of rain, Celia realised that they had reached a closer stage in their friendship.

"Nearly there," she told him. "This is our road."

"You girls seem to take every chance," he scolded.

He felt her shudder.

"What's wrong?" he asked.

"I don't know. Something terrible seemed to rush over me."

Suddenly she stopped to thrust her latchkey into his hand.

"Open the door for me," she said, "and tell me exactly what you see. I—I'm afraid to look."

Filled with uneasy curiosity Don unlocked the door and pushed it ajar while Celia closed her eyes. A private house had been converted into flats and the staircase which led to the upper storeys had been boarded up, with a separate entrance. Only room was left for a minute vestibule and a narrow passage on which the rooms opened. The nearest door was set cornerwise to the lobby whose walls were hung with grimed gilded paper.

"It's our Chinese ante-chamber. . . . Everything's all right. Cherry is here, for the light is on."

"You were an angel to see me home," she whispered. "Good-bye, darling."

Don knew that she had forgotten him in the rapture of her home-coming, so he closed and relocked the door, mechanically slipping the key into his coat pocket.

Walking on tiptoe in the hope of surprising her sister, Celia opened the door of the next room, which was hers, only to find it in dark-ness. The bathroom and then the kitchenette were also unlit, so there remained only the big bedroom at the end of the passage.

Celia entered it confidently expecting to see both Cherry and James. This time she met with a double disappointment as she gazed around her at the familiar old-rose carpet, the twin beds with dusty-pink satin coverlets and the veneered walnut toilet table with its big triple mirrors. Then she picked up from the floor a sapphire-blue velvet robe, trimmed with white fur.

She had arrived at the flat without even a dressing bag, sure of obtaining necessities for the night from her sister.

She was still wearing the fur coat she had bought in New York—recklessly spending all her surplus salary. She took it off and opened the door of her own little room.

The light from the passage showed her an uninviting interior—a stripped bed and a clutter of clothing thrown over every surface and piece of furniture. Too careful of her new property to add it to the communal lumber, she opened one-half of the wardrobe and hung it on an empty peg.

She was entering the lounge when she was startled by a dull thud—suggestive of the fall of some heavy object. It was impossible to locate it, so she stood, listening for it to be repeated.

As she sat and smoked her spirits began to droop from combined frustrated hope and fatigue. She was further depressed when she gazed around her with eyes which seemed to be newly-scaled. The room was more than untidy.

When she crossed over to the side table, she found evidence of further deterioration. There were too many bottles stacked amid a thick litter of cigarette stubs while every glass was dirty. . . Too tired to wash up, she searched amid the empties in the sideboard cupboard until she found a few tiny glasses of continental origin which were reserved for best occasions.

After she had sipped a small gin and lime, she felt brighter.

Then she remembered the sudden thrill of expectation which invariably heralded their reunion and she smiled.

"Yes, at this moment, Cherry is feeling very happy over me."

Even as the thought flashed across her mind, Cherry sat up in her bed at the nursing home and pushed her red hair back from her brow.

"Nurse," she cried, "I'm concerned about my sister."

The night nurse looked at her in surprise.

"I know she is in trouble," went on Cherry, "We're identical twins and very close. It's like this. She went to America before I knew that my young gentleman was on the way. Directly after, my father-in-law died and left us his furnished house at Purley. Of course, I wrote to her, telling her our new address. But now, I'm wondering if she got my letter."

"Does your sister know about the baby?" she asked.

"No," replied Cherry—her habitual smile breaking through—"I left him out of the letter. When Celia comes to Purley, Jas is going to tell her I've broken my leg and send her on here. But now I'm afraid. I kept seeing her in a terrible tainted place—all alone and in danger."

As though the twins had been speaking over an invisible telephone, the word "tainted" slipped into Celia's mind. It made her feel unclean and suggested the remedy of a bath.

"Go away at once." The warning seemed to in ring her her ears. "Go before it is too late."

"Nerves," she told herself as she resolutely turned on the tap, while the dingy cell filled with steam, mercifully dimming her vision. She undressed as though she were racing against time while the sense of being an intruder grew stronger.

As she soaked in the hot water, the teasing feeling that she might be surprised destroyed any sense of relaxation and further stimulated her brain to unpleasant activity.

"I'll wear Cherry's robe," she thought with a pleasing memory of the warmth of its quilted satin lining.

"Cherry's changed her make up," she reflected. "Why, what's this? Has she dyed her hair?

Although it was possible that Cherry had become a temporary brunette, an unpleasant suspicion began to shape in her mind. Hoping to disprove it, she rushed to the wardrobe which was crammed with clothes.

The first frock she saw told her the truth.

"That's not Cherry's frock. She's terrified of green. Nothing would induce her to wear it. . . . This isn't her flat any longer. The furniture is ours but strangers are living here. . . Horrible strangers. . . I must get away at once."

Half sobbing from lack of breath, she wriggled into her frock and then looked around for her precious fur coat. Rushing down the passage in a fury of impatience to escape, she burst through the door and tugged at the wardrobe. . . The next second she stifled a scream at the sight of a stiff white shape which had toppled sideways from the enclosed half of the clothes closet and was now propped up against her coat. It looked wedged into position, but as the door swung open wider, lack of support caused it to fall outwards.

It's chill and rigidity told her that it was a dead body and for a ghastly second she feared it might be Cherry. Her relief was almost empowering when she exposed the henna-tinted hair of a middle-aged woman whose congested face and protruding eyes proclaimed that she had been strangled.

"Murder," gasped Celia.

In spite of the waves of terror which rolled over her, her brain still functioned and she held on to see a clear purpose—to escape. Only a few yards divided her from the front door but—before she could reach the corridor, she shrank back into the room, just as a man entered the flat.

He was tall, bull-necked and broad-shouldered, and he wore country clothes—baggy plus-fours and a belted tweed coat. He turned into the lounge, but—to her dismay—he left its door open, so that he could see anyone who entered or left the apartment.

Suddenly two persons—a woman and a young man—entered the flat.

Celia was beginning to conclude that they could know nothing of their ghastly tenant, when Ronnie spoke nonchalantly.

"Who's the stiff?"

"Fricker's maid," reported the big man.

The big man turned to Ronnie. "Can you shift her? Get a car?"

"Can do," said the youth obligingly. "Pinched a Fiat yesterday. I'll run it round at two precisely, pick up the lady and shove it into the river from the first wharf. Tide should be about high."

Celia's knees shook as she listened, for the name of "Fricker" had given her the clue to the identity of the people in the next room. During the homeward voyage, she had heard a brief radio announcement of the murder of Lady Fricker—a well-known society hostess, notorious for her jewels. The pick of these had been stolen and their owner strangled, presumably to get the string of pearls she wore always, to preserve their virtue.

"They can't stay cooped up for hours on end," Celia reasoned. "The woman will go into her room and the men will wander."

As though to strengthen her hope, Ronnie spoke to his companions.

"Got a date. I'll be seeing you. Two sharp. . . Time for a quick drink."

Biting her lip, Celia heard him cross over to the table where she had left her glass.

"It's only one more dirty one," she thought. "He won't notice it. The big man didn't."

"What's the idea of thimbles?" he grumbled. "Holding back on your pals?"

"Well." The woman's thick voice choked in her surprise. "Where did that come from?"

"Search me." The youth sniffed noisily. "Someone's used it. Who's been here?"

"Only the Frenchy. We locked up when we went out to collect you."

Suddenly the front door-bell rang loudly. There was an urgency in its peal which filled Celia with hope.

"Don't answer it."

"Fool," said the big man contemptuously. "One might think you had something to hide."

Peeping through the crack, Celia watched him open the front door. The next second she felt electrified with joy at the sound of Don's voice.

"May I speak to Miss Steel?"

"Sorry," said the big man. "Afraid you've come to the wrong flat. I'll ask my missus." He raised his voice. "My dear, do you know anyone name of 'Steel' living in the building?"

"Yes," called the woman. "They had this flat before us. Two girls in the profession."

"Well, I guess she's moved since she gave me the address," he remarked, speaking with a stressed American accent. "Like a dame. Sorry. So long."

"Don never spoke with that accent," Celia reasoned.

She realised that she was now in even graver danger when the big man returned to the lounge.

"I'm wondering about that dame he was chasing," he said. "Someone's been drinking out of that glass."

"I'll look 'round," said the woman.

"Bath's full of water and the light is on," she panted. "She's been here all right."

Stimulated by the urgency of her plight, Celia's brain began to race. She knew that she must act swiftly and play "Simple Sailor" with all the histrionic talent she possessed. But first of all it was vital for her to reach the big bedroom before the woman went on with her search. She must make them believe that she had fallen asleep and knew nothing about the murdered woman in the small room.

"If they know I've been here, I'm sunk," she told herself.

Taking a chance, she sped noiselessly down the passage to the big room and dashed to the nearest of the twin beds. After rucking up the silk spreads and punching a hollow in the pillow she dragged on the blue velvet robe over her frock, since there was no time to change. Then, with a feeling that she was going to enter a tiger's cage, she rushed into the lounge, shouting her sister's name.

"Cherry! Cherry!"

"Cheerio, people. I suppose you're pals of Cherry's. Where is the old girl? Tight as usual? I'm just back from the States and I've come straight from the railway station."

She got no response to her overture as they continued to stare at her with a cold impersonal gaze.

"My robe," the woman shouted. "Take it off, you—. You've stolen my perfume, too. What are you doing in my flat?"

"Your flat?" asked Celia. "Do you mean my sister and her hubby aren't living here now? Oh, my godfather, it looks as if I've made a mistake. Listen, people."

She told them the facts of the story, hoping desperately that its truth would make it convincing, even while she tried to pose as a hard-boiled gold digger.

"Ta for the lend," she said coolly. "Well, I must be toddling. My mother told not to stay out late."

The men neither removed their eyes from her face nor moved from their positions, leaving it to the woman to protest.

"No, sister, it's not as simple as that. We got to know more about you. What else have you helped yourself to?"

"Frisk me and find out," said Celia, grateful for the education of the screen.

"You bet your life I will. But first you've got to tell me where you've been and what you've done here."

"Let's think." Celia puckered her brow. "Well, I had a drink or two—and a smoke or two—and a bath. Only one bath. Then I went to Cherry's room and had a lie-down on her bed and did a spot of shut-eye. I woke up when I heard my Yank ask for me at the front door."

Celia spoke casually, but she remembered Ronnie's argument that her silence was proof of ignorance and she felt that she was playing her trump card. She noticed the swift interchange of the men's glances although the woman appeared unimpressed.

"I'll check up on that," she said.

Left with the two men, Celia was conscious of a difference in their manner. She was sure that she had convinced them that she had blundered in by mistake and that her glaring indifference to discovery was proof of her lack of guilty knowledge.

"Didn't you want to see your Yank again?" asked the big man.

"Yet bet I'm going to see him," said Celia. "This is the lowdown. I'm aiming to marry the guy and I thought the robe would give him the wrong impression."

The big man nodded to Ronnie who gave her a playful slap.

"Clear out," he said. "Make it snappy"

Celia could hardly believe in her good fortune. In another minute she would be out of the terrible flat rushing to the shelter of the police station. Rushing down the passage, the woman gripped her arm and wrenched her away from the front door.

"Your mother wouldn't like you to get wet," she said with heavy sarcasm. "Where's your coat, dearie?"

"I—I haven't one," stammered Celia.

"Where's your coat?" persisted the woman. "You told us you came straight from the station. You couldn't make a journey with no coat."

"Of course not." Celia's brain whirled as she lied clumsily. "I must have left it in the taxi."

"Why did you take it off in the taxi?" asked the youth, with a leer. "Too hot in December?"

"Don't be a sap." Celia felt as though blazing theatre. "I told you I was going to marry the guy. I've sold him the yarn. I'm a doctor's daughter and been to high school."

"And that's exactly what you are, dear," said the woman—poisoned honey in her voice. "You've been putting on an act. You know where your coat is. You know it is hanging in the wardrobe in the next room. . . . So you know what else is there. . . ."

The silence that followed was broken only by the beating of the rain against the window. Staring at the impassive faces, Celia found it difficult to believe in her fate.

"So what?" said the woman.

"I must make the party for two," said the youth indifferently.

Celia had an agonized recollection of the purple face and bulging eyes of the murdered maid who was to be her fellow guest at the "party": but even as the picture—which forecast her own end—flashed through her brain, the big man's arm shot out, cracking her on the jaw. . . .

Darkness fell. She knew that she was dead, for she felt the wire biting into her throat; and then she saw stale river water bubbling up past a glass prison. . . . But instead of the peace of the grave, there was pandemonium all around her shouts, blows, curses, and once, the sound of a shot. Then—as she struggled back from annihilation to reality, she became aware of a whirling confusion. Gradually, as her brain cleared, she saw a wrecked room—men in uniform—and lastly, Don. She felt his arm around her as he pressed a glass to her lips.

"Throw it back," he invited.

She obeyed although her jaw was swelling rapidly and a tooth felt loose.

"I pocketed your latch-key by mistake," he told her. "When I found it, I thought I ought to bring it back at once. Didn't seem too safe to mail it, apart from the waste of time. Then the chap told me you were not at the flat, but I could see your bag lying behind the dragon on the chest. . . . Well, I knew if I started anything they'd only plug both of us. So I put on a dishonest-to-goodness American accent, hoping to fool you, in case you were listening, and I went off to collect reinforcements. We had the key so we were able to take them by surprise and that started the party. And what a party."

As he paused, a young constable—whose blackened eyes gave him an oddly glamorous appearance—crossed to the divan.

"Are you ready to tell us what happened, miss?" he asked.

Aware that she was about to present the C.I.D. with the Fricker murder gang on a platter, Celia spoke with stressed nonchalance—chiefly to keep herself from bursting into tears.

"Don't waste time on me. Just go into the next room and see what's inside the wardrobe. . . . You'll be surprised."

Sources

"Underground," *Pearson's Magazine* February 1928.

"At Twilight," *The Hartford Daily Courant*, May 25, 1930, *Pearson's Magazine* June 1930, *The Novel Magazine* January 1935

"River Justice," *The Los Angeles Times*, June 5, 1932.

"Waxworks," *Pearson's Magazine* December 1930, *Crime at Christmas* ed. Jack Adrian, Equation, 1988, *Silent Nights* ed. Martin Edwards, The British Library, 2015.

"Passengers," *Raleigh News and Observer* October 15 1933, *Bodies from the Library 4* ed. Tony Medawar, Collins Crime Club, 2021.

"Catastrophe," *The Hartford Daily Courant*, August 18, 1935.

"The Gilded Pupil," *The (New York) Daily News*, May 7, 1936.

"The Cellar," *Midland Empire Farmer*, February 18, 1937.

"Don't Dream on Midsummer's Eve," *The News and Observer*, Raleigh, NC, June 20, 1937.

"The Holiday," *Britannia and Eve* February 1938.

"Lightning Strikes Twice," *The (New York) Daily News*, October 16, 1938.

"The Royal Visit," *The (New York) Daily News*, May 7, 1939.

"Mabel's House," *Chicago Sunday Tribune*, April 21, 1940.

"Caged," *Chicago Sunday Tribune*, June 30, 1940.

"Blackout," *Chicago Sunday Tribune*, August 25, 1940 .

"The Baby Heir," *Chicago Sunday Tribune*, April 25, 1941

"White Cap," *Akron Beacon Journal* January 31 1942, *Bodies from the Library 2* ed. Tony Medawar, Collins Crime Club, 2019.

"The First Day," *Britannia and Eve* July 1943.

"You'll be Surprised…" *The Province* (Vancouver, British Columbia,) October 23, 1943

Blackout and Other Stories

Blackout and Other Stories is printed on 60-pound paper and is designed by G.E. Satheesh, Pondicherry, India. The type is Palatino Linotype. The cover is by Joshua Laboski. The first edition was published in two forms: trade softcover, perfect bound; and one hundred copies sewn in cloth. *Blackout* was printed by Southern Ohio Printers and bound by Cincinnati Bindery. The book was published in February 2025 by Crippen & Landru Publishers, Inc., Cincinnati, OH.

Crippen & Landru, Publishers
P. O. Box 532057
Cincinnati, OH 45253
Web: www.Crippenlandru.com
E-mail: orders@crippenlandru.com

Since 1994, CRIPPEN & LANDRU has published more than 100 first editions of short-story collections by important detective and mystery writers.

This is the best edited, most attractively packaged line of mystery books introduced in this decade. The books are equally valuable to collectors and readers. [Mystery Scene Magazine]

The specialty publisher with the most star-studded list is Crippen & Landru, which has produced short story collections by some of the biggest names in contemporary crime fi ction. [Ellery Queen's Mystery Magazine]

God bless Crippen & Landru. [The Strand Magazine]

A monument in the making is appearing year by year from Crippen & Landru, a small press devoted exclusively to publishing the criminous short story. [Alfred Hitchcock's Mystery Magazine]

Crippen & Landru Lost Classics

Peter Godfrey. *The Newtonian Egg.* 2002.

Craig Rice. *Murder, Mystery, and Malone.* 2002 eBook, $8.99

Charles B. Child. *The Sleuth of Baghdad.* 2002.

Stuart Palmer. *Hildegarde Withers, Uncollected Riddles.* 2002, eBook $8.99

Christianna Brand. *The Spotted Cat.* 2002

Raoul Whitfield. *Jo Gar's Casebook.* 2002.

William Campbell Gault. *Marksman.* 2003.

Gerald Kersh. *Karmesin.* 2003 eBook, $8.99

C. Daly King. *The Complete Curious Mr. Tarrant.* 2003, eBook $8.99

Helen McCloy. *The Pleasant Assassin.* 2003

William DeAndrea. *Murder - All Kinds.* 2003

Anthony Berkeley. *The Avenging Chance.* 2004

Joseph Commings. *Banner Deadlines.* 2004, eBook $8.99

Erle Stanley Gardner. *The Danger Zone.* 2004, eBook $8.99

T. S. Stribling. *Dr. Poggioli: Criminologist.* 2004, eBook $8.99

Margaret Millar. *The Couple Next Door.* 2004

Gladys Mitchell. *Sleuth's Alchemy.* 2005

Philip Warne/Howard Macy. *Who Was Guilty?* 2005, eBook $8.99

Dennis Lynds writing as Michael Collins. *Slot-Machine Kelly.* 2005

Julian Symons. *The Detections of Francis Quarles.* 200

Rafael Sabatini. *The Evidence of the Sword.* 2006 eBook, $8.99

Erle Stanley Gardner. *The Casebook of Sidney Zoom.* 2006, eBook $8.99

Ellis Peters. *The Trinity Cat.* 2006

Lloyd Biggle. *The Grandfather Rastin Mysteries.* 2007

Max Brand. *Masquerade.* 2007

Mignon Eberhart. *Dead Yesterday.* 2007

Hugh Pentecost. *The Battles of Jericho.* 2008

Victor Canning. *The Minerva Club.* 2009

Anthony Boucher and Denis Green. *The Casebook of Gregory Hood.* 2009

Vera Caspary. *The Murder in the Stork Club.* 2009

Michael Innes. *Appleby Talks About Crime.* 2010

Phillip Wylie. *Ten Thousand Blunt Instruments.* 2010

Erle Stanley Gardner. *The Exploits of the Patent Leather Kid.* 2010, eBook, $8.99

Vincent Cornier. *The Duel of Shadows.* 2011, eBook, $8.99

E. X. Ferrars. *The Casebook of Jonas P. Jonas.* 2012

Charlotte Armstrong. *Night Call.* 2014, eBook, $8.99

Phyllis Bentley. *Chain of Witnesses.* 2014

Patrick Quentin. *The Puzzles of Peter Duluth.* 2016, Clothbound $29, eBook $8.99

Frederick Irving Anderson. *The Purple Flame.* 2016, Clothbound $29, Trade Paperback $19

Anthony Gilbert. *Sequel to Murder.* 2017, Clothbound $29

James Holding. *The Zanzibar Shirt Mystery.* 2018, Clothbound $29 Q. Patrick. *The Cases of Lieutenant Trant.* 2019

Erle Stanley Gardner. *Hot Cash, Cold Clews.* 2020, Clothbound $32, Trade Paperback $22, eBook $8.99

Freeman Wills Crofts, *The 9.50 Up Express.* 2021, Clothbound $32, Trade Paperback $22, eBook $8.99

Stuart Palmer. *Hildegarde Withers, Final Riddles?* 2021, Clothbound $32, Trade Paperback $22, eBook $8.99

Patrick Quentin. *Hunt in the Dark.* 2021

William Brittain. *The Man Who Solved Mysteries.* 2022, Clothbound $32, Trade Paperback $1922, eBook $8.99

John Creasey. *Gideon and the Young Toughs.* 2022, Clothbound $35, Trade Paperback $20, eBook $8.99

Pierre Very. *The Secret of the Pointed Tower.* 2023, Clothbound $32, Trade Paperback $20

Anthony Berkeley. *The Avenging Chance and Even More Stories (Enlarged with Two Stories).* 2023, Trade Paperback $19, eBook $8.99

Richard and Francis Lockridge Flair for Murder, 2024, Clothbound $32, Trade Paperback $22

Ethel Lina White Blackout, 2025, Clothbound $32, Trade Paperback $22

Subscriptions

Subscribers agree to purchase each forthcoming publication, either the Regular Series or the Lost Classics or (preferably) both. Collectors can thereby guarantee receiving limited editions, and readers won't miss any favorite stories.

Subscribers receive a discount of 20% off the list price (and the same discount on our backlist) and a specially commissioned short story by a major writer in a deluxe edition as a gift at the end of the year.

The point for us is that, since customers don't pick and choose which books they want, we have a guaranteed sale even before the book is published, and that allows us to be more imaginative in choosing short story collections to issue.

That's worth the 20% discount for us. Sign up now and start saving. Email us at orders@crippenlandru.com or visit our website at www.crippenlandru.com on our subscription page.

www.ingramcontent.com/pod-product-compliance
Ingram Content Group UK Ltd.
Pitfield, Milton Keynes, MK11 3LW, UK
UKHW010830280525
6113UKWH00022B/246

9 781936 363919